To D

From Mum
(2006)

(700th anniversary
of coronation of
Robert the Bruce).

The author's early childhood was spent in Scotland's Highlands; through which she developed a lifetime's love of Scotland's wilderness, lavish history and affirmed culture.

Her working life was spent as a teacher of history.

She now lives and writes in Central Scotland.

GOOD KING
ROBERT'S TESTAMENT

Margaret E Wallace

Good King Robert's Testament

Vanguard Press

VANGUARD PAPERBACK

© Copyright 2005
Margaret E Wallace

The right of Margaret E Wallace to be identified as author of this work has been asserted by her in accordance with the Copyright, Designs and Patents Act 1988

All Rights Reserved

No reproduction, copy or transmission of this publication may be made without written permission.
No paragraph of this publication may be reproduced, copied or transmitted save with the written permission of the publisher, or in accordance with the provisions of the Copyright Act 1956 (as amended).

Any person who does any unauthorised act in relation to this publication may be liable to criminal prosecution and civil claims for damage.

A CIP catalogue record for this title is available from the British Library
ISBN 1 843861 97 6

Vanguard Press is an imprint of
Pegasus Elliot MacKenzie Publishers Ltd.
www.pegasuspublishers.com

First Published in 2005

Vanguard Press
Sheraton House Castle Park
Cambridge England

Printed & Bound in Great Britain

Dedication

For Roman, my inspiration

PROLOGUE

In the early autumn of the year 1305, the Scottish people learnt that Sir William Wallace, hero of Stirling and former Guardian of Scotland, had been found guilty of treason to the English king. The execution had been carried out immediately in London and the body quartered and displayed above the city gates of Stirling and Perth. Men paid homage to Wallace's memory according to their own hearts.

John Blair had been chaplain to Wallace and heard the news at St Andrews where he was attached to the household of Bishop Lamberton. He stopped his work in the library and hurried to the Bishop's private chapel, which he knew would be deserted at that hour of the day. He prostrated himself on the cold flags and lay before the altar, praying earnestly for the soul of his dead friend, until his whole body was stiff and aching with cold. When he finally arose to hurry back to his work, the grey floor glistened where his tears had fallen.

The knights, Malcolm and John Wallace, brothers of the murdered man, were at the castle of Robert Bruce, Earl of Carrick, at Lochmaben, when the messenger came at full gallop into the castle yard bringing word of the events in London. The news was not entirely unexpected. There had been rumours for the past few weeks that Sir John Stewart, Earl of Menteith, had betrayed Wallace to the English, and there was no doubting the truth of the messenger's tale. He had witnessed the execution and told his listeners every gory detail of Wallace's final moments. When Robert Bruce returned from the hunt he was not surprised either, for he too had heard whispers of Wallace's capture. However, his horror at Sir William's fate was genuine enough.

The Wallace brothers came to Bruce asking to be released from his service, that they might avenge their kinsmen's murder. He had refused to give his consent and urged patience. He said that he would aid their cause and would not allow Wallace's work to die with him for he had given his word to Wallace.

That night he slept alone, for he felt shame and guilt at the treachery of his own kind and for the death of a noble man. He lay thinking of his last meeting with William Wallace. It had been in midsummer when the strain of Wallace's fugitive life was beginning to show in the lines on his face and the flecks of grey in his hair and beard.

Wallace had pledged loyalty to Robert Bruce and Bruce had agreed that he would lead the quest for Scotland's freedom. Now, a Scot had betrayed Wallace.

Bruce closed his eyes. He admired King Edward of England, who was never rash, never allowed his head to rule his heart and was meticulous with his military planning. To be successful he must learn leadership from Edward of England. If he made his bid for power too soon he would follow Wallace to the scaffold. Before drifting into a restless sleep he had made his first plan. He would come to terms with his rival, Sir John Comyn, for the throne of Scotland.

***

In September 1305, Edward Plantagenet, King and Overlord of the Isles of Britain and Ireland, summoned a Parliament at Westminster and the ten Scottish commissioners, charged with the administration of that land, travelled to London to present themselves to him.

The English King was a contented man. He was powerful and recognized by all to be without equal. His enemies in Scotland had accepted his dominion or had been banished from that land and he was satisfied with the system of administration that he had set up for his Northern Kingdom. His nephew, the Earl of Richmond, was to be his viceroy in Scotland and both the chancellor and chamberlain were Englishmen but the councillors - bishops, abbots, earls and barons - were Scotsmen with much to lose and little to gain from defiance of his will. The head of William Wallace, traitor, outlaw and murderer of monks and nuns, had been placed on a spike above London Bridge as a warning to all who dare defy their king.

There was no king in Christendom who could boast such a prosperous and well ordered kingdom as his. It was true that the Scottish war had placed heavy demands on his exchequer and he had been forced to borrow heavily, but God willing he would repay his debts. His heir, Edward Prince of Wales, could expect to inherit a realm that was the envy of all.

Edward, his son, was a disappointment to him. He was weak and too fond of bestowing favours on his friends, but then a man could not choose his son. Responsibility changed men and the burdens of state might direct his son's energies away from foolish liaisons. Perhaps all would be well in the end. He sighed and thought of Robert Bruce, Earl of Carrick who was a fine man just like all the Bruce kinsmen. Robert's father and grandfather had ridden with King Edward on crusade to the

Holy Land. They had been good fighting men and he had honoured the Bruce family, giving in to any reasonable demands that they made. He had a soft spot for young Robert Bruce and at his royal command the Earl of Ulster had given his daughter Elizabeth as wife to the young man. Yet now it would appear Robert was scheming behind his back. Documents had been found on Wallace which suggested that Robert Bruce was a traitor. As a warning and to show his displeasure, King Edward had recently revoked the gift of land, which he had given to young Bruce. If he were wise Robert would heed the warning, but if treason were afoot Edward would not be sentimental. He would have them all, not just Robert, but all the Bruce family.

THE SUMMER KING

Dawn was breaking. It was bitterly cold. The skeletal bare branches of the trees were white with hoarfrost and the earth iron-hard. The rider picked his way carefully along the rutted track. A fall here for horse or rider would be a painful - perhaps a fatal affair. In the grey light he could see the silhouette of the Earl of Carrick's manor of Tottenham, in Middlesex and thought with pleasure of the fire he would sit beside in the great hall. At the gate, leading into the courtyard, a guard challenged him asking his name.

"My Lord, the Earl of Gloucester, sent me with an urgent message for your master."

A servant came out holding a burning torch so that the light fell on the horseman's face. Satisfied that all was well the servant opened the main gates and the messenger was permitted to enter.

Robert Bruce, Earl of Carrick, knew the Earl of Gloucester's messenger well. Peter Langley was the keeper of Gloucester's wardrobe and a trusted man. He would not have been sent out in such weather in midwinter without serious cause.

"My Lord sends you these gifts in return for what he received from you yesterday," said Langley. Cautiously Bruce took the offered leather pouch. He had last seen the Earl of Gloucester at the king's court during the Christmas feast and had not sent him any gifts since then. In the pouch was a pair of spurs and twelve pence. The spurs were the kind produced by any working blacksmith and used by common men, not a present for a great earl of the realm. Upon the money King Edward's head was clearly stamped. The message was clear, flee, flee from the king's anger. Bruce smiled at Langley, a pleasant, relaxed smile that belied the emotions and thoughts rushing through his mind.

"Warm and refresh yourself Peter and accept these for your trouble," he gave Langley the twelve pence. Quietly Bruce told his squire to saddle two horses and gave orders to his household that they should leave him in peace, for he intended to work on accounts in his chamber. Secretly the earl left his manor by a side gate and took the road leading to his estates in Essex. The local people recognized the great man and bowed as he passed by, but once safely in the forest of

Epping, he turned his horse northwards and at Hertford headed west then north again. Keeping to little used tracks he fled from King Edward's vengeance.

Later in the morning when the king's men arrived to arrest the Earl of Carrick, they were told that he had been seen riding towards his Essex manor and they galloped off, prepared to overtake their quarry. It was fortunate that the snow had not yet fallen, for on such hard ground the earl's tracks could not be followed.

For five days Bruce and his squire rode northwards hardly daring to stop and never when there was danger that they might be recognized. As they rested their horses close to the border by the banks of the River Lynne, they saw a horseman on the opposite side riding towards the ford. He hesitated before urging his beast into the icy waters of the ford for he knew both Bruce and his squire.

"Sir, that man is in the following of Sir John Comyn. I have seen him many times." Bruce looked with renewed interest at the horseman. With battleaxe gripped firmly he rode to intercept the traveller to ask where he was bound, for few men chose to travel at this time of the year without good cause. When the horseman saw Sir Robert's suspicious attitude he unstrapped his sword, spurred his horse and tried desperately to evade the encounter. Bruce yelled a warning to the rider, but the man continued, trying to put space between himself and his pursuer. As he rode he threw a pouch into the River but by chance, instead of sinking into the deep peaty pools, it landed on a large rock where there was little danger that its contents would be soaked by water.

When the earl drew alongside the fugitive he swung his battleaxe. It caught the fellow's shield, which was still strapped to his back, but the second blow cut deep into the back of the man's neck with such force that even his chain mail could not withstand the blow. He slumped forward over his horse's neck and Bruce caught the reins, turning the animal and ignoring the dying man still in the saddle as he watched his squire retrieve the leather pouch.

Bruce shook with rage as he read the letter which informed the English king of the bond agreed between the writer, Sir John Comyn and Sir Robert Bruce, The Earl of Carrick, "that we should work together and promote one another that one may wear the crown of Scotland." Comyn pleaded that the noble king should "forgive his lapse of loyalty and that he would hereafter be a loyal servant to the Lord King." The incriminating bond with Robert's own seal attached, which King Edward knew well, was enclosed. Never had the earl's young squire seen his master in such a black and evil temper as they flung the body of Comyn's messenger into a thicket. The horse, a fine bay gelding, they took with them.

Bruce was by nature a cheerful, generous man, quick to anger and quick to forgive. He was respected and admired by his followers and loved by many women but on this occasion his temper did not improve with the passing of time. For the remainder of their journey his squire rode silently behind his master, speaking only when it was required of him, while Bruce with a grim expression on his face, led the way. The earl considered himself an honourable man, particular in the execution of his duties to his king, his kinsmen and followers. He admired King Edward of England and his methods of government and he was angry and somewhat ashamed that Comyn should betray their alliance and conspiracy to take Scotland's crown from the old man.

Six days after his hurried departure from Tottenham, Bruce arrived at his castle of Lochmaben to be greeted by Elizabeth, his wife. She was in the great hall sitting close to the fire. Nigel, the youngest of his brothers, sat close by her reading aloud from a book. She arose smiling as Robert came to her. She was still very pale and the freckles across her nose and cheeks more pronounced than ever. The fine linen coif covering her hair framed her large, smiling, blue eyes. She wrapped her slender, long arms around her husband's neck and kissed his stubble cheek before burying her face into the, thick beaver fur of his cloak. For a few moments his black mood lifted and hugging her he playfully swung her around. Neither cared if their mutual affection should be seen by all their household.

"Your health has improved, Beth?" he whispered anxiously.

"Aye, better now that you have returned to me Robert."

Bruce smiled inwardly. His wife was not normally so mild in her speech. Plainly she could not be fully recovered from her miscarriage. He turned his back to the fire to warm himself. He was sure there would be snow in the night. It was already getting dark and heavily leaden, grey, snow clouds were forming across the hills.

Edward Bruce came onto the gallery overlooking the great hall and called to his elder brother. "What's brought you back across the border so quickly? We didn't expect to see you until the wild geese flew north again." Cheerfully he came to greet Robert, extending his hand.

Aware that so many were about, the earl put his arm around his wife's shoulders saying, "I had a great longing to see you all." Those who loved him knew that he would tell them the truth in due time.

Shouts of "father, father" could be heard and into the hall ran Marjorie Bruce with her skirts held high that she might run faster and her pretty chestnut plaits flying out behind her. Her father caught her in his arms. "Have you anything for me from England, father?" were her first words, for he always brought her a gift. The last time it had been a new pony and he had promised her a saddle for it. "Nay, sweetheart, your father has only brought himself this time, but I have not forgotten my promise to you."

Bruce sat in the great, carved chair which had been moved close to the fire and sipped the spiced, ruby wine feeling its warmth spreading throughout his tired body. Elizabeth had left with her steward to give orders to the servants and Marjorie sat close to her father while he warmed himself. The rage, which had earlier engulfed Robert, had given way to cold anger and he sat pondering how he should act towards John Comyn and his kin. He must speak with his brothers before rumours began to spread. He knew his household would already be whispering and wondering why their lord had returned early without a proper and fitting company of followers.

His wife returned to the warmth of the fire and saw her husband sitting deep in thought. She took her harp and began to sing in her clear, lilting voice. It was a gentle, little, love song that she knew he loved, and usually he would have joined in, his rich baritone voice blending so well with hers. On this evening he did not sing and it was Nigel who stood beside her and sang, his foot tapping out the rhythm.

When the song came to its sad end, Bruce excused himself and went to his chamber to remove his travel-stained clothes. His brothers followed him and picked up the letter, which Bruce had flung onto the settle. Their faces darkened as they read the contents. Edward, always ready to flex his muscles and swing his broadsword said, "By God Rob, the man is without honour. No doubt he hopes that by calling you the traitor he can sweep the Bruces aside and claim all power for himself. He was always cunning but I had thought he of all men would be loyal to Scotland." It was the dishonour and abuse of the Code of Chivalry that upset Robert Bruce most. Were they not both earls of the realm, both of Scotland's royal blood, born to rule?

Edward said, "The bugger sits in his castle at Dalswinton, Rob. Let's go now while he's still unprepared and deal with his treachery."

"Nay, you know that's not my way. I'll send a message to him asking him to meet me at a place of his choosing. Perhaps we can still come to an agreement."

"You're mad Rob. Why, the man has been caught red-handed double-dealing and you still think you can speak with him. Where's your sense? You carry honour too far."

"Maybe. Nevertheless, I will meet him at a place of his choosing so we can talk."

Edward still continued to argue saying that now was not the time for honour but Bruce would not listen and the following morning the knights Robert Boyd and John Wallace presented themselves at the gates of John Comyn's castle with a message from their lord.

Comyn sat in the great chair, which was covered with wolf skins to protect the earl from draughts. Around him stood his kinsmen and followers. Wallace and Boyd were no threat to the company for they had left their weapons at the entrance to the great hall as the custom of hospitality demanded. Comyn knew both men well, particularly Wallace, who had fought as courageously for Scotland as his brother Sir William and because of this, Comyn could not look them in the eyes. As they delivered their message he fiddled with the collar of a large hound sitting beside his chair. When they had finished speaking he said, "Tell Bruce I will gladly meet him at the Church of the Greyfriars in Dumfries where we will both be attending the 'Court Sessions." His uncle, Sir Robert Comyn shifted uneasily beside him and bent down to whisper into his ear, "Is that wise, John?" His nephew raised his hand for silence and said to Bruce's men, "Your lord and I will meet on the tenth of this month."

When Bruce's messengers had safely withdrawn, Red Comyn said to his uncle, "Bruce cannot know about my letter to the king. He's returned to Scotland because he senses danger at court, that's all. It's better that I meet and pacify him until the king orders his arrest. Besides, he'll not try anything in a Holy place". Robert Comyn was not convinced that Bruce was without suspicion. Why else should he suggest a meeting, but his nephew was a stubborn man, who did not take kindly even to sensible advice.

The tenth of February was a grey and bleak day. Snow lay in deep drifts where it had been blown by the wind. Its surface was frozen and crusty for fresh snow had not fallen on the previous night. The citizens of Dumfries were busy with their daily tasks but tried to keep indoors. If working outside was necessary they sought shelter from the wind in the lee of their houses. Fat with many layers of clothing, their faces were red from the raw, cold weather. They took little notice of the horsemen gathering outside Greyfriars Church. Up in the castle the sessions had begun and at such times it was a common sight to see great men come and go.

Comyn and his following were already waiting outside the church gates when Bruce and his men arrived but when they saw them approach, Comyn and his uncle, Sir Robert, dismounted and withdrew into the church. Bruce followed taking with him Christopher Seton, his brother-in-law.

John Comyn stood by the altar, his uncle waiting at a little distance. Comyn had removed his helmet and flung back his protective chain mail from his head and neck. He stood with bowed head as if in prayer. "Wait here by the door Christopher and see that no one enters," Bruce said, then he also walked to the altar and bowed towards the cross before confronting Comyn. "I thought you and I had a bargain John, on which we shook hands and set our seals." Comyn reddened but tried to bluff his way out of trouble. "You're very blunt, Bruce. I recall us agreeing to share our lands and honours should one of us become king. I do not think anything has changed."

"You say not, yet you chose to send your copy of our agreement to a third party." Robert Bruce withdrew the letter and bond from within his surcoat and flung them at Comyn's feet. Until that moment both men had hoped they could buy time and avoid confrontation, but the sight of the damning documents lying between them aroused such passion that both drew their daggers and flung themselves at each other. Bruce's dirk cut deep into Comyn's unprotected throat. The crimson blood splattered the white altar cloth before either Robert Comyn or Christopher Seton could intervene. Robert Comyn rushed to his nephew's side cutting with his sword at Bruce, but Seton caught the blow with his shield. The older man staggered backwards and before he could recover Christopher Seton had cut him down.

Bruce and Seton stood looking down at the Comyn kinsmen, one dead and the other, Sir John, lying in a growing pool of blood, undoubtedly dying. Bruce said, "My God, Christopher what have I done? I have broken the laws of sanctuary." "Come Rob, this can't be undone," and Seton pulled Bruce by the arm to urge him to leave. As they fled from the church two friars ran towards the altar, horror showing on their faces, the noise of their sandals slapping the flagstones and echoing around the empty church.

Outside the followers of Comyn waited, nervously gripping their battleaxes or claymores when Bruce ran out to his waiting men. Roger Kirkpatrick stood holding Bruce's horse and when his lord returned bloodstained he said, "What's happened, sir? Why the haste?" "I think I've killed Comyn and in such a place." "You only think, then I'd better make sure." He called to James Lindsay and together they walked hurriedly into the church. One of the friars had gone to get help but the other knelt by Sir John pressing his hand against the wound in the knight's neck. Roger Kirkpatrick took hold of the man by the back of his habit and pulled him roughly aside. Comyn opened his eyes when the pressure, which had been applied to his neck, was removed. A rattling sound came from his throat with each laboured breath he took. He was mortally wounded and could not be expected to survive. For a few brief moments Kirkpatrick stood hesitantly. To take a life on the altar steps was indeed a heinous sin. The friar got to his feet and with clasped hands called, "My Lord, think before you strike," but Kirkpatrick did not think any further and drove his broadsword deep into his victim's chest. James Lindsay had checked already that Sir Robert was dead and together both men hurried from the church.

This turn of events and the violation of the sacred building had shocked Robert Bruce who was a reverent man, but nothing could change his situation. He must strike and risk all now or run to his sister in Norway. Yet if he ran away all men's hands would be against him. He turned his horse calling loudly to his men, "On them," and charged Comyn's men.

When Robert Kirkpatrick and James Lindsay emerged from the church, Bruce's men had already slain many of Comyn's followers while the survivors were trying desperately to withdraw up the road towards the castle. Kirkpatrick and Lindsay mounted and sped off intent on cutting off their retreat.

The English guards on the battlements of Dumfries Castle heard the commotion down in the town well before the fleeing men came into view. The sergeant at arms, with a dozen or so of his men, galloped away to find out what the trouble was all about and to restore the king's peace; they did not return.

Sir Richard Siward, governor of Dumfries Castle, looked down from the walls at the fighting below. Plainly it was not a dispute between Scottish rabble in the town but men of rank fighting on horseback with arms and armour. As the fighting came closer he could see the coats of arms on the shields of the combatants. The Bruce and Comyn men were feuding again. He had heard that Bruce had returned to his castle a few days previously. Meanwhile as governor he had a duty to uphold the law and at this moment that meant securing the safety of the castle while the Court Sessions were in progress. "Shut the gates," he bellowed to the guards and the heavy, iron-bound gates were slammed shut.

Bruce and his followers arrived victorious and he called out to Siward, "Open the gates and I'll spare all within." Siward made no reply and withdrew from the ramparts. After a few moments Bruce called out his offer again but when there was still no reply and the gates remained firmly shut, he ordered Kirkpatrick to find brushwood suitable to burn the castle gates while his brother-in-law, Christopher Seton, organized burning arrows as a diversion.

Hearing the commotion, the citizens of Dumfries decided to defy the bitter weather and stood watching the fun from further down the road. Some of the hardy, young apprentices and journeymen climbed onto the parapet of the Lady Devorgilla's stone bridge over the River Nith where they had a better view. Whenever a fighting man received a blow a great cheer went up from the spectators whatever side the victim belonged to.

Within the castle the English, who had been caught by surprise, took up defensive positions and tried to put out the small fires started by the fire arrows that hissed over the castle wall. In the great hall the justices became alarmed by the noise outside, particularly when they were told that the castle was under attack from the followers of the Earl of Carrick. They decided to barricade the doors and make a defiant stand. A column of smoke, then flames and sparks began to rise above the castle gateway. Bruce was determined to gain entrance. Sir Richard ran up the steps to the battlements and cautiously looked down at the attackers who were dragging up more substantial logs and throwing them onto the fire in front of the gate. The Earl of Carrick saw the governor and called up, "Richard, surrender and you and all your men will be given a safe passage to England. Come, there are none that know of your plight who will make haste to aid you."

Bruce was right, of course. No one knew of the uprising, if an uprising it was and the garrison had but a handful of men. At this time of the year they were running low on supplies and could not sustain a siege. Flames began to leap high above the gatehouse and the heat could be felt on the inside. Once again he looked down at his attackers. They were excited. Some stood watching the flames and laughing, but none were in the mood to halt their attack. He called down to his men, "Open the gates and place your weapons in the centre of the yard."

Once inside the castle Bruce called to the justices to surrender. At first they tried to defy him until the thatch on the roof of the hall caught fire and was in danger of falling in upon them. Only then did they accept Bruce's offer of a boat to carry them safely across the Solway Firth to England.

They escorted Sir Richard from the castle to the quay to await the tide and as he left he said to Bruce, "Have you taken leave of your senses, Robert? When the King hears of this his revenge will be terrible. What can you hope to gain from your actions?" Bruce did not answer and nodded in farewell. As the English marched out young men from Dumfries came in and asked if they could join the earl and his men and fight for Scotland and Bruce laughed and said, "For sure, Scotland needs all the help she can get." Then he turned to his brother, Edward, "Take mounted men and ride now to Comyn's castle at Dalswinton and secure it before they have word of events here."

Robert Bruce spent a restless night. Now that the exhilaration of the day's events had ended, in the cold and dark the memory of his action in the church haunted him. He tossed and turned, listening to the wind howling around the castle walls. It was still black outside when he gave up all idea of sleep. His squire had been lying near the fire and jumped to his feet as his lord poked the embers and threw on a handful of kindling. Orange flames lit the chamber with dancing shadows.

"Go and find me food and drink, Harry. I need to think."

The young man left and Bruce fell onto his knees beside the bed, crossed himself and clasping his hands in prayer he recited the Pater Noster. Then he asked the Lord for his interception for the souls of the recently fallen, particularly for Sir John Comyn and begged for forgiveness for his own sin. Finally he prayed:

"Should it be your will Lord to spare your servant,

Humbly I will devote my life to the service of Scotland,

Never again will I seek my own desires and comforts

I will strive only for justice and freedom for this Kingdom,

To your glory."

Outside he could hear voices as his squire returned, accompanied by his brother, Nigel. As they sat for a while by the fire eating, Bruce said, "Nigel, take experienced men and for safety escort Elizabeth, Marjorie and the other womenfolk secretly to Bishop Wishert's manor at Stobo. I shall send word to you when it's safe to bring them to me."

When dawn broke, bleak, with flurries of snow in the air, Sir Robert Bruce accompanied by a mounted force rode out from Dumfries Castle for Paisley. News of his attack and capture of Dumfries Castle had already spread and men came from the villages, hills and forest to join him, but they did not come in great numbers as they had to Wallace's banner. Well, could he blame them for their lack of trust, so far he had done little to gain it.

Bishop Wishert was now an old man. All the years of Scotland's strife he had borne with fortitude, but it had taken its toll. He had always known that William Wallace could only be Scotland's

Champion, never her true king, but he had grown fond of the man and had admired the nobleness of his character. It had been Wallace's hope that Bruce would take up the challenge and wear the Scottish crown. The Bishop had pledged his support for the earl but after Wallace's betrayal and ignominious murder in August of the previous year Wishert had feared Bruce would forget Wallace's sacrifice and continue to live in the English king's shadow.

In the late afternoon of the day following his departure from Dumfries, Bruce knelt humbly before Bishop Wishert and made confession for his violent act, begging for forgiveness. Well, whether it was through accident or design, Bruce had struck his blow for freedom and the church must now give him support. "I absolve you from your sin." He made the sign of the cross above the bowed head. "Your penance must fit the seriousness of the sin but you may perform a more suitable penance when you have finished fighting for Scotland. Meanwhile, go to the chapel and keep vigil for the night and pray till dawn for the soul of Sir John. I will send word to all men of the church that they should give aid to you in your fight. In return you must swear solemnly that you will defend the liberties of our church in Scotland." Bruce held up his hand, "I do so swear."

That night in the chapel was long and cold. At its coldest they brought him a little wine to warm him and a soft cushion for his knees. He accepted the former but refused the offered cushion. He must accept just penance, although God knew that his knees were so stiff and sore from the cold flagstones on which he knelt and he wondered if he would ever stand upright again. Although he did genuinely repent his sin he found it hard to keep his mind on his prayers and consequently, by morning he had already made plans for his campaign. He must secure some of Scotland's strongholds and gain the support of other men of influence.

Sir Reginald Crawford who had been Sheriff of Ayr until an Englishman had been given the post, was ordered to collect men and to hold the castles at Ayr and Tibbers. Thomas Bruce rode immediately to Dunaverty Castle because it secured the entrance to the Clyde whilst Sir Robert Boyd set forth to capture Rothesay. As many fortresses and strongholds as possible in the west had to be seized before the English had time to rally and Bruce issued orders that all men of fighting age be ready within twenty four hours for mobilization.

Edward Bruce and John Wallace, followed by many mounted men rode to the castle of the Earl of Strathearn at Crieff. They were determined that he should join Robert on campaign and recognize

Bruce as the rightful heir to Scotland's throne, for Strathearn would bring many powerful supporters with him. Strathearn was warned of their approach and with twenty of his closest men, he rode into the hills hiding at a lodge that he used when he hunted deer. While Edward Bruce discussed with John Strathbogie, Earl of Atholl, how they would persuade the reluctant Strathearn to join them, Malcolm of Innerpeffray and his followers rode into the castle courtyard. Bruce's men crowded around them, broadswords drawn, for Sir Malcolm was among Strathearn's supporters.

Atholl, of a less fiery nature than Edward Bruce, stepped forward and with cautious courtesy greeted Malcolm. "Do you come as friend or foe, sir, for you should know that your lord has fled to the safety of the hills." "Aye, so I'm told, but although I've given my pledge to Strathearn and have supported him in all matters, my heart is with Scotland and I and my men have come to join The Bruce." For a moment even Edward Bruce was at a loss what to say. The tension lifted and it was Sir Malcolm who continued. "He'll have gone to ground in his lodge up in yon glen. We'll help you in your quest but we'd prefer to use persuasion rather than the sword for there are many of my followers who are kinsmen of my lord's kindred."

They arrived at the earl's hall as evening drew in. It was difficult to see in the darkness and Bruce ordered his men to spread out to prevent escape. The stone-built hall was long and low, with a turf roof. It was tucked into the foot of a hillside, a stream bubbled merrily close by. Atholl thought how well the hall blended into the surrounding boulder and fern-covered landscape and only the smell of wood smoke announced its occupation.

Edward Bruce stood just outside arrow's range and called out to Strathearn. "Come out man and let's talk in the open where all may see and hear us." For a while all was quiet and Atholl began to fear Strathearn intended to fight it out. Around him his men grew restless. Some withdrew an arrow from their quiver or unhooked a battleaxe from their saddle. They began whispering to one another looking for any vantage point where they might let fly their first arrow. Then they heard creaking from an opening door and light from the fire within flooded the entrance porch.

The men were silent as the earl of Strathearn walked out to meet Edward Bruce. The Earl it seemed was reluctant to join The Bruce's cause and raised many arguments. If Robert Bruce received absolution for Comyn's murder from the Holy Father in Rome, Strathearn argued, then he could support him but to pay homage to a man who had committed such an act before God's altar would put his soul in jeopardy. Surely Edward Bruce could - understand his problem, but Edward Bruce's patience had run out and his persuasion became more intimidating. When he threatened to burn Strathearn's manors and all his people with them, Strathearn gave in and he and his followers rode out with Bruce's men.

Three weeks after the murder of Sir John Comyn, King Edward received a message demanding that he recognize the Earl of Carrick as King of Scots. The English King, now a sick and tired, old man had taken to his bed. Mindful of their king's fragile health, his council sent a suitably worded reply. 'The only rightful King of Scotland is our liege, King Edward and Robert Bruce must return to the English crown all castles which he has unlawfully seized.' They sent their reply to Berwick where members of the king's Scottish council were meeting and it was they who forwarded the English reply to Bruce.

Bruce was at Paisley Abbey and smiled when he read the English king's letter. Well, it was no more than he expected. As for giving back the castles, he would take as many as he could. He pushed the letter across the table so that Bishop Wishert might read it and said, "The Bruce King Edward once knew would have considered his position, given back the castles and begged his king's forgiveness - which after careful thought the king would have granted. This Bruce will do no such thing - he'll defend himself with the longest stick he can find." The bishop smiled and was relieved that Bruce remained defiant.

In Berwick, William Lamberton, Bishop of St Andrews and President of the Scottish Council heard of Bruce's uprising and read his challenge to the English king with a wildly beating heart. At last here was a worthy successor to William Wallace. A man who would be king. In the bishop's service was a Benedictine monk, John Blair, who had been chaplain to Wallace and was himself a patriot. He called Blair to him, "John, go secretly to Paisley and tell Bruce that he must be crowned king with all haste. The ceremony should take place at Scone with as many to witness the act as possible. I will come for the inauguration by the 25th March, which will be the anniversary of the English attack on Berwick. Should I be delayed then Bishop Wishert must carry out the ceremony." Blair nodded. He had had many years' experience as messenger to the Scottish State.

When Wishert received Lamberton's message he ordered the royal coronation robes be prepared for the ceremony. They had been hidden from the English for the past ten years and were now brought up from the vaults. Then he sent word north to Bishop David Moray that he should also attend King Robert's enthronement at Scone.

In mid March Bruce left Paisley on his journey to his crowning and in his escort there were many men who proudly bore scars received fighting for Scotland. They had not travelled far when a man riding in some haste caught up with them. Bruce halted, perhaps the messenger brought bad news. The newcomer was a tall, dark, young man, who had seen about eighteen summers. He jumped from his horse and ignoring the mud, fell on his knees in front of Bruce.

"Sir, I'm James Douglas, son of William Douglas. Since my father's death in an English prison I've been reared in the household of Bishop Lamberton and he gave me permission to seek service in your company."

"Well, young Douglas, who's not heard of your father? If you conduct yourself as he did, Scotland will become famous throughout Christendom."

"Sir, I'll serve you loyally but beg you return to me my ancestral lands which the English king gave Clifford." Bruce thought for a few moments, scrutinizing the pale and serious, young face. Then he held out his hand, "God willing, James Douglas, your lands will be returned to you along with many honours, but I'll need your help to hasten the English on their way."

Douglas joined King Robert's party and he became Bruce's most trustworthy follower and a renowned warrior. The king did not forget his promise to Douglas and a friendship between them grew and lasted to the end of their days.

They arrived at the palace of Scone on the 22nd March and shortly after, Bishop Lamberton also joined them, having secretly left Berwick. Later Bishop Moray arrived, closely followed by Neil Bruce escorting the Lady Elizabeth, young Marjorie Bruce and other ladies of Bruce's following including his sister, Christina Seton.

Elizabeth Bruce stood on a bearskin in front of the fire with the long, brown fur partly covering her small feet. She wore only her shift. Her fiery, bronze hair hung in a thick, rippling cascade to her waist covering her slender, white arms. The light from the fire cast wild, dancing shadows around the walls, emphasizing the rich colours on the wall tapestries and bed covers.

"Come Beth, come to bed, as much as I enjoy watching you there in the firelight, I'll enjoy you more in bed." Elizabeth turned and gazed at her husband with her head slightly tilted to one side, as was her habit. "How can you be so jolly and think of love Robert, when you have brought us to such a predicament?"

For a few moments her husband made no reply but continued devouring her with his eyes. Her shift was made of the finest, linen gauze and the firelight emphasized the curves of her breasts and hips and every soft detail of her slender body. It was still Lent and a pious man should show restraint and curb his passions, but Elizabeth was a very beautiful woman. He laughed, threw back the bed covers, jumped from the bed and gathered her in his arms, pulling her down onto the bearskin and taking handfuls of her thick, silky hair. "Beth, it's not possible for me to take your scolding seriously, standing as you are, almost naked and looking so desirable." Elizabeth Bruce took a deep breath, intending to continue with her rebuke, but her husband was a very determined man in all things and he silenced her with his kisses and caresses.

On the 25th March 1306, the Feast of the Annunciation, Robert the Bruce, with dignity and solemnity, held his inauguration and became Robert I, King of Scotland. Dressed in the cherished gold and purple, royal robes that had been so carefully hidden by Bishop Wishert, Bruce was led to the chair of the Abbot of Scone, and there he was enthroned, for the sacred Stone of Scone was far away in London. At the appointed moment, when custom demanded that the Earl of Fife should place the crown upon the kingly head, Isabel, Countess of Buchan, acting on behalf of her brother, placed a circlet of gold upon King Robert's head. She stepped backwards from the dais, head lowered, eyes downcast, overcome with the emotion of the occasion then she paused, curtsied slowly and looked up at her king and his blue eyes smiled back at her. Isabel returned to her place beside the Earls of Lennox and Atholl with a wildly beating heart. The Earl of Strathearn stood nearby watching the lady. She was a fine looking women, not beautiful, but with a rounded body, ample breasts, dark, curling hair and when she smiled, which she often did, she had a dimple in each cheek and perfect, white teeth. It was well known that she and the earl, her husband, did not get on, but to leave her home and kinsfolk to crown her husband's enemy was indeed an heroic act and some might say a foolhardy one. She had arrived riding her husband's black destrier. Buchan was very proud of his string of warhorses and they were better housed and fed than many of his followers. Strathearn mused that the loss of the horse would anger him more than the loss of his wife.

The Bishop of St Andrews took Bruce by the hand and led him around the congregation that all might see their king and as he left the dais a shout arose, "God Save King Robert, God Save the King."

The celebration feast was sufficient to satisfy hungry men with many types of fish, both salt and freshwater, for it was still Lent. Isabel, Countess of Buchan, sat on the king's right and he toasted her liberally throughout the meal. Elizabeth, on his left, sat in silence and eventually he said, "Beth, why are you so glum, you're the most beautiful Queen Scotland has ever seen. Come love, smile and show all here that you are happy to be Queen to my King." She looked down twisting the rings on her fingers before replying, "Aye, maybe you'll be king for summer, but king of winter you'll not be."

Fortunately, only those sitting at the king's high table heard their queen's bitter words. The king made no reply and took a long drink from his goblet. A little later the queen said that she felt unwell and begged that all would forgive her if she withdrew. That night the king did not go to his wife's chamber but the sound of the king's voice and Isabel of Buchan's laughter could be heard coming from her chamber far into the night.

When King Edward heard the news of King Robert's coronation, his anger and sense of betrayal was intense. He had nurtured the Earl of Carrick, had enjoyed his company at court and had given the young man many gifts. Edward prided himself on his understanding of men and he had judged Bruce to be self-seeking and devious. A man of charm and knightly skills, but not inclined to raise his head above a parapet when the omens were against him. He could see now that this viper had been awaiting only the death of his liege lord King Edward, to strike and take the crown of Scotland for himself. Well, ill he might be, sometimes the angel of death did stand at the foot of his bed beckoning, but Robert Bruce had misjudged the situation if he thought the King of England would depart this life when there was a threat to his power. Ignoring the pleas from his doctors and council king Edward arose from his sick bed and began to plan another invasion of Scotland.

Throughout his long reign Edward had learnt that to wage a successful war, a king must have the full support of his army and the best way to do this was to play on men's ambition and greed. The promise of land and titles to a successful warrior would keep any army marching forward.

He sent out a general proclamation that on the feast of the Pentecost on the 22nd May, he would hold a great festival of Knighthood. His son the Prince of Wales would be knighted along with all eligible young men, before taking arms against Scotland. Nearly three hundred men presented themselves and amid great splendour in the Abbey of Westminster, each candidate knelt humbly before his king and was tapped upon each shoulder before arising a true knight of the realm. After the ceremony, in the Great Hall of Westminster, lit by a thousand candles, the newly created knights were wined, dined and entertained at their king's expense. Late in the evening when many were unable to stand without support, a huge golden dish was carried shoulder high into the hall. Upon it lay two swans held in place by shining golden chains. The old King rose and a hush fell upon the company.

"I swear before God and these swans to avenge the death of the Lord Comyn and thereafter never to bear arms against a fellow Christian, but to end my days on crusade." There was a roar of excitement and anticipation, then the Prince of Wales jumped to his feet.

"I swear before God and these royal birds, that I will never sleep more than two nights in the same place until I have reached Scotland and avenged Comyn."

Other young men stood unsteadily, swaying on their feet and pledging to avenge the Lord Comyn and destroy Bruce. The hubbub could be heard as far away as the City of London. The old king watched and listened to the excited, young voices. His friend and adviser Anthony Bek, Bishop of Durham, sat on his left hand and he turned to him and said, "Well Bek, Bruce will need a swift ship if he is to escape their onslaught."

Prospects of a new war in Scotland were met with general excitement and great expectation in southern England. War was a profitable business. The king's army would need food, carpenters to build siege engines and new ships to replace the many which would be lost at sea. Farmers, merchants and sea captains in the eastern counties of Suffolk, Norfolk and Lincolnshire smiled with satisfaction. The folk in the border counties of Northumberland, Cumberland and Westmorland shuddered and began to reinforce the fortifications of their towns and manors. The smiths in their forges set aside the peaceful, practical tasks, which they had been doing and worked late into the spring nights, forging weapons for war. In the market places, as people went about their daily duties, the only topic of conversation was the king's new war. Opinions were divided. Many dreaded sending their young men away to fight. If they left the Scots in peace surely they would leave them alone. Yet throughout the counties the reeves and other men of importance said that if Bruce was allowed to take what he wanted and to commit sacrilege in a Holy Place, who could tell where this business would end. They must put their trust in the old king who had not failed them yet.

Sir Henry Percy began to reinforce the garrison at Carlisle and took command of the western approaches on the border, whilst in Berwick, the Earl of Pembroke, sent out patrols to guard the border in the east.

In early summer the Prince of Wales left London in command of the English army. Veterans among his troops wondered if their young commander was man for the task, but the old King was to follow his army. He would lead them when the time came and they were sure he would bring them his usual victory. However, by early July, his party had only reached the Midlands and the strain on the king was plain. His warhorse was lead along by his squire while the king lay in a wagon surrounded by soft cushions to relieve the pain as the vehicle bumped along the rutted, dusty roads. For most of the time his eyes were closed and from his pallor and the perspiration on his brow it was plain to all that he was mortally ill.

As soon as the coronation celebrations were over, king Robert led his small company of knights and men at arms through the wild country to the northeast of Scotland. As he marched he tried to persuade men to follow him as their rightful king and fight for Scotland's freedom, but since his triumphal ride to his coronation, men's opinions had changed. Dumfries, Dalswinton and Tibbers Castles had been recaptured by the English and news spread that the English king and his son were marching north, intent on revenge. Scotland had known misery for so many years and since all men had paid homage to King Edward it could not be denied that he had imposed peace on the land and the Kingdom was once again beginning to prosper. Now here was another great man intent on starting the whole bloody business again. Moreover, rumour had it that the English had asked the Pope to excommunicate Bruce for his heinous murder of the Lord Comyn. To join Bruce would be a dangerous venture for both the body and the soul. So they listened to him, nodded their heads vigorously, agreeing with his arguments, but returned to their homes and did nothing. If Bruce and his men pressed them they gave provisions but few men came forward willingly to join Scotland's army. By midsummer, he had in his company one hundred and thirty five knights and five hundred archers and men at arms.

The Earl of Pembroke advanced through the lowlands of Scotland with three hundred knights and more than thirteen hundred foot soldiers, killing and burning as they went. The lands and manors of King Robert's supporters, Sir Michael Wymyss and Gilbert de la Hay, were particularly singled out by orders of King Edward. From Perth, the earl sent out patrols into the countryside, harrying and burning.

Pembroke had raised the dragon standard, a sign to the enemy that they would be offered no mercy and he intended to use his authority to the full. The uprising must be nipped in the bud now. Pembroke had known Bruce at court and had found him to be an amusing fellow, always ready to gamble on a game of dice and this treachery had surprised Pembroke. To judge from past experience, Bruce would not be man enough to continue the struggle once he realized the odds against him.

On a warm spring evening in late May, a patrol returned from Fife bringing prisoners with them. The captives were paraded before the earl. All were priests and Bishop Wishert of Glasgow was among them.

"Well, well, the king making bishop," the earl sneered. "The king will be delighted to see you, my lord."

The bishop was not a large man and was already well advanced in years. His captors had not treated him with kindness during his journey to Perth and he was dirty and tired. His clothes and face were smeared with dirt and blood from a gash on the side of his forehead. Nonetheless, he stood before the earl with dignity and did not beg for any special favours. The following day they sent him south, in chains, under close escort to be judged by the English king. A few days later, Bishop Lamberton was also captured and Pembroke smugly sent him to England. In due time the king could replace the vacant Bishoprics with his own men, for the earl was sure that the two Scottish clerics would not remain alive for long.

King Robert dismounted and led his wife's chestnut mare to a rocky outcrop shaded by rowan trees. A shallow, mountain River ran merrily by and on its mossy bank, where none could see them, he lifted her down from her mount.

She clung to him, fearful now that the time had come for them to part. They had had many partings in the three years of their marriage but this time he was leaving her to fight against the king whom her own father supported. The anger and jealousy, which she had felt towards Isabel, Countess of Buchan, had not passed but she would not allow it to blacken this precious moment of farewell. Gently he took hold of her chin and tilted her face up towards his. "My love, not so glum. I shall return and we will lay together as we did last night." She smiled wistfully for a few moments, remembering her joy when they had lain joined in love. Not for the first time, she thought how foolish she was to be jealous of his peccadilloes. She knew there were many, but she was his wife and none of them could take that away.

"Sweetheart, I'll return to you triumphant. Have no fear." He kissed the tips of her fingers and together they walked back to the assembled men.

Marjorie broke off her animated conversation with young James Douglas and rode to her father. "Father, please let me stay with you. I ride as well as any boy. Please don't send me away." Laughing, her father said, "Marjorie, you have a fine spirit, but your father must know you are safe within the walls of Kildrummy Castle." She pouted and looked over towards young Douglas, but later left in the company of other ladies without further argument, escorted by Nigel Bruce, her uncle.

Bruce continued to search the countryside for supporters but towards midsummer he withdrew to the city of Perth for there the English Earl of Pembroke held the castle. They arrived in the late afternoon on a hot, dusty day. The poor, living in their mud and thatch cots outside the city walls, scattered when Bruce and his men appeared. They had little to fear from either side for they had nothing worth stealing but the rags on their backs, but it was wise to put space between themselves and an English arrow.

When the English guards saw Bruce they sent word to the earl who came out onto the battlements, accompanied by Sir Ingram de Umfraville, ally and friend of the Comyn kinsfolk.

Bruce left his men and rode up to the gates calling out to the Earl, "Pembroke, bring out your men and fight now or surrender up the city to me." The English earl laughed, "You've the affront to offer such a challenge to me, when you've murdered my own sister's husband and are in command of such a puny force. Well, you were always a man to chance your arm. My men and I enjoy a good joke and we'll take you up on the offer tomorrow. We don't want to have blood on our hands on a Sunday. Anyway, it's too late in the day, besides which we haven't eaten. Come back in the morning." The earl did not wait for Bruce's reply and laughing and talking loudly with Sir Ingram, the two strolled along the parapet of the battlements.

Bruce turned his horse and rode irritably back to his waiting men who were not that far off and had heard the conversation. Edward Bruce said, "He was always a pompous ass. Let's make camp here out of arrows range, Rob, then he'll know we mean business."

"Nay, he's accepted the challenge and we have no siege engines nor other mighty weapons to lay siege to a city. The men are all hot and tired from the march. We'll withdraw and shelter for the night in the Methven woods. The English will still be here in the morning."

"Surely it would be wise to leave a picket here to watch them, Rob," suggested Edward. Robert Bruce looked at his brother and laughed, "Edward, why so suspicious, Pembroke is an honourable knight who has always followed the code of chivalry. We'll go and rest and prepare for tomorrow."

His small army camped for the night on high ground overlooking the River Almond. They dismounted and began preparing themselves and their horses for rest. The sun had already dipped down behind the hills but the evening air was still heavy with the scent of summer flowers and the sound of insects droning in the yellow broom. Many men took off their heavy chain mail while some went to the Riverbank, stripped off their clothes and swam, laughing and splashing in the sparkling water. As the evening wore on they lit fires to prepare food and here and there, according to their mood, the sound of singing mingled with the noise of sharpening of weapons and the cropping of the horses grazing the green grass by the Riverbank.

The Earl of Pembroke was an experienced soldier as well as a man of honour. In normal circumstances he would have kept his rendezvous the following day, but Bruce had relinquished his claim to chivalry when he killed a fellow knight in Greyfriars Abbey and turned traitor to his king. The earl did not consider it a dishonourable act to attack the Scottish rebels later that evening as dusk fell.

James Douglas was in the woods, the moon was out and by its silver light, he had tracked a boar. The animal led him to a small clearing, where it met others of its kind and together they were rooting among the ferns and tree roots. Douglas left his horse tethered by a beech tree and crouched by a thicket, watching his quarry. Slowly he placed an arrow in his bow but before he could let fly, the animals where startled by the sound of horses and the noise from bridles. Douglas froze. In the twilight he could see the ghostly shapes of riding men. It had to be the English and they were riding towards Bruce's camp. Silently he crept back to his mount. Riding as fast as the darkness and trees would permit, he returned to his comrades. When he was close and could see the flames of their campfires, he began to call out loudly, "Scots, to arms, Scots to arms. The English are coming." Confused, sleepy men searched for boots, broadswords and shields and stamped on the embers of their fires.

Robert Bruce had removed the saddle from his horse and was using it as a seat by the campfire. He was drinking wine and talking to Christopher Seton, when James Douglas galloped from the cover of the trees calling out his warning. Surely he was mistaken. Pembroke was well known for his honour and would not stoop to such trickery. Nonetheless, Bruce called out to his men to prepare themselves for battle as best they could. He had mounted his own destrier and was ready with broadsword and battleaxe as the English, led by the Earl of Pembroke and de Umfraville broke from the cover of Methven Wood.

Bruce galloped towards the English. The men who had already reached their saddles followed. He was always fearless in battle and cut to left and right as he rode towards Pembroke. The earl sat a large black stallion which was covered in almost as much armour as its rider, but when Bruce drew close he leant forward and drove his sword upwards so that the point went into the animal where neck joined chest and was unprotected. The horse fell back onto its haunches before collapsing onto its side pinning its master to the ground. Bruce turned his mount ready to strike a fatal blow to his fallen enemy but Sir Philip Mowbray, who had been riding close to the earl, rushed at Bruce and so violent was his attack that Bruce lost balance and control of his horse and fell from the saddle. Quickly he tried to remount but Mowbray took hold of the bridle and began calling "Help, Help, here I have the new king. Help!" Christopher Seton came to Bruce's aid and dealt such a blow to Mowbray that the Englishman toppled from his horse and, although not dead, lay stunned on the ground.

Taken by surprise and without the advantages of position or numbers, Bruce's situation was hopeless. The English concentrated their efforts on capturing Bruce and so fierce became the English attack that, surrounded by his closest comrades, Bruce was led from the battle into the safety of the woods. In the confusion, many of his men continued fighting, unable to break through the English ranks. A few crossed the River Almond and under cover of darkness, fled into the hills but as the grey light of dawn crept over the hills the full horror of the battle was revealed.

The Earl of Pembroke had been shaken by the fall from his horse and sat on a rock surveying the battlefield. Here and there wounded men groaned as they lay on the blood soaked turf and Pembroke could hear his men shouting to one another in the woods as they searched the thickets for fugitives. On the far side of the battlefield the captured common men at arms were being executed and their screams and pleas for mercy could be clearly heard. The earl stirred and walked over to the group of noble prisoners. Thomas Randolph, the young nephew of Robert Bruce, was among them. Randolph had seen sixteen summers and still had the slight build and soft cheeks of a boy. The earl knew him well and was perplexed. His orders were to treat all prisoners high or lowborn as outlaws. To send this boy south would lead to his execution. He called Randolph over and together they walked to the

Riverbank so that they might talk in private. "Tom, do you understand what trouble you're in? My duty is to send you south with the other prisoners, where you will suffer the punishment of an outlaw." Randolph flushed angrily, picked up a pebble and sent it spinning across the surface of the River. Then he turned and said, "The Bruce is my kinsman. How could I refuse to support him in his claim? He has an hereditary right to the crown of Scotland." The earl snapped back, "If you speak like that in front of others I cannot help you. If you love life you must say that because of your youth you have done the bidding of your kinsman without understanding the consequences."

Randolph looked defiantly at the earl and was ready to continue the argument but Pembroke raised his hand to silence him. "Don't dare to argue with me boy. Your position is impossible. Be guided by someone who has served the king and has a greater understanding of these matters. The Bruce is finished and will be hounded as an outlaw until there is no hiding place for him. If you give me your word that you'll accept loyal service to the English king, I'll stand surety for you." The lad turned his back so that the older man could not see his emotion. Then he mumbled, "Aye, I'll give you my word." The Earl of Pembroke turned and called to Sir Ingram who was standing at some distance. "Ingram, this youth was forced by virtue of his age and kindred to fight with Bruce. Witness his homage and he will fight with us." Then he said quietly to Randolph, "Come boy, use your commonsense." Reluctantly the young man fell on his knees before the two men. The earl held out his broadsword hilt downward and Randolph kissed it. "If you betray your promise lad, I'll kill you myself," said Pembroke.

Among the prisoners of noble birth were many of Robert Bruce's closest companions and they were forced to walk in chains behind their captors to Perth. Alexander Scrymgeour, who had triumphantly carried Scotland's standard before William Wallace after the battle of Stirling Bridge, was among the first to be marched south to Carlisle. There he was hung, drawn and quartered alongside Sir Hugh de la Haye and many others; their heads displayed on spikes over the city gates. Some men were captured whilst in hiding and they were taken to Berwick, where the same terrible fate awaited them. Sir Christopher Seton, brother-in-law to Robert the Bruce, was also amongst those who suffered.

Sir Simon Fraser had fought with Wallace and had been banished from the Kingdom of Scotland by King Edward. When he had heard of the Earl of Carrick's defiance he had secretly returned from hiding in France and had called out the men of the Selkirk Forest to join King

Robert and fight for Scotland. After the battle at Methven he fled with the survivors back towards the forests of Selkirk and for a few weeks continued to harry English patrols. One evening in August, greatly outnumbered, his men were surrounded and their leader captured and led away tied to his horse to begin the long journey south to London.

Fraser stood naked, his arms bound behind him. He stared defiantly at the English crowds who were in holiday mood, laughing and jeering at the condemned man. A group of entertainers loudly sang a popular song deriding Robert the Bruce and all Scotsmen. Fraser could hear the chorus above the hullabaloo,
"Oh, King Hobbe to the moors is gone,
To the town he dare not come."
A priest stood close by but Fraser did not listen to his words of comfort amid the din. They placed the rope around his neck and the hangman took the strain of the rope's end and hoisted him high. His legs thrashed as the pressure and choking in his throat became unbearable. The crowd swayed and rolled before his bulging eyes and a sharp pain gripped and tightened his chest, then blessed darkness descended on him. The crowd howled that the prisoner should not die before the real fun had begun. They released Fraser's limp body and threw a bucket of cold water over him but he did not recover. A man at arms cut a deep wound in Fraser's arm but still he did not stir. The Lord Clifford stepped forward prodding Fraser with the toe of his boot but there was no responding groan. "You were too heavy handed, you fool," he said to the hangman. Even though Fraser was already dead, he said, "Continue with the sentence."

To preserve it from decay the head of Sir Simon was plunged into a tub of tar before being placed on a spike on London Bridge beside the skull of his former comrade, William Wallace.

KING HOBBE OF THE MOORS

Robert Bruce awoke early. Leaving the shelter of the cave he emerged into a damp grey dawn. It was not cold, but the heavy rain of the previous day and night had drenched mountain and moor and in rocky crevices ferns bowed gracefully beneath the burden of wet foliage. Climbing down the bank he reached the River Almond which frothed merrily through the gorge over gleaming black rocks. He plunged his hands into a peaty pool and splashed water onto his face to relieve the pain in his head and his feeling of tiredness. He sat down on a fallen tree, holding his head in his hands and not for the first time, turned over in his mind the events since his inauguration as king. He laughed at himself, king, what a king. It had been his pride and foolish arrogance that had reduced brave men to this sorry state. He alone was to blame. The days since his defeat at Methven had not been easy. He had allowed himself to be led from the battlefield with shame and anger eating deeply into his heart. He had left behind many good men to retreat or die as their fate decreed. He was amazed that the men who had escaped with him and were also fugitives from Pembroke's searching patrols should continue to be so loyal to him.

He heard a movement a little way along the bank and rose, hand on dagger. James Douglas acknowledged his king with a slight bow before bending down by the bank. Bruce, instantly in control of his anguished thoughts, joined the young man who carried a small rod with line, weight and hook to which he was attaching a wriggling worm.

"Here sir, take my rod and I'll cut myself another. The trout are ready to be fed." He was friendly without the usual formality between king and subject. He did not wait for a reply but went over to a hazel, cut a branch and picked off the twigs and leaves. From his pouch he took another hook and line and together they stood quietly fishing for the brown, mountain trout. The day had brightened when the two men climbed back to their camp with eight fat fish to bake in the embers of the fire.

All that week Bruce's small force marched northeast through the mountains until they reached the banks of the River Dee. Daily fugitives from the defeat at Methven caught up with them bringing news of the retribution, which the English were inflicting on the Scots.

One day a small party of mounted men arrived leading two pack ponies laden with provisions they had captured from English troops. The kinsmen, Robert Boyd, John Wallace and Reginald Crawford were amongst the group. Bruce was relieved they at least had survived Methven. All three were hardened warriors, tough and resourceful, with many years' experience fighting the English, and he had great need of them.

Later when they sat around the fire with their king, John Wallace said, "Sir, the English lay the country waste and are raising dragon from Edinburgh to Glasgow. Neither young nor old are safe and you, my lord, have been declared an outlaw." "It'll go badly for our women folk if the English lay hands on them," said Robert Boyd. Each man sat silent for a while before the Earl of Atholl said, "Robert, the Queen, your daughter and sisters should not remain at Kildrummy. Pembroke is said to be marching towards it. It would be better if they were in some other place of safety." "Aye, this I have also been thinking. They are in grave danger now that the English have declared me an outlaw. Better they come under our protection," replied the king.

***

Christina Seton would have preferred to remain safely within the stout walls of Kildrummy castle. The comfort of a soft bed and hot food prepared in the kitchens were more attractive to her than venturing out into the mountains to sleep under the stars. However, when Atholl arrived and told them that Pembroke was marching towards Kildrummy, her first thought was to go to those whom she loved, for she had always been close to her brothers. She asked anxiously of her husband, Christopher Seton, but the Earl said when last he had heard, Seton had taken refuge in Loch Doon Castle and he could not say what had happened to him since. Christina could but hope that when she joined her brother's following, her husband would be among his men, for they had been married just a few months.

"Mother, please let me stay with my uncle and the other men, they'll never break through the walls here and Sir Robert Boyd says he'll help me improve my skill with the bow." Young Donald, Earl of Mar, looked pleadingly at his mother Christina. "Nay, Donald, we're going to your uncle. They tell me that the English are only a few days march away and will most certainly lay siege to this place. A castle under attack is not a pleasant place to be. Have no fear, you'll be able to practise your skill with arms later."

Early the following day, when the sun was beginning to lighten the eastern sky, the party of women led by Atholl rode across the drawbridge of Kildrummy Castle to rendezvous with their men folk at Inchaffray Abbey.

After the departure of his sisters and sister-in-law, Neil Bruce set about improving his stores and defences in readiness for a lengthy siege. Pembroke had lain waste the land to the south and was already in Aberdeen killing and burning. People from the surrounding country came to the castle driving their beasts before them and begging for protection, but Neil sent them away telling them to go into the mountains with as much as they could carry. "You'll be safer there, for be sure they'll bring their war machines and won't leave here empty-handed."

Towards the beginning of August the English forces were sighted. The main English army, commanded by the Prince of Wales, joined Pembroke and within a day of their arrival they began erecting four siege engines. They did not send out heralds to demand the defender's surrender and whenever one of Neil Bruce's men raised his head above the level of the parapet an arrow or bolt from a crossbow was dispatched towards him. Sir Robert Boyd had remained with Neil Bruce and cautiously Boyd raised his head so that he could watch the activity below. "I'm glad it's Kildrummy's walls which protect us from those," he said to Bruce, nodding towards the siege engines. "We must be grateful that King Edward himself decided to strengthen these before he went back to his own kingdom." He patted the thick protective walls of the castle. Crouching, he made his way along the parapet before running down the steps.

Boyd walked into the smithy for he had ordered the smith to make bolts for crossbows. He had always found the weapon very effective and had seen it used in France under siege. The smith was by the forge hammering and shaping a bolt when Boyd strode in. The smith was a typical tradesman, big and muscular, naked to the waist, his skin dirty from smoke and sweat. A blackened, leather apron, held in place by a wide leather belt, covered his front. He was a sullen looking fellow and ceased his work when he saw Boyd and plunged the hot metal into a bucket of water that hissed and bubbled as the iron cooled. When asked about the progress of his work, he answered abruptly with little pretence at civility. Boyd picked up one of the completed bolts lying on the ground and balanced it in his hand. As long as the man worked well he cared little about his manners.

The smith's young son, standing by the fire, stopped working the bellows and stood gazing at the knight. His father turned lashing out and caught the boy on the ear with the back of his hand. "Get on, who told you to stop work," he spat. The rasping, wheezing noise began again as the lad pressed the wooden bellows, the orange red charcoal glowing brightly in the dark smithy. Boyd, always direct in his ways, said sharply, "Why be such an oaf, I came but to enquire of your work." The man's face took on a subservient look, his eyes narrowed cunningly. "Sir, I meant nothing, the bolts will be ready, strong and sound," but as Boyd turned to go, the man made a crude sign behind his back and when he was sure that only his son could hear he, said, "It's their fight, not mine. I'll not die for them." Once again he began hammering at the metal with vigour.

***

Throughout the weeks of midsummer, Bruce and his men had remained hidden in the hills, living off the land, hunting the deer and fishing in the lochs and Rivers. As the weeks passed and no more fugitives from the battle joined them Bruce decided to retreat to the mountains and isles of the west. There at least would be friends, hiding places and time to gather their strength.

Since the battle Bruce had been melancholy and low in spirits. When his attention was not taken in hunting game for food or evading enemy patrols he would wander off a little distance from his men and sit gazing at the distant purple and brown hills thinking deeply on the events of the past months. The death of his friends and defeat in battle was God's punishment for his arrogance and sacrilege, of that he was sure. His confession and purification at Paisley had not been enough. God and his men needed to see him humble himself; all must be witnesses to his atonement.

By the middle of August they had arrived in the hills above the holy shrine of St Fillan and he called John Blair to him, "John, go to Abbot Maurice at Inchaffray Abbey and tell him that his king begs that he hears his confession." John Blair bowed but said nothing, for he knew how tormented Bruce was by his conscience. The abbot had heard that Robert Bruce and his men were in the area and when Blair arrived the Abbot did not wait to weigh the consequences to himself or his Abbey. His duty was quite clear and he left the safety of his religious house carrying with him in its reliquary the sacred staff of St Fillan.

Bruce waited on the hillside in a hazel grove. It was a beautiful day, the surrounding hills purple with flowering heather, the air heavy with perfume and the sweet aroma of pine trees and in the distance, the blue waters of Loch Earn sparkled in the sunlight. He could see the Abbot's procession progressing slowly through the valley, the silver reliquary, carried shoulder high on a bier, shone brightly. As they drew closer the words of the Agnus Dei, chanted by the holy men, could be heard above the sounds of the birds. Bruce rode out to meet them.

Bruce followed the abbot's instructions for his public atonement. He bathed in the River, covered himself with a loose flowing robe and with head and feet bare, climbed to the top of a circular mound built, some said, by the fairy folk. His men gathered around so that they might be witnesses to their king's penance. In full view of all, king Robert prostrated himself before Abbot Maurice. Slowly the abbot opened the holy reliquary and withdrew the Saint's sacred staff, which he held up high for all to see. The congregation was hushed, none dared to speak. Years later, when old men sat around their fires, telling tales of heroic King Robert, they said that when the holy relic touched his head and the spirit of the Holy Saint descended into him, the River ceased to flow. No ripple could be seen on its surface. The wind ceased to rustle the leaves on the trees and the birds stopped singing. Time stood still. Bruce lay prostrate, silent and humble and no one stirred. Quietly and with dignity the King arose and faced his men. In a loud voice he said. "My sins I truly repent." Then he placed his hand on his heart and said "When Scotland has no further use for this weak body I shall go on crusade to make amends for my hasty heart." At that moment, the sun came from behind a cloud and away on the far hills a capercaillie called. Once again the River began to dance merrily across the pebbles and boulders.

Just before dusk, news was brought to Bruce that the womenfolk were seen coming towards the Abbey. Immediately he rode out to greet them, eager to satisfy himself that all were unharmed. Elizabeth greeted her husband with joy but she was tired, her face pale and shining in the evening light. She could barely sit upright and held onto the saddle to keep her balance. Even the Lady Marjorie was less exuberant than usual and when her uncle, Edward Bruce took her bridle and led her the last mile, she did not object. They arrived at the abbey and Lady Wiseman, who was among the Queen's party, took Elizabeth's arm and gently, but firmly, led her to her chamber. When at last Bruce was permitted to visit his wife, she lay quietly in bed with her bronze hair spread loosely, dark against the flaxen pillow. The apothecary had given her a potion to induce sleep and her husband sat himself on the bed beside her. She smiled and held out her arms to him. "Rob, I am with child." Bruce bent forward embracing her, but when he let her go, she sunk back onto the pillow with tears in her eyes. "Oh, Rob, I'm so frightened, what will become of us? The King's vengeance is great and even my father will not save us from it when at last we're caught." Bruce bristled with anger and was about to reply sharply but remembering her condition he laughed, "Hush Beth, will you have us captured and executed without putting up a struggle? You must rest and in the morning you'll feel better. Where's your book?" He looked around the room and saw his wife's treasured book lying on a small table. It had been Robert's gift to her and both husband and wife enjoyed reading it together. Bound in red leather, the golden letters of the title, 'Chanson de geste de Fierabras,' shone in the glow of the brazier. He turned the beautifully illustrated pages, the borders decorated with animals, birds and entwined young lovers. "Sweetheart, perhaps we shouldn't read such a book within the Abbey," he laughed. "If the good monks come across it and read the tales and see these pictures, who can tell what they may do." He settled himself back on her bed and in response to her smile, read until she slept.

Bruce's marriage to Elizabeth de Berg had been a love match. He did not regret it but although many women had borne Robert Bruce children, all of whom he willingly accepted as his own, Elizabeth had not yet carried a child to its full time. That she was pregnant again at such a time was news that he would have preferred not to hear. He wanted a legitimate son and heir but not born while his parents were fugitives. He must get her to a place of safety.

The queen did not enjoy her rest and sanctuary at the Abbey for long. The following day her husband led his men westwards, the small group of women riding in the middle of the column protected by their men. They followed the bank of the Loch then turned north along the banks of the River Dochart. Now they were outside the sanctuary and protection of St Fillan and entering dangerous country, the territory of John of Lorn, son-in-law to the murdered John Comyn.

Marjorie Bruce rode her dappled, grey pony, chatting happily for much of the journey with James Douglas. She would gaze at him shyly from time to time from under lowered eyelids but her glances of admiration did not go unnoticed by the women riding with her. She had seen twelve summers and was reaching womanhood and followed young Douglas around like a puppy, laughing at his jokes and listening eagerly to everything he had to say. He was not a handsome man. His face long and pale with a heavy, lower jaw and straight black hair but women found his remoteness attractive.

Bruce had sent scouts along the tracks and as the army entered the valley leading to the narrow pass towards Tyndrum, Boyd and Gilbert de la Haye came towards them at full gallop shouting, "Ambush! Ambush!" The sides of the pass were steep, heavily wooded with the River running swiftly through and there was barely room for men to ride three abreast.

Bruce rode at the head of the column, the ladies in the middle were surrounded by mounted knights, whilst men without horses marched at the rear. No sooner had the shout of 'ambush' been heard, than the sloping sides of the pass came alive with running, jumping highlanders. Out from the cover of caves and rocks and from behind trees they hurled themselves downward towards Bruce and his followers, revenge in their hearts and plunder on their minds.

Marjorie Bruce was riding between James Douglas and John Wallace when the attack began. She looked up alarmed, her chatter to Douglas ceased. John Wallace snatched the reins from her grasp, taking control of her startled pony with his left hand, his battleaxe already firmly gripped in his right. The highland men had bare chests and thickly woven plaids wrapped around them and belted at the waist. As they jumped and ran down the hillside, they swung their Locharbar battleaxes shouting their wild battle cries. They were indeed a fierce sight for so young a maid. Douglas dug his spurs into his horse's flanks, manoeuvring the animal to face the challengers' attack while Wallace turned his horse and urged it forward, leading Marjorie back the way they had come. She clung onto her pony's mane, lying low over its neck, eyes tightly shut, she was led along the track. The noise was terrible. Horses were screaming as the highlanders swung their battleaxes at the frightened animals legs and bellies. Men shouted warnings to one another and there were cries of pain when the warning came too late. Marjorie heard a shout close to her and opened her eyes. A highlander was running by her side preparing to swing his mighty axe. "Oh, Holy Mother spare me," cried the young maid. Wallace, who was leading her, was a little in front. He slowed his pace turned in his saddle and hurled his battleaxe with such force and accuracy that it remained wedged in their attacker's chest even as he fell to the ground. His blood splattered the girl and the grey flanks of her pony.

Without pausing, Wallace pressed on, leading his charge away from danger. Marjorie from behind the nodding head of her pony, could see her stepmother with the Earl of Atholl at her side. Elizabeth Bruce had lost her white linen coif and her bronze hair, which had been plaited and bound around her head, had become untied allowing the two long plaits to fly out behind her. Through the trees Marjorie could see the peaceful waters of little Loch Dochart sparkling in the sunshine, tranquil and welcoming, whilst behind the sounds of battle continued. Wallace did not slacken the pace until they reached the shore of the loch and in the middle of the tranquil water, a small island offered safety for the fleeing women and their protectors. A boat had already left, ferrying her stepmother, aunts and young cousin Donald to the safety of a small, fortified tower. There was no other boat in sight. "Do you swim, lassie?" asked Wallace, as he urged the two beasts into the icy water of the loch. "No, No, Sir John, never have I swam." "Well, there's no time like the present so don't you be afraid. Once he begins to swim, slip out of your saddle and hold on to his mane." The animal had been a present from her father and she had a great affection for it. It had courage and she knew that for as long as it could, it would not let her down. Through the brown, peaty waters towards the sanctuary of the islet the two animals swam, the man and maid holding tightly to them. Once or twice Wallace, swimming beside Marjorie, put out his hand to steady and reassure the child but she did not panic and when her feet finally touched firm sand, the Earl of Atholl's page ran into the water to help her. She was so cold that through her blue lips her teeth chattered uncontrollably. Lady Wiseman ran to her and wrapped a cloak around her shaking shoulders. "There child, wrap yourself in this, you'll soon warm and at least you're safe." A little later Marjorie sat in the sun. Her back resting against a warm rock, she looked over the water to the wooded slopes of the glen where her father and his men could be heard and sometimes seen fighting. The Earl of Atholl, Wallace and the other men stood in a group on the shore watching helplessly.

The MacDougall clansmen tried desperately to capture Bruce and in the confined area it was impossible for him to organize his knights into an attacking force. Many men had their horses killed under them and were forced to fight on foot, but their heavy chain mail hampered their movements against the agile highlanders. Bruce hacked his way back along the narrow path towards Loch Dochart. The ground sloped away to the loch on one side and on the other a steep hillside was covered with pines, rocks and bracken. As he passed along the track, a man leapt down from the overhanging rocks. Bruce's horse reared when the fellow landed at its side. Bruce slashed with his sword using such force that his attacker's arm was severed, but before he had time to urge his horse forward, another man leapt at him, taking hold of his leg and trying desperately to pull him from the saddle. Bruce spurred his horse, shouting loudly to encourage it and as the big, frightened warhorse obeyed its master, Bruce's assailant lost his footing. His hand was caught between horse and rider and he was dragged along the stony track, shouting and cursing as he tried desperately to regain his balance. Then a third man jumped from an overhanging rock, landing behind Bruce, a knife clutched between his teeth. Before he had time to strike a blow, Bruce twisted around in his saddle and using the pommel of his broadsword he struck the highlander on the side of the head and pushed him from the back of his horse. His other attacker, who was still being dragged along at his side, was little more than a lad. Looking down Bruce could see the terror in the young eyes, but now was not the time for sentiment. He brought his sword up and down onto the tousled head and at the same time he moved his leg so that the boy was released.

As the evening drew in on the shore of Loch Dochart, it became clear that the highlanders were withdrawing back to the Tyndrum Pass and there would be no way through for as long as they controlled that area. That night Bruce took stock of his situation. He had lost many men, less than one hundred remained. Yet although the loss of friends and allies worried and upset him, it was the loss of their horses that would bring the greatest hardship. Without horses his army would cease to be a fighting force.

They rowed him over to the islet where he spent a restless night. Elizabeth pleaded that he should take flight and go north to the Orkneys and the safety of the Norwegian King's court, but Bruce sharply silenced her and by the morning had made his decision. The remaining horses were given to the women and an escort of men who would take them north to Orkney. Robert and his supporters would go west. He had come this far and would see it through to the end.

Sad farewells at an end, the women and their escort wearily rode northwards following stony highland tracks. At night they sought shelter in caves and among the crevices of rocks. There were no soft beds nor pillows, for the Earl did not dare announce their presence by seeking shelter at a manor or farmstead, particularly once they had arrived in the lands of the Earl of Ross. The journey was especially difficult for the queen who did not bother to hide her hatred and mistrust of the Countess of Fife, whilst to taunt the queen that lady took a delight in her own ability to fascinate men. No matter what their rank she would smile coyly, full of silent promises of joy to be expected in her company. By the time they had reached the Dornoch Firth, each man would gladly have faced the might of the English army single-handed, for one night with Isabelle of Fife. Sometimes she would gaze mockingly at the queen, challenging her. In her heart Elizabeth desired to fly at her rival and scratch out those eyes which had gazed up in passionate joy at Robert Bruce, but Elizabeth's character and training were such that she rode on in dignified silence. By the second week of their journey the effect on the queen, weakened by her pregnancy, was devastating and she withdrew into a shell of despondency.

Through the trees, Elizabeth glimpsed the sea sparkling in the rays of the evening sun. She was very weary and clung to the mane of her mount, a small, shaggy mountain pony. It was a spirited, tough beast, with a thick coat to withstand hard, highland winters and twitching ears always alert for the smallest unfamiliar sound, which would send his nimble hooves flying along the stony, mountain tracks. There were small twigs and leaves in his mane and tail and his legs, flanks and belly were coated in mud. She thought how furious her father would have been if he had seen one of his well-bred horses in such a condition. Oh! How her father and all her family would laugh to see her, daughter to the great Earl of Ulster, riding such a beast. Yet the animal made her feel secure for he picked his way carefully through glen and across moor with patient self-assurance.

The sergeant at arms turned in his saddle to look at her and called to the Earl of Atholl "Our lady, the queen is in need of rest, my lord." Atholl turned his mount and rode back to Elizabeth. Smiling, although tired himself, he said "Not far now, Madam." Elizabeth managed a smile in return but she could not hide her tiredness. Lady Wiseman riding behind the queen said, "She must rest for the night," then pausing she added, "We all need rest." The sergeant called out, "Shortly we'll be within the boundaries of the sanctuary of the Saint and his chapel, look, you can see its roof through the trees on the shore of the Firth." A short distance further along the track they came upon the sanctuary stone and each rider bent low from their saddle to touch the granite and claim the protection of the Saint for themselves.

They arrived at Tain on the shore of the Dornoch Firth as the sun completed its journey across the sky and lay low on the horizon, casting long shadows from rocks and trees. The earl escorted the queen into the safety of the small hospice. The building was built of stone, with a turf roof and fire ditch running through the middle of the hall, in the old style, so that all might benefit from its warmth. Four elderly canons attended the Saint's shrine, but there were few luxuries. In the corner of the hall was a closet bed, clean and warm, where the queen rested with the doors closed so that she was not disturbed by the noise from the hall. The quiet and darkness calmed her somewhat. The warmth of the bed eased her aching back and very shortly she sunk into a restless sleep. Once Lady Wiseman opened one of the doors and saw the queen tossing and turning. She withdrew, returning with a beaker of warm milk and honey and gently rousing her, said, "Drink this my dear, it will soothe you and help you rest quietly." Elizabeth drank the sweet, creamy potion but as she settled down she said, "Don't close the doors completely. It's so dark and lonely." A little later, from Elizabeth's soft regular breathing, Lady Wiseman knew that the queen was resting peacefully. The other members of their company had settled down to sleep. The earl, his squire and young Donald of Mar, who insisted on sleeping with the men, lay on the opposite side of the fire ditch, away from the ladies. The sergeant at arms and his men slept in the hayloft on the other side of the cloistered yard, but two could be heard outside on guard, walking up and down and occasionally calling to one another that all was well.

News that the Bruce women and Atholl were seeking shelter at the shrine of St Duthlac had reached the Earl of Ross early that same evening and immediately he left for Tain accompanied by many retainers. As he rode, he turned over in his mind the consequences of breaking the laws of sanctuary if he took the vagrants. The king would honour him, of that he was sure, and to take the women and Atholl would surely be permitted by God and the church. They were supporters of an outlaw who had committed murder within God's church and before his holy altar. Nay, there was no sacrilege, nor risk involved. His party arrived just before dawn. They did not stop when they arrived at the gates but rode into the cloister and quickly overcame the resistance from Atholl and his men and ignored the pleas from the canons to observe God and church laws.

The sounds of shouting and the clash of arms outside in the cloister awakened Elizabeth. Lady Wiseman opened wide the bed doors. She was very pale, her eyes wide with fear and her clothes in disarray, plainly she had slept in them. "My Lady, you must remain calm and dress yourself, for the Earl of Ross and his men are outside." The sounds of fighting men could plainly be heard and the other women were hurriedly tidying themselves, the two men were no longer in the hall. Elizabeth's auburn hair, which had not been brushed and plaited the previous night, hung around her bare arms in tangled layers. She picked up her blue, woollen dress but before she could put it over her head, the main door burst open and Ross and his men entered. He addressed himself to the young woman, "Madam, make yourself ready to come with me, for I intend to send you to the king." Elizabeth, standing in her linen shift, with her bare feet plainly visible and her unruly hair framing her white face, stared at the man, "Well, my lord, you are very gallant to break our sanctuary, do you fear nobody, not even God?" The earl coloured, but retorted, "Nay Madam, like your husband I will also answer to God on the Great Day of Judgement." The queen was about to make a reply to this but Lady Wiseman, true to her husband's name, put the queen's dress over her head and at the same time called out instructions to Marjorie Bruce to hurry in her preparations. Then she turned to the earl. "Sir, fugitives we may be but will you not allow us some privacy while we dress ourselves?" The earl did not answer but gave orders to some of his men to leave the hall whilst those who remained turned their backs. Only the earl remained watchful with his sword drawn. When the ladies asked if they could retire to the privy, the earl and a soldier, who was older than the majority, accompanied them. Of their own escort only the Earl of Atholl remained alive and he sat on the ground, for his left leg had sustained a deep wound, which one of the canons was trying to staunch. Before anyone could stop her, young Marjorie Bruce ran to the earl and kneeling beside him asked the canon his opinion of the earl's wound. "As long as it remains clean and free from putrid flesh and odours all will be well." he replied. "I will care for you uncle," said the young girl, but the Earl of Ross had placed his hand on her shoulder and she was not free to say more.

When all excuses to remain had been exhausted, the queen said to the earl, "Sir, will you not reconsider; permit us to remain here within the care of our Lord and these good men." But the earl replied angrily, justifying his actions. "You are on my lands and your menfolk have been declared outlaws. As long as you freely roam this kingdom you will be at the mercy of all men. This is for your own safety, Madam. The king will give you his protection and decide what your fate is to be." The Earl of Ross had known Elizabeth since she was a young maid and he did not wait to observe the expressions of despair and fear clouding her face but turned and gave orders for the party to depart.

THE SISTERHOOD

The English king's journey north took many weeks and by September he was resting at Lanercost Priory in Cumberland. As each new day dawned his councillors wondered if this would be his last. The king's old friend Anthony Bek, Bishop of Durham, sat constantly at his Lord's bedside ready to hear his last words and to give absolution to his master. Occasionally the king would rally and the gentlemen of the bedchamber would rearrange his pillows and raise him so that he could see out through the unshuttered window and across the fields to the Roman Emperor's great wall, stretching across his kingdom. Beyond rolled the distant northern hills of Scotland. Then he would murmur to Bek, "I believe I'm improving Anthony. Tomorrow I will be in the saddle again." Bek smiled and suggested that he read a passage from the Bible to his royal friend, but the king whispered, "No, let's talk about my Scottish venture and read me the letters from Pembroke. I must have a full picture of events." But the effort became too great and his voice trailed away, his head sank lower onto his pillows, his eyes closed and once again the king slept. Only the rattling in his chest as he struggled for breath announced that life was still present in the old man.

On a day in late September, when threatening, grey clouds hung above the hills and the wind tore dying leaves from trees and sent them whirling across cloister and fields, a messenger arrived and was ushered before Bishop Bek. He brought news that Elizabeth, wife to the outlaw Bruce, had been captured by the Earl of Ross and could be expected to arrive within the week. When the king heard the news he sat up in bed demanding wine and food, for he was sure that now it would only be a matter of time before Bruce himself was in his power and he was determined to live to see that day. He ate and drank a little and sent for his queen and the youngest of his sons, Thomas.

After the restless small boy had been taken away by his nurse and the queen had withdrawn, Anthony Bek came into the chamber and seated himself in the carved chair beside his master, while the king lay quietly planning his revenge on Robert Bruce and his kinsfolk. It was the king who spoke first. "I've heard that it's now common practice throughout Christendom to expose a prisoner on the battlements of a castle and allow the elements to do their worst." Bek looked shocked, for such methods had never been used in England before, but he said, "They tell me a cage is constructed and attached to the outer wall so that passers-by may see the occupant." "That, Bek, is what we will do with Mistress Bruce and her entourage, place them where all may view their humiliation." Bek did not answer immediately, but then said, "Do you think it wise, Sire? Remember whose daughter she is. You don't want to humiliate the Earl, her father, as well." Edward glared irritably at Bek, saying nothing and eventually told his servant to turn him onto his side. With his back towards his friend he quickly fell asleep. Bek pulled his chair to the fire and sat for sometime staring into the orange and blue flames, listening to the hiss as a flame found sap within a damp log. Punishment of Elizabeth Bruce had to be undertaken carefully. The Earl of Ulster has been a loyal supporter of the king since they had both fought together in France and it would not do to be too vindictive with his daughter. The King needed strong support now more than ever and when that young fool, the Prince of Wales, became king, the crown would need all the support it could get from a strong man like the Earl of Ulster. A few days later, just before Elizabeth Bruce and her escort were expected to cross the border, her father, the Earl of Ulster, with a large following of one hundred mounted men and as many again of foot soldiers, arrived at Lanercost. They made camp on the hillside at some little distance from the Priory and the following morning the earl, accompanied only by his squire and sons, asked for an audience with the king. They remained together for some little time and when the earl rode away, he was grim-faced and spoke to no one.

Once they left the high country behind them, Elizabeth and Marjorie Bruce journeyed in a covered carriage where prying eyes could not see them. The vehicle bumped and rattled slowly along the rutted roads and the few cushions they were given could not ease the bruising to Elizabeth's body and because they were not able to look out at the hills and forest, they passed the time telling one another stories and singing songs. At least while she rode with Marjorie she was free from the humiliating gaze of Isabelle of Fife. So tedious became the journey that Elizabeth almost looked forward to her arrival at Lanercost Priory.

Late on a September day their party clattered across the lowered drawbridge of Caerlaverock Castle. The evening was chill with the first hint of autumn and ground mist rolled silently across the flat lands from the Solway Firth. Elizabeth had felt unwell for some little while and when they pulled back the curtain so that she might get out she had continued to lie on her cushions with her eyes tightly closed. "Come Madam, we have arrived. Tomorrow we will be across the border," commanded the earl. "Go away, Sir, my stepmother feels unwell." Young Marjorie Bruce was nothing if not forthright. The earl replied, "Nonetheless Madam, you must alight. Surely you do not want to be removed by force." Elizabeth opened her eyes. She was deadly pale and her face shone in the twilight. "Sir William, please send my women to me, I am unwell." She looked imploringly at Ross, hoping that her familiarity with him would arouse old memories and soften him to show some charity, but William, the Earl of Ross, had been fighting all feelings of humanity since she had first become his prisoner and he did not intend to weaken now. He turned to his sergeant "Get her out of there." The sergeant was a Yorkshireman and his training and years of experience told him he should not stand any nonsense from the female, but during the journey south he had began to feel sorry for the poor thing. She always thanked him so prettily whenever he helped her in and out of the carriage, which had become her prison. She had not caused him any trouble and so he said kindly. "Come on m'lady, the sooner you're out of this ol' bone rattler, the sooner you'll get some good warm food inside you, then you'll feel better." She opened her eyes gazing beseechingly at him, tears rolling down her cheeks. "Sergeant, I really can't, I just can't." Marjorie, kneeling beside her tried to push the man away, but he leant forward and picked Elizabeth up, carrying her, like a child, into the great hall of the castle. She cried out in pain and immediately the sergeant felt the warm sticky blood on her clothing and his hands.

The other women, Lady Wiseman, Christina Seton, Mary Bruce and Isabelle of Fife had already been escorted into the hall when the sergeant came in carrying Elizabeth, with Marjorie running behind him. "The lady is unwell," he called. "Help me make her comfortable." He carried her close to the fire and lay her on a bench, pulling one of the cushions from a carved chair and placing it under her head. The women gathered around her whilst the sergeant withdrew for he guessed what ailed the lady and felt it was no place for him to be.

Elizabeth cried out again as pain gripped her. She could feel the blood spreading around her thighs and she began to shake uncontrollably. Lady Wiseman took hold of her hand. "There my dear, you hold on tight, the pain will soon pass."

Ross had stamped irritably into the hall. He was hungry and in no mood for any nonsense from his prisoners. He heard the commotion and turned angrily to his sergeant, "Well man, what is it now." "The lady is miscarrying, my lord." Ross swore, if this were so they would not cross the border next day. Lady Wiseman came to him, "Sir, we must find the Lady Elizabeth a more private place where we may care for her." Ross looked so bad tempered that she thought he was about to refuse her request and so she said, "Sir, it is possible that she will die without care, think who her father is." The earl did not answer, but called to the castle steward to find suitable quarters and assist the ladies.

They carried her to a small turret room. It was clean and dry with a bed, stool and clothes chest but otherwise lacked all luxury. There were no cushions nor wall hangings to lighten the grey stone walls and the only cheer came from the fire burning merrily, but it made the room very warm so that the women attending Elizabeth became very sleepy after their long ride.

Shortly after she had been put to bed she passed a tiny lifeless male infant. Hurriedly they wrapped him in a piece of cloth and gave him to a serving woman. She took him away and threw him onto the midden for, she said to herself, this is not a whole human child, blessed by a priest. It cannot be received into hallowed ground. The rubbish pit was good enough.

"There, there my dear," said Lady Wiseman. "Rest quietly, all will be well." Elizabeth continued weeping quietly. The bleeding appeared to have ceased but her back hurt so. It was as if an iron fist gripped her and clenched the whole of her lower back. They gave her some warmed wine diluted with water and sweetened with honey and spices, but she was still shaking so much that they had to hold the beaker or she would have spilled the liquid. A servant brought in a basket of hot stones wrapped in strips of woollen cloth and placed them by her cold feet. She could hardly feel her feet, not even when she wriggled her toes. Before healing sleep enveloped her she thought sadly of her babe. Once again God had taken her child. Why, oh why? Robert had sinned, that she could not deny, but the child, why punish the innocent? Now she would not hold him and kiss the tiny nose and eyes nor watch the small fingers clutching her breast. She murmured a prayer for his spirit. When the Great Day of Judgement came she would welcome her babe into her arms in Paradise; then she drifted into sleep.

In the cold light of dawn, with the promise of a fine day to come, the Earl of Ross gave orders for the escort and prisoners to prepare for their journey. He would not hear of Elizabeth Bruce remaining at the castle until her health improved. She would have plenty of time for that once they had arrived at Lanercost Priory. Lady Wiseman tried to plead with him, but he would not listen. The earl reasoned that with the tide so high, the boat voyage across the Firth would not be as taxing as the slow journey by road. Much to his relief, by mid morning, with a fair breeze, they had crossed the border into England.

Throughout their journey the Earl of Atholl had ridden among Ross's men. His feet were bound under his horse's belly and his hands tied to the pommel of his saddle. The wound in his leg had not healed and the effects of neglect and the weather, both rain and sun had caused it to swell. The wound was red along its outer edge and smelly puss escaped through onto the dirty bandaging. Only twice during the journey south had they allowed Marjorie Bruce to clean and bind his leg, indulging her because of her age, but he was kept apart from the grown women.

Ross sent a messenger in advance to the king and was not surprised that a guard, of the king's men, was waiting at the quay at Skimburness to conduct the Earl of Atholl to Carlisle Castle. Tormented by gloomy thoughts, Atholl was very weary and dejected. He had followed Robert Bruce because of kinship and affection, not for any noble ideals. In the days before 'Rob's madness' he had been such good company. Light-hearted and witty, there was no one quite like Robert for a jovial day's hunting and an evening of feasting with good wine, dancing and story telling – Rob had such a fund of amusing stories. There were few men or women who could resist his charm. It was his charm that persuaded one that something was right because Robert Bruce said so. Now, kinsmen were scattered, the women folk were in grave peril and only God and the English King knew what the future held for them all. It was his arrival at Carlisle Castle which forced him to think about the present and for a while to forget his sad reminiscing.

Elizabeth Bruce had developed a fever and lay without understanding during the journey to Lanercost. Her sister-in-law, Christina Seton, who was herself advanced in pregnancy and Lady Wiseman, nursed Elizabeth, taking turns to wipe her flushed face with damp cloths and spooning small drops of liquid into the pale, slightly parted lips. As the wagon lurched along the sick woman cried out, sometimes calling the name of her old nurse and often talking to herself in Gaelic. When they entered the gates of Lanercost her father, encamped on the hillside, joined Ross's escort, took charge of the female prisoners and saw them safely installed in chambers in the hospice. When he saw his daughter's condition he went immediately to Archbishop Bek demanding that the Royal doctors attend her.

The Earl of Ulster's reconciliation with King Edward had

occurred in this manner. After his first encounter with the English King, Richard, the Red Earl of Ulster had ridden back to his men in a high rage. The king had been irritable and vindictive when they had spoken about Elizabeth. She would be punished along with the rest of them. Ulster had reasoned that his girl could not be held responsible for her husband's act of treason. Anyone who knew Bruce, and the king knew him well, understood that Bruce was his own man, not influenced by a woman and Elizabeth was a loyal wife. "What ingratitude," the earl had shouted loudly. "All these years I've given him loyal service and now the pig-headed ass intends to insult my family by punishing my daughter for Bruce's crimes." The earl ground his teeth together and drove his spurs into his startled mount's flanks, forcing it to canter the final short distance into camp. The earl stormed into his tent flinging his mantle onto his heavily carved chair. His sons stood in the entrance. Their father's mood was uncertain and they chose not to speak. The earl broke the silence saying to his eldest son, "William, give the order to break camp now. I want to be away within the hour. His son hesitated, "Aren't you going to see the King again, Sir? We can't leave Beth to her fate." His father glared at him. "Do as I say, the king will understand when he is told we are already withdrawing and marching north towards the border. Get a message to Murdoch, order him to heave to and anchor somewhere near the mouth of the Solway."

His men had been busy preparing their evening meals when the order came to break camp. The noise and confusion as tents were packed and horses prepared could be heard in the Abbey. Finally, surrounded by his bodyguard and kinsmen the earl led his force northwards.

They marched late into the night. It was raining heavily and the men grumbled among themselves, unsure where they were going and why the 'ole fella' had disturbed their evening meal. The earl was known for his quick temper, but he was a fair man, reasonable in his demands. "Someone sent a wasp up his arse," was the general view. They were ordered to bivouac for the night and found shelter where they could in the lee of rocks or under the branches of trees. As dawn crept grey and silent over the eastern hills the men, who had spent an uncomfortable night, were already moving around trying to bring the circulation back into their numb bodies. The earl made no allowance for hunger or cold and as soon as the horses were ready he mounted and rode westwards towards the estuary of the Solway Firth. They rode along the coast to Burgh le Sands where his galleys were at anchor. With the ebbing tide and a light wind he sailed along the coast and around the point to Bowness, anchoring for the night where they could not easily be ambushed.

The Bishop of Durham had watched the Ulstermen's departure with a worried frown on his face. He understood the challenge thrown to the king and Bek knew that he must act on his master's behalf. Ulster must not be allowed to join the rebels in the north. A rebellion can so easily become a just cause. He hurried to his master's bedside, but found it surrounded by the king's doctors. The patient lay with eyes closed, his face translucent and shining eerily in the failing evening light. Symons, the king's most trusted physician whispered to Bek. "After the earl stormed from the chamber, His Majesty swooned and has remained as you see him." Bek stood watching for a while before leaving to seek out the king's council. Early the following morning a troop of the king's men, accompanied by Archbishop Bek, left Lanercost and two days later they found the earl's fleet at anchor off Bowness point.

The earl was still smarting from his last conversation with the king and was in no mood to throw caution to the wind and greet Edward's closest friend as if no insult had occurred. During the morning the Earl and his men could be seen sitting in the stern of their boats fishing for the flounder which abounded on the sandy seabed. The Archbishop, with many years' experience of manipulation and intrigue, concealed his irritation and found a sheltered rock where he sat and waited. Every hour or so he sent his clerk to the beach to hail the earl. The earl refused to speak with Bek until well beyond noon when he grudgingly agreed to allow the Archbishop to send a galley out to him so that they might talk, but he refused absolutely to come ashore himself. The Archbishop had taken the precaution of ordering a vessel to sail from Burgh. The crew rowed as close to the shore as possible, but still lay offshore and Bek would be unable to board without getting wet. His men carried him through the grey water and although he did not look in their direction Bek knew that de Burgh and all his men had lined the side of their boats to watch his discomfort. "If you value your skins, don't stumble," hissed Bek, to the men who had formed the cat's cradle, which carried him above the water. His feet and lower legs became numb from the cold water, whilst an occasional wave, higher than the rest, soaked through his robes freezing his buttocks. His men delivered him safely to the waiting vessel and he was rowed out to the Ulsterman.

The earl sat under the awning surrounded by his sons and kinsmen. Across his knees lay his long handled battleaxe, a favourite weapon and of great value. The axehead was highly polished and engraved with Celtic designs, which twisted and swirled around the blade like the Tree of Life. Its shaft was also carved with animals of many species. Bek had always thought it rather a contradiction to decorate so deadly a weapon.

The Archbishop, far from being a man devoted to the Christian ethic of peace, regularly led Edward's knights into battle and never shrunk from violence to gain the advantage. On this occasion, however, his instincts told him that if he was to retain the earl's loyalty for his master he must adopt a conciliatory pose. So he stood alone and unarmed, wearing his Bishop's robes before Richard de Burgh who said, "I see they've sent an important message with an important messenger." Bek shrugged and began, "I've come with this message." He did not mention that it was from the council and not the king, "Mindful of your loyalty and friendship and aware that you gave your daughter to the traitor, Bruce, on the King's advice, leniency will be shown to the Lady Elizabeth." The earl's face relaxed, "The lady, however, should remain within the king's protection and given a modest household until Bruce, her husband, answers for his crimes. Then she will be free to return to her father's house."

The earl sat for a while considering his reply. It could not be too long before his daughter became a widow. For that matter it would not be long before they might expect a new king. What then? "This must be binding on whoever sits on the throne of England," said the Earl. "It has already been agreed," was the reply. De Burgh knew that he would accept these terms but intended to make them wait for their answer. The two men had known one another for more than twenty years but he wanted Bek and the king's advisers to know how close they had been to losing their strongest and ablest, ally. So he said, "I'll give you my reply tomorrow." Refreshment was not offered and once again Bek was forced to climb into his own galley to be rowed towards his waiting men and carried ashore. Only when dry sand was beneath his feet did he feel that his dignity was safely restored.

The earl watched the retreating vessel before ordering his men to sail his war galleys away from the land, for that stretch of the coastline was busy with merchant ships. When the light began to fade they sailed back, anchoring some miles further south from Bowness and the following morning, when Bek checked the horizon the earl's ships were nowhere to be seen. For a moment he felt a slight tightness in his chest; surely the fool had not sailed north after all. He regained his composure; de Burgh was too experienced to throw everything away on an impulse.

Bek sat down to wait. By the middle of the morning his patience and faith were rewarded when the flotilla of war galleys sailed into view.

The doctors stood around the sick women's bed, acutely aware of her father's fiery temper. The lady's fever still raged, her cheeks red, her lips dry and cracked. Elizabeth opened her eyes, gazing at the men but without any understanding. Her eyes, the colour of a summer sky, which had always sparkled, had lost all lustre. The earl entered noisily, "well, is there improvement?" The sound of her father's commanding voice awakened Elizabeth to her surroundings and she gazed up at her father as he bent over her. "Come, come, Lizzy. It saddens your father to see you so down. Show them all what the de Burghs are made of." Elizabeth recognized her father's pet name for her and felt the pressure of his strong, hard hand on hers. It revived and comforted her. When he cradled her in his arm and held a cup of warmed, spiced wine and honey to her lips she drunk a few drops. The earl turned his awesome gaze upon the doctors; they would do their best for her.

Elizabeth did not die but lay in her chamber for many weeks with recurring fevers, with little understanding of the world and unable to walk. Her father and his men remained encamped even though the autumn of 1306 was wet and cold, with high winds blowing the leaves early from the trees and revealing the bright, scarlet-red rowan berries hanging in clusters and awaiting the hungry birds. Visits from her sister-in-law, stepdaughter, father and brothers tired her, but strengthened her spirit. Indeed many people showed Elizabeth kindness not because she was the daughter of a great man, but because of her courage, uncomplaining nature and readiness to thank even the most humble servant for their service to her. One morning in early November, when she had been carried from her bed and was seated close to the brightly burning fire, the woman hired to wash her personal linen came quietly into the room. "Lady, Wilfred, sergeant to the Earl of Ross, asks that you accept this holy relic of St Ninian. He trusts that it will bring you health and good luck." She paused and untied the small leather bag and emptied a fragment of yellowed bone onto the palm of her hand. "Wilfred said it was his mother's and brought her good fortune many times. Wilfred leaves with the earl but wishes you well." Elizabeth remembered the tough sergeant at arms who had tried in his own way to ease her suffering on their journey through Scotland. She accepted the relic and said she would keep it on a chain around her neck so that the Saint might watch over her. From her little finger, now so thin, she took a gold band, studded with garnets. "Give this to Wilfred. Tell him I have cherished it for many years. I wish him a safe journey and good fortune in his life." Before the woman could go, Elizabeth gripped her hand very firmly for one who had been so ill. "Tell me, is there news of my husband?" The woman looked fearfully around before replying. "He's still at large and some say he is in the western isles. Please let me go, my lady, it's dangerous for me." She scrambled to her feet and fled fearful of Archbishop Bek's spies.

About the same time as Wilfred's departure, others were also preparing to leave the relative security of the Priory. The king, still determined to exact vengeance on his female prisoners, had ordered the construction of three timber cages with lattice sides and wooden roofs coated in tar. The pens had been attached to the outside of the towers of the castles of Roxburgh, Berwick and London and the prisoners Isabelle Countess of Fife, Mary Bruce and the young maid Marjorie, who had seen only twelve summers, were to be imprisoned in them. The Earl of Ulster and his following were still encamped at the Priory so they did not tell Elizabeth about the fate of the two women and Bruce's daughter for fear that Elizabeth's fragile recovery might cease.

Isabel of Buchan realized early in her captivity that for her part in the seizure of the Scottish crown by Bruce, she would be singled out for a fitting punishment. At first she had feared death would be her penalty, but when she realized that this would not be the case, she grew bold again. She tossed her head provocatively, curved her mouth into the bow of a smile and with her mocking eyes obtained small privileges to ease her captivity. Her physical appeal did not move Archbishop Bek however, who was the power behind the throne while the king remained prostrate. Bek was cold and unyielding. When the English woman, who was her jailer, told Isabel that she was to be moved to a prison especially prepared for her in Berwick Castle, she demanded to see the Archbishop. At first they made excuses but one pleasant October morning she was escorted to the refractory. Bek sat behind a carved table. His face was without expression as he scrutinized the young woman before him. "You have been demanding to see me." Isabel ignored his hostility, saying sweetly, "Your Eminence, I do not demand, but ask that you send word to my husband for he has not replied to my message." "Nor will he, lady, but he has sent word to me. The earl, your husband says that you have dishonoured his name and betrayed his person and he is happy for you to answer to the king for your betrayal." Bek watched for her reaction, for the tears, hysteria and disbelief but was disappointed. The woman remained composed before replying, "If that's the case, God help all the virtuous women left in my husband's castle, if I'm not there he'll mount them even in Lent." Bek stared coldly at her, ignoring her crude innuendo and said, "You are to be placed in Berwick Castle, a confinement that is suited to your crimes and await the king's pleasure.

The following morning she was escorted from the safety of the Priory by men, hand picked by the Archbishop for the meanness of their characters. She was mounted on an old piebald mare, which had not gone beyond a slow walk for many years. Around Isabel's neck they hung a placard informing the citizen's of England who could read that she was 'whore to Robert Bruce.' She kept her head up and tried to urge her unwilling nag to move with more haste so that she might avoid the dung and other muck which was thrown at her, but the animal ignored Isabel's pounding heels and plodded slowly onwards much to the amusement of her escort. By the time they arrived at Berwick even Isabel's indomitable self-confidence was bruised by her mistreatment.

Outside the drawbridge the escort stopped and gazed upwards at the grey walls rising towards the sky, uncompromising and pitiless. At the top of the west tower and jutting out from it was a cage. At that distance it looked like a wicker basket into which people put broody hens before they hung them on the branch of a tree. The soldier riding beside her had the same thought for he leered at Isabel and said, "A fine cage, for a fine bird." He jerked the reins of her mount and led her across the drawbridge.

Every day, no matter what the weather, Isabel remained in her cage, without chair or stool to sit on. Her only privacy was a tiny wooden room built within the tower with a thin straw filled mattress and a leather bucket that she herself emptied each day. As the first grey light crept above the horizon the English woman responsible for her took her to her cage and there she remained to suffer the gaze of all whom passed below.

The Scots, who once lived and traded within the town of Berwick had been driven from their homes by King Edward's men and the new English population rejoiced in the prosperity which came to them through Berwick harbour. They were happy to stand and jeer at their king's enemy, even if it was only a woman. Often they would call up to her telling her the latest news, "Atholl has been executed, hung drawn and quartered. " Another would add, "He was still alive when they cut off his balls." "Alive right up to the end," screamed a woman. "I'd have cut your tits off," yelled a man.

One December day when she was so cold that she could no longer feel her feet, even though she had been stamping them so vigorously that her cage creaked, one of her regular tormentors hailed her from below and called up. "King Hobb's run off to Norway and left his whore to pay for his crimes." He laughed and began to saunter back the way he had come. For the first time Isabel forgot who she was and screamed back every abuse which she could think of and because there was nothing in her cage to use she took off her shoes and hurled them through the bars at the retreating figure. One fell into the moat, the other harmlessly on the path. For a few days she was left without shoes, but when the governor heard that his prisoner had feet covered in chilblains and a feverish cold and cough, he ordered them to give her a pair of leather boots. On the path below Isabel's cage, a guard was ordered to move on any spectators who became a nuisance.

On the morning of Christmas Day, Isabel sat on the floor of her cage with her back against the castle wall listening to the church bells of Berwick calling the virtuous folk to the celebration of Christ's birth. She could no longer hold back her misery and the tears rolled silently down her thin cheeks. The priest had heard her confession and had given her absolution on the previous evening when she had tried to remain resolute and defiant, but God himself must surely know that today, of all days, she could pretend no longer. She wore all the clothes she possessed, layer upon layer. Her feet pulled up under her many skirts, her hands tucked into her sleeves and her head and neck well covered with scarves and hoods. Only the smallest amount of face was visible and that was pinched with cold. The wind from the north swooped around the castle walls. If it found an open door or unlatched shutter it slammed them shut and howled like an unshriven soul. When it discovered Isabel's cage it vent its fury on the timber construction so that she feared it would be torn away from the wall and she would be sent flying through the air with her skirts billowing around her. Then her tormentors would shake their heads and say that it was true, she had been a witch, and when they found her body they would burn it and then her soul would not enter into Paradise. She closed her eyes burying her head onto her drawn-up knees and, not for the first time, asked God to release her from her burden.

When twilight crept across the frozen land they came to take her to her nightly prison. That evening instead of the usual thin ale and dry bread there was a beaker of wine and a wedge of game pie with a thick slice of freshly baked bread. The woman who guarded her said grudgingly "An act of Christian charity from the governor, but I say it's a waste of good food. You can't last for long, sitting out there in the cold. I expect to find you frozen each time I come for you." Isabel did not bother to reply and slowly nibbled the pie. She did not eat it all but wrapped some in her coif; she would eat it the following day in her cage. She had not drunk strong wine for some months and it made her feel sick and lighth-headed. She soaked the bread in it, slowly sucking the pulp and by the time the beaker was drained she felt warm, her eyelids drooping and she curled up under the thin bedcover and slept, for the first time since her capture, without nightmares. The following morning they came for her as usual and took her out into a white world, the snow lying in heavy drifts where the wind had blown it.

Mary Bruce suffered the same cruel imprisonment as Isabel but at Roxburgh Castle. Mary was not a large woman, small and dark, 'ma petite oiseau' her father had always called her and by mid winter she had become thin and her large dark eyes hollow within her pale pointed little face. The woman who acted as her jailer told the governor that she would surely die before the winter was over. The worried governor consulted his confessor. The king had not ordered him to kill the prisoner just detain her and who could say what the king might want in the future. When the Christmas feast arrived Mary Bruce remained within the tower, lying on her straw mattress and warmed by a charcoal brazier, which they brought in. They gave her hot broth with a few small pieces of chicken in it and better quality bread, soft and sometimes still warm from the bakery. She regained some of her strength and by mid January was back in her cage "just like a little blackbird on her perch," one of the guards said.

The king was adamant that Marjorie Bruce should receive the same fearful punishment as the older women. Bek, always careful to consider the position of the church, pointed out that imprisoning a young maid for her father's sins would offend the Holy Father and condemn the king throughout Christendom as barbaric.

"You're sure the Pope will condemn me if I'm over harsh with the girl?" Asked the king one morning. "I'm sure of it." Edward sucked on a tooth that was worrying him; a cage had already been built for Marjorie in London. He could wait, she would go to London and await the arrival of her father. So Marjorie, Lady Wiseman, Christina Seton and her young son Donald, Earl of Mar, left the warmth and security of the Priory on the long journey to London. If Marjorie had known that her imprisonment would last for so many years would she have set out with such exuberance and good humour? Lady Wiseman said the truth when she had answered Marjorie's question, as they left Lanercost, "Will we see Scotland again, d'you think?" "Only God can tell us our destiny, my dear." Marjorie looked down and leaning forward rearranged the bridle around her horse's mane and ears so that none should see her expression. Determinedly she rode onwards.

Christina Seton expected her child at the feast of Christmas and when she began her journey south she was already very heavy, but was in good spirits for she could feel the child moving within her. Her boy, Donald, rode at the side of her wagon. At least they were together.

During the journey Marjorie and Donald often fought, Lady Wiseman had said, "Oh, between cousins, it's to be expected." Marjorie was quite an accomplished horsewoman and had a great fondness for animals. If Donald wanted to annoy Marjorie the weapon was easily to hand. He would position himself in front of Marjorie and begin to ill-treat his pony, hitting its ears with a switch of hazel, pulling its head and neck hard back, holding it on a very short rein and repeatedly hitting the startled animal. Marjorie would flare up and the two would argue while Donald laughed loudly. The welfare of his pony meant nothing to him, but annoying 'mad Marj' was real fun. Then the boy would let the pony have its head and jog off up the track, while Lady Wiseman tried to calm an irate Marjorie.

One afternoon, when Donald had grown particularly bored and was very hungry he began his game again, whipping his pony and with each swipe of the hazel branch he chanted "mad Marj, mad Marj." Marjorie gave a shout, spurred her pony and charged him. Although he was a good three years younger than his cousin, he was a very quick boy. He let his pony have its head and fled up the path with Marjorie after him. This was too much for their escort. The captain and two men at arms galloped after the pair and when the captain had taken hold of Donald's reins he leant forward and administered a heavy clout around the boy's ear which knocked him from his pony and sent him sprawling into a puddle. "Anymore nonsense from you lad, we'll gag you and make you walk. Now mount and keep quiet." There were tears in Donald's eyes, but he did as he was told and remained sulkily quiet thereafter. Everybody, both Scots and English, excepting his mother, thought Donald of Mar had deserved it.

They had travelled for a fortnight when they were told that they should now say goodbye to the Lady Christina Seton, who would be confined at the Convent of Sixhills, in Lincolnshire. "And my son, where is he going?" Asked a tearful Christina. "He'll continue to London lady and will be reared with other children at court," she was told. Christina began to scream and cling to Donald, but the English women who cared for her pulled them apart. "Now, now, lady, he'll be safe at court, he'll learn his lessons and discipline, don't you worry."

Christina continued sobbing and leant over the side of the wagon to watch her son until he was out of sight.

The Convent of Sixhills was a wealthy house and the holy women were not unkind to Christina but she became very melancholic, refusing to eat and at night-time she could be heard crying for many hours. Just before Christmas, Christina went into labour and was delivered of a stillborn daughter.

The king's doctors lacked the courage to pronounce Elizabeth Bruce fit for a journey, since her father and his men were still encamped just outside the Priory. It was well into 1307 before pressure from the king forced them to admit that she could make the journey south to imprisonment in Burstwick manor by the estuary of the River Humber. Only when she had left, would her father break camp and patrol the sea between Scotland and Ireland, as ally of the English King to search for the king's enemy, his son-in-law.

For a frail woman to undertake such a journey in midwinter was hard, but her father ordered the finest, strongest wagon furnished with a couch, feather mattress, cushions and the warmest covers and furs. The message to her escort, servants and two elderly waiting women was clear. 'You'll answer to the Earl of Ulster if some harm comes to his daughter.' Everyone knew that the old king was mortally sick and his son a weak man. So they took good care of her. Before she left, her father came to her to say his farewells. "Well my girl, you've cost your father dearly, if that husband of yours is ever in a position to do so, I'll make him pay for all of this," he waved his hand around at the fine equipment. "You see if I don't." Elizabeth laughed and wound her arms around her father's neck. "You're the best of fathers. I hope Rob survives long enough to thank you."

They had to cut across the Pennines, through wild cold and windswept hills and moorland. The track was so bad the wagon wheels were loosened by rocks or became firmly stuck in the mud, which had slid down from the hills. Then Elizabeth was forced to alight while the men whipped, pulled and pushed the poor horses until the wagon was clear. Wet and cold, Elizabeth was then allowed back into her shelter until the next time.

The king's manor of Burstwick was on the bleak and windswept estuary of the River Humber. It was an old estate once held by the Earl Torstig, brother to King Harold, but it had had many lords since and although the King stayed there whenever he journeyed to and from York, the estate had an old-fashioned air. The buildings were timber framed with wattle and daub infill and thatched roofs. The great hall was the oldest building and many of its beams were blackened with smoke. The fire was in the old style, central with a vent in the roof to allow the smoke to escape. When the wind blew in from the sea, as it often did in that part of the country, then the smoke was swept back into the hall below, making the eyes of those who sat inside on a winter's evening smart. Outside there were many other barns and storehouses, brewhouse, bakery, dairy and weaving shed and beside a small chapel dedicated to St Helen was another smaller women's hall and it was there that Elizabeth was confined. A deep moat surrounded the buildings.

Away from the prying eyes of her father's spies Elizabeth was to be given no comforts or considerations. She was not to suffer or be placed in physical danger, but she was to be left in no doubt of the king's displeasure.

The women's hall had no furniture. There was a straw mattress in the corner, but the bed and other soft furnishings in the wagon were quickly unloaded and carried into the great hall and were no doubt used by the estate steward and his family, mused Elizabeth. Her clothing went the same way so that she was left with only what she wore. She protested but the steward's reply was blunt. "You'll not be treated like a queen here, but for your father you'd be awaiting the executioner like the rest of the traitors." The following day a spinning wheel was brought into the hall. The steward stood in the doorway. "If you want to eat you must earn it, as we all do. The wool will be brought to you each day." He left, not waiting for her reply.

The following day she stood looking at the heap of wool. She had learnt how to spin but as the daughter and wife of Earls of the Realm she had not spun often and it was a task which held little joy for her. "Don't you stand gawking at it," said the most unpleasant of her women. "If you want to eat today you'll have to get a move on." There was no alternative for Elizabeth and as the months went by she became accustomed to the work. When the weather turned brighter she was allowed to spin outside. There she could smell the sea on the breeze, hear the larks calling high over the fields, and when hay-making came the sweet smell of the fresh cut meadow grass calmed and lifted her spirits.

One day in late June, she sat at her spinning in the shade of an elder tree. Her two women, sitting nearby had fallen asleep. A horseman rode across the drawbridge. She recognized him immediately as her father's squire but he rode passed Elizabeth without glancing in her direction. She smiled to herself and thought that it must be difficult to recognize her. She wore an old linen shift covered by a sleeveless wadmal dress the colour of dusty oatmeal, tied at the waist with a leather thong. They had given her a pair of leather shoes but no cloak to cover her bare arms nor a coif or kerchief to cover her hair. Her wonderful, thick. bronze hair, which had been the envy of all women and a joy to her husband was combed each morning and tightly pulled back into a thick plait. She had neither ornaments nor jewels to set her apart from any serving woman on the estate.

The steward's young daughter ran over to her women with a message and Elizabeth was ordered to leave her work and taken to the great hall. Her father's man sat at the bench, food and drink before him. At first he made no movement, then recognition came into his eyes and he jumped to his feet. "My lady," He gasped with astonishment. "Did you not recognize me, Ralph, sitting at my spinning, for I remember you." The man's face reddened and he turned angrily on the steward. "You told me the Lady Elizabeth was well and in good spirits." The steward was a middle-aged man, balding, with a permanent scowl across his face. He was an official who knew he had carried out his instructions meticulously. The woman had not been ill-treated. He had a clear conscious and replied, "The lady is the King's prisoner and I have carried out my duty. She is given fish, fowl and game in due season, wood for her fire and a priest to hear her confession." Ralph replied, "Look at her! She's my lord's daughter whom I know well, yet I didn't recognize her." "Nonetheless, she has all I am prepared to give her, without the authority of the king," spat the steward. Elizabeth knew the steward to be uncompromising so she said to Ralph, "I'm well and all that he says is true." Ralph directed his reply to the steward. "Well I'm not satisfied that her circumstances will be acceptable to her father, who at this moment searches for the king's enemy, Robert Bruce. He demands that she write to him." He said to the steward, "Bring parchment, that the Lady Elizabeth may tell her father of her plight." The steward shrugged, but had the writing materials produced and Elizabeth sat herself on a cushioned bench to write her letter. Her women sat close by but she knew that neither could read nor write. She tried to be cheerful, for her father had done his best for her, but Ralph, sitting by her side, said, "Be honest with your father, madam. If he doesn't know of your distress these wretches will become even harsher with you." So she told him about the straw mattress and that she had neither clothes nor cover for her head. "You tell him the rest Ralph, I cannot write such sad things." She walked out into the yard with the young man to his waiting horse. In front of the unfriendly eyes he bowed to her and at the gatehouse he turned and waved, her letter safely in the pouch on his belt.

Nothing changed after the visit. The steward continued to observe his duty as he saw it and Elizabeth continued with her daily routine, spinning the wool from the estate flock. The summer wore on, warm and sunny but in July a troop of the king's men rode in. Their captain was Peter Gavaston, whom Elizabeth had often seen in the company of the Prince of Wales, for Gavaston's cousin, Piers was a favourite of Prince Edward. Gavaston walked with confidence into the great hall and a few moments later one of Elizabeth's serving women came scurrying out. "The old king is dead. The Lord Edward is our king now," she cried.

HIS WEIGHT IN GOLD

The Prince of Wales became bored with the lack of progress in the siege of Kildrummy Castle. Since it had begun in early August he had thrown everything he had at the defenders. Every kind of siege engine, scaling ladder, battering ram and grappling iron had been used and to be fair his men had not lacked courage, throwing themselves into their task with enthusiasm. He had offered a purse full of gold to the first man to succeed in breaching the castle, but all to no avail. Kildrummy was a fortress of such strength that it was capable of withstanding a besieging army well into the following year and Edward could not spare the time. Some other means must be found. The fortress must be taken from within. He would speak to Pembroke about the matter.

The earl had been thinking along the same lines. The walls of Kildrummy Castle had been reinforced to King Edward's exacting standards five years previously, for he had intended that it would be Englishmen sitting safely within it. Pembroke's spies told him that the castle storehouses were full and supplies would last for many months. Whilst he and the prince sat idly outside the castle walls, what might Bruce be up to? He sent detachments of troops into the surrounding countryside carrying the dragon standard with orders to kill or burn every house, barn, man, woman, child and beast and hoped that news of the devastation would lure the defenders out. If Neil Bruce felt compassion for the people's plight still he could not be diverted and remained resolutely within the castle walls.

Bored by inactivity the prince went hunting with his friends and left the everyday command to Pembroke. When the weather was fair, the heir to the English throne could be found in the surrounding hills and glens and any wild creature, which had so far escaped the hunger of the people, fell victim to his falcons or hunting dogs.

By the first week of September a typical siege routine was in force and the Earl of Pembroke's patience bore fruit. One bright morning a young lad was brought to him. The boy said they called him Duggie. He had seen ten summers and his father was the smith within the fortress. "My father sent me with a message for your honour." The earl continued to stare coldly at the lad until the poor boy, uncertain what to do next, looked up at the sergeant standing beside him. "Go on then lad, tell his lordship what you told me," said the soldier. The boy's face reddened and he began to mumble his message. "Speak up boy," the sergeant gave him a shove, "His Lordship hasn't got all day." Duggie tried again this time speaking more clearly. "My da says he'll help you get into yon." He indicated the menacing fortress behind him. The earl lent forward in his chair, interested in what the boy was saying. "Oh, he'll turn traitor, will he? And how much will this cost me?" "He says he wants gold, as much as he can carry." Duggie, having unburdened himself of his father's message breathed a deep sigh. "You can tell your father that men do business with men. I make no bargains with lads, if you can get out so can he. Take him away sergeant and guard him well till dark." Duggie went reluctantly with the soldier. His father would be angry with him for not coaxing the English Earl to agree to his terms without the necessity of involving himself in the negotiations. His father had also told him that for bringing such important news the earl would reward him; so far there had been nothing. The sergeant gave the boy a push propelling him into the portly abdomen of the earl's cook. "You stay here boy, if you value your skin. Don't you go running off, not till I tells you." The food being prepared smelt so good and Duggie had not eaten that day. "Here boy, you turn this here spit and you'll have some when it be ready," said the cook. Duggie sat himself down beside the meat and turned the roasting piglet. The sergeant wandered off satisfied, for he had never known a boy who was not hungry.

Later that night Duggie repeated the earl's message. He expected a blow from his father, but the smith mumbled under his breath and continued pounding the glowing metal on his forge.

In the early hours of the morning the craftsman stood before the Earl of Pembroke explaining that the only way to hasten the fall of Kildrummy was the destruction of its stores. The castle itself could not be sabotaged for it was so strongly built and its guards alert. "And what reward do you want?" demanded Pembroke. "As my boy said, as much gold as I can carry, Sir." The earl did not say anything for a while, but sat scrutinizing the big, strong man. Then he said, "This castle will be costly to take." It was still dark when the smith made his way back, swimming the moat and slipping through the postern gate, opened by a sleepy Duggie. All that day the smith hammered away in his forge. Boyd and Neil Bruce, carrying out their daily inspection of the castle, came by during mid morning, enquiring if all was well. Otherwise the day progressed normally enough for a castle under siege.

Late that night, when a bank of cloud covered the moon, a dark figure poured a trail of pitch against the timber wall of the main storehouse and set fire to it. A guard on the wall by the gatehouse noticed the first flames and raised the alarm. Men roused themselves quickly, forming a chain from the well to the fire but the weather had been fair for the past week and the timbers and thatch burned with vigour. The light breeze carried sparks into the night sky and they flitted like fireflies across to the other barn roofs. Before long, the area where most of the provisions were stored was well ablaze. In the nearby stable block the horses began stamping and kicking wildly, neighing to each other in a frantic attempt to get out. Men, badly needed to fight the fire, left the chain to help release and control the frightened beasts. Everywhere was confusion and panic, yet such a short time before, the castle had been quietly slumbering. Now its peace was shattered by the noise of crackling flames, shouting men, panic stricken-horses, frightened squealing pigs, barking dogs and above all this noise the cheering and shouting which came from the other side of the wall.

The English, awakened by the fire, were jumping up and down waving weapons and banging the hilts of their swords on their shields. The flames and din could be heard and seen many miles away. The Earl of Pembroke's sergeant at arms, who had taken part in many campaigns, stood watching the flames leaping above the castle walls. "Now they're for it," he murmured.

The fire gained such a hold that Bruce ordered the removal of whatever could be grabbed before the fire did its worst. By mid morning the area where once well-stocked storehouses had stood was a heap of smouldering ash and charred beams. Weary men with blackened faces, many with burnt hands and arms, stood in small groups staring at the devastation and discussing their fates.

Neil Bruce was a young man who had joined his brother's rebellion out of loyalty to his kinsman rather than military ambition. He was the kind of man who was loved by all, but Robert Boyd had the military experience which Neil lacked nor, was he too proud to turn to the older man for advice. Boyd accepted the situation and did not bear a grudge towards the young man. Therefore, it was not surprising that the garrison looked to Boyd to get them out of their situation. There was a lot of talk about how the fire had started and most agreed that it must have been started deliberately, but by whom? Suspicion and despondency hung like a cloud over the men.

In the late afternoon a herald rode up to the drawbridge and hailed the defenders. Bruce stood on the ramparts of the gatehouse, Boyd beside him. "My lord, the Earl of Pembroke offers you your lives for your immediate surrender." Boyd said to Neil, "Tell them that it's an important decision needing thought and you'll give him your reply at first light." Bruce delivered the message to the herald, then turning to Boyd he said, "Come Rob, let's have a glass of wine from the one barrel we saved, while we are still free men." Both men knew there would be no relief sent to them. To accept mercy from the enemy was their only hope.

The following day Pembroke agreed that the lives of the defending Scots would be spared if they surrendered without bloodshed. Just before noon the great gates swung open, the drawbridge slowly lowered and two abreast, the defenders crossed over, discarding their weapons in a pile at the feet of the waiting English. Bruce and Boyd were the last to leave and taken directly to Prince Edward, who had returned early from the hunt to watch the humiliation of surrender.

Prince Edward and Neil Bruce had known one another since boyhood, but Bruce's honest open character had never appealed to the Prince's group of self-seeking friends or to the streak of cruelty, which often displayed itself in England's future king. "Your brother's treachery has led his kinsmen into deep shit," said the prince. "Now you'll pay for his treachery for I doubt my father will be forgiving." "We surrendered on terms," said Neil, "The lord king, will honour that." "Oh you think so do you? It was Pembroke who made those terms, not the king." Neil flashed angrily and Pembroke, standing nearby looked uneasy. Robert Boyd, more experienced in the ways of the world, continued staring impassively at the ground, but from that moment he decided he would not remain a prisoner for long. The prince continued, "I'll send you both to the king, he'll decide your futures. He turned to Pembroke's sergeant at arms, "Hold these men secure but apart."

When they had gone the prince turned angrily on Pembroke. "Why offer them mercy? They were in no position to demand conditions." "You weren't here, my lord, to express your preferences and this way they've surrendered without further loss of life. You wanted to finish it quickly, did you not?" "Yes, but not on their terms. I cannot agree Pembroke." "So what would you suggest, send them all back again and continue the siege?" snapped Pembroke. Without waiting for the prince's reply he turned and stamped out into the warm sunshine where the air was still pungent with the smell of burning.

The Scots sat in a group of about sixty men and Pembroke stopped to look at them. They were relaxed and quite unaware that they were prisoners of a man capable of deception and double-dealing. His sergeant came to him, "My lord, the smith wants to remind you of his promised reward. He also asks that you take his son into your service." Pembroke looked surprised, "what do you think, is he a capable lad?" "He'll not make a good fighting man, Sir, but he pleases your cook." He nodded in that direction where once again the boy was turning the spit. "The smith is tired of fatherhood, my lord." Pembroke replied "Promise nothing but do not move the boy on and tell the cook to find chores for him."

The earl had business with the armourer but when he arrived the prince was already there issuing orders to the man. "What's this?" asked Pembroke, indicating the piles of charcoal and gold. The prince smiled, he had already forgotten the earlier disagreement with the earl and took his arm, guiding him to one side. "I'm preparing a surprise for our Scottish traitor." He indicated the smith who sat on an upturned fish barrel at some distance from them. "But first it's time for archery practice." The earl noticed the activity near the prisoners. Archers were taking up positions around them and the prisoners themselves were becoming restless, nudging one another while some of the more experienced men got to their feet ready to face what might come. Angrily he turned on the prince. "I gave these men my word that I would spare their lives." "I choose not to, Pembroke. If we let them go they'll all return to Bruce and I'll be damned before I allow that to happen." He nodded to his archery sergeant and amid shouts and screams from the doomed men and the whirr from the flights of arrows, death rained down from the gentle, blue sky. When all was over, a willow warbler began to sing in its bower among the reeds by the moat.

The archers moved among the bodies stripping them of their clothes and boots. One man's misfortune was always another man's gain. They dug a deep pit where later in the day the bodies were thrown and at Pembroke's order, a priest said mass before the bodies were covered.

The smith watched the carnage without any feelings of guilt, but with a growing feeling of suspicion and fear creeping through him. Once again he sat down on the upturned barrel to think. He had to have some reward he reasoned, for he would be a marked man now. Gold would give him a new start in some other part of the kingdom. He would remind the earl again, but if there were no sign of his reward soon he would have to make a run for it. Before he could carry out his resolve an escort of the prince's men came over to him. "Come on turncoat, it's your turn now." The smith looked alarmed and tried to argue, continuing to sit firmly on the barrel as if it might offer some protection from retribution, but they grabbed him by the arms and propelled him towards their master. The smith, frightened by their rough treatment called out to Pembroke, "Sir, what's this? I did what I could to help your lordship overcome your enemies." The earl looked the other way, caught his sergeant's eye and said "Send a man to the cook and make sure the boy remains where he is, no matter what happens. I don't want his death on my conscience as well."

The prince and his men laughed at the smith's efforts to free himself and said, "You'll receive what is due to you. Did you think we would not keep our word? Look, the gold is ready and waiting. As much as you can carry." The terrified man looked at the armourer still busy at his furnace. Four moulds with small spouts and long wooden handles to make pouring easier were ready. They were being kept hot by the edge of the fire just like a woman keeps a stew warm ready for her man when he comes in from the fields. The prince ordered, "Bring him over so we may give him his reward." The prisoner kicked and struggled as he was dragged closer to the fire. There they flung him on top of a dusty wagon, securing his arms and legs with manacles tightly to make movement impossible. A soldier knelt and wedged his victim's head between his own knees and firmly held the smith's nose. As the smith opened his mouth to breath and calling in terror for mercy, the armourer began to pour the gleaming golden stream into his open mouth. The screaming ceased. He did not suffer for long and when the gold had formed into an ingot it was removed from his body. Then they hung him near the entrance to the castle as a warning to all. In the camp the cook had taken Duggie by the arm and led him to a corner where they could not be overheard. "Your father ain't with us no more lad. Don't you go asking no questions and stay close by me. You understand?" Duggie's mother had died years before and he had learnt early in his life that people come and go and it was wise not to become attached to anyone. So he nodded to the cook, who said, "Don't you do nothing daft now," then satisfied, the cook let the boy go.

The earl left a garrison at Kildrummy, then they withdrew. Duggie was amongst the camp followers for he had nowhere else to go. As he passed the castle the mutilated body of his father swung gently on the ropes end and Duggie swallowed hard, wiping away a tear. He followed the others, leaving his father and childhood behind him.

Since his capture Robert Boyd had been kept in chains, his hands and feet manacled. It was clear to him that his life would be forfeit, no ransom would be demanded and the massacre of his companions had confirmed his fears. When the army began marching south-west towards Stirling he remained alert for an opportunity to escape. One late afternoon when they had stopped to rest and eat, Boyd was allowed to dismount and they gave him water and bread. Two men were set to guard him and he tried to engage them in conversation, asking about Neil Bruce, whom he had not seen since they were first parted, but his guards scowled and refused to speak. Not far off he could see the cooks hastily preparing food and he caught sight of the smith's young lad amongst them. After a while the boy walked near to where Boyd was resting, carrying a bucket and heading for the burn which bubbled merrily over rocks, on its way to a small lochen. The lad returned, this time a little closer to Boyd, with a full bucket, the water spilling over the sides as he walked up the sloping path. Sir Robert called out to him in the Highland tongue that his guards could not understand. "Hey, Duggie, you saw how they repaid your father? They'll do the same to me too laddie. Without your help I'm a dead man." "How can I help that?" called Duggie with little sign of respect. The English guards had jumped to their feet when their prisoner began to speak "Shut up you," yelled one, but Boyd called again. "At night time lad. I need to get away when it's dark and I'll need a horse. You must warn the Lord Bruce to escape as well, Duggie." One of the angry soldiers called to Duggie, "Clear off boy, if you don't want my knife in your throat." Duggie scuttled away with his bucket that was now half full whilst the other soldier caught Boyd a blow just below his ear, with his clenched fist, which sent Boyd sprawling. After a while he was able to sit again but the blow left him with a ringing sound in his ear and he was unable to hear properly for many weeks.

Duggie spent the following two days thinking. He could not remember his mother, and his father had never shown him love. Whenever he had the time, free from helping his father at his work, Duggie had spent his leisure with the men at the fortress, running small errands, listening to their yarns and grateful for any small kindness shown to him. Yet he fitted into English camp life just as well and his life was in less peril if he remained with the winning side. Yet his father was still his father and they had killed him.

When they reached Stirling, some of the army remained there to reinforce the garrison while a strong escort, with Neil Bruce in their midst, left for Edinburgh. Duggie's friend, the cook, told him they were taking Neil Bruce to Berwick. The remaining army continued its slow progress southwards. Their ultimate destination was Dumfries and the border country, where the old English King lay in his bed awaiting death. As they went they harried and plundered and the Prince of Wales and his followers were particularly savage with any Scot who did not pay homage to King Edward and to his heir, who would shortly replace his father.

When Duggie was on some errand which took him close to Robert Boyd, the man would look knowingly at him trying to catch the lad's eye, but Duggie would turn his head away for he had not made up his mind what he would do.

It was an act of unnecessary cruelty, which the prince and his friends were so fond of perpetrating, which made up Duggie's mind. The cook told him to take a basket of apples to the prince's squire who would transfer the fruit to a bowl. "Just you wait for the basket lad," the cook had said. The prince and his favourite, the Lord Piers Gavaston, surrounded by their friends, were relaxing in the prince's pavilion. A finely carved oak, table stood nearby with a silver bowl on it and a small, charcoal brazier close by. The prince and Gavaston sat at a gaming table, a chest set in front of them. The prince was concentrating deeply on the game but Gavaston, who was losing, was searching for some activity to distract his master.

The prince's squire was watching the game and took no notice of Duggie who, since he knew no better, decided to hurry his task along. Instead of leaving the basket, he began to transfer the fruit into the silver bowl himself. The apples had been washed and polished and the boy's grimy fingers contrasted with the crimson blush on their skins. He concentrated, carefully placing them into a pyramid shape as he had seen the steward do. When the Lord Gavaston shouted in horror, "My God! Just look at the boy's hands," Duggie jumped, dropped the basket and knocked over the fruit, which cascaded off the table and rolled across the ground in many directions.

Edward of Canarvon was a tall, athletic man, with piercing, blue eyes and the straight, thin nose of his Norman ancestors. Gavaston's interruption came just when the prince was about to declare checkmate, but it was impossible for him to show annoyance, worse still anger to his dear friend so he directed his fury at Duggie. Gavaston said, "Imagine where those hands have been." Duggie would have run, but in the past he had found that punishment administered after a search was usually worse than staying and facing whatever was dealt out now. He stood looking at the Prince and his friends, not really understanding what all the fuss was about. "Come here boy," ordered Edward. Duggie stood rooted to the spot until one of the princes's following caught him by the arm and propelled him towards Edward. At last Duggie found his tongue. "Sir, I meant no harm. I was told to bring the apples." The cold face showed neither interest nor compassion for the lad. "Look at your hands boy." Duggie looked down at his thin, grey hands, the dirt embedded into the skin and under the nails. Then he noticed the hands of the great Lord and his followers, tanned, strong and clean, their nails clear and polished. "When you work in the service of a great Lord you must have a clean person, boy. When something is dirty you clean it and there are two things that purify boy, fire and water." Duggie was not sure what purify meant, but he guessed it had something to do with the muck on his hands. How could you have clean hands when you did all the dirty work was a question which flashed through his mind, but since the mighty Lord had finished speaking, perhaps it was better he put distance between himself and them. He gave a small bow and tried to back away, but the grip on his shoulder remained firm. The prince nodded to Duggie's guard, who pulled the boy close to the small brazier, the charcoal glowing red and orange. "Your hands need something strong to clean them." Too late Duggie sensed danger. His guard, who stood behind him took hold of Duggie's twig-thin arms and plunged the boy's hands into the charcoal. Immediately he let the struggling boy go and the whole audience taking their cue from the Lord Edward, began to laugh.

The whole incident lasted just a few moments, but the pain made Duggie wild and he dashed from the pavilion and directly past Boyd, who was sitting in the shade of a mature oak. Boyd called to him in Gaelic. "Hey, Duggie, why so much haste?" The lad's dirty face had white streaks from the many tears, which rolled down. He ran over to Boyd and holding out his hands said, "I did nothing wrong, look what he had them do to me. I'll no stay with such men as these." In a glance Boyd took in the blackened, burned palms and fingertips on which blisters had already formed. "Run to yon wee waterfall laddie and keep your hands under the gushing water. It'll ease the pain and help them to heal quickly." Duggie stood looking at the man for his father had always rubbed goose fat on his burns. "Go on, be quick about it," commanded the man. Duggie, his hands throbbing, turned and ran to the stream and sitting down, allowed the cascade to pummel his wounds with cold, crystal droplets. Gradually numbness replaced the burning and his hands looked white and clean. Boyd called to the boy. "Hey, Duggie, come here and tear strips from my under shirt to bind your hands?" One of Boyd's guards nodded and he himself tore the cloth, which Boyd offered Duggie. The guard said, "Soak the cloth in the stream before you bind your hands," and Duggie did as he was bid. The man followed him and took from around his neck a kerchief that he tore in two and bound on the outside of the boy's wet bandaging. He did not say anything to Duggie, but later he said to his comrade, "Those shits have so little to do they have fun torturing boys." That night, when most of the camp was asleep, someone stole a knife and horse and when morning came the guards, who had been on duty with the prisoner Boyd, were found with their throats slit, whilst Boyd and the boy Duggie had disappeared.

It had been no easy task putting distance between himself and the English whilst he was still chained, but once away and into the hills Boyd had smashed the chain links and although the manacles were still attached, at least he had free movement. He turned his horse's head towards the west and with the boy behind him they began their search for Bruce.

THE WANDERERS

It was a tranquil scene, the calm waters of Loch Lomond reflecting the sky and hills. The small boat was low in the water and heavily laden. A rower and two passengers balanced between bow and stern. Just ahead and on each side of the craft were swimmers. Occasionally one would stop and hold the edge of the boat to rest and catch their breath before striking out once again towards the further shore.

Robert Bruce was the first to be ferried across to the western shore of the loch. He sat in the hollow of the gently rising land warming himself in the sunshine. In his hand rested his wife's book, her parting gift to him. Half a dozen of his men sat around admiring the pictures whilst the king read aloud the adventures and loves of the Lord Roland and his men. It was an excitingly erotic story about battle-hardened men. The way in which Bruce read, the intonations in his voice and wickedly suggestive pauses in the light-hearted story, helped to relax the men. Then someone said, "This story could almost be ourselves, except we're not having the love." Everybody laughed. They could almost forget their perilous situation and for a while each man escaped into his own daydreams.

Then Bruce aroused them and they built a fire to dry themselves, for although the weather was warm and sunny, after such a long swim the skin on their arms and legs was raised into small peaks like the skin of freshly plucked geese before roasting. They still had small quantities of oatmeal and Crawford, Wallace and others began to make flat oatcakes. They shaped them in their hands before balancing the cake on the flat blade of their broadswords and cooked them in the embers of the fire. In this way they could cook six at a time. The cakes were somewhat burnt, covered in ash and crumbled easily but for all that, were welcomed by hungry men. James Douglas who had rowed back and forth across the loch twice before giving up his place to another, spent his time picking blaeberries. These he added to the collection of oatcakes. When they were warm some began fishing, perching on rocks and casting out their lines. In happier times, the small fish they caught would have been despised and thrown back with the command to grow before daring to return to their bait. Now, hunger gripped them and fish of all sizes were welcome, rolled in oats and thrust into the orange embers.

It took nearly the whole morning for the fugitives to swim or row across the loch but Bruce could not allow them to rest for long in such an exposed area, for they were still hunted by the English and liegemen of the Comyn kinsfolk. When they were all safely across they made for the hills. They were in the Earl of Lennox's land and at least here they should be among friends, but who could say who held sway in the earl's land since the battle at Methven. Robert had had no news of Lennox's fate since he had left him on the battlefield, so they proceeded with caution, using whatever cover could be found.

That night they slept on a tree-covered hillside, close to a tumbling burn. Douglas and others searched around for game but although they could hear the capercaillie clucking away among the trees they were unsuccessful in catching any and were forced to retreat back to their camp by dusk fall. Away on the far hillside they could hear the stags calling to one another. There were neither manors nor other settlement closeby, and they risked a fire. Trying not to think of their hunger they sat watching the pictures in the flames and telling stories.

In the grey light of dawn, Bruce said, "Today we'll hunt. These hills are alive with fine deer which Lennox would not begrudge us. Douglas, you have a canny knowledge of wild things. Take a party of men and beat the hillside. I'll lead the hunting party." The hunters moved away from the shelter of the trees and across the hill. When Bruce and his men were in place he sounded his hunting horn as a signal to the beaters, then he sat down to wait quietly, sunk in his own thoughts. He looked at the detail and workmanship on the horn. It had been a gift to his father when Robert's elder sister Isabelle had been taken as a bride to King Eric of Norway. The horn itself was from the wild mountain sheep and it curled round in a circle. Carved with hunting scenes and runic signs it must have been crafted when the Norsemen followed the old ways, before they became Christian. The mouthpiece was of silver and Bruce had been told that the magnificent instrument once belonged to King Olaf himself and that the silver came from the royal silver mines at Kongsberg. When it was blown, it had a remarkably clear call that could be heard at a great distance. Bruce was very fond of it.

He was aroused from his contemplation by the shouting of the beaters. Two fine stags were thundering towards them. Wallace, in command of the skilled archers, stepped from their hiding place behind the rocks and bracken and sent a flight of arrows into the leading stag. The animal was pierced in many places and Bruce ran forward. It was nearly on him, the fear showing in the beast's wild eyes. Bruce threw his lance with full force into its broad chest, the animal staggered and fell into the heather, yet it was still alive. William Wiseman who was close by, ran to it and hacked at its neck to sever the main artery so that death would come quickly. The kill had taken only minutes but was sufficient time to allow the other fleeing stag to disappear into the cover. One animal would be little between so many but they had to be satisfied. They felled a young birch and used its trunk to secure the animal while they carried it away to a safe place where they might butcher and roast it. Further along the glen there was a rocky outcrop, which offered some shelter and laughing, and cheerful at the prospect of freshly killed venison they traversed the hillside. They had nearly reached their goal when dark figures appeared on the crest of the hill in front of them. The day was overcast, the visibility poor and at that distance they could not distinguish the newcomers. Bruce halted his men, they were out of arrow range and he had no desire to take on Comyn supporters. The men needed rest and support before he rallied them once again. He barely had time to put his thoughts into words before a shrill call from a hunting horn was heard from the brow of the hill. Three horsemen appeared and following a narrow path, rode down the hillside at some speed. From the way their cloaks flew out behind them, they were men of some wealth and importance. As they came nearer it was with great relief and considerable excitement that he recognized Lennox himself. Throwing all caution and kingly dignity to the wind he snatched his soft, woollen cap from off his head, threw it high into the air and cried out, "God be praised, it's Lennox." Lennox jumped from his horse and they threw their arms around each other's shoulders and in unison said, "I thought you were dead." Then they laughed, relieved but embarrassed by their emotion. Lennox said, "I recognized the sound of your hunting horn, Robert, it was always so distinctive."

That evening, safely within Lennox's hunting lodge, and sitting before a large fire, well filled with venison, fish, bread and ale, Bruce's mood became somewhat lighter. It was true that Lennox could not give him news of his old friends and he offered little hope that more survivors would appear from Methven but seeing his friend encouraged him to believe that all was not hopeless.

Since Lennox had last seen Bruce he had changed. All his kingly and knightly trappings had been discarded. Shield and ensignia had disappeared into a peaty bog, whilst he had flung his chainmail into Loch Dochart. Nothing distinguished Bruce from any other fighting man. His padded, knee-length haubeek had no costly decoration and was dirty and torn whilst his legs were kept warm with plain, woollen leggings. Bruce saw Lennox scrutinizing his appearance and laughingly took hold of a handful of his unkept beard. "Aye, I'm not quite the man I once was, the women would think twice before falling into my arms." Then he said with a serious face, "Have you heard anything of my wife and daughter? I sent the women north to Orkney to the care of Bishop Moray, from there they'll take ship to Norway." "Nay Rob, I've kept my head well down since coming to my own lands. They tell me that Pembroke and Prince Edward have raised the dragon flag and are burning and pillaging from the Tay to the Moray lands, but I'll tell my men to keep their ears open." Bruce sat quietly for a while before saying, "Malcolm, I must lay low. If I get to the west I can rally support among the Islanders and the men of Ulster but I'll need ships and supplies."

Malcolm of Lennox sat listening to his king's plans. He had first met Robert Bruce at the English court when they were both beardless youths and he had fallen under the spell of Bruce's wit and charm. He had tried to emulate the Bruce style himself causing much amusement and taunts from other boys, but Lennox's puppy love had developed into a genuine affection for Bruce the man.

The Campbell brothers, Neil and Donald, who knew the area well, volunteered to search for vessels. They knew men who owed them favours and they promised to rendezvous with Bruce and Lennox one week from that day. Accompanied by other men from Lennox, they left the following morning.

Travelling by night Bruce and his supporters kept their rendezvous with the Campbells, just north of Cardross, on the banks of the Clyde. A strip of marshy land jutting out into the Clyde sheltered fine, sandy beaches and protecting any moored craft. The month of August had been the worst that any could remember, so cold, windy and wet which made their journey doubly difficult.

Bruce's arrival at Cardross coincided with the first days of September and a change in the weather. The Clyde sparkled with sunshine diamonds and seabirds swooped and wheeled on the warm south-westerly breeze. It was early morning and fishing boats were already bobbing in the swell of the retreating tide. Not far from the shore and moored in the shallows were four wargalleys with furled sails. From the beach Bruce inspected the sturdy vessels. Judging from the barrels and packages stowed aft they were well provisioned and he turned to the two Campbell brothers, "How did you manage this, they're almost new." Neil laughed, "They're a gift from Angus MacDonald, you my lord, are his new ally against the MacDougalls." He began to wade out to the nearest ship, but called over his shoulder, "Angus would trade with the devil if it meant that the MacDougalls would be the losers," he added "my lord," as a polite afterthought and Bruce laughed.

It was a tight squeeze with seventeen or eighteen men to each boat. As they pulled away from the shore, there was a lot of splashing, cursing and laughing. Men unaccustomed to oars who would normally expect others to do the rowing for them, tried to synchronize their stroke to comrades who were as much at home with sail and oar as they were with sword and lance. Hugh Lovell, who held the inland manor of Harwick dug deeply into the water, putting such effort into bringing his oar to the surface that he slide from his bench, showering the man behind him with spray. "Hey Lovell, warn me before you try to catch your next crab." Hamlin of Troup, was a local Clyde man who rowed skilfully. He sat in front of Hugh and called over his shoulder, "You're not suppose to move the whole of the Clyde, just skim below its surface. Then you'll help to move this beauty and not kill yourself with the effort." That first morning as men adapted to each other's style and strengths, friendships and tempers were tested. Rowing was tiring work and they had had meagre diets for many weeks. Once on the open water, travelling in secret was impossible and if they were caught in the Firth by Comyn or English warships they would need to pull together. They depended on each other and Bruce depended on them.

Bruce took the steering board of the leading vessel. Lennox in the second ship came behind, whilst the remaining two, captained by Bruce's brothers Tom and Alexander, positioned themselves in the rear, side by side. The flotilla kept to the middle channel, between the land, until Rothesay was well behind them. Only then did Bruce, with a deep sense of relief, order the sail to be raised and tacking before the wind, they sailed around the north shore of Arran.

The men new to rowing were fearful that the oars would be dragged away by the force of waves and current and they gripped the oars so tightly that even their battle scared-hands became sore with blisters and they were forced to bind them.

The voyage to Arran had taken two full days and in the narrow waters of the Firth they had not dared put ashore to rest, but had taken it in turns to sleep and keep watch. Ears and eyes straining in the darkness for the slightest sound of a creaking oar, slap of wave on bow or smothered curse. At dusk, they lashed their boats together so they could not drift apart in the strong currents and they began rowing when the first rays of the sun rose above the eastern hills. Often they saw people running along the shoreline, waving and cheering and in this way Bruce understood that the common people of Scotland had not forgotten him.

As dusk began to fall on the fourth night, Bruce risked mooring in a sheltered bay on the north Arran coast overlooking the peninsular of Kintyre. A River cut deeply into the land, the surrounding hillsides covered in birch trees. The tide was out and seaweed-covered rocks offered a retreat for resting seals. Each animal relaxed in the final rays of the retreating sun, warming their broad backs and through lazy, half-closed eyes, watched the ships glide into the bay. Their sails were furled and tired men took to the oars to guide the boats closer to shore. The seals slid into the water swimming gracefully away. One or two heads broke the surface, whiskers twitching with droplets of water, watching the intruders. Darkness crept across the land and fires were lit along the shoreline. The animals flipped their tails and disappeared into the murky sea.

A guard on the battlements of Dunverty Castle hailed the war galleys of Robert Bruce. The weather still held fine, the sea calm. Angus and Donald MacDonald stood on the jetty to welcome them. It was a bonnie sight to see a friendly face. Many of Bruce's tough campaigners had lumps in their throats and one or two turned and gazed out to sea so that none should see the moistness of their eyes.

For the first time since the ambush at Dalry, Bruce was made to feel like a king. He climbed onto the jetty and the MacDonald brothers, lords of the Clan, welcomed him. He knew that his appearance did not inspire awe in a subject, all his kingly trappings jettisoned as they had fled across his realm. He smiled inwardly, 'Aye, but it was his realm.' He had lurked in so many caves and hidden by so many waterfalls that he had almost forgotten who he was. He squared his shoulders and prepared to greet the MacDonald kinsfolk as their king. They fell to their knees and below the castle walls they vowed allegiance to King Robert.

The MacDonald brothers were fierce-looking men, large and dark with black hair and bushy beards and eyebrows. For generations, the MacDonalds and the MacDougalls, kinsmen of the Comyns, had been violent rivals. Anyone who was an enemy of the MacDougall was a friend of theirs. If that man was also King of Scotland all the better.

Later Bruce sat in his chamber with some of his companions,

Lennox, Douglas, his brothers and one or two others. He had bathed, trimmed his hair and beard and clean leggings had been found for him but he had refused all other luxury or adornment for his person. He sat on a window seat staring out onto the moonlit sea below. "Our enemies will be on our trail already, we'll have to be away with all haste." There were grunts of agreement from around the room but all the men were so tired and relaxed after the hardships of the past three months, no one made any sensible reply.

Bruce remained at Dunverty for three days, receiving vows of allegiance from the men of Kintyre. On the third day a fishing boat arrived at the jetty, the crew brought news of the enemy. "My lord, the English have launched many warships from the Solway and they're sailing along the coast. When we left Ayr they were but a day's sail away. They say they're commanded by Menteith, betrayer of the Lord Wallace." The messenger was Robert Wallace, the youngest of Sir Richard Wallace's brood and cousin to the murdered Sir William. Robert Wallace had barely reached manhood but begged Bruce to accept him into his following. Bruce scrutinized the youth. All of the Wallace kinsmen were hardy, fighting men so he said, "You've a lot to live up to, but keep close to Douglas, he'll be your mentor." Douglas, older by two or three years, gazed coldly at the young Wallace and said, "Do what I say as soon as I say it and we'll get along just fine." Later John Wallace, brother to Sir William, watched his cousin as he trailed behind Douglas who was organizing the stowing of Bruce's provisions and he said to Gilbert Hay, "Sparks will fly before he settles to taking orders, he was always a headstrong fellow." "Aye, Douglas will give the lad short shrift if he's slow to do his bidding."

That evening Bruce called Douglas to him and said, "We'll be leaving tonight James, when there are fewer eyes around to see us, but I want you to go back to the mainland to my lands of Carrick and collect my Michaelmas rents. I'm in sore need of money. Men and arms don't come cheaply." Douglas was about to reply and it was plain from his expression that he was not happy with the task but Bruce raised his hand, "James, before I can defeat the English I'll need to subdue the Comyns and their allies. I can't do this without money. Take young Wallace with you and raise what you can but hide it well." Bruce held out his ring with his family seal on it. "For you, it may help. I know it's not a task to your liking but I trust few others with such an important matter.

There was heavy cloud that night but just as dawn began to touch the eastern sky with only the yawning night guard watching their departure. Four warships set sail. With trimmed sails and tacking into a brisk south-westerly wind they faced the uncertain weather of the Irish Sea. Shortly afterwards a fishing vessel manned by Douglas, Robert Wallace and John Kynmouth followed. Douglas steered east, keeping watch for the reported English fleet and trusting to God that they would reach the Ayrshire coast before they were spotted.

Crawford stood at the prow of his vessel, holding tightly the thick mooring rope. He yelled over his shoulder to the heaving rowers, "Pull, pull." The wind whipped his commands away, "Pull." With their final effort the keel crunched on the stony bottom. Crawford jumped over the edge, rope in hand and splashing through the frothing surf he pulled the rope. Other men joined him trying to secure the ship; at least in the bay there was some shelter and at least they had not lost a vessel. They had landed on the Isle of Rathlin. Not quite the destination Bruce had intended but it would suffice till the storm abated.

Sir Hugh Bissett, Lord of Antrim and Rathlin had received the news from his allies the MacDonalds, that Bruce had broken out from the Comyn and English grip and was heading for Ireland, but had expected him on the mainland of Antrim.

Sir Hugh had always adopted a pragmatic approach to the politics between Scotland and England. He preferred the judicial approach and remained on the winning side, but his family had been allied to the MacDonalds since Sir Hugh's grandfather's day, united in a hatred of the MacDougalls. Bruce's cause did appear forlorn at present but if the Bissett kindred provided men and arms and rallied support for King Robert of Scotland, who could tell what high rewards might be theirs?

Bruce, whose behaviour towards his companions was always relaxed and unassuming, had adopted the attitude of monarch to subject towards the shrewd Bissett. There would be no opportunity for Bissett to encourage doubt in the minds of any man present that the inaugurated King of Scotland could be denied homage. Bruce ordered his men to bring all the people of Rathlin, young, old, men and women, to the Bissett manor to witness their Lord's homage to his King. Afterwards each man bowed his knee before King Robert and promised him loyalty. In return the king vowed to protect them, their families, land and homesteads.

Rathlin was a small island and could not support many extra men for long and Bruce, his companions and a few young men from Rathlin returned to Antrim with Sir Hugh. During the remaining weeks of September and early October, Bruce toured the lands of the Bissetts and Stewarts. He spoke to the people himself, as their king, and listened to their troubles and in this way he gathered many supporters. By the second week of October, he had three hundred men, warships and supplies pledged to fight for Scotland's cause.

One evening he announced that it was his intention to sail for Kintyre. There were many voices raised against this. Menteith, in charge of the English fleet, was last heard of laying siege to Dunverty Castle and sending troops to harry the people living around the coastal land of Kintyre. It was Alexander Bruce who expressed all their thoughts. "Rob, as long as you remain free and active Scotland's cause is not lost. We can't risk your capture. Let Tom and I take the men to Kintyre and strike if and when we can, whilst you with a small bodyguard, take refuge in the isles." Around the room men said "Here, here," or "That's right, I agree." Bruce allowed them to voice their opinions, then when all men who wanted to, had been heard, he said "There's a deal of truth in what you say. Perhaps I would be more useful gathering men. My kinswoman, the Lady Christiana will assist, of that I am sure." So it was agreed that Bruce would take one hundred men as a bodyguard and seek protection in Scotland's Western Islands. His brothers, Thomas and Alexander would take command of the remaining men and sail for Kintyre. Bruce was firm in his orders, however, "Do not seek out the enemy needlessly. Every man is precious. We can't afford to lose one on a potentially unfruitful encounter."

That night, before he slept, John Wallace, not for the first time, thought of his dead brother. What would his thoughts have been on the changes in Bruce since his fateful encounter in Gray Friars Kirk? William Wallace had last seen Bruce in early summer 1305. Then Bruce was a cynical opportunistic nobleman, but as William would have said "hardship and tragedy change a man." After his brother's death he had been uncertain about following Bruce because Bruce had never shown steadfast loyalty to the Scottish cause, only self-interest. Now in just eight months, if John Wallace were honest, he would admit that he would follow anywhere Bruce led, just as he had his brother and for many of the same reasons.

When news had reached King Edward that Bruce and his following had broken out of the Scottish mainland he turned peevishly on Anthony Bek. "What are my son and Pembroke thinking of? Don't they have enough men to catch a handful of renegades? I'm told Bruce rows around the coast, in full view, smiling and waving at the population." "My Lord, you must order a fleet to intercept him before he has a chance to hide himself away for the winter on one of those wretched islands. We'll never find him then." "Whom have we in command?" asked the king. "Sir John Menteith, an able man who knows the islands well." The king sighed and closed his eyes, tired with the effort of talking. Menteith, one of his Scottish Lords, he did not want a Scot to have sole charge for apprehending Bruce. He had trusted Bruce and look where that had got him. No, it would have to be a joint command between Scot and Englishman. "Order the fleet to leave Skimburness immediately and not to return until they've found that man. Share the command between Menteith and Sir John Botetourt."

By the third week of September the English were besieging Dunverty Castle, confident in the knowledge that they had Bruce holed up inside. They had not seen him on the battlements but their informant assured them that the trail ended here. Every morning, Menteith himself with four or five galleys sailed up the coast, landed and harried the homesteads within easy reach, burning, killing, and driving off the livestock, but nothing happened at the castle and no attacking force sallied forth from within. If the English sent in a flight of arrows they were acknowledged by a similar display from the castle, otherwise everything remained quiet. Menteith and Botetourt sent a message to Skimburness demanding a siege engine be sent immediately before the winter gales began.

In the first week of October, when the English had been there for a little over a week, three wargalleys rounded the point off the sound of Kintyre. They rowed at a leisurely pace, their captains standing at the prow and did not hesitate when they saw the English but came on as if they were coming to pay their neighbours a visit. The captain of the leading vessel hailed them. "Ahoy, the land." The men near the jetty ran to their weapons and many put arrows to their bows. Botetourt ran to the jetty calling out, "Who are you?" The boats were very close to the land and Botetourt could see that the occupants were Scots. "The MacDonald of the MacDonalds," came the reply. The oarsmen tried to keep the vessels out from the jetty while the two commanders faced each other. Angus MacDonald, red in the face and standing precariously on the edge of his galley, hanging onto the prow with one hand, the other stuck into his belt, yelled, "What do you fools think you're doing here? We have no argument with King Edward. We've always been his most loyal subjects. Get off my land." "You are harbouring the king's enemy, Robert Bruce," shouted back Botetourt. "Show me the man who says that Englishman and I'll boil him alive." "I say you are MacDonald, for he was seen coming this way." Angus MacDonald began to laugh. His attitude was one of outraged innocence. "You've been sent on a wild goose chase. I'll show you myself that he is not here. You may search every corner and every barrel of my castle." Then he coolly rowed ashore followed by the other vessels. Botetourt was dumbstruck by the man's behaviour and beyond ordering his men to be prepared for treachery he followed Macdonald into the castle. Now that its commander had returned, the gates opened and the silent sombre place became a hive of excited activity.

Angus took the Englishman by the arm and led him into the great hall. As he walked he called out, "Donald, where are you lad?" A young man came running in. "Uncle, I'm here." Botetourt had seen him standing on the battlements and although they had hailed him many times he had never replied. "This is my nephew, a good lad but witless, although he can use the bow well. Now boy, have you had any visitors here while I've been away?" "No uncle, we locked the gates and waited for your return just like you told me to." Botetourt was exasperated, "Why didn't you open the gates for the King's forces?" Donald looked vaguely at the Englishman and said to Angus, "You didn't tell me to do that uncle."

It was plain Bruce was not hiding at Dunverty and there was no evidence that he had ever been. That evening when Menteith returned they sat together discussing their situation. "It's true that the MacDonalds have always been loyal to King Edward," said Botetourt. "True enough, but then the MacDougalls fought for King John Balliol, now they fight with the Comyns and the Comyns are loyal to King Edward. I find it hard to believe that the MacDonalds and the MacDougalls would ever be on the same side." said Menteith. "Well, I don't believe that we should pick a quarrel with Macdonald if we're sure that Bruce is not here." "Aye in that you're right although they've just persuaded us to waste a week, simply by ignoring us. So what now?" replied Botetourt. "I for one have no desire to go back to face the king empty-handed. We should sail along the west coast of Kintyre and up to Lorne. We can search the caves and islands as we go and might get a sighting if he's not expecting us," replied Menteith.

Late in the afternoon on the following day, the MacDonalds waved goodbye to the English fleet and John Menteith had the unpleasant feeling that as soon as the fleet was out of sight the MacDonalds would fall around laughing and in this he was right.

TO SEEK KING ROBIN

In command of six sturdy galleys, Bruce played hide-and-seek with the English fleet through the islands of the west coast. He had an ally in the weather with heavy seas and mist which numbed all sounds and senses. MacDonalds out on fishing trips told him when the English sailed north through the sound of Iona and Bruce altered course and sailed along the western coast of that island. The English sailed east into the sea lochs off the Isle of Mull, no doubt to search the caves and coves. Bruce hurried north to Staffa, the creaking and splashing from the oars echoing through the arches and chambers of that strange place and onwards, weaving in and out of islets, whilst Menteith and Botetourt continued to search doggedly. Bruce's vessels slipped between the rocky headland off Coll and at last he began to feel safe from detection. That night they rested in their boats, ears straining for the slightest unusual noise, and at first light under a full canvas sailed for Barra. There was a heavy swell but visibility was good and by midday the coasts of Barra and South Uist could be seen. In the late afternoon the sails were lowered and the vessels glided gracefully into the bay with Castle Kisimul towering above them.

Menteith and the English fleet, exhausted by their thorough search of the islands, sailed into the Firth of Lorne to Dunstaffnage Castle where they took council with Sir John MacDougall of Lorne.

Sir John was annoyed and made a great issue of his attack on Bruce at Dalry and now the English had allowed Bruce to escape into the islands. With winter closing in, Sir John was not keen to put to sea. Reluctantly he agreed to make another search and sent half of his fleet north to search the northern isles and the Cape, perhaps Bruce had slipped passed and was making for Orkney. In command of his remaining vessels he sailed southwards. By the end of November the three commanders, who had intercepted and questioned every merchant and fishing vessel in the area, were confident that Bruce was not hiding in their sector. Menteith, certain that his cold, wet and despondent men would mutiny if he did not return to port, sailed for Ayr.

There were many rumours that Bruce was in Ulster seeking men for ship service. No sooner had Menteith made harbour than they received news that three men were busy in Ulster buying stores of wine. Their informant was sure they were agents for Bruce. Menteith ignored the grumbling and sullen looks of his men and put to sea and in spite of heavy weather made Ulster in good time.

The Earl of Ulster's men had apprehended the merchants in Derry, which was Stewart territory, and they were brought before Menteith for questioning. He sat staring at the three. Certainly they were lowland Scots, Menteith could vouch for that. They were in a sorry state, covered in dried blood and dirt. When captured they had indignantly and loudly protested their innocence, which had irritated their captors, and they had received many blows and kicks. When they heard that they were being taken to Sir John Menteith, they ceased trying to explain and lapsed into sullen silence. Before their forced march and ill-treatment they had been prosperous men, well fed and wearing strong, leather boots. They did not have the appearance of living a vagrant's life. Menteith said, "You have been buying quantities of wine, for whom?" The elder of the men, his face red with anger, glared at the earl. "Sir, my name is Osborne and I am attached to the Earl of Pembroke's household. These two," he indicated his companions, "are the earl's sworn men. I have orders to buy wine and beef, provisions for King Edward's men. Your men have taken the earl's gold and beaten and humiliated me. I demand my freedom and the return of the money." Botetourt had come into the chamber during the prisoner's tirade and whispered into Menteith's ear. "I've seen this man in Pembroke's following." Menteith paused to compose his thoughts before saying, "You were reported to us as agents for Bruce, plainly you didn't announce who your master was or you wouldn't be in this position now." The prisoner replied, "Whoever informed you is no friend of King Edward for you have wasted valuable time. I was ordered not to make too much noise about my business, you know the price always goes up if the sale is to representatives of the king." Menteith reddened but otherwise kept his composure. "You'll return with us to Skimburness and we'll report to the king, meanwhile, complete your business here."

After this disappointment the English fleet returned to harbour. As well as this humiliation, Menteith and Botetourt had to face the king's anger when he heard Osborne's version of his capture and imprisonment. The Earl of Pembroke and his men had recently arrived in Ayr and it was with relief that Menteith joined him, glad to be out of the king's reach.

The Lady Christiana MacRuarie greeted her kinsmen King Robert with a splendid feast. There was hardly space on the tables so full were they with fish, fowl and game and all washed down with good Burgundian wine. The great hall of Kisimul was filled to overflowing and for those men who could not find seats with their comrades, there were benches and boards laid in the women's hall.

The king sat in the high chair, the lady beside him. They had dressed Bruce in a sumptuous royal blue surcoat, its velvet material from Venice was of the smoothest texture. The coat was long, to the ankles, and of generous cut with full sleeves, the hems and neck edged with otter skin. He had always been considered a comely man but after all his wanderings he had lost weight, his face gaunt, tanned by sun and wind and his blue eyes keener. Christiana thought how he had changed since she had last seen him and when they were alone she had said, "You look just like the great, white–tailed fish eagle who swoops down and plucks salmon from the sea, for its eyes see everything." Bruce relaxed and smiled good naturedly. They had last met when she was a guest at his marriage to Elizabeth and since then Christiana had been widowed. She had the dark, thick hair and blue-grey eyes so often seen among the people of the western isles, but since he last saw her, she had grown fuller around hips and breasts yet he thought her still a bonnie woman. After months of male company, it was a pleasure to have her paying him compliments and sitting by his side. She had a young son, born after the death of his father and Christiana loved the child deeply. He was the only one left to her after many pregnancies. She talked a great deal about the little lad and had confided in Bruce her fears for the boy's future should anything happen to her. She had inherited her father's lands, the Isles of Uist, Rum and many others as well as large estates on the mainland. "He will inherit all my lands," she had said. Bruce had patted her hand. "You must let me find you another husband Chrissy, who will fill your life with more children. You are still young and very comely." Christiana had smiled, "Nay, my lord, I would prefer to remain free and unwed. Donald and I never lived that kindly together that I wish to undertake marriage again." In earlier times Bruce would have joked and teased the lady about her disillusion with men but he had more pressing matters on his mind and knew that Donald of Mar had been a harsh man.

He had had no news of his wife and daughter and on that first night, Bruce was able to eat and drink to excess and listen with a quiet mind to the bard and minstrels. As the evening wore on many men fell asleep where they sat with their heads on the tables, surrounded by the debris of the meal while the dogs ran around their legs fighting over the discarded remains.

Since his hardships had began Bruce usually slept soundly, his mind giving way to his body's exhaustion but on this night, in spite of the wine, he lay wakeful and restless, thinking about his wife and Marjorie and his own hotheaded actions at Greyfriars. Eventually when morning was nearly upon them, he fell asleep.

During the weeks of Advent, in spite of the winter gales, Christiana rode with Bruce throughout Barra and Uist and her men paid him homage and promised their support.

Late on a cold, grey afternoon when Bruce had been at Kisimal for about a week, a galley arrived. Ruairi MacRuarie, Christiana's half-brother, by their father's mistress, was in command. He was a very young man and bursting to tell everyone the news, which he had heard in Kirkwall. Bruce was sitting with Christiana when Ruairi found him. "My lord, I have news of your lady and daughter." Bruce leant forward in his chair. "It is not good news Sir, the party sought sanctuary at Tain and it was granted, but the Earl of Ross broke the church laws, slaughtered the queen's escort and the women and Earl of Atholl were taken prisoner and escorted to the English king." Silence fell upon those gathered in the hall. Slowly the king stood up, an expression of horror on his face. "Have you more?" asked the king. "It is said that the Earl of Atholl has been sent to London for execution and the castle of Kildrummy fell in September, they say it was betrayed from within." "And the garrison?" asked Bruce. "Pembroke pledged his word for their safety, but the Prince Edward gave the order for their murder. Only your brother was taken south." "What became of the men at Methven?" said the king. By this time even Ruairi, who was notorious for his brash and careless attitude, realized the enormity of what he said and began to blush. "The men of Methven also suffered, my lord. Simon Fraser is already executed in London and Christopher Seton they took to Dumfries to carry out the deed." He was about to continue with his seemingly endless list of misfortunes but his sister laid her hand on his arm and said, "Now, now, Ruairi spare our guests, let them speak to you alone when you may answer all their questions." The men in the hall sat quietly and when they did speak it was in hushed tones. Bruce walked quickly from the hall and sat for a long time on the headland, gazing out to sea until it was dark. The following day he continued travelling around the land talking to the men and receiving their homage. He must win the crown, which he had already taken, or die.

Christmas came and he joined in the games, dancing and laughing at Patrick the jester, who had developed a repertoire of English jokes for his guests. On Twelfth Night, Bruce danced the circle dance with Christiana's hand in his. It was so enjoyable and when it came to an end they collapsed onto the bench laughing and breathless for the hall had become very hot, packed with so many people. Bruce slipped his arm around Christiana's shoulders, more the action of an old friend than a lover. Christiana stiffened her gentle face, adopting a worried expression. Robert, whose own sufferings had made him more aware of other people's, patted Christiana's shoulder and said, "Your husband has a great deal to answer for Christiana. I mean you no harm, you know." The lady relaxed and smiled up at her king.

Three days later King Robert's fleet of twenty galleys set sail from Barra. Christiana stood on the jetty until they were far out to sea. There had been tears in her eyes as Bruce had taken her hand and kissed the fingertips, "Without your help I could not go now. You are cold Chrissy, go you in," he said. She had smiled up at him. "Then, my lord I regret giving so much, for I am sending you all into danger." Bruce made no reply.

Now there were others who willingly took the steerboard and Bruce sat by the carved prow, keeping watch for enemy craft as they sailed south towards Rathlin where he would take command of more galleys.

Hugh Bissett greeted him with respect and openly told Bruce that during the Christmas feast he had received orders from the English king to sail immediately and search for Bruce. "They are out in force, my lord. I hear there are three fleets and one is already at sea cruising through the western isles, you were lucky to evade them. Menteith is busy rowing up and down the Firth of Clyde whilst I am told that the Earl of Pembroke has grown tired of Prince Edward's so-called jokes and has command of many ships, harboured at Ayr awaiting news of you." "So, the prince is still endearing himself to everybody with his glib tongue is he?" said Bruce. "Aye, they tell me he refers to my lord Pembroke as 'Joseph the Jew,' because he's so dark." Bruce laughed. Although Pembroke had once been a friend he could not forget the underhanded lie on the battlements of Perth and his own disgrace at Methven. "What are you doing about your orders Hugh?" asked Bruce. Bissett laughed. "I can't go to sea yet, half my fleet are in Dublin and many that remain have been damaged by recent storms. It's doubtful if they'll be ready to put to sea before the spring comes." Then they both laughed, for Bruce had seen Bissett's large and excellent fleet moored in the harbour that very morning.

In the last day of January amidst swirling mist Bruce's fleet slipped past Dunaverty Castle, now garrisoned by Englishmen and around the southern tip of Arran and run his ships onto the sandy Arran beach in the shadow of the rocky isle which the local people called Holy Island. Fields sloped down to the sea and tucked away, sheltered by rocks and trees, was a farmstead. The woman, followed by five children came down to the water's edge asking who the newcomers were. Edward Bruce stepped forward, "Seafarers mother, seeking safe haven from the mist. Friends live hereabouts have you heard of any newcomers?" The woman looked around at the galleys full of strong and purposeful warriors and knew who they were, but it was wise to appear innocent, so she said. "Aye, I have seen men, hardy like yourselves, they went up through yonder hills and my man says they live well protected and comfortable. For sure they have never bothered us." Then she smiled. "Someone attacked the governor's men and stole their goods. My man says it was themselves." Edward said, "your man has a lot to say." The woman bit her lip, perhaps she had been too forward, but one of the other men said, without showing any anger, "Will you show us where the men are?" "Aye sir," she turned to her old mother, "You take care of the little ones until my man returns, mother." She wrapped her baby tightly in a lamb's fleece and with her daughter's help strapped him to her back, took a sturdy staff and stepped briskly along the path leading through the trees and to the glen. Edward Bruce and half of the men remained with the galleys but the king followed closely behind the woman. As they ascended the sheep path, the mist grew thicker, clinging to Bruce's cloak and where it touched his beard it formed into droplets of water. It was cold, the dampness eating into joints and sinews. They had gained the top of the hill and continued through a wooded glen. Then she turned to Bruce and pointed to a thicket, but Bruce said "Wait mother, it's unwise to rush in on armed men without introducing yourself first." His hunting horn hung at his belt and he put this to his lips and blew twice. Immediately there was a shout from behind a rocky outcrop and two heads popped up above the granite. "Is that yourself then my lord?" called James Douglas from the safety of the rock. "Aye James and is that yourself safe and well?" Douglas and Boyd scrambled from behind their cover followed by other figures.

Very quickly the newcomers were taken to a small cottage hidden by gorse and bracken. Soon they were seated comfortably around the fire and offered food and wine, which had formerly belonged to the English garrison. The woman sat herself in a corner of the little hut and turning her back on the men offered her babe the breast. She ate the food and drunk the wine offered to her and then she and the babe fell asleep. "Well Robert, tell us of your adventures, for it's a joy to me that you are safe," said Bruce. Robert Boyd related his tale of treachery and murder and his own escape from Prince Edward's army. "Come forward Duggie lad and show yourself," ordered Boyd. The boy had been sitting in the shadows but came forward with confidence holding his right hand behind his back because it was still bandaged and hurt him. "I could not help your brother sir," said the lad. At first Bruce made no reply for he guessed what Neil's fate would be and he was overcome with emotion but when he gained his composure, he said, "Ah well! At least you are safe Rob and can carry on the fight." Just as he finished speaking someone roared from the forest edge, "Hey, you in there. Where's ma woman?" At first they had thought the bellow came from an angry red stag, but a few moments later a small, fiery man burst into the hut, quickly followed by two of Douglas's men. Everyone jumped to their feet, daggers in hands but the intruder rushed past them all and swooped on the woman who was woken with the noise. The baby began to cry and the intruder turned to the astonished group. "What'd think you're doing with ma Moira? Ma bairns are all alone with none but the ole woman and Moira up here and not yet churched." The man was red in the face with rage and his beard and hair matched his colouring. Douglas stepped forward, "Watch your tongue in front of noble lords," but Moira's husband stood his ground, boldly staring back at Douglas. "Up your arse," he roared, "This is ma wife and bairn. You've put them in danger." Douglas was about to strike but the king stepped forward and holding up his hands said, "Would you deny your wife the honour of serving her king?" For a moment everybody thought the irate husband would continue with his fighting talk, but he remained silent and Bruce continued. "Your lassie has come to no harm and I am in her debt." He turned to Douglas who had managed to collect some of the Earldom of Carrick's rents. "Give this man one merk of silver," then he said to the furious husband, "Perhaps this will pay the priest extra at your wife's purification that he may keep away evil spirits from the mother and child? Grudgingly the man accepted the money.

It was now quite dark and impossible for Moira and her man to return to their farm that night and the farmer drank so heavily of the strong wine which he was unused too, that Moira whispered rather loudly, "Murdo, you're drunk." Murdo, in an even louder whisper said, "I'm no drunk and if I am it's not every day I'll drink wi ma king." By morning he was so enthusiastic about King Robert and the fight against English rule that Moira feared he would join the ranks of fighting men and leave her alone with the farm and all the children to manage.

Bruce prepared his plans, King Edward lay mortally sick, indeed was perhaps already dead, it had to be now. He sent messengers to his brothers encamped in Arran. Tom and Alexander would make a landing in Loch Ryan and move towards Dumfries, whilst he and Edward would land further up the coast south of Turnberry. A spy was hurriedly sent to the mainland to judge the mood of the people.

Fifteen galleys had left for Loch Ryan, commanded by Bruce's brothers and accompanied by Reginald Crawford and men of Kintyre and Ulster. So far no news had come through about the success or otherwise of their mission and Bruce was ready to depart for the mainland. He walked restlessly, backwards and forwards along the beach, unusually agitated and nervous. It was a late afternoon in early February with a heavy overcast sky and the first of the galleys were already afloat and riding the gentle swell. The men were eager to get back to the mainland and were ready for action. All being well they would make landfall under cover of darkness, but the news was not good. The English garrison at Turnberry Castle had an iron grip on the surrounding population, its commander, Sir Henry Percy, was well known as an uncompromising and callous man. Indeed, men who had been Bruce's most loyal and trusted tenants were cowed by Percy's tyranny whilst just up the coast at Ayr, Pembroke and Menteith were waiting for news of Bruce's landing. Bruce spoke to his men. "There'll be no battles, no laying siege, no glory, we'll strike and depart. I want the English and their Comyn friends looking over their shoulders day and night." They put to sea leaving the safety of Arran behind them.

Turnberry garrison was large and men not on duty were billeted in farms and manors in the surrounding area. They felt so confident they did not stand watch. Bruce knew the country well. Under cover of darkness his men took up their positions. When the moon came from behind the clouds he began the attack. It was unexpected and ferocious. High up on the battlements of Turnberry Castle, Percy, who had been woken by the noise, listened to the screams, pleading, clash of arms, and later general rejoicing of Scottish voices, but he did not open the castle gates to send out a relieving force. In the darkness he could not tell the numbers of the enemy nor exactly where they were, for the sounds came from all around the castle walls.

All Englishmen found in the area were executed and the Scots were able to take away large quantities of much needed supplies, both food and equipment. Then they fled into the Carrick hills and by morning the area was once more peaceful. The supplies were hidden and Bruce divided his men into smaller fighting groups with orders to scour the area for recruits. "I prefer men to come willingly," he said to his commanders, "But if they hang back, use force to remind them of their obligations to their liege lord". By these means Bruce was able to increase the numbers of his group.

Thomas and Alexander Bruce had sailed to Loch Ryan and landed under the cover of sea mist. There were over one hundred warriors, including many Irishmen and Reginald Crawford and John Wallace. They had made good time and it was late afternoon when they cautiously entered the loch. Lookouts standing on the prow of each vessel watched the land for signs of the enemy. The mist wrapped itself around the low hills but low on the western horizon a watery sun tried to break through the clouds. The only sound came from the flapping canvas as the men loosened the rigging and prepared to furl the huge square sail and the splash of oars dipping into the water. Landing would be the most dangerous time for an ambush.

They landed where the trees grew close to the water's edge. Once ashore the men began unloading stores, hiding them among the trees until they could be moved to safer cover inland.

The sun had not disappeared below the horizon and from the cover of the trees, men of Dougal MacDougall of Galloway, Comyn supporters, appeared. They had advanced silently and were upon Bruce's force before they were aware of danger. Caught in the open, casualties were great. Alexander Bruce, Master of Cambridge University and Dean of Glasgow, was a man of learning, more at home with his legal and Holy books than fighting in hostile country. It was his loyalty to his kinsmen, which had brought him to the fight and he was quickly overpowered. His brother, Thomas, fought furiously, receiving a wound which entered just below his ribs on the right side and forced him to drop his broad sword. He staggered backwards but regained his balance. A battleaxe lay discarded on the sandy beach and he scooped it up warding off his opponent's weapons with his shield and trying to defend himself with the axe, which, with difficulty, he swung around his head. As the weapon cut through the air it sang a deadly song until one of his opponents rushed at him with a pike. Thomas took aim and let fly. The axe rang out loudly as it somersaulted through the air and caught the pikeman at the side of the neck almost severing his head from his body and he fell lifeless. At the same moment, someone caught Thomas a heavy blow from behind. Stunned, he fell to the ground.

The Irishmen were commanded by their own chieftain, who was

overcome by MacDougall's followers, but Sir Reginald Crawford, realizing the hopelessness of their situation, tried to organize a retreat. With a few men he struggled to relaunch the galleys. Two of the vessels were re-floated and those men who could do so climbed aboard. Crawford waded into the inky water shouting commands but before boarding, he looked back at the scene of devastation. The remaining vessels had been set alight by MacDougall's men, each detail clearly etched in the light from the fires. Some men still fought, and grotesque bodies littered the sand. Then Crawford saw Thomas Bruce. Unable to stand, he was crawling along the water's edge towards the vessels. Crawford shouted to the steersman, "Wait if you can," and he waded back towards Bruce. Reaching the young man safely, he pulled him onto his own back and struggled towards the still waiting galley. It was MacDougall himself who saw Crawford's attempt to escape and with a bellow of "Forward, take them alive" he and his men rushed towards the pair. The galley's oarsmen, unable to help, pulled away from the shore and were swallowed up in the darkness.

MacDougall was a fiery individual, greedy for power. The Bruce brothers and Crawford were separated from the other prisoners and forced to watch the slaying of their men. Alexander Bruce made the sign of the cross and prayed loudly for the reception of their souls into Paradise, but MacDougall rushed at the young cleric and gave him such a blow to the side of the head that Alexander fell to the ground. "Their souls can rot in hell," snapped MacDougall.

The severed heads of the Irish chieftain and MacQuillian of Kintyre were wrapped in sacking and placed in baskets. Then MacDougall and all his men rode triumphantly along the coastal path, past Luce Bay and followed the Solway Firth to Calaverock Castle, where MacDougall, his followers, prisoners and severed heads crossed over to England.

At Carlisle the prisoners were placed in the castle dungeons, whilst the decaying trophies of war were carried to Prince Edward, who was resting from the worst excesses of the winter weather at Wetheral Priory. When he heard the good news, he issued orders that the prisoners should be executed immediately. His confessor said, "But my lord, remember Alexander Bruce is a cleric, if the Holy Father, in Rome should hear.....," but before he could continue with his warning Edward turned away adopting his bored, slightly irritated air saying, "Bruce has forfeited any rights he may have had. He must suffer as other traitors do." Later the priest thought about this. 'Yes, yes, there was truth in what his master said, Bruce had waived his rights by taking up the sword.'

When they dragged Thomas Bruce through the streets of Carlisle, to his execution, he was already close to death and burning with fever from the wound he had received, and was barely able to stand. His brother Alexander helped to support the dying man up the steps to the gallows and Thomas whispered his confession to him through fever-cracked lips. Sir Reginald Crawford, patriot and uncle to Sir William Wallace, was executed with them. The watching crowd was not very large. Since the beginning of the Bruce rebellion, just one year previously, there had been a steady flow of executions and Carlisle's population showed little enthusiasm. They needed something new and excitingly different to make them wait around in the wet and cold.

After the ravaging of the lands around the castle of Turnberry Robert Bruce and his men disappeared into the surrounding Carrick Hills. The lands were Bruce's own earldom and he knew the people and they him, but fear of the reprisals which the English would undoubtedly take frightened them and they could not be persuaded to join him. They used all manner of excuses and he was forced to order his men to use harsh treatment. James Douglas was the most feared of Bruce's captains and he never left a settlement empty-handed. Occasionally after one of Douglas' visits, crying and wailing could be heard and a male body swung from the branch of a nearby tree. Such news spreads quickly and gradually when men heard that Douglas was in the area, before his arrival, they discussed among themselves who should join Bruce's following from among their community. When Douglas arrived a man would be ready with his weapons, to follow Bruce. In this manner Bruce began to collect together a fighting force.

High in the hills where there were fine views of the surrounding land, Bruce had a small camp within a cave. One day, when he had been in the area for about three weeks, William Wiseman came running up the narrow path, "My lord, you've a visitor." Wiseman was smiling broadly so Bruce said, "Plainly it's a guest who'll bring me pleasure." "Oh aye, this guest will bring you much joy." "Who is it then?" called Bruce, but Wiseman, still smiling was already returning back the way he had come and to add to Bruce's sense of anticipation Wiseman whistled as he went. To satisfy his curiosity, Bruce clambered onto a nearby rock and peered through the trees down the path leading into the glen. He caught glimpses of horsemen but could not distinguish their identity. When he heard the sound of horses hooves on the stony path he walked down to greet his guests. Even before he saw them, he heard talking and above the sounds of the men's voices the unmistakable laughter of a woman. He quickened his pace, leaping across puddles and boggy, moss–soaked ground until around a bend in the track the cavalcade came into view. Edward Bruce led the procession and at his side rode Christine, Robert's own bonnie Christine. How long had it been since he had last seen her? He could not remember but she looked just as she had then. She wore a wine red mantle edged with squirrel, the hood pulled up to protect her yellow hair, wisps of it escaped and blew across her broad forehead. When she saw Robert standing in the middle of the path, hands on hips, smiling and welcoming, as he had always been, her heart jumped with joy. He lifted her from her pony, scrutinizing her from head to toe. He had lost so many loved ones, yet here was Christine standing before him. She remembered that now Robert was her king, and she curtsied and showed him great respect in front of the men. "Nay, Christine rise up. It is my pleasure to see you," and taking her by the arm he led her back to his camp. As they walked he said. "You're a joy to behold Christine. You haven't changed one bit." She laughed "That's not true Robert. When you left me last I was screaming at you and threw a flagon of my best wine at your retreating back." "Christine, you shame me." She said laughing, "That, my lord, is because you should be."

When they arrived at the camp Christine turned to the men, about forty in number, who rode with her. "Kinsmen, this is your King, Robert of Scotland." They, having dismounted fell on their knees and pledged themselves to him as his liegemen.

By the time they had fed their horses and prepared food, it was late in the afternoon. A fine, gentle rain fell and Christine asked Bruce if he would walk with her. As they climbed to the top of the bolder–strewn hill she told him about their children, Robert and Christine. She was very proud of them. They rested for a while, leaning against a large rock and there Bruce, unable to control his impatient passion any longer held Christine close, kissing her face and neck and searching her familiar body with his hands, but she pulled away from him. He, with surprise in his voice said thickly, "What, are you still angry with me Christine?" "Nay, my anger with your roaming ways diminished with the years. I always knew that I could never be your wife, but I have brought you news that will give me no pleasure to tell. For a few moments she turned her gaze away from him, dreading the pain which she was about to inflict. "Your wife has lain at Lanercost Priory, hovering like a bird between life and death. None knew how it would end with her. Your child was stillborn and now that she is better she has been taken south, no one knows where. Only the power of her father saved her." Christine did not look at him while she spoke and continued, "Your sister Mary and the Lady Isabelle have been hung in cages on the castle walls at Berwick and Roxburgh, for all to see and jeer at, and your sister Christina is in a convent in Lincolnshire." Bruce had turned away from her so that she could not see the tears in his eyes. Christine put her arms around him, but he said "And my daughter, what have they done to her?" "She has been imprisoned in the Tower in London." Robert Bruce turned ashen, "Is there any more?" "Aye my love, there is, which I will tell you and then if you wish, I will leave you in peace. At the raid at Loch Ryan the MacDougalls lay in wait for your men and your brothers were captured and executed at Carlisle last week. Two ships only have returned to Arran from Loch Ryan." Bruce swayed slightly, but caught hold of a nearby rock to support himself and from his deep breathing and wild eyes it was plain he was deeply affected. The despair was clearly heard in his voice when he said, "Was it so wrong to want the crown of Scotland? Punish me, Lord, if you must but why all the innocent?" He straightened himself, breathing deeply, but the pain remained on his face. Then he turned and put his arms around her and they stood for some time like that. Dusk fell, and the rain became heavier. Bruce said, "Go back to the camp Christine and warm yourself and tell Edward to join me. Don't worry if I don't return tonight."

By Bruce's camp was a windowless stone byre with a turf roof and raised floor on each side of the door. Sacks had been filled with moss and bracken and that night Christine of Carrick slept there alone. It was a fine winter's day when she awoke and the smell of wood smoke and roasting meat hung in the air. Christine wandered over to some of her own men and began helping them to prepare their meal and much of her day was spent in this manner. Edward Bruce came back to the camp about midday but spent time talking to James Douglas.

Christine was perched on a large rock within the cave entrance and as darkness fell Bruce came back into camp and sat beside her. A bright fire burnt cheerfully and she drank a beaker of mead, a wonderfully warming drink, thick with honey and perfumed with herbs. The rich golden liquor was part of the bounty Bruce's men now enjoyed and had belonged to the English at Turnberry. Bruce was quieter than usual but had regained his composure and listened to the songs and storytelling which went on around the fire. Two of Christine's men were accomplished musicians and played haunting tunes on the pipe and drum, the notes spiralling upwards with the smoke from the fire, and lifted the spirits of the listeners, before floating away into the night.

Had it not been for the recent sad news it would have been a pleasant evening.

Robert Bruce spent that night with Christine. By the light of a small brazier she removed her clothes and Bruce sat and watched her. When she was quite naked she unbraided her hair so that it fell around her shoulders in heavy waves. Then Robert leant forward and swept it back on either side so that he could gaze upon her. "You were always a lovely woman Christine. I have not treated you as well as I might." "Aye, Robert, that's true, but we'll not speak of it now." She said this smiling, in a matter-of-fact way, and he being a good-natured man accepted her rebuke knowing it to be true. Then he kissed her with passion. That night Bruce found great pleasure with Christine of Carrick whilst she murmured, "Oh, what perfect bliss, Rob." Early the following day she rode back to her manor whilst Bruce and his men moved camp.

Late one afternoon James Douglas arrived in camp in a great hurry. He had been out recruiting men, but the speed with which he climbed the winding track to Bruce's lair indicated that he brought news of great importance. Bruce hailed him saying, "What dragons are after you?" Douglas scrambled up the steep slope and upon reaching the top, between deep gasps for breath said. "My lord, not an hour's march from here is an English patrol. They've bivouacked for the night by the small loch close by Palnure Burn. They have many pack ponies. If we attack with speed we'll have the advantage of surprise." Douglas began drawing with a stick on the muddy path an outline of the terrain and the position of the English. Edward Bruce came over and quite soon all the men had gathered around Bruce. "Take only the weapons you'll need and we'll leave now, following the burn and resting here." He placed a pebble on Douglas's drawing. "We'll attack at first light before they have had time to breakfast or take an arrow from a quiver." The camp was tense whilst each man collected what he needed and within a short space of time since Douglas's arrival, they had left the camp.

Duggie had become Boyd's shadow and before leaving Sir Robert said, "If we're not back by noon tomorrow take, what you need from here and go to the Lady Christine of Carrick, she'll tell you what to do." Boyd followed the other men into the forest and Duggie looked pensively after him.

A cold, dripping, misty dawn awoke both Scots and English. The former spent the night hidden around their enemy in a semicircle and awaiting a signal from their commander. Some of the English yawning, stretching and scratching crawled from beneath their blankets, but their commander was not yet up and about and so many of his men stayed snuggly wrapped in their blankets.

Bruce launched his attack silently. On his command, Douglas, Boyd and others skilled with the bow crept close, as Douglas later said, "Within spitting distance." Their first victims died so quietly that many Englishmen continued sleeping through the initial attack. The horses and pack animals were driven away and Bruce and his men, remembering their comrades at Loch Ryan, indulged themselves in an orgy of killing. A handful of men were allowed to escape into the forest "They can take news of their defeat to their masters," said Bruce, as he leant against a convenient rock and surveyed the scene of battle.

Within days news of Bruce's attack reached the old king. He lay in his bed in Lanercost where the task of breaking the news was left to Bek who had had many years' experience of dealing with such things. The king was too weak to flare up into one of his rages and looked at Bek with sadness, sighed and said, "Twenty years or more I've worked to unite these two kingdoms – all wasted." "My, lord, it was an encounter of no consequence. Eastern and northern Scotland are yours and Bruce, with a handful of men, remains defiant only in the southwest." "True, but so long as he remains free I fear he's a danger to our power and when I'm gone all will fall to him," replied Edward. "Then we must hope Our Lord spares you for many years yet," said Bek smoothly, but it worried him for he had never heard his master so despondent before. The king lay silent. The only sound came from the guard, coughing and stamping his feet outside the door. When Bek thought his master had fallen asleep he arose, but Edward said, "Anthony, write a letter to Pembroke, with copies to all sheriffs and captains throughout Scotland. Tell them they are being too harsh with their interpretation of my wishes and they must show more mercy in all matters concerning the Scots. Issue proclamations throughout Scotland that all who have given aid to Robert Bruce through fear will be pardoned. Perhaps that'll put an end to their support of him. Also send Pembroke a private letter ordering him to put more energy into searching for Bruce." The old king lay back on his pillows, his eyes firmly closed, the effort of saying so much had exhausted him, but before he slept he said, almost as an aside, "Anthony, they're all waiting for me to die."

Sir John Wallace was present at Loch Ryan and had fought at the edge of the fray. He had defeated his opponent and realized the hopelessness of the situation. Without other means of escape open to him, he ran into the Loch and swam after the departing galleys. He called to them, but they showed no sign of hearing him before they were swallowed up by the darkness. Wallace swam further along the loch and eventually took cover in the forest. Shivering with cold, he crept among the rocks and fallen trees where he had some relief from the fine drizzle which had begun to fall. It was a wretched night and when the grey dawn came, Wallace crept stiffly from his hiding place. His clothes were still damp and in order to keep warm he ran through the forest and up the glen in a northerly direction, keeping the sea on his left and avoiding manors and farms. Whenever he saw people, or wood smoke filled his nostrils, he hid himself until the danger had past. At the head of Glen App, he turned northeast following burns and tracks. He was entering country that he had known well when he had ridden with his brother and if he could but keep up the pace he would soon be in Carrick country. He had his bow, axe and knife with him but neither food nor drink. He drunk from the burns and lochens but by the end of the second day he was very hungry. He was climbing down a steep stony track when he caught a glimpse through the trees of a young stag drinking at the edge of a lochen. Taking care not to dislodge stones, he hid behind a large rock, silently loosened his bow and took an arrow from his quiver, placed it to his bow, stepped from cover and let fly. The arrow flew straight to its target entering just behind the left shoulder. A second arrow caught its victim before it could speed away and it collapsed onto the grassy bank, legs jerking. Wallace finished the deed quickly and then built a small fire at the forest edge and settled down to his meal.

Wallace's need for food had been so pressing he had not taken his usual precautions before leaving the sanctuary of the forest. It was not a large loch and on the opposite hillside an English patrol, sergeant and ten men, on their way south to Dumfries, halted when they saw the stag fall and silently watched Wallace as he prepared his meal. The tantalising smell of roasting venison drifted across the still water. "Sarg, he can't eat all that." The sergeant agreed that fresh meat was better then the dried pork they had in their pouches and they could spare the time to relieve the Scotsman of his kill. Stealthily they moved around and behind Wallace, who sat watching a pair of buzzards soaring above the waters of the loch, no doubt waiting for him to move on when they could have their share of the fallen stag.

As the first stars appeared in the sky and Wallace sat, clearly silhouetted by the flames from the fire, the Englishmen attacked. The sergeant had heard about the failed Bruce landing at Loch Ryan and although he could not persuade Wallace to speak, he was very suspicious that the big tough-looking Scot was an escaped renegade. So they bound Wallace and continued their journey towards Dumfries, the prisoner maintaining a brooding silence. It was in Dumfries Castle that Sir Richard Siward, back at his post as governor of the castle, recognized Wallace. In spite of the king's order to his commanders in Scotland to show leniency, Wallace was taken to London for execution.

On a fine spring day in early April, Sir John Wallace faced the London crowds. The young man who had stood with his brother above the bridge at Stirling watching the advancing English army, and who had refused to seek pardon from the English King was about to pay the penalty for his defiance. Crown officials witnessing the execution noted that the crowd was not as large or as vocal as they would have expected for the execution of Wallace's brother. Perhaps the rumours were correct. The people believed the old king was being too harsh and were tiring of the spectacles. Just before the noose was placed around the man's neck, voices called from the crowd, "Why can't the poor sod speak?" "Let him have his final say," and "Shame on you, give the bugger a chance to speak." Seagrave, who had attended the execution of William Wallace, nodded to the hangman.

Wallace gazed around at the now silent crowd. After all the rough treatment on the long journey from Scotland, he was weak and could barely raise his voice to make himself heard. He took a deep breath and in as loud a voice as he could muster he said, "You've seen many standing here during this past year because we're Scots, of Scotland born and we die for Scotland. Would you do less for your homes. We do not have a quarrel with you, but with your leaders and those I have left behind will continue to fight for freedom." Seagrave had heard enough, the rope was placed over the prisoner's head and he was jerked into the air. There was neither whistling nor cheering from the crowd, but a groan escaped from a thousand throats and someone called out "Poor bleeder," and many turned and walked away before the executioner had finished his butchery. Those who remained crossed themselves and murmured a prayer for the departing soul.

King Edward had written another of his letters to the Earl of Pembroke, demanding to know what steps Pembroke was taking to apprehend Bruce and the other traitors. The earl, a meticulous and hardworking commander, groaned. It irritated him that he had been foolish enough to allow Bruce to escape at Methven and he knew that once The Prince of Wales wore the crown, the situation would deteriorate further. The earl considered the heir to the throne insufferable and he had every intention of retiring to his estates, on the grounds of ill health, once the old king's time was up. In the meantime if he could quell the Bruce uprising it would make his own future plans more realistic. Bruce's tenacity surprised him. From previous experience he would have expected Bruce to sue for peace and beg for pardon with his usual carefree charm and, if that proved impossible, have disappeared to Norway by now. Yet a little over a year after the murder of John Comyn, Bruce was still free in the Carrick Hills drumming up a growing support from the people, raiding English supplies and keeping English troops holed up behind garrison walls. Well, spring had arrived and he would get Bruce now before his forces grew any stronger. Pembroke ordered a meeting of his captains.

Pembroke gazed along the table at the assembled men. Clifford, Percy and Botetourt he knew well, all good, sound men from solid English families. He knew their strengths and weaknesses and how far he could push them, but the Scots he viewed with mistrust. Why were they here? Greed, or fear like Sir John Menteith, responsible for William Wallace's betrayal. Or could it be revenge, like young David, the new Earl of Atholl, who blamed Bruce for his father's execution? "Well gentlemen, the king grows impatient and demands to know our plans. He accuses us of cowardice. Has anyone fresh news of Bruce's whereabouts?" No one spoke, not even Percy, a bombastic fellow, who could normally be relied upon to voice some sort of opinion. They presented blank stares and when the earl turned his gaze on each of them, they shifted uneasily in their chairs. "Surely one of you has some information, we're paying our informants enough." They remained silent. No one wanted to venture the first opinion. It was not that they lacked valour nor loyalty. The English cause, they knew to be a just one, but they had spent the past nine months searching both land and sea for Bruce and always when they arrived at his camp he had flown the coup, as if he was laughing at them. Meanwhile, support for Bruce and his cronies grew amongst the common folk. Eventually Sir John Mowbray said, "I've heard that Bruce has been seen by the Blackwater of Dee, heading towards Glen Trool."

Pembroke arose and strode irritably to the window niche to gaze out across the sea. It was a wonderful, bright day, full of the promise of spring and the Isle of Arran, dressed in fresh green, lay quietly in the sparkling, sapphire sea. From Bruce's last known position to move north–west to Loch Trool would be a logical move. The earl turned to face his captains. "We'll send a mounted force of Northumbrians to find

Bruce. If they don't stop him it'll be their homes he'll attack when he turns on England."

The week had been dry and fair when three hundred of the finest seasoned warriors from Northumberland rode out from Turnberry Castle, led jointly by Sir Robert Clifford and Sir John de Vaux, to find and engage Bruce. They were used to the type of difficult country, which they would encounter.

Pembroke had toyed with the idea of leading the raid himself but an ambush by Bruce was always a possibility and Menteith had persuaded Pembroke that if such a noble prisoner were to fall into Scottish hands his ransom would be embarrassingly high. Pembroke was forced to see the common sense of the argument and waited impatiently for a satisfactory outcome.

Clifford's company travelled at speed through the rolling coastal country with a MacDougall as their guide. The local people had no idea of the column's intended destination particularly when they took the rode leading to Dumfries, but when Clifford gave orders to take to the Galloway Hills, Bruce's supporters ran ahead to warn him.

Since leaving Turnberry, de Vaux had irritated Clifford. They could not agree on the smallest point. He countermanded Clifford's orders, complained that Clifford did not consult him and when Clifford did, he could not agree with Clifford's point of view and argued incessantly. By the time the column neared Glen Trool, Clifford wanted to get the campaign over and done with as quickly as possible and vowed to avoid any further joint commands with the self-righteous bugger. They had been out for a week or more searching the hills and for once the commanders were in agreement, if they could not find a fresh trail by the following day, they would return to Ayr for news.

Glen Trool was narrow and steeply pine–clad, whilst the waters of its loch filled the glen. A track ran along one side. Trool looked harmless enough, its waters sparkling in the gentle, April sun. A dog and bitch otter played on the opposite bank and Clifford watched them for a while for he rode at a leisurely pace by the water's edge. A sergeant with an escort of men had been sent ahead and Clifford could see them, the sun glinting on their helmets, at the Loch head. The sergeant had dismounted and he and his men were at rest by the water's edge, their horses waiting in the shade. The scene was very normal. He quickened his pace. Perhaps this would be a pleasant place to camp for the night. The column was spread out along the track and Clifford turned in his saddle and shouted, "Close the line there." His men quickened their pace.

The vanguard, including the two commanders, had joined the sergeant and his men and all had begun to dismount when the first arrow struck the sergeant. No one had heard the attacking Scots coming out from their hiding places along the tree-lined track.

It was more a rout than a battle and ended as quickly as it had begun. The riderless horses were driven off. Men without horses jumped up behind their fleeing comrades and many Northumbrians had to fight their way back along the track and out of the glen on foot. It was a disorderly retreat, which left the tough north countrymen humiliated and bad-tempered.

A roll-call showed that they appeared to have lost more horses than men and the sergeant was one of the few casualties. He had been a popular man, of good kindred and his kinsmen and comrades were keen to follow Bruce's trail back into the hills, but Clifford would not hear of such foolhardiness. They bivouacked that night with the guards doubled, allowing stragglers time to catch up. With a failure to report Clifford was in a dangerous mood. He had not yet eaten but had drunk heavily. De Vaux swaggered over to him. "I hear the men are keen to strike back. An excellent plan, something Bruce won't be expecting. We should go now and not wait for the morning." De Vaux must already have heard Clifford rejecting such rashness yet here he was opposing him again and within the hearing of the men. "I'll not sanction more losses without a definite sighting," snapped Clifford, but de Vaux was not going to be put off. "Are you unwilling to track Bruce to his lair? Is this another example of what our lord the king has accused us of? Well you might be frightened of the Scots, but I'm not." Defiantly he stood in front of Clifford. His intention was clear, to take sole command of men, eager to avenge their comrades, and to humiliate Clifford. Clifford's mailed fist landed squarely on De Vaux's chin. The men stood around watching. A good fight would clear the air and raise their spirits. De Vaux sprawled on the ground. He clambered to his feet and swung at Clifford who, inspite of his heavy chain mail, nimbly dodged the blow and again swung his fist. It looked as if their audience was in for an invigorating entertainment and they became noisy, shouting encouragement to the combatants. De Vaux was younger and smaller than Clifford and tried to draw his dagger but some of the older men watching the spectacle moved in to stop the fight. As they were pulled apart, De Vaux noisily vowed to seek satisfaction from Clifford, but his personal servants took him away and after that the two commanders adopted a morose silence. When their duties demanded that they communicate, messages were taken backwards and forwards by their aides and the Northumbrians, who had at first found this amusing, became despondent and quarrels broke out among the ranks. It was a very demoralized company of men who returned to Ayr.

When the Earl of Pembroke heard reports of the fiasco at Glen Trool, both men blaming each other, he exploded into one of his rare bouts of rage. "What ingratitude," he had stormed. Clifford, of all the king's men had much to lose. He had been handsomely rewarded by the king and had been given all the lands that had been the inheritance of the traitor James Douglas. It was only the king's poor health which prevented Pembroke from sending a damning report about the affair to his master. Something had to be done and next time he would do the job himself.

During April Bruce moved steadily northwards. As he progressed he gathered more men and by the end of April was encamped near Loudoun Hill. He had begun to train his men to stand and fight together. Because he was within striking distance of Ayr, he sent out raiding parties led by his brother Edward and James Douglas, with orders to harass the English. Strike and retreat commanded Bruce.

At his headquarters in Ayr the Earl of Pembroke fretted. The knowledge that his brother-in-laws murderer camped just over the hill was insufferable. On the first day of May he called Alexander Abernethy to him, a Scot, but a man whom he trusted. He said, "Bruce becomes bolder yet we never get close enough to him. If he's not stopped now he'll slip through and once beyond the Forth he'll have the freedom of the north and help from the McDonalds. We must call him out to meet us know." Abernethy could understand the logic but so far Bruce had been an elusive and wily adversary evading all serious encounters. "How do you suggest we do that, my lord, the people are more frightened of him than they are of us. They'll not betray him." Pembroke replied, "I'll challenge him. Last year I humiliated him and the chance to defeat me will, I believe, lure him into the open. You issue the challenge and give him this." The earl lay a leather glove, embossed with his coat of arms, on the table. "Take this and say, if your cause is just come out into the open and face Pembroke." Abernethy, a kinsmen of Comyn was anxious to play his part in the downfall of Bruce and with a small escort and a banner of truce held high, he left Ayr hastily.

Douglas shadowed the herald for a whole morning before he came down from the hills to challenge Abernethy. The gauntlet was flung onto the track between the two groups of men and Pembroke's challenge delivered. Before returning to his master, Douglas shadowed the English back to the gates of Ayr.

Bruce looked across the gentle slope of Loudoun Hill. Above him soared its jagged crags. On each side of the hillside the land was bog and shifting, mossy pools. He watched his men as they drew up into two companies, cheerful and confident. He sensed their mood. They were ready for this trial of strength. He could hear them laughing and calling to one another as they tested the staves which they had driven into the ground in front of their schiltrom. One hundred mounted men, under the command of Robert Boyd, waited out of sight but ready when needed.

In the valley Pembroke, like Bruce, was overseeing his forces. The English had arrived in the late afternoon of the previous day and since first light had been moving into attacking formation. The earl himself had reconnoitred the field of battle and now regretted being so foolhardy offering the challenge, for Bruce had chosen the site well and it would not be an easy task to get at him. It had been dry for the past week and the open ground between his men and the enemy was firm but there was no denying the fact that the battlefront was very narrow and to left and right were stretches of wet moor land. His spies told him that Bruce had less than five hundred men all on foot and perhaps the sheer weight of numbers and the discipline of his Englishmen would overcome the faults of the terrain. He had been forced to abandon the traditional battle formation of vanguard with left and right flanks and had divided his two thousand men into vanguard and rearguard. What the earl could not see, what none of the English could see were the three parallel ditches dug in front of the Scottish pikemen.

In that quiet moment before he ordered the advance, Pembroke contemplated the scene before him. The men were in perfectly ordered ranks, their horses standing patiently, their rider's armour shining in the early morning sun. Pembroke sat on his warhorse, a fine chestnut, with white feathering around his hooves. He was fond of the beast and lent forward to pull the animal's ears and rearrange its mane.

King Robert of Scotland dressed in a short chain mail surcoat, taken from the body of the Northumbrian sergeant at Loch Trool, stood beside James Douglas in the front rank of pikemen. His brother Edward commanded the second schiltrom. John Blair, who through all the troubled months of Bruce's wanderings had shared his hardships had given Bruce absolution and now stood with the boys, smiths and other camp followers, well behind the fighting men. The light-hearted banter had ceased. All eyes watched the enemy.

The English trumpets sounded, the vanguard began its advance.

The walk, trot, canter and then the full gallop, lances sloped, heads well down over their horses' necks and with a mighty roar as if from one throat they thundered towards their foe. Above the fearful din the waiting Scots heard the clear call of King Robert's hunting horn. Together they sloped their pikes towards the enemy and braced their backs for the impact.

It was the forward ranks of the English who floundered into the trenches, whilst the men behind, at full gallop were unable to turn their animals and crashed into their comrades. A few evaded the mêlée and reached the schiltrom, but were met by a wall of pikes and turning, found their escape blocked by dead or dying men and horses in and around the ditches. Pembroke, watching was powerless to do anything. The Scots remained in good order, moving from their positions only under command. Then in tight formation they stabbed and hacked at their enemy.

The English rearguard had already began its advance before the fleeing vanguard turned and hurtled back towards them. In the confusion the normally disciplined and orderly English army fled back towards Ayr in panic. Bruce's pikemen made no attempt to break ranks and follow, but Boyd and his horsemen slipped from their hiding place and at full gallop, sped towards Pembroke in an attempt to cut off his retreat and prevent him from rallying his fleeing men. Pembroke realized the danger and retreated towards Bothwell Castle some leagues along the road. For a few days, Boyd and his men enjoyed the experience of laying siege to the castle and preventing the English commander in Scotland going about his business. Occasionally the earl climbed up to the battlements staring across the country and expecting to see a relief column. The week drew to an end and Pembroke, with no sign of the expected help from the Earl of Gloucester began to think that the king had good reason for his complaints about his commanders' handling of Scottish affairs. After watching the horizon he would glare down at Boyd and his motley collection of horsemen. Clenching his fists in his frustration, he stamped back to his quarters talking to himself under his breath, "Where's Gloucester, hasn't the man any balls?" Wisely his men did not ask him any questions until he had regained his normally calm composure.

On the fifth morning, while the earl was still in bed, his squire rushed in "Sir, they've gone. Disappeared like thieves in the night," but Pembroke, who had been humiliated by the experience for long enough, just grunted.

After the battle at Loudoun, exhilarated by their victory, the Scots felt they deserved a celebratory drink and with gusto set about the captured English ale and wine, but King Robert, that charming and generous leader, said he would hang any man who became drunk. His men grumbled bitterly so that the king said, "Do you want to be in a drunken stupor, with your sore heads in your hands when the English return? For be sure their shame will bring them back."

Pembroke had waited in vein for the relief column, not because The Earl of Gloucester lacked courage but because the enemy prevented him from sending help.

Gloucester had taken command of the garrison at Ayr immediately he heard the news of the defeat. He was angry, but sufficiently in command of himself to send out spies before making any decisions to retaliate and his spies told him that Bruce was still encamped by Louden. Three days later Gloucester marched out of Ayr with cavalry and lightly armed foot soldiers. His intention was to attack whilst the Scots were celebrating their victory.

Bruce waited long enough for Gloucester to hear that the Scottish army was still camped at Loudoun before he gave the order to strike camp. As the sun's first light crept above the eastern hills, the Scottish forces positioned themselves in the forest along either side of the road at Galstones and awaited Gloucester. The air was fragrant with the sweet scent of bluebells carpeting the woodland and once the men had settled, hidden in thickets and behind rocks and bracken, the birds continued their dawn chorus. Everything appeared calm and normal. Bruce sat with Lennox and James Douglas under a beech tree. They took turns to rest while they awaited the enemy, dozing in the dappled sunlight filtering through the overhanging branches. It grew pleasantly warm and insects droned above the moist, moss-covered rocks. A man ran towards them through the trees. "My lord, they're sighted," he gasped. Bruce turned to James Douglas, "Go with him and await my signal."

When Gloucester's troops were within Bruce's ambush and still unaware of danger, Bruce sounded his horn. So unexpected and ferocious was the confrontation that once again the English cavalry turned, scattering their own foot soldiers and fled back the way they had come. Bruce's men mopped up the stragglers and wounded before they followed the main army back to Ayr and that night the Scots celebrated around the walls of Ayr Castle, singing, shouting, banging and generally making as much noise as possible. Neither friend nor foe slept. At first light when the sergeant of the watch looked out from Ayr Castle battlements their noisy neighbours had faded away with the darkness.

Lying on his bed at Lanercost, King Edward heard of the humiliation of Pembroke and Gloucester and ordered his doctors to prepare him so that he might travel. They protested loudly, "My lord, you must rest, if you move the pain will return." "Am I surrounded by fools?" snapped the king in a voice stronger than he had used for some time. "Prepare one of your concoctions, master doctor and get me out of this bed. I will review my army at Carlisle in May." It was foolhardy to argue with the King, and the chief physician hurried away to his chamber to mix precious ingredients to ease the king's pain. A spoonful of musk, a pinch of ground amber, a dash of gold and silver, two pinches of herbs and five drops of rare poppy syrup.

They dressed the king, as he lay on his bed, helpless like a babe. His long thin limbs were like brittle branches on an old oak, his ribs and collarbones protruding through his yellow skin. Only his ice-blue eyes remained alert, the iron determination shining through his pain. He could not bear the weight of his armour so they dressed him in rich velvets with warm fur trimmings before carrying him to a waiting carriage. For the first time in nearly nine months King Edward left the safety of Lanercost and his procession moved slowly towards Carlisle.

On the Feast of Pentecost, astride his favourite warhorse the king reviewed the army with two squires riding on each side helping to support him throughout the ceremony. The army looked a grand sight drawn up in disciplined ranks on the plains outside the city walls of Carlisle. A brisk breeze blowing off the Solway buffeted the pennants and banners. These are the best men that the shires of England can give me, thought the king. With these men behind me, Bruce and his bunch would have no hiding place. He found the strength to lean forward to pat his mount. "You're getting fat old fella or are you getting old like your master? I'll try to exercise you more now I'm out and about."

Sight of the old king boosted army morale. "All would be well now that Longshanks was back in the saddle," they said to each other around their camp fires. But the effort proved too much for the king's frail body and the day following they carried an exhausted king to his chamber in Carlisle Castle where he remained well past midsummer's day.

While King Edward rested in Carlisle, Bruce continued roaming through the hills, harrying the farms and manors of English supporters and ambushing English patrols sent out by Pembroke.

At the beginning of July once again King Edward left his sick bed and riding his powerful black stallion, led his army towards Scotland as he had done so many times before. Each step taken by the mighty beast sent waves of burning pain through his body, forcing him to grind his teeth to prevent himself from crying out aloud. Slowly the army marched towards the border, stopping often to let the king rest. The men found the slow advance irritating for the sooner they got the Scottish business over and done with, the sooner they could go home. After three days they had covered just six leagues and camped for the night at Burgh le Sands. An exhausted king was put to bed.

"At this speed Harry, we'll not be over the border before harvest time," said a Lancastrian archer. His comrade replied "Well I ain't stopping longer than my forty days service. My crops won't harvest themselves. These fine folks have little time for our worries, they've others to do their work for them. They'll not run short of food during the winter." The two men continued grumbling about the unfair deal that God had bestowed on them and why in His wisdom he had made them humble men. "Stop rambling on about things you can't alter," ordered the sergeant. "Too much time on your hands you have, so you won't worry about taking the first watch. That'll give you something to think about."

The following morning when the king's personal servants lifted him gently in his bed so that they could prepare him for the day's march, a low groan escaped from his lips and Edward's spirit passed into his Lord's keeping.

CROSSING THE RUBICON

When King Robert heard the news of the English king's death he laughed out loud. He hooted and shook with merriment until the tears ran down his cheeks and into his beard. He staggered to a fallen tree and sat on its trunk wiping his eyes and chuckling to himself whilst his men watched their commander's glee with surprise, but when he had gained control of his emotions, he said, "I don't laugh because my enemy is dead, but with his death we'll gain freedom. Now we can tackle our real enemies, the Comyns and their kinsmen." Then he raised his arms looking upwards towards heaven "Alleluia, God smiles on us. Where's John Blair? We must all thank God." The men knelt around their king and John Blair led them in prayer, giving thanks that with a change of King in England their own efforts might be blessed, for they all knew Edward II would not be the man his father was.

Within days of the English King's death, King Robert's men attacked manors and settlements in Galloway and continued throughout the harvest month sweeping Galloway with fire and sword. They killed the leading men of the MacDougalls and avenged the ambush of King Robert's brothers at Loch Ryan. Their attacks came quickly like lightening in a summer storm, rolling across the Galloway hills and ending before the MacDougall men had rallied. Crops and homes were burnt, livestock driven off and the common farming people did not wait for help, certain that it would not come. Driving their livestock before them they trekked south over the border carrying a few possessions with them. In England they took refuge in the Cumbrian forests. Those who remained in Scotland pleaded with King Robert for a truce and paid him, with money and weapons, to be left in peace.

When the king was satisfied that Galloway was subdued he marched northwards to attack his enemies in Argyll and Ross-shire, but he left James Douglas in Galloway to ensure that the MacDougalls did not forget from whom their peace came. As he marched, he received tribute and homage from common folk while at the same time his triumphs brought cautious men out from behind their castle walls and tentatively they raised their standards to follow their king.

At Cardross, on the northern bank of the Clyde where his roaming life had begun the previous year, the king met his old friend Angus Og MacDonald, whose support in the early months had been so welcome. "Angus, you old rogue." Angus beamed at his king, his clothes and beard covered in brim from the salt spray, and the king embraced him. Angus had arrived in command of a fleet of thirty galleys to support Robert. "Will you sail with us, my lord, for it'll be more comfortable than marching north however fleet of foot you are." "Nay, Angus my place is at the head of my men, but now that I've a horse to carry my weight it's not such a hardship."

That night they feasted on venison, salmon and all manner of fine food and afterwards danced with their camp followers who had recently grown in number, and because they had lived fugitive lives for so long they indulged themselves in the heather with the women. Bruce quietened his conscience, "Before a fight to the death, even a common man may relax, why not a king?" he said to himself.

The following day Angus and his galleys shadowed the king's advance along the Firth of Lorne to Loch Linnhe, where it was his intention to do battle with John of Lorne.

At his castle of Dunstaffnage, John MacDougall, Lord of Lorne had taken to his bed. He was genuinely ill and embarrassed that his followers would laugh behind his back and call him a coward. He lay depressed and despondent surely every one knew that he did not lack courage. In his sick bed he lay debating how he could show loyalty to his Comyn kinsmen and yet keep his lands intact. "Move over laddie," he pushed the large deerhound stretched out on the bed beside him. The dog yawned and rolled onto its back expecting to be fondled. Its companion, lying on the floor by the bedside jumped up, perhaps it would be its turn to lie beside its master. It rested its snout on the edge of the bed, watching Sir John with sad, brown eyes. MacDougall patted it, moving painfully and pulling the bed covers away from under the dog, so that the weight of the covers did not lie so heavily on his sore legs and continued to think about his problems. He must gain time, but how? He was in the middle of composing a letter when his wife swept into the chamber. She screamed when she saw the two dogs sprawling on her husband's bed, for the other had taken advantage of his master's preoccupation. Lady MacDougall ran towards the offending beasts but they, quicker than she, jumped from the bed and fled past their mistress and out through the door before she could lay hands on them. "John, you do it deliberately because I have forbidden them to sleep in your chamber." As she spoke she adopted her characteristic pose; one hand on her ample hip while the other was free to wag a finger under his nose. Sir John lay back with a resigned expression on his face, but his silence irritated her even more and she began to attack him with greater vigour. The dogs forgotten, she delved deep into her memories reliving her husband's misdemeanours with relish. Eventually when she drew breath he declared, "Oh Joan, go and whip the steward with your tongue for I am cold and there are no logs for the fire. Besides, the dogs do no harm and I like them." "They smell," she screamed as she flounced from his sight. He pulled the covers up around his shoulders and continued pondering the text of his letter. That afternoon his letters were carried to his neighbours but there was no response to them, neither men nor weapons arrived from his allies.

Days passed and spies told him that Bruce's forces could be expected daily. There was nothing for it. He must lead his men out to meet Bruce. Much to his wife's noisy disapproval, John MacDougall left his bed and succeeded in mounting his horse, but he had barely left the castle courtyard before the pain in his lower abdomen and back became so intense that he slumped forward in his saddle. It had been a brave, but abortive attempt to inspire his men with confidence and they led him back into his castle.

King Robert sat listening to the stories brought back by his spies. John MacDougall was ill and in his bed. Without their leader the MacDougall kinsmen would not attack and would sit behind their walls defying King Robert. If that happened, it would tie up his forces until Christmas. In a Highland winter it would be a disaster and would lose him more men and beasts from cold and exhaustion than a Lochaber axe. Robert Bruce turned to his brother and said, "MacDougall can wait. We'll finish off Comyn of Buchan first, which will give MacDougall something to think about while we're away." The king took his forces up to the walls of Dunstaffnage Castle and sent his brother to negotiate a truce.

John MacDougall, was a desperate man and agreed to a nine month's truce for which he paid Robert Bruce one thousand Scottish pounds if he would leave him in peace. Silently he prayed Bruce would honour the agreement and march north. John knew eventually he must fight, for his mother had been aunt to the murdered John Comyn. When his men told him that they had followed Bruce's army up to the castle of Inverlochy he breathed a deep sigh of relief.

Bruce sat down at Comyn's gates at Inverlochy and daily, men from the surrounding hills came to pay him homage as their king, but by the end of October his patience was running out. Besieging a castle was futile without the benefits of siege engines.

He was rowed out to see Angus Og, on Loch Linnhe which guarded Inverlochy's waterfront and they discussed a night attack from the water. Bruce declared he wanted to avoid heavy casualties and said that with so many men coming to his standard, there must be one who had a kinsman serving within the castle. Angus agreed and promised to make enquiries and arrange for the fall of the castle. So it was through deception that Inverlochy fell to the king's forces with little loss of life on either side.

King Robert had felt unwell for a few days, feverish, with a headache and hard little lumps in his groin and the pits of his arms. His brother and squire said it was an ague brought on by dampness and cold, night air. Once they were on the march again he was sure to get better. In this they were right and the small eruptions in such a tender and personal area of his body disappeared as they marched through the Great Glen.

At Urqhurt, exhilarated by their recent triumphs, he halted at the castle and ordered the defenders, as their king, to surrender. The garrison was aware that outside help would not be forthcoming and reasoned that their lives would be spared if they surrendered early, rather than late. They left their posts and paid homage to King Robert as their liege lord.

After their surrender, Bruce gazed up at the damp grey walls of Urqhurt glistening with rime in the chill autumn weather. They had a brooding and menacing air standing guard beside the deep, peaty waters of the loch. The old woman that somehow managed to keep up with his men, earning her living washing clothes and binding wounds, said that the castle was guardian of the beastie of the loch. "Well," said Bruce indicating the castle, "I'll just have to incur the beasts displeasure, for its guardian must go." He nodded to his men and they moved into the castle, burning what would burn and dismantling walls and buildings. "It'll not be used against me again," he mumbled to himself. The old washerwoman stood watching the destruction with wide, fearful eyes. "Well Morag, will the monster of the loch come from its lair tonight and carry me away?" laughed the king. "Och my lord! No good will come of this. The wee manie in yonder water will avenge his own." The king being a good-humoured man, smiled and ignoring her foreboding led his men towards the head of the glen leaving his brother in charge of the final destruction of Urqhurt. Morag followed along behind, shaking her head and looking fearfully in the direction of the Loch. The men close to her laughed and as the days and weeks went by it did look as if soothesaying was not one of Morag's strengths.

At the head of the Great Loch the Bishop of Moray, and many other men who had returned from exile in Orkney awaited Bruce. All were fully armed and ready to do battle against the king's enemies. Among them was Alexander Pilche who had followed Andrew Moray and William Wallace into battle at Stirling Bridge. Pilche pledged himself to the king and Bruce knew he would be as loyal a follower to him as he had been to Moray and Wallace.

When he heard of Bruce's rapid advance Sir Reginald Cheyne, the English governor of Inverness Castle had left his post and headed south, leaving the defenders leaderless. Many of the citizens of Inverness had already left carrying whatever they could move and herding their pigs and cattle before them. The wealthy burgesses boarded galleys in the Moray Firth, whilst the poor took the coastal road north hoping to reach the territory of the Earl of Ross before Bruce and his men overtook them.

When Bruce's men arrived at the gates of Inverness they found the town inhabited by the sick and hopeless and the garrison indecisive. For two days they held Bruce at bay, but it became impossible to put out fires before more fire arrows came over the walls and Gilbert Glencarnie, sheriff of Inverness, called the men together. "Look here, I'm not frightened of dying, but only if I need to. Lord Cheyne has left us and Ross's men haven't appeared. Who agrees to throw in their lot with Bruce?" They sat around discussing Glencarnie's point of view whilst the buildings around them burned.

Outside Bruce's men begun piling brush wood and logs against the main gate to burn the defenders out. Edward Bruce was overseeing the activity when he was hailed from the battlements. "Hold the fire," called Glencarnie. "Offer us suitable terms and we'll surrender and save you further trouble." Edward stepped backwards, the better to see the speaker. "Well now, I see no reason why we should give you anything, for the castle will be ours without your help." In normal circumstances the sheriff would have taken up the challenge, but he could hear from the man's speech and manner that he was a nobleman and there would be little point in picking a fight with him. One of his men edged along the battlements and gingerly raised his head above the parapet. "My lord sheriff, that's Edward Bruce. Take care what you say or we're all done for." Glencarnie looked with renewed interest at Bruce who continued organizing the firing of the castle gate. He took a deep breath and called out "My lord, my men and I offer to surrender on your terms." Bruce could hear the man was a Scot, but from the border country and so he said, "You must pay homage to your king and serve him without pay for as long as he wishes."

The sheriff, with all the fighting men and craftsmen of the castle, knelt with bare heads before their king and pledged allegiance while behind them the town and castle of Inverness burnt furiously.

That same day Bruce's army marched towards Nairn and the men from the garrison at Inverness marched with them. The men of Nairn hesitated. They were uncertain which way their allegiance should go but the men from the garrison of Inverness, all hale and hearty, stood before the gates and shouted their support of the noble King Robert. Slowly the gates of Nairn swung open. The king ordered the destruction of Nairn and the flames could be seen many leagues away.

Earl William of Ross had been following Bruce's progress through the Great Glen with growing alarm and when refugees from Inverness began arriving in his lands he called out his men, stationing more than three thousand around his borders to await Bruce's attack. He heard the men of Inverness and Nairn had been fairly treated but he had little hope for himself. Bruce must know of his part in the capture of Elizabeth de Burgh. Ross sent messages to John MacDougall, appealing for his help, but expected nothing since he had not rallied to MacDougall's side and MacDougall was still reported to be sick.

In the third week of November, when the snow had already fallen thickly on the mountains and all sensible men should have been in their homes dozing by their fires, a messenger arrived from Bruce offering Ross peace until the following Whitsun. Ross reasoned that he could not expect help because the new English king was in France attending his marriage. If Reginald Chayne had remained at his post, Ross would have fought Bruce but he needed allies. His mind was made up, he agreed to accept Bruce's truce until June of the following year.

Edward Bruce was surprised that his brother had offered a truce to the man who had handed his wife and daughter to the English king. "What are you thinking of Rob, let's get the bastard now. Think of the legitimate sons you could be fathering while she wastes her youth in England." Edward looked exasperated, but Robert said, "They'll all fall into my hands in God's good time. We mustn't lose sight of our real enemy. John Comyn of Buchan and his kinsmen must be lured out to fight. English Edward will soon wake up to what is happening up here and then he'll march north in force to aid the Comyns." Edward Bruce laughed, "Rob, Edward of Carnarvon is a pretty boy in the jousting field, but hasn't the stomach for all out war." "Aye, but what he lacks in persistence he'll make up with numbers and equipment." It was only then that Edward Bruce fully understood his brother's policy of destroying all captured castles. Robert said, "The English need their fortresses to conduct their kind of warfare, but we Scots must adapt to our own land and make the English follow our tune." Edward Bruce, an impatient man, did not think deeply. He rarely gave himself time to listen to other people's views, but after he left his brother he realized it was the first time he had heard Robert use the familiar term 'we Scots.'

Sir John Mowbray and his forces had reached the north–east by the central route having been informed of Bruce's march through the north, but the full significance of the Bruce's manoeuvres had escaped him. "He must be brought to the field now, John," he said to Sir John Comyn, Earl of Buchan. "The longer we hesitate the more support he gains from the rabble and since he does not rely on horse nor siege engine, it matters little to him what manner of support he controls." Buchan said, "My men are already mustered and David Strathbogie is but two days march away." "Well, where is Bruce now?" asked Mowbray. "He has spent two days at Concarn and has burnt the estates of Duncan of Frendraught. Duncan has been shadowing Bruce since he left Elgin. Now Bruce is marching through his own lands of the Garioch and his own men there are flocking to his banner." Buchan related this with despair in his voice and Mowbray, irritated by the Scotsman's gloomy manner replied, "Well, he's not won the war yet and he won't if you buck up. When David arrives we'll all march on Bruce."

After leaving Nairn, King Robert surrounded Elgin but because of its strength he was unable neither to defeat nor intimidate the English defenders, so he burnt the surrounding countryside, then marched on to Inverurie.

It was the last week of Advent and snow had fallen so thickly that it lay in deep drifts against manor walls and in the crevices of rocks. From his own choice the King walked with his men whilst his recently acquired warhorse was led along with its saddle girths loosened. During the short daylight hours of mid winter his men struggled through the driving blizzard which swept in from the north–east, with the wind on their backs. Lennox, marching beside the king said, "Frendraught and his men have been seen again up in the hills. They match our pace." The king replied, "He'll not attack until he's joined by Buchan and Mowbray. Besides this weather affects them as it does us." Lennox thought that to be true. So long as Frendraught kept his quarry in sight he would be more concerned with surviving the elements than attacking them. Besides, Bruce had marched his men along the open road, forcing Frendraught to follow paths across the open hill tops and floundering through snow drifts and across open, snow-covered fields.

Bruce halted his men. The short winter day was coming to a close. The strong wind blew flurries of snow from the drifts, which swirled round and round covering both men and beasts. It had grown noticeably colder and by nightfall the surface of the snow would be frozen into a crisp crust but they were nearing Inverurie where they could shelter for the night. Robert felt very tired, his head ached and his legs felt so heavy he could barely put one foot in front of the other. His horse stood quietly beside him and he found himself leaning against it for support. He patted the animal's strong neck. "Not far now, laddie." He raised his arm to indicate forward, took a step and fell into the snow. His brother, Lennox, Boyd and others gathered around him. An arrow had not struck him. He attempted to get to his feet but fell again. He laughed in an embarrassed way, but however hard he tried, could not walk. The girths on his horse were tightened and they manhandled him into the saddle. The animal, with head lowered and ears flattened, walked doggedly onwards, his master swaying from side to side and in danger of falling off, until his brother took hold of the martingale and lead the beast carefully towards Inverurie.

The manor of Inverurie was not large but was well managed. The long, low house, a style often seen in those parts, was snug and warm, built to withstand the harsh northern winters. It had small shuttered windows and a doorway so low that a man was forced to bend when entering. At one end of the hall a door lead through into a byre, where the over-wintering cows and last spring's calves and plough oxen could be heard placidly munching hay. In the centre of the main room was a fire pit with a chain and hook hanging from a beam to support a caldron. On each side of the fire, spikes had been driven into the earthen floor and a roasting spit stretched between them. A small pig was being roasted when the king arrived. Along the back wall was a bench and trestle table and at the other end of the main chamber was a box bed. Around the outside yard were many more outhouses, brewing house, bakery, weaving house and a barn with a firebox for drying grain after a wet summer.

Bruce had visited the manor many times before, which was just as well, for when they arrived he had slumped forward and lay across his horse's neck his arms hanging down loosely on each side. Edward Bruce and Lennox carried him to the box bed. They did not remove his chained surcoat nor boots, for whom could say what Frendraught might do during the long hours of darkness? They offered him mead and bread but he would accept neither.

Outside men could be found in every nook and cranny of the estate and township of Inverurie and Edward Bruce, Lennox, Wiseman and others went around posting guards. The clouds had cleared and a full moon reflected the white landscape, casting dark shadows across the fields. "Let's hope it stays like this all night," said Edward. "Aye, it certainly is clear. God help them tonight." Lennox indicated the camp fires of Frendraught and his men at the top of the hill. Edward replied uncompromisingly. "If they freeze from the cold it'll save us a job. Just look at that." The three men stood watching the sky lit by the flashing lights on the northern horizon. For a Moray man like Wiseman the northern lights were not a unique sight, but he had to admit they were magnificent.

Bruce and Wiseman stayed to supervise the first watch but Lennox went back to the house. The king's squire was leaning over his Lord holding a beaker of water while his master sipped. Lennox told the king what arrangements had been made for lookout and enquired after his health. The king grinned, "I'll be well in the morning." His face was flushed like a man far-gone in drink. They were about to close the doors to his bed but he ordered them to be left wide so that he might be aware of the comings and goings.

As soon as it was light the king staggered from his bed, determined to be seen by his men and enemy upon the hills, for he feared the outcome from both if they suspected his illness was in any way serious. Lennox tried to persuade him to remain where he was but he said, "They're used to seeing and talking to me, I must go." They helped him walk around in his usual way, talking to men as they prepared their food, waving to the guards in outlying posts and walking out into the open, a tempting target for Frendraught out on the hillside.

Frendraught and his men blew into their hands, waving their arms around like the sails of windmills and stamping their feet vigorously to warm themselves. Frendraught glared down at the tall figure of King Robert. He took a bow from one of his men and sent an arrow whistling through the clear air towards Bruce. The distance was too great and the arrow fell short, but King Robert gazed up at his enemy, smiled, raised his shoulders and held out his arms provocatively. The king turned to Lennox and said "Take half a dozen archers as near to them as possible and send over a flight. It'll give us all some amusement."

Then they helped him back to his bed. His body, arms, legs and head ached. His head was so sore he could hardly hold it up and his eyes were painful, particularly in the strong light of the reflecting snow. They offered him food, but he did not want it, his throat was so sore he could barely swallow. He accepted sips of water, but that was all that passed his lips that day.

Lennox took his best archers further along the road to a small copse and under cover of the trees they drew closer to Frendraught's position and sent in a flight of arrows. They did not see the results of their attack but heard a cry of pain as they ran back to their comrades with enemy arrows hurrying them on their way. They reached the road and were forced to bend low holding their shields over their heads for protection. The rest of the day passed peacefully enough, both warring parties were pleased to rest. On the hillside Frendraught's men cut branches from nearby trees to make more adequate shelter for the night.

During the night the king's condition deteriorated and he tossed on his bed mumbling to himself but the following morning once again he made a supreme effort and walked around Inverurie, cheerfully hailing his men and showing himself to the enemy on the hills. When he reached the safety of his lodgings his legs gave way and they carried him to his bed. Edward Bruce leant over his brother and Robert whispered, "You must lead them to a defensive position at Slioch. Take command, Edward". Then the king closed his eyes and gave himself up to the pain which gripped his body in its vice.

In the barn, where their enemy could not see them they built a litter for the King and the following morning before it was light, Edward Bruce led King Robert's army in a withdrawal from Inverurie. The king was carried on a litter, the men of the schiltrom surrounding him and they took refuge in the wooded marshland of Slioch. Frendraught hurriedly struck camp, sent a message to the Earl of Buchan and in the half-light of winter followed his quarry.

Once again the King of Scots hid, like a fugitive, in marshy woodland in a charcoal burner's bothy with a small brazier beside him. More snow fell that night, it was bitterly cold and their situation was serious. The following day was Christmas Day.

The Earl Buchan was preparing to leave when the new Earl of Atholl, accompanied by Sir John Mowbray and their men, joined him. David Strathbogie, Earl of Atholl, had changed sides and had sworn allegiance to the English cause. He was angry with Robert Bruce whom he felt had sacrificed his father needlessly and for a hopeless cause in which the Strathbogies should not have been involved.

The Earl of Buchan looked across to Slioch. "Well we can't send the horses in," he said to Mowbray. "We'll have to get the archers to soften them up and force them to move," replied Mowbray. Every man who could use a bow was ordered onto the high ground, but it was without cover, a cold, bleak expanse of snow-covered moor with neither tree nor rock for shelter. As the archers took up position, with the enemy well within range, some grumbled. "It's not right, asking us to kill a fellow Christian on Our Lord's birthday," but the sergeant told them to "shut up and keep their minds on the job," and obediently that is what they did, their arrows rained down upon the silent enemy. As soon as an arrow left the bow a new one replaced it, but for some time there was no replying salvo. "Move forward," roared Buchan. "You heard, move forward," roared the sergeants. The archers moved further down the slope. That was the moment Edward Bruce had been waiting for. The shrill tones of King Robert's hunting horn sang through the forest and his archers, who until this moment had hidden beneath their shields, released their arrows. Mark your man, the Lord Edward Bruce had said and without shelter on the exposed hillside the men of Buchan fell, their blood staining the snow crimson.

Hurriedly Buchan withdrew his forces and retired to his own lands remaining there for the next seven days of the Christmas festival but he was angry and humiliated. King Robert remained helpless at Slioch, cared for by John Blair and his squire. From time to time he drank a little water but food and wine he would not take. On the last day of December a man on lookout came to the bothy where the King lay. He was breathless from running and floundering through snowdrifts, his clothes covered in snow. He was taken before Edward Bruce. "My lord, the Comyns, they've been seen coming in large numbers. They come from the east and will be here within the hour. The king was still helpless, unable to walk or ride a horse but Edward Bruce acted without hesitation. He ordered the men to form into three tightly packed schiltroms. Shields held upward to protect their heads, pikes sloping outwards. In the middle schiltrom they carried Bruce's litter and they marched purposely up the road towards Huntly. At the head of the army Edward Bruce rode his brother's horse, while the king's squire rode behind carrying King Robert's standard. Lennox led the horsemen and carried Edward Bruce's pennant. It was still bitterly cold and the road was difficult to march along but when they were close to the junction of the road which lead down to Old Meldrum one of the scouts came running towards him. "My lord, the men of Buchan are within sight." Bruce stopped, turned his mount and called out. "We go forward. Keep in close formation and do not stop."

When the Comyn men saw Bruce's force marching purposefully straight towards them, diverting neither to left nor right, bristling with pikes, and ready to do battle, they were alarmed and uncertain. Their commander was as indecisive as his men and immediately they turned and retreated hurriedly back the way they had come but Bruce's men gained on them and the Comyn men broke ranks and spread out onto the hillside. Only when they felt themselves safe did they turn to watch the enemy continue briskly along the road towards Huntly.

When the earl realized he had been duped and intimidated by his enemy, forced to watch it march past him, his anger and shame was intense and he raged against everyone whom he felt could be held responsible for his misfortune. David Strathbogie urged they attack Bruce in the rear immediately, but with their men in disarray and the bad weather against using mounted troops, the earl ordered a withdrawal. He would find more supporters and then meet Bruce again.

The king's sudden illness had been a surprise to everyone. For the first few days after his collapse they had been confused and had adopted a defensive attitude, but once Edward Bruce had seized the advantage and the enemy scattered at their approach, a renewed vigour and self-assurance entered the king's men.

They took refuge in the Earl of Atholl's manor of Huntly, which was not a large manor, but the hall and outbuildings were strong with a palisade surrounding them and a deep moat beyond that. The barns were not full but there was sufficient for a week or two and there was plenty of kindling and dry wood. For the first time in over a week the King's chain mail was removed. As they exposed his body to the air he shook with ague and it was then that they saw the pink rash on his trunk and in his groins were hard, raised lumps similar to those he had complained of in earlier weeks. They lit a good fire and ordered Morag to make a broth to give the king strength. Then they placed him in the master's soft, warm bed. During the next few weeks he recovered a little, sitting up in bed and able to hold conversations with his captains, but he could not walk.

The stores were running low and King Robert, anxious to continue the momentum of his advance, sent out scouts to spy on the enemy and they returned promptly with news that the Earl of Buchan was at Meldrum awaiting reinforcements from Sir David Brechin of Angus. The king decided to engage Buchan in battle immediately. He would not wait for reinforcements or the spring to arrive.

At the end of January King Robert was carried back to Inverurie in his litter. Outposts were established and spies sent out and when the Earl of Buchan heard that Bruce was once again in the neighbourhood he also sent out spies.

Within a week of Bruce's arrival at Inverurie a prisoner was brought before the Earl of Buchan at his camp at Meldrum. The earl questioned the terrified man. "How many men does Robert Bruce have? Are they short of food? Who are Bruce's commanders?" The man had already been badly treated and gave answers as best he could until he had cried out. "Mercy lord. I'll answer what I can." "Then give me information I can use," snapped Buchan. "Lord, I have news that is worth my life," pleaded the prisoner. "If I deem it worthy, we'll see," replied the earl. The prisoner took a deep breath and began. "The Lord Robert Bruce is sick, mortally sick and has been these past four weeks. When we march his brother leads us carrying the Lord Robert's standard, whilst he himself is carried on a litter, hidden within the schiltrom." The earl jumped to his feet, his face contorted with a mixture of hatred, anger and disbelief and sprung at the prisoner grabbing him by the throat. "You lie, we've seen him lead his troops." "Nay, nay lord, that was Sir Edward riding Sir Robert's horse. You were meant to believe it was Robert Bruce but he is too ill even to sit his horse." The earl turned back to his chair waving his hand to the guards to dispose of the prisoner whilst he sat and thought. If this was true and none could say until they had defeated Bruce, then they should attack now before he has time for his health to improve.

Early the following morning, before it was fully light, a force of fifty foot soldiers, most of them archers, left Meldrum. Their task was to assess Bruce's fighting ability. Many were survivors of the encounter at Siloch and they were determined not to be made fools of by Bruce's men again.

Edward Bruce had set up outposts along the junction of the road from Inverurie to Huntly and Inverurie to Meldrum and it was his men on the Meldrum road who were attacked early that morning. Volleys of arrows whirred through the silent snow–covered landscape. A man crouching by the fire and two completing their guard duties were the first to fall. Their enemy, with howls and roars sprung their attack. There was no time to muster or organize a defence. One of the lads, who had seen fifteen winters, had been sent to the burn, at a point where it was not completely frozen, to collect water. When the attack was launched he was struggling back up the snow-covered slope. He dropped his bucket and ran towards the camp, floundering through the deep snow, falling, sliding and slipping. He could see his two older brothers fighting desperately against a group of Buchan's men. His eldest brother swung his lochaber battleaxe around his head and caught one of his attackers such a mighty blow on the neck that his head was cut from his shoulders and he fell without a sound. The lad was exhilarated by that event and was about to cheer, when he lost his balance and fell into a deep drift. When he had succeeded in struggling to his feet his brothers had fallen, overwhelmed by the ferocity of the attack and the weight of numbers. For a few seconds the boy stood watching the scene, but he could see no signs of life from the two bodies lying side by side. He fought back his tears, turned and slid down the way he had come and along the road to Inverurie.

Buchan's men sent a number of arrows speeding after him and he could hear them shouting from the hillside, but he reached the outskirts of the manor safely. It was the big sergeant who rode with the Earl of Lennox who caught him. "Now lad, what ails you." The boy looked a sorry state covered in snow and so out of breath he could hardly speak. The men had gathered around him before he could say, "The enemy jumped us. They've all gone, my brothers included." He was near to tears, but before so many older men he fought to control the flow. The sergeant took over. "Arm yourselves and watch the road and hillsides. Come lad, calm yourself and run to the Lord Edward Bruce. Tell him we are watching the approaches and await his command. Be quick then you may avenge your brothers." The man's calm and businesslike manner gave the boy courage and he ran to the long house where the king and his brother were quartered.

The king lay quietly in his bed listening to the tale. Immediately his brother left to order the men to arms ready for battle. The king told his squire and other men to dress him in his armour and to prepare his warhorse, for he would lead his men. They tried to argue with him, but he abruptly quietened them and when the Lord Edward returned, the king had been carried outside and was being lifted into the saddle. "What are you doing?" said Edward Bruce, a disbelieving expression on his face. The king replied, "This will be our turning point, I feel it in my bones. If we finish Buchan the rest will follow like lambs." His voice was still weak but there was such a ring of determination in it that Edward knew it would be pointless to oppose him. Yet in spite of his determination the king could not sit upright in the saddle nor did he have the strength in his legs to command his mount. His squire rode on his right carrying his personal standard, whilst his brother's squire rode on his left and between them they gave support to their king. When the men had formed into their schiltroms, King Robert lead them from Inverurie towards Meldrum, his brother and captains ranged on either side. John Blair stood at the junction of the Meldrum road. As they passed by he said a blessing, sprinkling Holy Water over the marching men. They crossed themselves and murmured their own special prayers to God.

Buchan and his captains were elated by their early success against Bruce's outpost. The news that Bruce was near to death and his army confused and leaderless, inspired Buchan's forces with confidence and great expectation and they marched purposefully forward. Less than a league from Inverurie a scout came running back to the earl. "My lord, they're nearly on us. Just around that bend and coming at speed." "Who is, man?" demanded Buchan. "Bruce, my lord. He leads his men towards us." At that moment outriders of Bruce's force appeared, caught sight of their enemy, turned and rode back shouting warnings as they went. Buchan stopped his advance ordering his captains to take up positions on the gently sloping hills along the road's edge. The earl thought to himself, 'So they think they can trick me again. Well, we'll see if it's the murderer himself or his brother who leads the Bruce men.'

Buchan's forces had not had time to reform into fighting formation before Bruce's army appeared and halted well within arrow's range. Robert Bruce was clearly seen fully armed and at the head of his men. Both sides eyed each other and King Robert pulled back the chain mail covering his head and neck. The Earl of Buchan could see that it truly was Robert Bruce, for not only did the earl recognize him, but he also recognized Edward Bruce who had joined his brother at the head of their army. The two could be seen conversing with each other. At that very moment Robert Bruce replaced his mail and drew his broadsword. His squire blew on Bruce's hunting horn and a mighty roar arose from three thousand throats as King Robert's men began their attack. In tight disciplined formation, they marched at speed holding shields high for protection against arrows.

They covered the ground between them at an alarming pace. Sir John Mowbray, who rode with Buchan, ordered his archers to fire at will. Suddenly Bruce's men veered off the road and raced up the hillside towards him, their shields lowered, their pike's bristling out from their formation. They were intent on joining battle. When Buchan's men saw their enemy, they turned and fled. Bruce's schiltroms followed and ploughed through the enemy ranks, scattering, trampling and disorganizing.

Buchan watched the disintegration of his own forces and Bruce's schiltrom advancing rapidly and he also turned and fled with all his followers, back the way they had come. Through Meldrum, with the enemy still pressing them onwards, to Fyrie Castle. Buchan was a fugitive fleeing across his own lands with the battle cries and trumpet calls of his enemy ringing in his ears.

Outside the gates of Fyrie Castle, Edward Bruce sat down with many men to beseige Buchan, while Lennox, Wiseman, Barclay and other knights harried the earl's lands, burning, killing and looting, until only those who claimed King Robert as their liege lord remained. The earl stared out from the battlements of Fyrie, watching the columns of smoke on the horizon and listening to the stories from the few refugees whom Edward Bruce permitted to enter the castle. He went to his chamber a sad and broken man.

After the rout at Meldrum, King Robert had ridden back to the manor of Huntly where he ordered the destruction of Buchan to continue until all men had submitted to his lordship. At Huntly the king's health gradually improved and while he remained there many men came to him to pay homage and seek his service.

The Earl of Buchan fled south to England, but John Mowbray, and the Earl of Atholl, having shaken off his pursuers, rallied their men and with great determination followed Bruce who had now left Huntly and returned north, striking at the enemy strongholds wherever he could. Mowbray and Atholl adopted Bruce's tactics, swooping down on outposts whenever they could and when Bruce attacked the castles at Tarradale and Slain, they sat in the hills awaiting their opportunity. When Mowbray and Atholl heard that Bruces's men were attacking Elgin they hurried to the aid of the defenders and arrived in time to prevent the surrender of the castle. There they remained for Elgin was a fortress, which the English did not want to lose. The men sat around the castle yard in small groups, dejected and listless, even the bright sunny weather could not raise their spirits and as the sergeant said to Mowbray, "They're fearful my lord. So far north and surrounded by enemies, they can see no escape." "Will they fight when the time comes?" asked Mowbray. "Aye they'll fight. They're good men." "Then set those men who are not guarding the walls to repair the storehouses. Keep them busy. Don't let them think too much," ordered Sir John.

One afternoon when Mowbray was inspecting the repairs that had been carried out, he heard one of the men whistling and said to the sergeant, "They sound more cheerful, Alan!" The sergeant replied, "Aye, let's hope King Hobbe remains away for some weeks yet." Mowbray, however, was sure that they would be seeing their enemy very soon for that morning he had heard that Duffus Castle had fallen to Bruce. A few days later his fears were realized when on a glorious afternoon in late May, Bruce's forces came into view with King Hobbe himself leading them.

Bruce had many foot soldiers, archers, horsemen and pack animals carrying scaling ladders and pulling battering rams and for a week the garrison held off their attackers. Yet with such short nights Bruce gave the garrison little time to rest and while half of his own men rested the others kept up the attack, forcing Mowbray onto the battlements day and night. Sometimes he caught a few winks of sleep with his back resting against a buttress and his mantle wrapped around him against a night chill, but as soon as the first light crept above the eastern horizon, Mowbray jumped to his task again. The attacks were launched simultaneously around the walls and in this way Bruce kept the castle's defenders at their posts until fatigue overcame them.

After seven days softening up his enemy, King Robert rode to the castle gates and called out to Mowbray and Atholl. "Surrender! You've no chance of reinforcement. The English King has left you to fend for yourselves. He expects your loyalty but leaves you to face his enemies without his help or guidance." Mowbray looked down at the big man sitting confidently and robustly on his warhorse. There was no evidence of the illness that had afflicted him earlier in the year, and there certainly was truth in what Bruce said. They could not expect relief. "What you say is true, but a man cannot easily change allegiance without careful thought," shouted Mowbray. "Aye, then I give you time to think," replied the king and turned his horse.

Mowbray climbed slowly down the battlement steps and across to the great hall. Surrender would be a bitter draught to swallow. He flung himself into the master's chair. It was dark and cool away from the bright sunshine, soothing for his tired eyes. The steward brought him mild ale and he sat back in the chair, legs stretched out in front of him drinking the cool nectar and gazing up at the soot-covered rafters, thinking about his predicament.

He had ridden with Wallace against the English and fought for Scotland's freedom for ten years or more but when his lord, the Red Comyn, had finally sworn allegiance to the old English King he had followed him and fought with the Comyns. To surrender to Bruce now and pay him homage would guarantee his own life for the time being. Yet Bruce was a murderer and usurper of the throne. Mowbrays had been allied to the Comyns for well over one hundred years. Mowbrays had married Comyns. Yet without English help, Bruce would triumph of that he was sure. There would be no room in Scotland for both Comyn and Bruce and the outcome would be that Mowbrays would be the losers. They would forfeit their estates, but to kiss the Bruce sword and fight alongside his former enemies would be no easy task.

His chin gradually sunk onto his chest, his eyes closed and for a short while he slept. The sergeant woke Mowbray. "My lord, King Hobbe returns to the castle walls demanding your answer." "Well Alan, it seems I must make a decision for us all. Could you fight for Bruce?" The sergeant, a prudent man said, "Men like us follow our lord's wish."

When Mowbray reached the top of the battlement steps and saw Bruce's army spread out around the walls, scaling ladders and battering rams ready for immediate action, he knew there was only one answer he could give. His men paid homage to their king and were permitted to take up arms in the king's pay and Sir John and Atholl were taken into the king's custody. Then the king ordered the destruction of Nairn Castle.

Throughout his campaign King Robert's greatest problem had been the provision of weapons for his growing army. When his followers were few, he kept them supplied with weapons captured from the enemy, but it was always a hit and miss affair, not worthy of an army of Scotland. Smiths followed the army now and repaired all body armour, weapons and gear, but a smith can only forge if he has the raw materials to hand. Scotland lacked iron ore and buying it from other parts of Christendom required access to merchants and ships. The capture of Aberdeen was the obvious answer. The citizens of Aberdeen had followed Wallace in his fight for Scotland's freedom and Bruce was sure they would follow him if he gave them the opportunity.

Bruce called Alexander Pilche to him. "Master Pilche, you have kinsmen and friends among the burghers of Aberdeen. Take men and ride to that city. Tell them if they hand over their city to me, I'll double their trade and buy all they have. Oh, and point out what effect a siege will have on their trade and profits." Then the king smiled. "I'm sure you'll know what to say to make them see sense.

When the king's army was sighted from the city walls of Aberdeen the gates opened. The army spread out around the city and a pavilion was set up for the king where leading merchants greeted him and paid him homage. In Aberdeen Castle the men were restless. They had had an easygoing relationship with the citizens and now that they had handed the city over to Bruce the castle was besieged and vulnerable.

A few days after Bruces's arrival, James Douglas and his followers, excited after their campaign in Galloway, joined the king. When the commander of the castle looked out from the battlements, the besieging army stretched away onto the horizon and he returned to the great hall a worried man. The following day the Earl of Lennox rode up, as he had every morning, and in the name of King Robert ordered them to surrender. This time the commander agreed. Later the king rode through the gates of the seaport, leading his captains in triumph along the streets, lined with cheering citizens and up to the castle where the defenders came out and in front of all paid homage to King Robert.

During the days that followed, the king called John Blair to him and dictated many letters to the mayors of the cities of Hamberg, Lubeck and Bergen, explaining that Aberdeen was now in the hands of its lawful king. He welcomed the merchants of those cities to trade with his subjects. Later as John Blair sat quietly making copies of the king's despatches he remembered his dear friend, William Wallace. Ten years it was since he had written similar letters to those same cities, inviting trade with the Community of Scotland. Poor Wallace, his success had been short-lived, thwarted by men of superior rank. Of course, William's noble nature had been his undoing. John sighed, the perversity of the human character never ceased to amaze him. He continued with his writing.

The king halted the army near Glen Dochart. It had been two years since he had last met the MacDougalls in that glen and it was here that he had parted from Elizabeth and Marjorie. When he thought back to those days it seemed to him like a dream. Those were the days when he had practised for the battles in which he was now engaged. Now he was ready to meet John of Lorn. The truce had ended and this time he would meet him on his terms.

James Douglas had been riding in the company of his own men and the king sent a message inviting him to eat that night. Dinner was a noisy, jolly affair and when they sat with full goblets the king said, "John MacDougall will wait in ambush at the Brander Pass because it's the most difficult part of his territory to march through before reaching his castle of Dunstaffnage. He'll try the same techniques he used before, when he met us at Glen Dochart. Take your highlanders and wait in ambush on the higher slopes of Cruachan. Make sure that when I march through the pass with the army MacDougall and his men regret they ever crossed Robert Bruce."

The slopes of Cruachan fell steeply into Loch Awe, its waters were very still and blue in the early morning sunlight with the River Awe flowing merrily into it. If anyone, with time to spare, had stood on the summit of Cruachan and gazed around they would have seen spread before them the lochs, forests, glens, mountains and corries of western Scotland and the isles. Out towards Loch Linnhe a white–tailed eagle called plaintively, twee-oo, twee-oo, a lonely, sad call as it soared on currents of warm, morning air. Close to the bank of the loch a family of otters, mother and two young were about their daily business and in the silence one could hear the mother's soft whistle to her kittens. Among a cluster of Caledonian pines, on the northern bank of the loch, a lynx had a den, but she did not leave its protection and kept her two young kittens close by her. She could smell danger on the wind and her sharp ears heard the noise of snapping branches and twigs.

The MacDougall men had arrived well before light, positioning themselves on the slopes of Cruachan overlooking the narrow path and settled to await Bruce and his army. Their lord, Sir John had not completely regained his health and he remained in a galley on Loch Awe, unable to take any part in the forthcoming battle. His old friend Gillespie Maclaclan took command of the men.

King Robert's army marched at a leisurely pace. From their behaviour there was no hint of caution and at the rear of the army were baggage wagons, more appropriate to the slow-moving English army than King Robert's lightening attackers. Gillespie himself sent the first arrow flying downward towards the enemy and the men of Argyll launched their attack. Arrows, stones and boulders crashed into Bruce's men. As the Argyll men leapt from their hiding places behind rocks, thickets and trees and ran down the hillside brandishing their locharber battleaxes, they were in turn attacked from the rear by Douglas's men who had been hiding higher up the mountainside for the past two nights.

The King's men turned, clambering up the rocky hillside to meet their enemies, now caught between the two. Douglas's men jumped down the rocky paths, shouting their battle cries and brandishing sword and battleaxe. Bruce, who knew how important success in this campaign would be, dismounted and led his men to the enemy. The fighting was ferocious. Mercy was not given on either side. Bruce hoped to encounter Sir John of Lorn, but that chieftain was not to seen. The mountainside was so steep and strewn with loose stones that many MacDougalls lost their footing as they struggled with their opponents and fell to the path below where camp followers finished them off. Some fell into the deep waters at the foot of Cruachan. James Douglas, quick to cease any advantage, with a dozen of his best archers positioned on a large rock and a clear view of the battle, carefully picked their targets and dispatched them one by one.

Gillespie blew his hunting horn and began to run down the hillside towards the bridge over the River Awe, the only means of escape. His intention was to destroy the bridge and retreat to the MacDougall castle of Dunstaffnage, but his force was so outnumbered and outmanoeuvred, that his men followed him across the bridge, leaving it intact. The MacDougalls fled, streaming along the road to the castle now held by the old earl, Alexander, father to John MacDougall, but the king's men were so close behind that when the gates were slammed shut, many kinsmen and followers were left outside to face the fury of their enemy.

Earl Alexander sat, as he always did, in his carved, high-backed chair, gazing through the window and across the castle walls towards Mull. It was the old chief's favourite view. Once he had been a large, powerfully-built man, but in his old age he had become gaunt, his beard and whatever hair remained to him, snow white. When he had become ill, three years previously, the left side of his body had become paralysed and although he was able to walk unsteadily, leaning on a stout staff, his left arm hung loosely at his side and he dragged his left leg as he walked. His speech was slurred and he looked a sad figure.

For a week the castle withstood the attacks of the king's army, but Sir John of Lorne had not arrived with a relief force and Gillespie told Earl Alexander they could not hope to hold the castle, now overflowing with survivors from the battle and many of their families. They must surrender to Bruce. Dunstaffage was the place of the Earl's birth and it was with a heavy heart that he surrendered it into Bruce hands. He thought sadly of his dead wife who was a Comyn by birth. Now at the end of his life he would have to kneel before her nephew's murderer and pay him homage. His daughter and servants came into the chamber. Since she had been widowed, she had cared for her father and like her mother was well known for her sharp and haughty nature. "They're ready for you father. Let me see that you look your best." She walked around the old man, tidying his hair and checking his robes. His fine, red, woollen surcoat fell to his ankles and was embroidered in gold and silver threads. Around his waist he wore a wide, red, leather belt embossed with silver and when his servants helped him to his feet he looked, as indeed he was, a distinguished chieftain. One of the servants carried him like a child down the steep stairway to the great hall, for he was unable to walk down by himself.

King Robert sat on the raised dais in the earl's high chair. He wore chain mail with the golden circlet of kingship on his head and looked a warrior king. The hall was packed with the king's followers and many of the MacDougall barons and chiefs were there to pay homage to the king. As Earl Alexander entered, the noise abated. He refused the offer of assistance from his daughter and servants and clutching his staff tightly, walked slowly up to Bruce, pausing here and there to rest. Nothing was said and the king sat staring straight ahead. Slowly the old man sank onto his knees, wobbling and swaying dangerously, so that all watching were sure he would fall on his face. His daughter jumped forward, running to his aid, but once again irritably he refused any assistance. When he was finally kneeling before the king, he kissed the hilt of Bruce's outstretched sword and in a quaking voice repeated the oath of allegiance. Rising to his feet he accepted a chair to watch as his MacDougall kindred and liegemen paid homage to Bruce, before they filed out into the warm, sunlit courtyard. Most of his followers had left the hall when Sir Alexander began to retrace his painful steps, but his daughter turned on the king and snapped, " This was not well done my lord, my father is a very sick old man. Was it necessary to humiliate him so?" James Douglas stepped angrily from his king's side, his arm raised as if to strike the unhappy woman, but the king said, "Sir James, the lady is distressed." Then to the woman he said, "Madam, were I in your place I would have said the same, but as it is I fear it was necessary that your father's homage be seen by many. Tonight we feast at my expense and your father will be my honoured guest and I beg that you attend as my lady." The king was as good as his word and paid special attention to his two guests. Although he did not win them over, the lady had to admit to her father that Robert Bruce was a most charming and generous enemy and that his behaviour took some of the sting from her humiliation.

After Sir John MacDougall of Lorn had watched the defeat of his forces, he ordered his men to row him to his fortress of Inchconnell and from there he escaped to the Isle of Man. King Robert did not harry, burn or pillage the earl's lands, but provisioned the castle and left Earl Alexander and his daughter in peace, with a close guard to watch them. Then the king set about wooing the men of Argyll while Sir James Douglas spent eight months with his followers, winning control of his own lands in Douglasdale, Clydesdale and the Selkirk forest as far as Jedburgh.

When James Douglas returned to his king in the spring of 1308, he was a most successful and hardened warrior with a reputation for pitiless cunning.

"Well James," said the king when they met, "Tell me about your campaign." "My lord, I took my Douglas' castles first. I met kinsmen and tenants from my lands and they helped me to secure my heritage. We took all weapons and treasure, destroyed the castles and any provisions, as were your instructions. All the Englishmen have been killed and we put fear into their hearts, they'll not be so eager to step over the border again. While I campaigned in the Selkirk forest we ambushed an English patrol and I captured a prisoner whom I've brought to you. He's arrogant and abusive but I believe you'll be pleased with him." He turned to his sergeant, telling him to bring in the prisoner. "I've captured your sister's son, Randolph, my lord," He was about to add that the young man had been argumentative and abusive ever since his capture, but when he saw the expression of pleasure and relief on the king's face he said nothing.

After the battle at Methven, when he had given his pledge to the Earl of Pembroke, Randolph lived at the English Court and had been in the following of various English nobles. The previous Christmas he had been with the Prince of Wales and admired him enormously. Edward was so accomplished on the jousting field, so knowledgeable about fashion and style and his wit so sharp that in his company Randolph hung onto every word that came from the great man. So enchanted was Randolph that he tried to emulate the prince's bored and lofty behaviour. After his capture, he treated James Douglas, who was a similar age to himself, with disdain. Compared to his beloved, cultured prince, James Douglas was an uncouth peasant, an outlaw, a man without honour, who murdered secretly like a fox in the night. Douglas did not obey the noble rules of chivalry and Randolph would not allow himself to be associated with Douglas in any way.

When they brought him before his uncle he adopted a cold and surly attitude, but the king greeted Thomas in a friendly way. "Well lad, it's a pleasure to have you with us and I'm going to leave you in James's care, for you will become great comrades." The king ignored the expression of despair that spread across Douglas's face, who had been pleased to be rid of the haughty sod but, before the king could say anymore Randolph spoke. "I'm pledged to King Edward II. I can't fight with his enemies." The king replied "Come Tom, you're a Scot, your lands are in Scotland, your kin are Scots and your mother bore you for nine months beneath her Scottish heart. Would you deny all of this?" The king swept his arm around to emphasis peaks, glens and rushing waters of the Scottish landscape. Thomas retorted, "You wage war against your rightful lord, King Edward, yet you fight not in open battle like a true knight but skulk in moors and forests where none may get at you. I don't want to be a Scot if this is what Scots do." His uncle looked at him with a cynical smile on his face. "Open battle you may yet see, but before that all men must put to good advantage those weapons which they have to hand. I see that the English have bent your ear and persuaded you to renounce your heritage. It's your youth that's to blame. James, take my nephew into your custody and guard him well."

As the king turned to leave he said to Randolph, "Perhaps time will show you the error of your ways."

As the months went by the relationship of guard and captive between the two young men changed and James Douglas and Thomas Randolph became good comrades, although they remained jealous of the affection which the king had for the other. Thomas learned a great deal about the nature of warfare from Douglas, but it was from the older knights, Boyd, Lennox and others that he learnt that King Robert was a noble and courageous leader.

That autumn while King Robert progressed through Argyll, he learned that his brother Edward's campaign in Galloway had been so successful that Dougal MacDougall had sent his family and other kinsfolk over the border to England for safety. A steady stream of refugees fled into England, but MacDougall himself refused to be ousted from his lands and continued to defy Edward Bruce from the safety of Dumfries Castle. When the king heard this, he ordered Douglas, Lindsey and Boyd to join his brother and to take Thomas Randolph with them but before they left, the king said, "If he attempts to rejoin the English send him back to me for punishment."

King Robert once again turned his attention to the north marching through the Great Glen and as he neared Inverness, men guessed who his next victim would be. The imminent arrival of King Robert sent the Earl of Ross into a frenzy of activity. He called his men to arms and they stood on watch around his territory day and night and he sent out messengers asking his friends, neighbours and kinsmen for help but in spite of all his arrangements he doubted he would be able to stand against Bruce. After careful thought he contacted his cousin, Thomas Bishop of Dundee and Bishop David Mowbray asking them to intervene on his behalf with the king. They arranged that Ross publicly admit his offences against the king and his kinsfolk and in return the king permitted the earl to retain his lands and gave him a gift of land that had previously belonged to the King's enemies. For both, it was a most satisfactory outcome.

With Ross no longer a threat, King Robert travelled to Auldearn near Nairn where, for the first time in three years, he relaxed. The Earl of Ross, as a sign of his good faith, had sent the king a gift of a pair of hunting dogs and a fine falcon and the king rode out with his companions, flying his falcon with his hunting dogs trotting at his horse's hooves. Men, who had formerly run away when Bruce and his forces appeared in the area, now sought their king's favour. Wool and cloth merchants from Inverness arrived with gifts of finally–woven, woollen, Flanders cloth, an ankle length surcoat of royal blue, a colour he had been fond of in happier times and fine linen drawers and undershirt to ease the chaffing from his chain mail.

Since his illness he had been prone to sores on his legs which did not heal as quickly as he would have liked and resting and sleeping in a soft, dry bed eased the discomfort he felt from the weeping sores.

One morning, two messengers sent by Alexander Pilche, arrived from Aberdeen. "Master Pilche and other merchants have commissioned me to make this gift for you, my lord, in recognition of their loyalty," said one of the men. He offered the king a box inlaid with walrus ivory. Inside the box, lying on a silken cushion, was a gold brooch about the size of a man's fist, engraved and inlaid with garnets and fresh water pearls. It was beautifully crafted, fit for a king. The goldsmith, with some pride said, "It's made from Scottish gold and gems, my lord." "It's indeed a fine gift, master smith. From whom did you learn your craft?" My apprenticeship was under a skilled smith in Aberdeen, but as a journeyman I travelled to Danzig and improved my craft in that town." The king replied, "It's such craftsmen as yourself that Scotland needs. Your name?" "I'm Neil, son of Duncan of Aberdeen." "Well Neil, son of Duncan, in the future I hope you will use your skills to serve the crown."

Neil's companion represented a body of merchants and ships' masters departing for Lubeck and Hamberg with a cargo of wool and furs. They hoped to trade for iron ore and weapons and came to ask their king for letters of introduction. He listened intently to him before saying, "I'll order my clerks to prepare an introduction and when you return I'll purchase your goods. God's speed and a safe return from your enterprise."

On All Saints Eve the Earl of Ross, accompanied by his barons, lairds and followers attended their king at Auldearn. There the earl prostrated himself at his king's feet and confessed to his numerous sins against King Robert's womenfolk and kinsmen. His lord the king forgave Ross and received his oath of allegiance. As a pledge of the good will which was to be between them it was agreed that as soon as matters of state permitted, a marriage would be arranged between the earl's eldest son, Hugh and the king's youngest sister, Matilda when the maid reached marriageable age. That evening the two men signed the betrothal contract before attending a great feast held to celebrate the king's victories in his northern lands.

The extraordinary year of 1308 drew to its close. During that year King Robert had seen such changes to his fortunes that he found it hard to believe it could be so. Lately he had been able to deal with matters arising with the government of his kingdom. There had been correspondence and petitions from many men and there was now too much work for John Blair and the king appointed a chancellor to attend to his administration, Bernard, Abbot of Kilwinning, an able and humane man.

During the third week of Lent, Edward Bruce returned from Galloway bringing guests with him for the King. Dusk was falling when Robert went out into the courtyard and from the light of the torches he saw Christine. In spite of her weariness her face beamed with happiness when she saw her beloved. Behind her rode their son. "Christine, my bonnie lass," the king lifted her from her mount, tears in his eyes, for he was so overcome with emotion. Then he turned to his son, a strong lad with an open face and steady gaze. He was big for his age of nine winters and within the sight and hearing of all, the king acknowledged his son. "Well Robert, get down so that your father may see you properly." The boy dismounted, throwing back his cloak from his head and shoulders and went down onto his knees before his father, as his mother had instructed him. "Come lad, get off the cold cobbles," said his father as he placed his arm around the boy. A small figure burst from the group and flung her arms around the king's legs. "Father, father, have a look at me too." The man laughed and pulling back the hood from the little maid's face scooped her up in his arms gazing into the small face with its delicately pointed chin, sparkling blue eyes and mass of chestnut curls. "So my little Christine have you come to see your father too?" he said.

When the children had been taken away to be fed, King Robert led their mother to his chamber and he flung himself upon her with such impatient passion that afterwards she had laughed and said, "Good heavens Robert, you've still got your boots on." He looked down at his half-clothed body, his naked legs with his draws hanging in cascades around his ankles and his heavy leather boots, covered in mud, still encasing his feet. They both laughed and Robert said, "I'll try to behave with the dignity that befits a king later tonight." To which Christine laughed and wantonly said, "I loved you just the way you were." That night Christine dined with her lord as his lady and she and her children remained in his household throughout the winter months.

One evening when the Earl of Lennox sat playing chess with the king he said, "Robert it's not safe for Christine and your children to return to her own manor. When you go on campaign you must find a place of safety for them." The king did not reply, but early in March the Earl of Lennox escorted Christine, her children, a tutor and numerous servants westward to the safety of a Lennox manor.

In April the king rode to St Andrew's to meet a secret delegation sent by the English king. Edward proposed a truce between the two kingdoms and since it was convenient to be free from fear of attack, for the time being King Robert agreed. A truce was signed between the two kingdoms which was to last for nine months.

King Robert called his first parliament and all those earls, barons, lairds and chiefs who were within his peace attended. With them the king discussed Scotland's trade with the Hanseatic towns and relations with their good friend the king of Norway but before parliament closed, he put before them his triumph, a letter, recently received from King Philip of France and addressed to Robert Bruce, the King of Scots. It was the first occasion on which he was addressed by that title by a fellow king and when the French emissary had arrived Robert had found it difficult to restrain his desire to run up to the nearest battlement and shout his news to the surrounding town. Instead he grasped Edward's arm and laughed. "Not only does he recognize my kingship, but asks me to go on crusade with him to the Holy Land. One day I will be recognized by all of Christendom and shall ride with kings to Jerusalem." Edward also laughed but said, "Meanwhile brother, there is still the small question of the English."

WHAT ABOUT THE ENGLISH?

After his father's death Edward II's inheritance was a prosperous land, albeit with debts which his father had incurred during his Scottish wars. Edward left Percy, Clifford and other commanders in the north to continue with his business - the capture of Robert Bruce and the other rebels - whilst he travelled to London where he was reunited with his lover, Piers Gavaston. In the last months of the old king's life Gavaston had been banished to Poitier. He returned with all haste and Edward was elated to have Piers by his side once again. To show his true love for Piers, Edward bestowed the royal title of Duke of Cornwall on him and for appearance's sake married Piers to his royal cousin Margaret, but before the new king could complete his father's work in Scotland, he married his betrothed, Isabella, a princess of France. While he was away he left the care and administration of England in Gavaston's hands. The English nobles, who should have enjoyed that privilege, ground their teeth together with anger and plotted in their castles against the king but when he returned to England his only interest was Gavaston, compounding his nobles' anger and jealousy. The queen's uncles and brother, who were to be guests of honour and witness the crowning, accompanied the king and queen from France.

Isabella was just sixteen and very excited. She spent many happy hours trying on her coronation robes and discussing with her ladies how to wear her hair to her best advantage on the day. Her old nurse held Isabella's thick, black hair up around her pretty, oval face showing to advantage her long, slender neck, whilst Isabella gazed at herself in her hand mirror. The English earls would be wearing cloth of gold for the ceremony and Isabella was to wear silver and red silk, with her creamy skin and dark hair her ladies all agreed that the loveliness of their queen would dazzle both her husband and his subjects.

On a chill and misty day at the end of February, when swirling, clinging, white fog rolled up the marshes and over the River Thames, Edward held his coronation. The citizens of London Town gathered outside Westminster to watch their nobles come and go and to admire their fine clothes and noisy confidence. Isabella ordered her sleek, black, Arab mare to be prepared. It was indeed a beautiful animal with slender legs, a neat head, large, intelligent eyes and alert, twitching ears. Its red and silver, embossed saddle and bridle and other accouchements had small silver bells attached which jingled merrily whenever it moved or shook its head.

Isabella had arisen early. Her husband had not shared her bed since their arrival in England and she was free from the unpleasant reminiscence of her troubled first night as a bride. Before her marriage her nurse had told her what to expect and her ladies said that since her husband was such a strong and handsome man she would find it most enjoyable and would yearn for the following night. She would have screamed if she were forced to gaze upon the face of a man who had bad breath and pimples and she had admired his looks. On her wedding night she had sat in her marriage bed with nervous apprehension, waiting for them to lead in Edward. He had climbed into the bed without a glance at the young maid beside him. It was mid winter, but the room was very stuffy with so many members of their families and nobles jostling one another to witness the first night consummation. The heavy, royal–blue, brocade curtains were pulled around the bed which made it so dark she could not see the man as he fumbled at her shift, squeezing her nipples and forcing her legs apart with his knee as he lay her down. A more sensitive husband would have recognized her fear and calmed her with tender caresses, but Edward carried out his duty and cared little for the finer points of love-making. Isabella lay as rigid as a soldier before his captain and gave a cry of pain as he entered, ejected and withdrew, his duty at an end. Outside the curtains their audience relaxed and Edward called out. "It's done my lords, England flourishes in France." Some of his English nobles called out "Well done Sire," before they all filed from the room, leaving the married pair their privacy. Then Edward pulled back the curtain, letting in the light from the fire and looked down, scrutinizing Isabella's slender, young body. "Let's hope you quicken early," he said without a smile or any show of tenderness. Then he turned on his side and fell asleep, whilst Isabella continued to stare at the canopy above the bed. "Was that it?" She felt rather cheated, but of what she was not sure. Well at least she would be a queen.

When they had arrived in England they had been met by her husband's favourite, Piers Gavaston and her uncles told her that the two men were lovers, but that she should not worry for he was not a threat to her. She was to remember that as queen and future mother of the heir the Church protected her. Besides, many of the king's English nobles hated Gavaston and his days might yet be numbered.

Isabella's joy at her coronation was short-lived. The king ordered that the coronation procession enter Westminster Abbey by the side door. The young queen who had been practising how to wave royally, for her new subjects, was rushed into the Confessor's Abbey without time to see or be seen. Her husband barely noticed her, having eyes only for Piers, who was regally dressed in royal purple. Around his waist he wore a magnificent belt decorated with cameos set in gold and walking haughtily in front of his king, carried the crown of Edward the Confessor on a crimson cushion. The belt Isabella reconized, for it had been given to her as part of her dowry. As she walked slowly behind her husband, she thought how difficult it was to know which man was the king. During the tedious ceremony many of the nobles whispered behind their hands. The Earl of Warwick was heard to say, "Why the Archbishop bothered to come I don't know, we've Gavaston to perform the crowning."

A splendid banquet had been prepared in the great hall of the palace of Westminster. The Abbey had been so cold and outside the weather so grey and damp that the palace, lit by thousands of sweet beeswax candles was warm and the revellers quickly became intoxicated with the spirit of Bacchus. Isabella sat on her husband's left, her kinsmen beside her whilst Piers Gavaston sat on his king's right in the place of honour. Edward barely glanced in Isabella's direction and directed all his attention towards his lover, but as the banquet wore on and wine flowed, tempers grew shorter. The sight of Gavaston preening himself in the seat of honour infuriated the Earl of Lancaster. Red in the face, he rose unsteadily to his feet. Pushing back his heavy chair he staggered around the table towards Gavaston shouting, "I'm going to kill that cunt, let me at him," but Lancaster's friends jumped up, pulling him back to his seat and were heard to say, "Not yet Thomas, not on a feast day." Lancaster in his drunken state continued to mumble, "The cunt, I'll get him," before his head sunk onto his trencher and he began snoring loudly. The king in, deep conversation with Piers, hardly noticed the commotion.

Isabella's uncles watched their niece's husband with growing contempt until Charles de Valois said loudly, "At least that peacock cannot produce heirs, he'll have to turn in this direction for that." Isabella, who had been watching the jugglers, turned to Edward to pass a comment about the entertainers but Edward did not turn towards her so that she was forced to pull his sleeve to attract his attention. Irritably he pushed her hand away and continued listening to Piers who was telling him a very funny story. That was too much for the Duke de Valois. He stood up, took his niece by the hand and gesturing to the rest of the French entourage, swept from the hall, loudly saying, "We'll return when His Majesty has the time for us."

That night, after the queen's ladies had paid elaborate attention to her toilet and night attire, Isabella lay in her bed waiting. She knew she looked desirable with her midnight-black hair spread out on the white, linen pillow. Freshly bathed, her skin smelt of lily of the valley from the sweet smelling oils they had rubbed onto her. As time passed and he did not appear she began to sob. Her old nurse came in to her and sat on the bed, patting her hand and talking to her about old familiar times in France until the young wife fell asleep. In the morning her uncle said, "Well, did he come?" She looked down at her feet and slowly shook her head. Hesitatingly she said, "Does he not find me beautiful?" "Niece, that man would not find Helen of Troy lovely. He is besotted. He'll not get his heir this way."

Edward's behaviour at his coronation feast set the pattern for his married life. So long as Piers Gavaston was around he had time only for him and was too busy, both day and night, with his dear brother Piers to consider his responsibilities towards his wife and kingdom. All his attention and energy focused on his lover and how to keep him safe from his nobles. They continued to hate Piers Gavaston and plotted and schemed how best to dispose of him. Christmas arrived and Edward and Gavaston spent it at the royal manor of Langley in Hertfordshire, which was the king's favourite residence, whilst the queen and her court remained at Westminster.

In February the king opened the new session of Parliament. His nobles were ready for him, brandishing lists of complaints against the king's dearest friend. For good measure they accused the king of mismanagement of the kingdom and losing most of Scotland, which had been won by his father. To emphasize their determination they stationed their armed retainers around parliament and Edward had little alternative but to hand over the administration of the kingdom to a committee of earls and bishops. Stunned by the turn of events, Edward decided to begin a new offensive against Robert Bruce, when the truce came to an end. He would take dear Piers with him and that would keep him safe from the murderous nobles.

The Earls of Gloucester and Surrey responded to their king's call to arms and Piers, of course, but his other earls refused to attend muster and Edward was forced to rely on the veterans of the Scottish wars, Sir

John Seagrave, Clifford and Percy. The wealthy merchants of the City of London, anxious to protect their trade, paid for one hundred crossbow men to march with the king and remain in Berwick to protect that town from attack by the Scots. John of Lorn, who had recently escaped from Robert Bruce, had fled to the English king and promised to attack Argyll by sea.

Preparations for invasion took so long it was nearly autumn before the army was mustered and marched into Scotland. With the cold weather about to arrive, many of the king's commanders shook their heads but King Edward was not deterred, Piers was safely riding at his side, secure from their enemies. Throughout a damp and misty October the king led his army through the lowlands, seeking Bruce and visiting English–held castles. On All Soul's Day they reached Linlithgow with no sign of Bruce and his army. The surrounding country through which they had passed had been emptied of all food for both man and beast and as the English army advanced, the Scots retreated into the hills and forests. Each night men on guard duty and others in outlying pickets disappeared and the army's rearguard was under constant attack by the Scots,.

On one occasion Sir John Seagrave sent out a raiding party to search for food, particularly fodder for the horses. The force comprised of three hundred Welsh and English archers with a small company of horsemen to protect them. They marched west, into the Clyde valley towards Renfrew, but they saw no one and the Scots had already burned the farms and manors.

In the late afternoon, when the men were tired from their long day without sign of plunder, their captain decided to return to the main army. As they sat resting in a heavily wooded valley the Scots, led by Edward Bruce, emerged from their hiding places among the trees and attacked furiously. Arrows fell among the English before they had time to form defensive ranks and they were forced to scatter and seek cover, but the Scots, with the advantage of surprise, pursued them through the trees. The mounted English troopers, unable to launch an adequate defensive attack, pulled out, shouting to their comrades that they would bring help and at full gallop fled back towards the main army followed by a hail of arrows. As they neared their camp they made such a hullabaloo their comrades could hear the uproar from a great distance even above the noise of their own camp clatter. Seagrave, commander of the rearguard, listened to their tale and led a large company out to rescue his men. Too late! The place of ambush was silent and deserted by the living. Even the songbirds had ceased to sing. Only the lonely, keening call of a curlew and the squabbling squawks of the crows, as they scavenged among the grotesque corpses, broke the silence. The bodies had been stripped, their weapons taken, but of the murderous Scots there was no sign. Not being able to force Bruce out into the open increased the king's frustration.

King Edward's problems continued and throughout the following spring and summer, his nobles hated his dear brother Piers and would not obey their king's commands. One night when he was alone with Gavaston Edward said, "My dear fellow, recently I've been considering recognizing Bruce's kingship and making peace with him." An expression of horror spread across Gavaston's arrogant face. "Edward you cannot give away half of your inheritance. We still have a firm grip on the south-east of Scotland. Take time to consider." It was this manner of speaking, as if he shared the crown with the king, that had gained him the hatred of England's nobles, but the besotted Edward ignored the familiarities. "Piers, if I could come to terms with Bruce I would make it a condition that you'd receive his protection. Some corner within his Kingdom where we would meet from time to time. Remember I still have his wife and family, pawns to buy you estates and security in his land," but Gavaston cried, "No, no, this will not do, to live so far away from you, never. Why, you have said yourself I am your dearest brother." His sincerity so touched Edward that tears appeared in his blue eyes and he embraced his lover.

Edward left Gavaston at Stirling Castle, which was still in English hands, with orders to reinforce the defences and hold the town at all costs. He returned with his weary army to Berwick where he was joined by Isabella, but when autumn came, much to Isabella's dismay they were again joined by Gavaston and as usual the king paid his lover every attention and compliment.

No sooner had the English army crossed the border into the North Country than King Robert and his men thundered across the Solway into Cumberland attacking many manors and settlements. Whenever they met with resistance they burned the defenders in their houses, but if the houses were deserted King Robert's men were satisfied to herd the livestock back across the border to their own people. The Scots marched as far as the manor of Haltwhistle, before returning to their own land carrying everything which could be moved.

King Robert laughed with his brother Edward and slapped him on the shoulder, "What a success Edward, they're completely defenceless. We'll go back next week before they've had time to catch their breaths, but we'll go along the eastern coast instead." True to his word, King

Robert led an army of horsemen, through the wild country of Northumberland attacking from Harbottle to Corbridge, burning and plundering, through Redesdale and up the Tyne Valley to Newcastle until the whole county was alight. Northumbrians, tough, hardy men, well used to striking blow for blow stood their ground, but their women, children and farms were vulnerable. Their king and his nobles were too busy bickering in the safety of the southern counties to give them any support and when the chill, autumn winds blew in from the north sea they sued with the Scots for a truce. This was to last until the following spring and they paid King Robert two thousand English pounds to seal the bargain.

The Scottish king kept his word and left Northumberland in peace that winter. Instead he encouraged his captains to attack the lands of the Earl of Dunbar who still clung obstinately to his English alliance. When the spring of 1312 arrived, the truce at an end, the Scots returned to Northumberland in greater numbers than before, and still King Edward did not send his soldiers to the north to support their countrymen. He cared little for his responsibilities to the common folk for he was too busy protecting Gavaston from his noble lords. Once again the farmers and merchants of the northern shires paid tribute to their enemy, the King of Scots, to leave them in peace but did not pay their taxes to their own king for they had nothing left to give.

The King's cousin, the Earl of Lancaster, contemptuous of Edward's infatuation with Gavaston, raised an army with the sole purpose of capturing the most hated man in England. Gavaston had arrived in Newcastle to stay with the King and Queen and when Edward heard that Lancaster was marching north, he left with Piers taking a boat down the coast to Scarborough. The queen and other members of his court were left in Newcastle. Piers took sanctuary in Scarborough Castle whilst Edward began desperately to search Yorkshire for reinforcements but whilst he was away, the Earls of Pembroke and Surrey, accompanied by Lord Percy arrived and lay siege to Scarborough Castle.

Gavaston stared moodily from the ramparts out towards the sea. Scarborough was built on top of the cliffs, a formidable fortress. The great bay curved around in a wide arch, the sea lapping the sandy beach. Sea birds glided noisily overhead and Gavaston contemplated their carefree flight as he considered his own future. The castle stores were low and if Edward did not return within the week he could not hold out. Below him the Earl of Pembroke's forces rested because it was Sunday. On the outskirts of the camp he could see the earl's pavilion, striped blue and red canvas and outside Pembroke's falcons sat on their perch, hoods covering their eyes, ready for their masters return from mass, when he would exercise them as he did every Sunday.

Gavaston's ego was so great he failed to understand the hatred the nobles felt for him and in his arrogance he did not comprehend the danger. Yet he had cunning and a natural intelligence. Although to amuse Edward, he had poked fun at the earl of Pembroke, his instinct told him that of all the noble earls who had taken arms against their king, Pembroke was the most honest and honourable. Gavaston made up his mind that if he had to surrender it would be to Pembroke. The following week, when the king had not returned, Gavaston sent a herald to Pembroke and received the earl's oath, given on the Sacrament, that in return for guaranteeing the safety of Piers Gavaston, the castle would be surrendered into his hands.

Pembroke escorted Gavaston south where Parliament would decide his future. They arrived at the earl's manor of Wallingford where he lodged Gavaston, under guard, while the earl visited his wife who lay sick a few miles away at Deddington. The following day, before Pembroke had returned, the Earl of Warwick appeared at the manor gates and ignoring the protests of Pembroke's men, took custody of the prisoner and led him away to his own castle at Warwick.

The Earls of Warwick, Lancaster and Hereford were determined that Gavaston would not slither away for a few months of comfortable banishment on one of the king's estates in Gascony and return when the hue and cry had died down. They threw him into the darkest dungeon of Warwick Castle. By the light of a smoking torch, thrust into an iron wall sconce, he could see and hear water running down the slimegreen walls. Manacled by his wrists and ankles, his only companions during his waiting period were the scurrying, black rats, nibbling their way through the wet straw that covered the earthen floor. After three days in captivity Gavaston, always so fastidious about his appearance, emerged in a sorry state. Early on a fine, bright morning they brought him blinking into the castle yard. Warwick, Lancaster and others were waiting. Ignoring his cries that Pembroke had promised him safe conduct, they tied him to a grey palfrey and led him from the castle to his execution.

Bad news travels fast and when the king heard that his dearest brother had been murdered by Lancaster and others on Blacklow Hill, he collapsed with grief and despair and shut himself away in his chamber for many hours. The Earls of Pembroke and Surrey, furious that an oath of safe conduct had been dishonoured rode, with all their men, to join the king. Their action strengthened the king's position and averted civil war, but Edward vowed he would avenge the death of Piers when the opportunity came.

The remaining months of summer and autumn proved difficult for Edward. He missed the easy fellowship he had enjoyed with Piers. He rode to his manor of Langley in Hertfordshire, and rowed, fished and swam in the River Gade. The parkland and farm of Langley had always pleased him and there he indulged his interest in animal husbandry and the companionship of the estate's peasants helped him to forget the loneliness of kingship. In this way king Edward nursed his grief.

Isabella had been distraught when her husband and his lover had left her in Newcastle and it was Lord Percy and the Earl of Pembroke who had come to her rescue and escorted her south to her husband at Langley Manor. Her abandonment was more distressing because she was three months pregnant with her first child. Pembroke said little but everyone, except the king himself, noticed his frosty disapproval of the king's actions. When the queen gave birth to a healthy son, on a misty day in November, Edward and the people rejoiced and everybody, from the king to the humblest of his subjects, were sure that the problems of the past few years had come to an end.

Sir Philip Mowbray, governor of Stirling Castle, had withstood a siege for many months and without relief knew he could not hold the fortress for King Edward indefinitely. If the Earl of Pembroke had still been in command in Scotland, Sir Philip would have felt more confident, but as things stood he fretted and sent messages to his king with regular monotony. By mid summer 1313 he was desperate. He had not received any orders and on this particular day stood on the battlements watching the activities of the Scots far below commanded by Edward Bruce. It was a grey day with a westerly wind, threatening rain before the evening. His eye was caught by a group of horsemen riding towards the main entrance. As they drew closer he recognized the pennant of Edward Bruce and saw him among the group. Mowbray rattled down the steps to the courtyard in time to witness the opening of the postern gate. His sergeant called, "My lord, it's Edward Bruce, who says he has a proposition to put before you." Sir Philip, tired of waiting for instructions from the king and aware that his men's spirits were at a low ebb, knew he needed a miracle to break the present impasse.

Edward Bruce, affable even when enduring a lengthy siege said, "Mowbray, this situation is as unpleasant for us as it is for you. Surrender and I guarantee you and all your men safe conduct to the border." "Mowbray replied, "This is no more than you have offered me before," but Bruce would not be put off and said, "Face facts, your king has much to occupy his mind and he's forgotten you." There was something in what Bruce said, but the garrison had hung on this long and he was loathed to give up now. Bruce, watching Mowbray's expression said, "Look here, this siege is tiresome to us, but time is on our side not yours and we'll win eventually, surely you know that. Without relief you can't survive, must you sit it out until you're all bags of bones." "I'll not surrender without my king's command," Mowbray persisted. Edward Bruce drew a deep breath. An idea had been formulating in his mind for the past hour and he said, "Mowbray, I'm a reasonable man. Give me your word that you'll surrender Stirling to its rightful Lord, King Robert of Scotland, one year and a day from now, on St John's day, if your king has not relieved you by that date. I for my part, give my word to raise the siege tomorrow." Mowbray looked stunned. It was a novel idea, but dangerous since King Edward had not acknowledged any of his messages since the previous autumn. He voiced his fears, "If I make such a bargain how will my lord king know? Many times I have sent despatches, but only you know if my messengers have got through your camp." Edward smiled, "For sure we have stopped two, but the others?" he shrugged. Then he said. "We have known one another a long time, give me your pledge and you yourself may have an escort to the border and be your own messenger to your king." The bargain was struck and the following morning the Scottish army began to lift their siege of Stirling Castle, while Sir Philip Mowbray began his journey south to put Edward Bruce's challenge before his king.

Edward was at Langley enjoying the pleasures of harvest time. He listened to Bruce's ultimatum with mixed feelings. At first he was angry at Bruce's bare-faced cheek, but as he considered more deeply he came to the conclusion that another invasion of Scotland was not only long overdue, but could be a godsend. Full-scale victory over the rebellious Scots would enable him to reinforce his authority over Lancaster and the rest of his rebellious nobles. Perhaps without realizing it Bruce had given him the opportunity he needed.

When the harvest had been safely gathered in, Edward sent out writs to his nobles and sheriffs to muster their men and supplies at Berwick by the first week of June 1314. Throughout the autumn and winter Edward enthusiastically prepared for war. All east coast ports mobilized shipping in readiness to ferry supplies up the east coast to Edinburgh and from all over England wagons, carts, horses and oxen rolled their slow and weary way towards Berwick. Archers from Wales, men at arms from Shropshire and Warwickshire, foot soldiers sent and paid for by the citizens of London, veterans from other wars as well as raw, untrained fellows eager for plunder. Smiths, cooks, furriers, carpenters, washerwomen and prostitutes all made their way north for the grand invasion and destruction of the king's enemies. When all these multitudes of men, women and beasts had assembled, the organizing of the army began. The knights into their battalions, men at arms and archers commanded and chivvied into place by their constables, until the army like a mighty beast was ready to move forward across the border to reclaim Scotland for the English king.

FOR FREEDOM ALONE

"You said what?" Robert had stormed when he first heard that Edward had raised the siege of Stirling and issued a challenge to the English. Never had Edward Bruce seen his brother so angry. "You bloody fool! Now I'm committed to a full scale battle which I don't want and which I'm not sure we can win." "Rob, see sense," persisted his brother. "Keeping men around Stirling throughout the winter is a waste of time." Robert was red in the face and had been shouting and blustering at Edward Bruce for sometime. When finely he had control of himself he said. "Can you not understand we can't fight England in open battle. We can't match their wealth or numbers. Why do you think I've played my game of attack and withdraw for so long? I thought you at least understood." The two men were alone in the king's chamber at Scone. In slightly more measured tones the king continued. "Well it's done now and we must prepare." Edward replied in a chastened voice, "You know you can depend on me."

The years between the first parliament at St Andrews to Edward Bruce issuing his foolhardy challenge at the gates of Stirling Castle, in the summer of 1313, had been busy and productive for King Robert. He had little time for merrymaking, laughter or the joys of hunting. Comyn supporters, lead by the Earl of Dunbar, still opposed him particularly in the south–east of Scotland. Scotland's administration, neglected for so many years, had to be re-established and taxes long overdue collected but Scotland was an impoverished kingdom and little enough reached King Robert's exchequer.

During the campaigning seasons Edward Bruce, Robert Boyd, James Douglas and on occasions King Robert himself, attacked England's northern counties. They stole cattle, removed property, burnt, plundered and when necessary killed, until the English in Northumberland and Cumberland, willingly paid ransom to the Scottish commanders to be left in peace. With the English money King Robert purchased weapons from English merchants, who secretly did business with their own king's enemy and on early morning tides vessels slipped silently away from Dunwich, Kings Lynn and other eastern ports bound for Aberdeen and captained by shrewd men of business.

King Robert continued harrying his enemies, refusing to face them in open battle and he opposed the deployment of men to besiege fortresses. Success was never guaranteed unless the defending English had been weakened beforehand by weeks of short rations and prolonged fighting.

In the autumn of 1313 the King of Scots rode again into northern England, driving off cattle and demanding ransom money. When he returned in November he sent out writs to his nobles to assemble at Linlithgow to discuss the king's plans for the continuation of the war against England. The weather was golden and crisp, unusually pleasant for the time of year as the earls, barons and lairds came at their king's bidding. The king set before them his requirements for the spring, he did not demand, he was too intelligent and experienced in the manipulation of men to antagonize them, but neither did he give them the opportunity to put forward objections. When the time came for departure to their estates and manors, their spirits were high and they were united in their determination. At long last they would meet their enemy openly and they were in no doubt that they would be led by a man proven to be an invincible warrior.

Before the king threw himself into planning and training for the forthcoming trial of strength, he allowed himself the luxury of family celebrations; marriages between his family and the family of the Earl of Ross. It was no easy task to persuade Edward to honour his betrothal vow to Ross's daughter. During the past year Edward had fallen in love with Isabel, the youngest sister of David Earl of Atholl and the lovers had met alone secretly on many occasions, the young maid flying to him like a bird on joyful wings at Edward's bidding. Now she was pregnant and Edward was anxious to marry the girl, but on this occasion he could not move his brother who commanded him to honour his pledge to Ross whom he would not have offended. He told Edward, "I'll need all the support I can get from the northern barons and there must be a link between Ross and the royal house," To make doubly sure, he ordered the marriage to take place between his youngest sister Matilda and Ross's son Hugh.

Edward Bruce had to choose between loyalty to his kinsman or his sweetheart and wisely he chose the former, presenting himself at the Abbey of Scone looking as impressive as his noble brother, the king. His young bride hardly dared to look at him and kept her eyes fixed on his boots, occasionally glancing up with shy, apprehensive eyes. Their kinsfolk bedded the pair, the young wife tense with anticipation of the unknown. Edward indulgently laughed and stroked her cheek. "Relax little one," he had said and the king and her parents standing at the foot of the bed had all smiled reassuringly. Her father had said "God bless you both," then she was left alone with her husband.

Matilda Bruce had spent her childhood with her mother who, after the death of her Bruce husband had remarried Sir Richard Wallace. For safety, Sir Richard had taken his bride and stepdaughter to his estate on Arran, for the Wallace kinsmen had been marked men when the English held sway in Scotland. Later, on the king's advice, he had sought safety with the Lady Christiana in the far isles of the west and Matilda had known her brother only through the stories of his deeds told when the family sat down to eat. Like all Bruce kinsfolk she was a fine-looking girl, tall and slender, with thick, yellow hair and a full, humorous mouth. On her wedding night she was as apprehensive as her new sister-in-law, but Hugh of Ross was well pleased with his bride and was not so bold and experienced a man as Edward Bruce. They came to their bridal bed on equal terms and grew together in love.

The king left the wedding celebrations a happy man and as he explained to his Christine later that night, "If I should fall, when I encounter the English, my brother Edward will inherit Scotland and I hope produce a legitimate son." "Hush dearest, murmured Christine sleepily, her head lying on his shoulder, do not speak of your death, it will bring bad luck. At that remark Robert had laughed saying, "My girl, there is no such thing as luck, only common sense and hard fighting."

In his own chamber the Earl of Atholl lay awake for many hours, going over and over in his mind the harm that the Bruce family had done to his own kindred in past years, although they always pretended to be his friends. His father's years of loyalty to Bruce had brought him to the gallows, suffering the death of a traitor in London. Now his sister, gentle foolish Isabel, branded a whore and left with child because of her love and loyalty to another Bruce. When he had last seen his sister he had told her of her lover's desertion. Her anguished screams had echoed around the castle walls until her old nurse had said, "Hush, hush my dove, do you want to harm your child?" Isabel had continued to wail saying she did not care if her child died. Everybody within her brother's castle knew of Isabel's disgrace. One or two said she was to blame, running to him in that way, but most sadly shook their heads, Sir Edward was after all the king's brother. In her distress she had begged her brother to speak to Edward Bruce and tell him that she and the child had first claim to his loyalty. Edward had replied, "Were I free to marry as I please there is no lass in Scotland I would rather wed than Isabel, but as it is I wed for Scotland." He might have added, I am to be my brother's heir, therefore I must please him, but David Strathbogie stormed out of Edward's chamber and as he stood witness to Edward Bruce's marriage to Ross's sister he vowed that one day he would take revenge on the Bruce kinsmen.

A short while after this the king was guest at another marriage. At Sir Richard Wallace's manor of Riccarton the marriage of his niece Margaret to Sir Thomas Shaw was celebrated. The family chapel was barely large enough to permit close family and their royal guest to enter. At the chapel door the bride's hand was placed into her husband's. Then the priest led the pair to the altar to receive God's Sacrament and blessing on their union. Afterwards Bruce congratulated them, they made a fine couple. Tom Shaw was proud and content with his Margaret. Whilst she smiled at the young husband for they had loved one another since their childhood. Eleanor Wallace, the king's stepmother, remarked, "He's a fortunate man to marry a maid equal to him in fortune and character. I'm sure they'll live contentedly together." Later, at the bridal feast, when the king toasted the wedded pair, he remembered Margaret's father, Sir William Wallace, who had given up so much for Scotland. Then he thought about his own wife and daughter, still imprisoned in England and compared himself with Wallace. Wallace had given all for love of Scotland whilst he had lost all for love of himself. Before leaving Riccarton he prayed alone in the chapel for guidance in the months to come.

While he awaited the arrival of King Edward and his army King Robert decided to take the castles still left in English hands. Then the English king would have nowhere to run to. It was true, in the past he had opposed deploying his men to besiege fortresses and had taken castles by guile, but now the fewer footholds the English had the better.

In mid winter, on a moonless night, King Robert himself led an attack to recover the port of Berwick. Scaling ladders were successfully attached to the walls and the king directed his men in hushed tones. Their weapons had been carefully strapped to their backs where they were unable to clatter and clang and give warning to an alert guard. Carefully, in the darkness, the men began their climb. Occasionally the rope swung and the wooden steps knocked against the wall, but they continued slowly, not daring to allow their boots to scrape on the rocky surface.

The attack was unexpected and the English garrison were hiding from the winter weather in the gatehouse, kitchens and great hall, in fact anywhere where a good fire burned merrily, but far below in the courtyard one restless creature did hear the noises made by the invaders. A garrison dog kicked out because he had picked a fight with the commander's hound, prowled around seeking shelter from the bitter weather. Ears alert and nose twitching, he heard the approaching Scots and began to bark, running backward and forwards and jumping up and down excitedly. Finally he stood on his hind legs, front paws on the wall, head thrown back, loudly proclaiming his anger and alarm. The men in the gatehouse nearest to the commotion heard the noise. "Has that dog found another nest of rats?" roared the sergeant, who stamped outside carrying the wooden bar used to wedge the door shut. His intention was to throw the wood at the offending animal, but when he saw the dog's agitated behaviour he was certain that this time it was two-legged rats that disturbed his peace. The man quietened the dog and stood for a few moments listening before ordering his men onto the battlements and sounding the alarm. The Scots lost the advantage of surprise and the men who had rushed forward to be the first into Berwick Castle tried to scramble down. The English dislodged the ladder and threw spears, stones and whatever else came to hand in the darkness onto the heads of their enemy.

In the cold light of morning they found the ladders lying in crumbled heaps at the foot of the walls and the commander ordered them to be hung symbolically on a pillory in the centre of Berwick town. That day the dog became the hero of the castle and was made a great fuss of by the men whom he had saved. When he stretched himself in front of the kitchen fire, well fed and contented, none of the cooks dare put their boot behind him to move him on.

After the disappointment at Berwick king Robert moved his forces north to Perth, another fortress still under English control. Perth had been under pressure for sometime, vulnerable since the fall of Dundee, but because of the strength of its walls and towers and the surrounding moat it remained firm.

The king arrived just before Christmas and positioned his army around the city walls, preparing to starve Perth into submission. His men built makeshift huts for protection from the easterly wind and dug deep and wide trenches between themselves and the city walls with sharpened staves embedded into the pit bottoms. The only safe route in and out of the city was along the roads leading from the city gates and these they guarded securely.

The garrison were professional soldiers who had not been paid for many months. They had not been re-supplied from England since the early autumn and now their rations would be cut so they watched the Scots with alarm. After completing their preparations, the Scots sat down around their campfires and sang and told stories. King Robert launched two daylight attacks but after the failure of both he appeared to lose heart and under the watchful eyes and to the relief of his enemy he gave the order to break camp. Armour and weapons were stowed away into wagons, supplies packed onto ponies, shelters burnt and to the accompaniment of jeers and whistles from the watching garrison on the castle walls, King Robert's army turned their backs on Perth and marched away.

Sir William Oliphant, garrison commander, watched with mixed feelings. He was a Scot and had held Stirling Castle with great courage against King Edward 1. He had suffered starvation and bombardment from the English siege engines and when the castle fell the English king imprisoned him for four years, refusing all offers of ransom from his family. He had obtained his freedom after swearing on the Holy book that he would return to Scotland to hold Perth Castle for the English. A man of honour, he held firm to his vow, but as he watched the retreating banners of Scotland he found it hard to conceal his disappointment. Nonetheless, that night and for a week following, he doubled the guards and only when he was sure that the Scottish army had truly departed did he order an oxen to be killed and allowed his men as much ale as they could drink by way of celebration.

The Earl of Strathearn was also lodged at Perth and although Oliphant always showed Strathearn the respect due to his position, there was little love lost between the two men. Strathearn was morose and moody, dwelling on the loss of his younger sons as hostages of the English and the betrayal of his eldest son who followed King Robert. The earl's wife, the Lady Agnes, was daughter to a Comyn and her bitterness towards the Bruce king constantly spilled out and she tortured herself and the earl, her husband, about Robert Bruce and his hostile pursuit of her kinsmen. Oliphant tried to avoid the earl and his lady whenever possible and dreaded a prolonged siege, although he was sure that Lady Agnes could have hurled fire and brimstone from her own lips at Bruce and his men. Now King Robert had departed and he did not expect to see him again until spring.

King Robert led his army eastwards until the towers and battlements of Perth were no longer on the horizon. They arrived at a forest and he ordered his men to camp among the trees and build shelters for themselves. They could not imagine why they should make camp in the middle of nowhere for there was no target worth attacking that they could see.

At Perth, the Christmas feast passed pleasantly. King Robert and his men had gone and although the English king had not sent the garrison's pay or reinforcements, at least they were alive. By Twelfth Night the garrison was relaxed and full of Christmas cheer and the following morning they awoke to find themselves prisoners of King Robert.

The fall of Perth had been achieved in this manner. When King Robert had laid siege to Perth he had had some small hope that Oliphant, once renowned for his fiercely patriotic stand against the old English king at Stirling Castle, and the Earl of Strathearn, would surrender because of the lack of support from their English master. King Robert had personally spoken to both men, but one held doggedly to his vow whilst the other suffered under the burden of his wife's tongue. However, there were other men living in Perth who held to King Robert's cause. One such was a tanner who carried on his business on the banks of the Tay. He was in his middle years, with a large family relying on him, but when he was young he had marched with Wallace and was a veteran of Stirling and Falkirk. One dark, wet night he made his way to the Scottish lines and asked to see the king.

The king received Peter the Tanner with friendship and over tankards of ale Peter told his king what he most wanted to hear. Perth Castle was built with the River Tay acting as a natural moat on its south side and a cut had been dug around the remaining walls, into which the Tay flowed forming a moat. Peter's tannery was close to the castle walls and he had noticed that along the upper reach of the moat, before it ran back into the River, it was sufficiently shallow to allow a man to wade through it. The shallows usually coincided with the ebb of the tide going down the Firth when the water level was sufficient to make a difference. "I'll show you the way across," Peter had offered, but the king said "A crossing must be made at night, when the flow of water coincides with a moonless sky, but you may show my men where the ford is to be found."

Alexander Pilche, merchant turned warrior, from Inverness, was amongst the king's most trusted followers. He knew Perth well. Dressed in his short wadmal surcoat and cloak of poor, thin wool, the following day he went with Peter to his tannery. Peter said that Alexander was a distant cousin to his wife and had come to Perth to work. That story covered Pilche's sudden appearance and his lodging with the family. Alexander did not rush his survey but a few nights later he returned to his king with his good news.

The following day Alexander returned to Perth, to continue his spying, and the king gave orders to break camp. They bided their time in the forest east of Perth for two weeks, but on Twelfth Night, when the garrison at Perth was enjoying the final night of festivities, the king himself led his men to the edge of the moat. Arrayed in heavy chain mail and helm surmounted by a golden circlet, King Robert tested the moat bottom and took his first step into the cold, murky shallows. With each cautious step he probed the muddy bottom in front of him with his lance. In the middle the water came up to his neck, but each careful step took him closer to the further bank. It was bitterly cold, and he found it hard to keep his teeth from chattering loudly. His men followed closely, acting as a human bridge and passed across ladders to scale the walls. Occasionally they heard shouts and laughter from within the castle which reassured the king that the garrison was unsuspecting. Carefully, so very carefully and quietly they fixed their ladders to the walls and the king, his teeth clenched to stop their chatter, led his men up the dark, slippery wall to the battlements.

The men were in the great hall, watching mummers enacting an exciting Christmas story. The garrison fool had blackened his face with soot and disguised as an infidel pranced up and down on the tables waving a stick with a stuffed sheep's bladder attached to it. Whenever he found a drunken man with his head lolling on the table he brought the bladder down with some force on the tousled head and the audience rocked with laughter. A large fire blazed in the hearth and ale and wine flowed freely. Everybody was very hot and in varying degrees of drunkenness so that they had opened the main door to allow in the cold, night air. It was the foolish Moor who first saw King Robert in the doorway flanked by his captains. The fool stood on the table, a bewildered expression on his face, his arm raised with the wand and attached bladder swinging backwards and forwards. Slowly the revellers became aware of the intruders.

Each man had his dagger on the table to cut meat and bread but as custom demanded, all other weapons had been left at the entrance to the hall. In their bemused state some struggled to their feet but just as many remained where they sat. Some tables and benches were knocked over and Oliphant's chair crashed backwards as he jumped to his feet. The king's men entered into the hall, but few of the defenders were prepared to take on an impossible fight and the castle was taken with little loss of life.

Malaise of Strathearn, with the point of his sword pressed into the castle steward's chest demanded, to know where his father the Earl of Strathearn could be found since he was not among the men in the hall. The king had ordered Malaise to find his father before Douglas or Randolph could lay their hands on him.

The earl had retired early with an attack of indigestion, his lady with one of her headaches. When their eldest son burst into their chamber Lady Agnes was already in bed whilst her husband sat by the fire. He had begun to undress, his boots kicked off and his long, black, fine-woollen surcoat lay on the clothes chest, across its breast his family crest embroidered in gold thread shone in the light from the fire. Lady Strathearn gave a shrill cry and the earl jumped to his feet as their son entered the room. The young man lay aside his broadsword and with his men guarding the doorway he walked swiftly to his mother and put his arm around her shaking shoulders. "Now, mother all is well, no harm will come to you." The lady kept repeating "Oh, Malais, my son." Meanwhile the earl had regained his composure. "Our own son has come to arrest us," he snorted in disgust and looked at the men in the doorway, some of whom he recognized. "I see my men have also deserted their lord. Was I not a fair man to you all?" His son held up his hand to stop his father's angry recrimination. "Father you must come with me to the king and pay him your allegiance while you still can." "You dare to tell your own father what he must do?" he snapped back, but his wife began to cry loudly again and shouting, "Robert Bruce killed your cousin. He's been excommunicated by the Holy Father in Rome and is outside God's mercy, you can't ask your father to kneel before such a man." Her son glanced at his men before saying "Hush mother. Father you must come now before the King sends for you." His father grudgingly saw the wisdom of his son's suggestion and began slowly to dress himself. When the Lady Agnes saw that her husband intended to pay homage to the Bruce she began to make such a noise that when her ladies came to her, the men left the chamber with much relief and the sound from their heavy boots as they clattered down the steps of the tower drowned her wailing.

The king sat by the fire warming himself, Oliphant standing defiantly before him. "Come, Sir William, offer me your sword and you may have your honourable freedom." "My lord, I pledged myself to the King of England. I can't ignore my oath on the Holy Book, besides that he has my young sister hostage, I'll not forget my responsibilities to her." The king understood the man's dilemma. "You're an obstinate fool, but honest, unlike your English master who has left you and your men without support." He shrugged, "But have it your own way, in time perhaps you'll see sense."

Then the king turned his attention to Strathearn, who. prompted by his son. knelt before the king and pledged his allegiance, but the king did not look as benign as he had with Oliphant and said, "Because of your son's loyalty and because I understand your family allegiances I'll grant you your life, but your earldom and estates I give to your son and place you in his keeping. Don't leave the boundaries of his lands without my permission." Strathearn looked stunned, and was about to protest but felt the pressure of his son's hand on his shoulder and the hostility on the faces of the men who surrounded the king. He looked and felt a broken man, torn between loyalty to his wife's kinsmen, his youngest son's hostages in England and his eldest son who followed Bruce. Now no man trusted his word and his family was split in two.

The new young earl escorted his silent parents to his lands, but before returning to King Robert he begged them both to live quietly. His mother turned her angry gaze away from her first born but his father gave his word for next time the Bruce would not be so generous.

The English garrison were offered their lives and told that those who wished could pay homage to Bruce and fight for Scotland and there were some who did this, but the remaining men were given an escort to the border. As they left, King Robert's men began the destruction of Perth Castle. The English king would find no sanctuary there if he passed that way.

It was late on a March afternoon during the third week of Lent. The governor of Edinburgh Castle, and some of his men had retired to the tiny chapel of St Margaret to observe mass. Whilst there, they heard the commotion from the east gate, the Scots were launching yet another attack. The worshippers saw no need to hurry unduly to retrieve their weapons and shields from the church doorway, because the path leading up to the east gate was so narrow and precarious they were confident the Scots would withdraw again before dusk. They had attacked and withdrawn many times before.

This time the fighting was more determined than on previous occasions. Battering rams were used and in spite of the missiles raining down on them they pressed on with their attack. Each time splinters fell from the thick, iron-bound gates, the attackers cheered loudly and made a great deal of fuss. They continued their attack with such confidence that the governor was forced to order men from other sections of the walls to come to the aid of their comrades on the east gate.

The north wall of Edinburgh Castle was a rocky precipice offering no possibility of attack and it was from this area that the guards were withdrawn, leaving it undefended. From the cover of the rocks and trees, at the foot of the edifice, crept six men and with nimble, skilful movements they began to climb the rock face. Fingers and toes found crevices deep enough to grip and slowly, carefully they crawled their way upwards to the foot of the castle walls. They had not dared to hope that they would reach that far without being observed. Each man had a rope tied to his belt and that was tied to a rope ladder, once these were secured, men waiting below began scrambling up the first stage. Meanwhile the six climbers had begun the more difficult task, climbing the castle wall to secure their hold on the fortress. The English defenders, preoccupied with the open Scottish attack on the east gate, were taken by surprise. They found the enemy at their rear and there was such confusion that the east gate was opened from within and the main Scottish attackers poured through, massacring and plundering until the flames could be seen many miles away like a beacon on the craggy summit. English ships, lying in the Forth, hastily raised anchor and rowed out into the Forth away from danger, but they had already unloaded their provisions for the English king's army. Quantities of wine, salted meat, wheat and beans lay on the quay or in the king's warehouses, awaiting his arrival. Thomas Randolph, commander of the Scottish army, took charge of the captured provisions and arranged for their transportation to the Torwood, ready for the muster of the main Scottish army in the late spring. When this was done he ordered the destruction of the castle. The advancing English army would not have the protection of its thick walls, but he left the tiny chapel of St Margaret, he could not bring himself to order its destruction since it would serve no military purpose.

While the men of Scotland mustered at the Torwood, the men of England backed by Welsh archers were nearing their destination. Berwick was still in English hands and the atmosphere among the assembled army was one of excitement. Their king had promised lands and position in Scotland and much plunder when victory was theirs. They were confident of victory. The Scots could not stand and face such a mighty army as the English king commanded. Two and a half thousand heavily armoured knights, at least fifteen thousand foot soldiers and so many Welsh archers that no one was quite sure of their numbers. Supply wagons, herds of beef cattle with drovers, washerwomen and prostitutes, the numbers were so great that when the king gave the order to advance across the border the column stretched behind him for many miles. The men were organized into companies from each county, town and village, with a constable leading and occasionally he rode up and down the ranks, bullying or chiding men in danger of being left behind. The pace set was a steady twenty miles each day. Like a huge, fiery dragon, the army set forth prepared to settle the problem of the Scots once and for all.

From the beginning of May the Scottish lords began to arrive in the Torwood, west of Falkirk. There was plenty of cover from the trees and rocky outcrops and to the west was the safety of the hills, excellent country for foot soldiers. The old Roman highway connecting Edinburgh to Stirling ran through it and it was along that route that the English army would have to march to relieve Stirling Castle. King Robert allowed time to train his men and had raised every penny possible to purchase weapons and supplies. What he could not purchase he stole from northern England. The men of Carrick, Moray and Clydesdale sat around their fires sharpening pikes and staves and chatting to comrades from the isles and highlands.

When all had arrived, there were in the Scottish ranks five hundred lightly armed horsemen, six thousand infantry, and as half as many again supporting smiths, cooks and furriers. The king's spies reported the size and strength of the enemy but it came as no surprise, he knew he could never match English numbers. His army must defeat the English with discipline and force of arms. He recalled seeing Wallace camped by Irvine, training his pikemen, bellowing instructions to move forward, stand, level pikes, take the force. At the time it had amused him, now it was from Wallace he took his inspiration, not the chivalrous knights who had taught him the arts of warfare when he was a boy. His own grandfather and the old Earl of Gloucester had taught him to control a spirited stallion and to fight in close combat with mace and lance. He was surprised their spirits did not haunt him as he arranged his pikemen into companies and began training them to move together on command, pikes bristling like giant hedgehogs. The four companies each had a commander who fought with his men. The king's own schiltrom was made up of men from the west, brought to him by the Lady Christiana of the isles.

When the news had reached the isles that the king needed men for his fight against the English king, Rhuri Macgillivery, Christiana's half brother, refused to stir himself to lead the men of Uist and the isles. He had laughed. Who could say that King Robert would win? When his sister heard, she was furious and threatened to lead her men herself. This had caused Rhuri to laugh even louder and he continued pursuing his own business, until rumours spread among his household that the

Lady Christiana had ordered her smith to forge a helmet and shield suitable for her to wear in battle. They told Rhuri that she could be seen in the courtyard each morning practising with a two-handed claymore, her sergeant, with a grin on his face, defending himself as she tried to cut and hack at his shield. The claymore was as long as the lady herself and the men, who came daily to watch, wondered that she could raise the weapon at all. Eventually the sergeant, who bore the brunt of his comrades jokes said, "Lady, if you insist making Rhuri Macgillivery a laughing stock use a battleaxe, that at least is shorter than you are."

Her brother continued to view the whole episode as a joke and refused to muster the men, but his sister's persistence gained the grudging respect of the islesmen. In all weathers she was out arranging stores, weapons and galleys to transport her men to the mainland and continued practising with her battleaxe, wearing a shining new helmet, her hair in a long plait down her back.

The time for departure arrived, the galleys rode the crystal clear waters by the lady's castle in Uist and the whole island was in a hubbub of excitement. That night at dinner, the lady stood up and said, "Those who should lead you to battle have lost courage, but I haven't. The weather's fine and that's a good omen. We'll sail at first light and our king will reward you."

Before dawn had lit the sky, there was great activity by the galleys. The lady arrived followed by the men whom she had asked to be her captains. She wore a white, linen shift with a simple, woollen kirtle over such as serving women wore. A brown wadmel cloak was draped around her shoulders and all was held in place by an unadorned, leather thong. She did not wear the snow-white linen coif of a married lady, but a kerchief covered her plaited hair. No finery set her apart from any other, except for her father's crested ring, which she wore on a cord around her neck because it was too big for her fingers. Her men were respectful and silent, no one nudged or winked at his comrade and they raised a cheer when she said farewell to her young son and women, for other than her chaplain she took no attendants with her. Her son stood for a long time watching his mother. She had commanded him not to be tearful for one day he would lead the men of Uist, Moydart and the isles. Bravely he waved because his nurse said that his mother was a very special lady.

When Rhuri heard that his half-sister really had gone forth with her men he was wild with rage, never had he believed she would carry out her threat. She had made a fool of him. The men in his household stood together in small groups talking quietly and when he approached, they moved away and made no attempt to hold a conversation with their chief. An air of contemptuous disapproval settled over his household. With bad grace Rhuri admitted defeat and prepared to join King Robert. His little fleet arrived on the mainland a week after his sister's arrival, but she had not wasted any time and only by long marches could he hope to catch her up. On a wet and blustery afternoon they caught sight of her force. Rhuri spurred on his pony so that he could talk to her before his own men caught them up and tongues started wagging.

Christiana was silent and continued leading her men so that her brother was forced to match his pace to hers. Her silence made him even angrier for she placed him in the wrong. "This is no place for a woman, now I'm here you can return." "I've come this far Rhuri, I'll not turn back. Remember it's my son who will be chief one day and I want him to inherit the respect that our father's name had." Rhuri, red in the face, ground his teeth together with rage and looked as if he was about to strike her. He could not change her mind and it was plain that her men gave her their full support. Brother and sister remained aloof from each other but they joined their forces and marched to the Torwood together.

The arrival of the Lady of the Isles, with a large following of men, caused a stir in the camp. Upon hearing the news the king sent for her and to stop all jealousy, he also sent for Rhuri and greeted them together, although the whole camp knew of Rhuri Macgillivery's reticence to join his king. The king pretended he knew nothing of the circumstances of Christiana's arrival and treated Rhuri as a great and honoured chief, who had responded to his king's call with praiseworthy speed. Wisely, the lady wore a royal–blue, woollen kirtle embroidered at wrist and hems and hid her hair beneath a fine gauze coif. She wore no warlike garb but all noticed that her father's ring hung on a silver chain around her neck, not on her half-brother's finger. After the initial meeting with the king, Rhuri relaxed, adopting his usual swagger and began to enjoy the large gathering of men.

Christiana showed little interest in the problems of war and nothing more was seen of the helmet and battleaxe. After a few days she said to the king that the journey had tired her and that with his permission she would retire to her estates. The king laughed "Chrissy, you're a very cunning woman, no one has given me so much loyalty as yourself. Be sure I'll watch over you and your son's interest. I'll take command of your islesmen myself and will fight with them when the time comes, but I have a favour to ask of you. Take in your charge Sir William Oliphant, he's a stubborn man, but honourable. He was in the custody of Angus Og, but his captivity will be easier spent with a more gentle captor." When the lady took her leave Sir William rode with her, escorted by a number of Angus's men. Sir William had given the lady his pledge not to escape and the king was satisfied that he would not betray his trust. The king watched them leave and smiled to himself, for he had observed the mutual glances of interest which had passed between Christiana and her captive. 'Well, she'd led the life of a nun long enough,' he said to himself.

The king was as good as his word. Men from the islands, Ulster and the western highlands formed the king's schiltrom and he made Rhuri his aide and honoured him so that the wild tales of cunning and cowardice were silenced by his favour. Rhuri, for his part, served the king and Scotland well from that time onwards.

In recent years the Earl of Ulster had received letters from his daughter Elizabeth, begging him to intercede with the English king on her behalf, but King Edward could not be moved in his determination to keep the wife of Robert Bruce in custody. It was true that he had eased her burden somewhat by moving her to the Convent of Sixhills in Lincolnshire and had allowed Bruce's daughter to be taken from her prison in the Tower at London, to join her stepmother, but beyond this concession the king could not be moved. The Earl of Ulster's private hope was for a Scottish victory, but he admitted to himself that it would need a miracle of biblical proportions if Scotland's David were to gain victory against England's Gallioph, but God's actions had always been a mystery to the earl. Otherwise how could you account for Bruce's surprising success against all odds for so long? So the earl had secretly sent men to fight for Scotland whilst he himself commanded war galleys, guarding the sea route between Ireland and south-west Scotland, for the English king. Whenever a sail was sighted towards starboard, the earl and his captains watched the portside. In this way many opportunities to capture Angus Og and Scottish merchant ships were lost and this was as much assistance as the earl was prepared to give his son-in-law.

In the Torwood, the training of Scotland's army quickened pace. Sir Robert Keith, commanding the small force of lightly armed men, carried out mock cavalry charges towards each schiltrom, thundering at full gallop, making as much of a din as possible, towards their own men. Above the noise, Bruce and his other captains shouted commands at the solid ranks of men, STAND! LOWER PIKES! PREPARE! READY! But before impact the horsemen wheeled to left and right flanks. Then the pikemen moved forward on command, pikes lowered in attacking position. They found this action exhilarating and laughed and talked about it around their fires and there was a great sense of brotherhood among them.

When the king heard that the English had crossed the border and could be expected within the week, he rode around the Torwood, Bannock and the King's New Park testing the ground with his lance. He commanded Sir Robert Keith to ride his mounted men back and forth across the marshy ground surrounding the Bannockburn, testing it for its suitability for heavy cavalry. He divided the schiltroms, whilst two trained, two dug pits and ditches on each side of the road along which the enemy would be forced to march. The pits were covered with branches, bracken and loose turf. In this way the English would be forced to bunch up and would have no room for manoeuvre.

Scotland's destiny was achieved in this manner. The English army arrived at Falkirk on 22 June, just two days before the bargain made by Sir Philip Mowbray expired. Then King Robert ordered his men to retreat northwards from the Torwood and reassemble in the New Park, closer to Stirling Castle and close to the sacred shrine of St Ninian. There they blocked the English advance to Stirling and because of the hidden pits, the English king was forced to swing his army around to the east and into the marshy ground. The Bannockburn was at his back, whilst his foe faced him on the high ground with the shelter of the Torwood protecting their backs. King Edward halted his vanguard, allowing the column to close up in preparation for battle.

James Douglas, Robert Keith and a small band of mounted men watched their enemies. The sunlight flashed on armour, shields and helms. Both men recognized knights of renown amid the leading ranks of the English. Sir Robert had once been on friendly terms with the Earl of Pembroke, Clifford and Sir Marmaduke de Tweng and it was sad to think they were now on opposing sides, but each man had to follow his conscience and interests. They returned to their king and described the size and splendour of the English army. The king said, "It's necessary for us to know what we're facing, but spread the word that the English looked badly disciplined and without resolve. That'll keep our men in good heart."

At midday, while King Edward was resting, Sir Philip Mowbray, commander of Stirling Castle arrived. Edward Bruce had given him a safe conduct that he might seek out his lord, King Edward. Sir Philip beamed at the king and made no real effort to conceal the relief he felt. He knew well the terrain around Stirling and without doubt Bruce's army commanded the best ground. "Sire, thank God you have arrived before midsummer's eve. For sure there's no need for you to progress further. Under my agreement with Bruce you may re-supply the garrison without hinder." The king stared coldly at Mowbray, "Are you daring to suggest that having brought the army this far we return home without engaging the enemy, which is we are told half the size of our own?" Sir Philip looked embarrassed at his blunder, "Sire, the field of battle will not be easy. The terrain...." but he got no further. The king raised his hand in a dismissive action and turned to the Earl of Pembroke. "My lord Pembroke, send for all your captains and we'll discuss the forthcoming battle." While he awaited his staff the king said to Anthony Bek, Archbishop of York, his father's old friend and advisor. "What would my father have said Bek?" Bek smiled, "he would say, go forward and grind them into the ground. Your prestige in the kingdom and throughout Christendom will suffer if you don't. Besides, Scotland is a poverty-stricken place and Bruce can't employ cavalry nor archers and it was they who won your father his victory at Falkirk."

With the archbishop's words of reassurance ringing in his ears King Edward spoke with authority when his commanders arrived. When they heard that Mowbray had proposed they shun battle there was uproar around the table. The servants, squires and grooms outside the king's pavilion stopped what they were doing to listen to the raised voices and watched contemptuously as Sir Philip, red–faced and humiliated, left the meeting to return to his command at Stirling Castle.

After Sir Philip's banishment the meeting continued noisily. Everybody was keen to do battle, but disagreed how it should be fought. The king appointed another of his favourites, Gilbert de Clare, the young Earl of Gloucester, to command the vanguard, the most prestigious command in the army. Around the table thunderous faces glared at the king and Gloucester. Once again the king was giving an inexperienced boy the highest honour. The Earl of Hereford slammed his fist down on the table. "This is an outrage, my lord. As Constable of England it's my hereditary right to command the vanguard," he blustered. Around the table voices were raised in agreement. The king looked at Pembroke who nodded his head in agreement with the earl's statement. The outcome of the dispute was that Hereford and Gloucester would hold joint command, but Hereford glared at young Gloucester and said threateningly to Robert Clifford sitting beside him, "Just let that puppy countermand my orders." Arguments continued over the order of battle and many of the experienced warriors present felt increasing exasperation and concern because of their king's indecisiveness. Spirits were lifted somewhat when it was announced that the Earl of Atholl had arrived in the camp bringing with him Bruce's supplies which had been stored at Cambuskenneth.

Atholl had continued to harbour ideas of revenge for Edward Bruce's dishonourable treatment of his sister Isabelle. Early that morning, with the most faithful of his kinsmen and followers, he left Bruce's camp and attacked the Scottish supply depot, killing its commander and guards before riding triumphantly to the English camp. Atholl confirmed that Bruce had no cavalry to oppose King Edward's mighty force and that the Scots would fight on foot. This information boosted English morale further and that afternoon the army struck camp and began its final advance towards Stirling.

The vanguard, with its joint commanders, advanced along the old Roman road to attack the Scottish positions in the New Park, while a second brigade under the dual command of Clifford and Beaumont, circled around to the east. Their task was to relieve Stirling Castle whether Mowbray wanted it or not.

The vanguard expected to advance rapidly, but was slowed down by Bruce's camouflaged pits. Their intention had been to attack on a broad front but they were forced to close ranks along the road and ride in a column, three abreast, splashing through the ford of the Bannockburn. Under cover of the trees, on the top of the gently sloping hill of the New Park, the Scots waited. Once into the open, Gloucester and Hereford quickened the pace, both men determined to lead the vanguard into battle. Hereford tried to block Gloucester's progress. After all, a Bohen had led the vanguard of all victorious English armies for the past two hundred years and he could see no reason why this should change now. Gloucester, furious at the older man's pig-headedness increased his speed and took the lead.

Suddenly, on the brow of the hill, a horseman rode out from the trees and casually walked his mount along the edge of the wood. The rider rode a grey palfrey and wore chain mail and a light helmet surmounted by a gold, ornamental circlet of kingship could be clearly seen. The bright Scottish gold glinted in the sunshine. Simultaneously, the Earl of Hereford's young nephew, Henry, spotted the solitary rider and noticed Gloucester had overtaken his uncle in the race for leadership. The glory of the family name had to be upheld at all costs and Henry lowered his lance, spurred his horse and sped towards the King of Scots.

The Scottish pikemen, watching from the cover of the trees held their breath. Honour demanded that King Robert should not retreat from his enemy. As young Henry Bohen thundered towards his victim, lance sloped, body crouching low along his horse's neck, the watching Scots hardly dared to take further breath and watched silently as their king, on his small-boned gelding, took up the challenge. He collected his horse urging it into a controlled canter. The Englishman drew closer, riding as if towards a champion equally matched in the jousting. They met but Sir Henry in his youthful eagerness had misjudged the position of his lance to the unequal size of his opponent's pony and missed the noble king, but Bruce stood up in his stirrups and with great force brought his battleaxe down onto the young man's head. The helmet was split in two and the axe cut deeply into the unprotected head. The huge warhorse continued unchecked towards the woods, its master's body lolling in the saddle. From the trees a great roar arose from the men of King Robert's schiltrom, who were formed up ready to take on England's vanguard. The Earl of Hereford, witness to the defeat and death of his nephew, realized the danger they faced and shouted to his men to retreat. He need not have worried for the Scottish commander-in-chief was not yet ready for a serious encounter with his enemy. Quickly he brought his men under control. They were elated by their first taste of blood and satisfied themselves with catcalls and shouting abuse at the retreating English cavalry. Meanwhile King Robert sat quietly watching the enemy. His pony, excited by the encounter, danced restlessly, swishing its tail and tossing its head, breathing heavily through flared nostrils while it worried its bit. Sir Robert Keith rode up, "My lord, that was magnificent, but if it had turned out otherwise what would have been the outcome for Scotland? You mustn't place yourself in such peril," but Bruce replied. "Look, it's broken my axe." He had wrenched his axe free from its victim, but the shaft was split down its length. "I've had this axe since I gained my spurs," he lamented. There was a sorrowful expression on his face as he inspected the weapon closely and shrugged off Keith's chiding of his foolhardy action. He indicated his men and said, "If I don't face unequal odds, I can't expect them to."

Very shortly after this king Robert saw the second cavalry brigade led by Clifford and de Beaumont riding to the relief of Stirling. Thomas Randolph, Earl of Moray, had arrived just moments before, eager to congratulate his king, but the king said sharply, "Thomas, look yonder, your men need you. Cut off the English." Randolph saw the sun glinting on English armour and crestfallen for leaving his post, he rushed back to his schiltrom and assembled them ready to block the enemy's path.

When Clifford saw the Scots blocking his way he halted his men and the two forces glared across the divide between them. The Scots were in their massed formation, front ranks kneeling, their comrades standing behind them with pikes at the ready. The silence was broken by the sound of English visors being slammed shut ready for battle. Then the Scots banged on their shields with the butts of their pikes chanting, "SCOTLAND, SCOTLAND!"

In the English ranks, Sir William Deyncourt, who had not previously had experience fighting against the Scots said, "They must be joking, just look at that rabble," but Clifford, who had fought gallantly against Bruce for many years snapped, "Reserve your opinion until you have tested their muscle." Clifford raised his arm high to indicate the advance and set spur to his horse. The trot, the canter, each stallion in a race to be in the lead, faster, faster to the gallop, lances lowered for the impact, until they careered headlong into the formation of pikes. Sir William's bold words had taken him into the lead and he was among the first to be killed. His body fell from his plunging horse. His horse screaming with legs thrashing in its agony fell onto its side, pinning its master underneath. The Scots, with their backs braced against the impact, held firm. Without panic each man stood his ground. Clifford shouted to the trumpeter to sound the retreat and reform, leaving the ground littered with dead and dying men and horses. Once again the Scots taunted their enemy. "SCOTLAND, SCOTLAND." Once more the mighty warhorses thundered across the open ground towards the enemy, but they were unable to break the formation, their lances too short to reach the front ranks. Again they withdrew leaving behind the sad debris of war. Desperate to make some impression on the jeering Scots from a short distance, the English began to hurl their maces into the enemy, but as the deadly weapons flew through the air, Scottish shields were raised to meet the threat. The maces were piled up in the centre of the schiltrom and Thomas Randolph, inspecting the collection said, "They'll run out of maces shortly."

From his vantage point King Robert watched the mounting frustration of the English and said to James Douglas, "Take your division to the top of the slope where the English can see you, but don't join battle unless Randolph and the men of Moray need help." Douglas, accompanied by young Walter Stewart and their men, jogged to the top of the rise and roared their encouragement to Randolph's men below, cheering each time an English knight fell. Clifford called off the attack and angrily returned to his king while the Scots laughed them on their way. Exhilaration engulfed all the Scots. They had withstood an English cavalry charge and what they had done once they could do again.

The evening drew into the short northern midsummer's night.

King Robert sat at the campfire with his commanders, Keith, Boyd, James Douglas, his brother and young Walter Stewart, whose eager face beamed with unconcealed admiration for the older men. Randolph sat beside his king and Rhuri Macgillivery sat closeby, for he had taken a liking to the earl. In all the excitement no one had noticed that the Earl of Atholl had not been seen for some time.

"Friends," said the king, "It's time for us to decide. We've been successful today but we haven't faced the full force of the enemy. Tomorrow the English king will throw everything he's got at us. The noble Lord Wallace tried to stand against their might at Falkirk and failed. If we withdraw now, they'll keep Stirling, but we can still attack them as and when we wish and by autumn they'll have run out of food and hunger will drive them home. If we make a stand tomorrow we risk everything. So, I say to you who have so much to lose, decide and I will abide by your decision." They had listened intently to their king and he expected them to discuss the situation at some length, but almost before the last words had left his lips his captains clamoured loudly to stand on the morrow. They agreed all or nothing. Walter Stewart said, "Can we attack them now Sir, when they least expect it?" and the king laughed saying, "Patience lad." To the gathered assembly he said, "Let's drink to our success tomorrow." He left his commanders and rode around his army, chatting to the men and acknowledging their greetings.

Before he retired to snatch an hour of sleep his brother brought Sir Alexander Seton to him. Seton was a Scot, who had ridden with the English and he had been caught coming through the lines from the English side. After Clifford had returned at the head of his angry cavalry, Seton had watched the demoralized English foot soldiers, drinking and fighting drunkenly among themselves, without their commanders making any efforts to restraint them. He decided then that it was time to change his coat and ride with the Scots. "My lord, I offer you my sword. King Edward is not a fit commander and he'll bring ruin on his men. Attack now for his grip on his army is weak."

In the English camp King Edward sat listening to Clifford and the Earls of Hereford and Gloucester recount their encounters with the Scots. It was a setback but nothing more. He turned for advice to Pembroke who said, "My lord, we mustn't underestimate Bruce. I suggest we move the army to firmer ground away from these pits. If we cross the Bannock and reassemble on the opposite bank we'll have a better chance of forming ranks," but the king's new favourite Hugh Despenser, who sat beside the king said. "The ground there is too narrow for the cavalry." "That's true," argued Pembroke, "but here we'll flounder in the bogs and our beasts will break legs in Bruce's pits." All the earls agreed with Pembroke mainly because it made sense, but also because Despenser was opposed to the plan.

It was not quite dark when King Edward's vanguard moved forward across the boggy ground, but the firm ground was sufficient for the cavalry only. The infantry, archers and welsh knifemen, along with the baggage train, were forced to spend the short night in the marshland, wet, cold and very irritable. They raided the wagons carrying flasks of wine, which were passed around the camp to drown their sorrows and spent the night drinking and quarrelling. As the eastern sky lightened the English infantry held their heads in their hands, peering at their sergeants through bloodshot eyes. The sergeants kicked many archers into wakefulness or threw buckets of water over them. "Wake up you farts, how can you pull your bows when you see two of everything?"

King Robert awoke as a breathless messenger ran to him. "The Lord Atholl has attacked our stores, stolen our supplies and killed all who were there, my lord." The king's face had an expression of disbelief. His old friend's son, turned traitor and at such a time. Of course, there had been that trouble a few months earlier with Atholl's young sister and Edward and it was true that Atholl had been aloof since then, but the king had never dreamt he would seek revenge on the Bruce kinsmen in such a manner. Now they must claim victory in the forthcoming battle and capture the English stores or starve themselves. Well, he supposed, there was no use crying over spilt milk, the day must progress.

He made his confession to the Abbot of Inchaffray and kissed the Holy Staff of St Fillen, who surely had been responsible for bringing him safely through his turbulent years as King of Scots. Now for sure the Holy Saint would guide Scotland to victory. Bernard, Abbot of Arbroath was also present and carried St Columba's casket to confer the saint's blessing on the army. King Robert spoke to his men and Benedictine monks read written copies of the king's speech to those who could not hear his words.

"My lords and people. We set great store by freedom and we have suffered many hardships for eight years and more for our right to this kingdom, to honour and liberty. These armed lords who you see before you have already insolently ordered our destruction. They do not believe that we are able to resist. They glory in their horses, baggage trains and other worldly goods, but this is a blessed day, on which St John the Baptist was born. With Christ the Lord going before us we will conquer and bring an end to these years of warfare."

Then the king knighted certain men who had impressed him with their steadfast courage. Among them were Walter Stewart and Tom Shaw for the king had grown fond of Shaw, son-in-law to the dead Wallace, who so many years before had also brought Scotland to battle.

The Scots advanced from the cover of the woods in the New Park, their banners fluttering bravely in a light wind with the Abbot of Inchaffray walking before them, bearing a cross. They arranged themselves into their schiltroms and the Abbot lowered his hands as a sign for them to kneel. In full view of their enemy, with heads bent, they said the paternoster.

King Edward watched, amazed as the Scots emerged from the cover of the trees and formed ranks. "Sir Ingram, I do believe the devils intend to fight us!" Ingram replied, "I can't believe they'll take on our cavalry. Surely not!" But when the whole of the Scot's army knelt, the English king, thinking he had misunderstood the situation, laughed and exclaimed loudly. "No! Yon folk kneel to ask mercy of us," but Ingram replied, "True sire, but not I think from you. They appeal to our Lord for his mercy. They'll win or die." "So be it then," said the king. He turned to his trumpeter and ordered the advance.

The English vanguard, drawn up on the dry, narrow ground was forced to bunch behind each other and in some places were six deep which was the only way they could fit into the available land, instead of the usual two orderly rows of heavily armoured knights. At the sound of the trumpet the Earl of Gloucester moved forward.

At the brim of the rising ground three, schiltroms faced their enemy. The central division, under the command of Randolph, to his right Edward Bruce's divison, whilst James Douglas and the newly knighted Walter Stewart took up position on the left flank. King Robert, in command of his Islesmen and men from Clydesdale, held his division hidden among the trees. Rhuri Macgillivery stood with his men in this schiltrom eager to meet the English in battle. Since his arrival in the Torwood, Rhuri had become a close admirer of the king and was very excited to be fighting with him. Standing in the second rank, as close to his king as his lowly status permitted, was Moira's fiery man, from the Isle of Arran. He was as ready to attack the king's enemies as once he had been to attack the king himself.

King Robert raised his hunting horn to his lips and blew one long, loud note. The Scottish advance began. Moving forward, the men in the front ranks saw quite clearly the English thundering towards them. Fear lurked in the pit of their stomachs and many prayed over and over again "Hail Mary full of Grace, Hail Mary full of Grace," but none broke rank. Their eyes set steady on the enemy, they marched determinedly forward with pikes sloped, bristling like huge hedgehogs. Then above the noise of the approaching English, the Scots commanders and chiefs roared, "STAND!" To a man they halted, the front ranks knelt and each soldier braced his back to withstand the impact when the English would collide into their pikes.

The English crashed into the forest of steel-tipped pikes and above the terrifying noise of men's yells and the impact of arms, could be heard the screams of wounded and dying horses. Amid the first casualties of that terrible scene was the Earl of Gloucester, whose stepfather had warned Robert Bruce, Earl of Carrick, that King Edward 1 had ordered his arrest. Quite close to Gloucester lay the body of Robert Clifford, veteran of so many Scottish campaigns and half hidden by his fallen horse lay young Sir John Comyn, son of the murdered Comyn of Greyfriars.

In the constricted confines of the battlefield, littered by so many corpses of men and horses, the vanguard found it impossible to withdraw and regroup while the ranks in the rear were unable to reach the enemy at all. Once again the three schiltroms moved forward, forcing the English to retreat back towards the banks of the Bannock. The Earl of Pembroke raised his visor and gazed around the field of battle. If they failed to scatter the Scots formation the cavalry would be pushed into the bog and waters. Their only defence was his Welsh archers who had taken up their positions on the north bank of a small burn which flowed into the Bannock. Pembroke turned to his young squire. "Ride to the commander of the archers and order him to send arrows into the Scots."

King Robert, watching from the trees, saw the effect the arrows were having on the tightly packed Scots, their flight adding to the noise of battle. He sent an urgent message to Sir Robert Keith and his horsemen, hidden from the sight of the English. 'Attack the archers with all haste.'

Keith circled around approaching the archers from the rear. So absorbed were they with the task in hand that Keith was upon them before they noticed. The Welsh survivors scattered, running in panic towards their own infantry who, so far, had not been involved in the battle. Confused and leaderless, the archers continued running to the safety of the baggage train and took no further part in the battle.

King Robert watched the fleeing archers and was relieved when Keith called off his men before they could penetrate too far into the English lines and ordered his own archers, picked men from the Forest of Selkirk, to advance and take up the Welshmen's vacant positions. Once in place they covered the English cavalry with arrows causing confusion and many deaths among the closely packed knights.

The division commanded by James Douglas and Walter Stewart received the most casualties from English arrows and although they still held firmly to their formation, many fine men fell.

King Robert dismounted, joined his men, crossed himself and led them forward to assist Douglas. Once again the mass of spearmen pushed forward, driving the English before them, until the four Scottish divisions joined together in one huge wall of pikes forcing their enemy back into the waters of the Bannockburn.

The English were so tightly packed they were unable to fight or manoeuvre, indeed it took all their strength and skill to keep their horses steady on the blood–soaked slippery ground. Many men tried to escape across the Bannockburn, but in places the banks were steep and the land above soft and boggy and the terrified animals floundered around in the water and mud. What had been a fighting retreat swiftly turned into blind stampede with men and animals beyond the control of their constables and sergeants. At that crucial moment Englishmen, who were still aware of the battle and events around them, noticed, from the woods upon the brow of the hill, another fresh division of Scotsmen running towards the battle. This surge of fresh men drove all heart from the English and they fled in panic from the battlefield. They could not know that the latest men to join the battle were only King Robert's supporting folk. Cooks, smiths and boys who ran errands and were keen to join in the victory.

Many men fell in the crush but those who succeeded crossing over the River still had to make their way across the marshy land before reaching the comparative safety of the Torwood and onwards to the banks of the River Forth. Bruce's camp followers and local people chased them relentlessly, ready to pounce on the wounded and exhausted men.

King Robert ordered his fighting men to stay by the battlefield for he feared the English, scattered and vulnerable at the moment, might reform and attack later. The king surveyed the sad scene. He was relieved it had all ended well, but his joy was tempered by sadness because too many good men had perished. When the last Englishman had left the kingdom then he would feel joyful.

Edward of England had fought bravely on the field of battle and he resisted his noble's demands to leave while he safely could. His horse had received a death wound and Edward was forced to mount a beast roaming riderless in the fray. The Earl of Pembroke, aware of impending defeat, boldly took his king's rein and with the help of Sir Giles D'Argentan, dragged Edward from the battlefield and along the road to Stirling. With his bodyguard around him the tired, defeated king arrived at the castle gates, but Mowbray, who had been watching from the ramparts, refused to open the castle gates. "My lord, if I give you sanctuary for sure you'll fall into King Robert's hands." This was the first time anyone had dared to refer to Robert Bruce as king in Edward's presence. Edward's face, already flushed from the hard fighting went redder still, but Pembroke would not allow irrelevant protocol to hinder their progress and shouted. "Come man, surely this castle is strong enough to hold the king." Mowbray and Pembroke were old comrades and Mowbray replied, "Now the king has left the field I am duty bound to surrender, I gave my word. Besides, if the king is captured think of the strife it will cause in England." That was true, Pembroke could see that. The king must be taken to a place of safety and then home with all speed. The castle of Dunbar was the only possible place. Surrounded by five hundred of his knights king Edward was taken to Dunbar and James Douglas, with lightly armed horsemen, followed the king's party at some distance. Douglas passed through the Torwood and met Abernethy, who had missed both the battle and the king's party. He was in command of reinforcements to join King Edward against King Robert. When Abernethy heard about the English defeat and King Edward's flight from the field he sighed loudly. He was a Scot. Kinsmen by marriage to the Comyn kindred and the men he led were all Scots. As far as Abernethy could see there was little point now in being pig-headed. King Robert had won the day and Comyn resistance was broken. He would do the only sensible thing and join his forces to James Douglas. Together they continued chasing the English king from Scotland.

The Earl of Pembroke and Giles D'Argentan did not leave Scotland with their king. Both men were experienced warriors and they watched as Edward was led away to safety, then they turned their horses back towards the battlefield. Neither man's courage could be questioned but their motives and intentions were quite different. As they cantered back towards the sound of battle, D'Argentan talked angrily to himself. "Never, no never, have I run away from a battle and I don't intend to now, damn them." Pembroke, listening to the knight's indignant grumbling said, "Save what you can from the mess, Giles. There's nothing to be gained fighting to the death." D'Argentan did not reply but spurred on his horse and as he galloped off towards the battle he raised his hand in salute to Pembroke. The earl continued riding at a steady pace, veering slightly to the east to miss the mossy land where the small stream flowed into the Bannock. He would come around from the flank and begin to round up his Welshmen. Unlike D'Argentan he believed his duty lay in getting as many of his men home as possible.

For a few moments he sat astride his mud and sweat–covered destiere quietly looking at the scene of battle. Corpses of the dead, both men and beasts, lay grotesquely piled on top of each other. Here and there a fallen horse, still alive, would lift its head and whinny pathetically. On the opposite side of the battlefield the Scots searched amongst the bodies. Carts had been brought close to the field and the bodies of fallen knights were already piled onto the timbers to be taken for burial. It was late in the evening and the sun was sinking low behind the western hills. Soon the short night would hide the terrible scene from human sight. Pembroke pulled his horse's head around and cantered towards Torwood where he expected to find his Welshmen. Throughout the following day his men sought his protection and guidance and when the earl was sure he had rallied as many as remained in the area, he led them back through Scotland by the western route. Many times they were attacked and the weak and wounded killed. Food was impossible to find, even wild creatures of the moors and forests had disappeared. Occasionally birds were brought down by a well aimed stone from a welsh sling, but these fed few men. One by one they butchered their horses until Pembroke gave the order for his own trusted mount to be pollaxed. Without food men could neither march nor defend themselves. The column passed Louden, the place of Pembroke's humiliation by Bruce seven years previously. Marching on foot with his men, he paused to look towards the valley where Bruce had dug his trenches. "Damn him, the cunning bastard," he murmured. To admit the superiority of the Scot as a fighting man he could not, which brought him to the only other conclusion, the English command and battle tactics were inferior.

By the time the Welshmen had fought their way to the Solway Firth the earl, the most experienced and loyal of King Edward's commanders was weary of war. Weakened with a sickness in his bowels, thin and pale from the long march, he arrived barefoot and exhausted at Carlisle, when the harvest month of August was drawing to a close.

The holy brothers at Lanercost Priory took him to the same

chamber where the noble king Edward I had once rested and Pembroke drank the bitter potion offered to him, relieved to be laying in the soft, feather bed. His young squire, standing by the window, gazed out towards the northern hills. His master called to him from the bed. "Piers, go and rest and when you've recovered ride with haste to my lady and tell her that I live and will be with her before the leaves fall."

Marie, Lady Pembroke, had already heard of England's defeat in Scotland, when her husband's squire arrived to tell her that her lord lived and was recovering in the north. Immediately she ordered her servants to prepare her horse and with a large bodyguard from among her kinsmen and servants and accompanied by her eldest daughter, she set out for the north for Marie of Pembroke was a loving and loyal wife and intended to nurse her husband herself.

On a brisk, early, autumn day when the leaves where whirling across the track leading to Lanercost Priory, Brother Alan, the gatekeeper ran in with the news that a large party of wealthy people were approaching. Pembroke who had recovered some of his strength, was sitting in the window recess. His spirits were somewhat lighter and he was regaining some of his former vigour. He heard the shouting and arose to see what all the fuss was about. Marie had already dismounted and stood by her beast, stretching her back, as was her way after a long ride. The earl and his lady lived comfortably together and when she saw her husband walking into the yard she gave a cry of joy to see him and ran to him, throwing her arms around his neck and burying her head onto his shoulder. "My sweet, you have come so far to greet your husband." "How could I leave you here alone and I not knowing if you would live or die? Piers told me of your march through Scotland." His daughter stood by her father awaiting his kiss and then the three walked to his chamber. The earl could be heard saying, "Now Marie tell me, how are my sons?"

After the great defeat at Bannockburn, Pembroke vowed never again would he go on campaign to Scotland, then he recollected that he had made that vow once before, but he continued to be a loyal subject to his king for the rest of his life.

James Douglas continued to harry the English fugitives throughout southern Scotland, but King Robert remained at Bannock. He ordered the body of the young Earl of Gloucester be placed before the altar in the tiny chapel of St Ninian where the king kept vigil for the night over the body. Many times during the short hours of darkness he prayed for the soul of the young man and remembered that his father had sent the warning spurs and coins to him years before.

"Oh Lord Jesus,

Did I but know then what my hasty actions would bring to my kinsfolk and this land.

Could I have continued with my arrogant quest?

Yet with your help Lord, this land is free."

Abbot Bernard of Arbroath came into the chapel. In the dim light from the four wax candles burning at each corner of the body he saw his king, who turned tired, red–rimmed eyes towards the cleric. "You must rest my lord, " said the abbot, but the king replied. "If I were to stand vigil for one year and carry this knight's body barefoot to his home, I could not repay my debt to his kindred."

When dawn came the king ordered that the bodies of Gloucester and Robert Clifford, his old adversary, be sent to Berwick where their families could claim them for burial. To the English king he returned his shield and the privy seal which had been taken from the body of Edward's shield bearer.

Now that the English were on the run and Stirling was his, how could he get his womenfolk back? It was the capture of the Earl of Hereford who gave King Robert his chief hostage. Such an important man could be used to bargain for the return of his loved ones.

The capture of Hereford had come about in this manner. English knights who had been separated from the king's bodyguard sped south–west to avoid Douglas and his avenging mounted troops. Constantly harried by local people three days after Bannock, the exhausted and disgruntled Hereford and other knights sought sanctuary at Bothwell Castle, which was held for the English king. The governor welcomed them with smiles, food and the promise of a guide and provisions for the journey home but in the early morning the governor and his men set upon their guests, tied each man to his horse and led them back through a jeering population to King Robert.

MY ANE FOLK

Elizabeth de Burgh, Marjorie Bruce and Christina Bruce, queen, daughter and sister of the Scottish king knelt before the altar in the chapel of the convent of Sixhills in Lincolnshire. It had been a warm and sunlit day when the messenger from Elizabeth's father arrived with the news of King Edward's defeat and flight from Scotland. The women were not sure how they should react. It was eight years since they had last seen their homes and kinsfolk and their treatment was less harsh than in the early years of their captivity, yet they were still prisoners. Their movements restricted, their conversations reported. Elizabeth often said to her sister-in-law, "What a blessing we have no power Chrissy, I do believe sometimes that they've forgotten us altogether." "Aye, maybe, but men are free to follow their own desires, while we sit here and each year that passes brings us nearer to old age. Now who can say what will happen to us?"

Six years earlier, Elizabeth had left the bleak windswept manor, on the banks of the River Humber, for the convent nestling in the rich farmland of the rolling Lincolnshire Wolds. Christina was already there and Marjorie had joined them shortly afterwards from her prison in the Tower. Once or twice a year, one or other of the Earl of Ulster's men visited Sixhills, bringing news and gifts from Elizabeth's kinsfolk. Other than these small diversions they led quiet lives. Each season passed without change. They were accepted in the religious community and each woman had found a small niche for herself in which to pass the days.

Elizabeth, forced during her early captivity to spin, spent time with the lay sisters embroidering fine cushions and wall hangings, commissioned by wealthy lords and merchants. When the weather was pleasant she wandered into the abbey gardens taking deep breaths of the warm lavender and rose-scented air. She collected herbs and vegetables from which she prepared dyes for her skeins of wool and there she would be sure to find Christina, hidden under a large, brimmed hat, sleeves rolled up, her strong slender body hidden beneath a coarse, wadmal dress. Christina's hands were always covered in soil, her nails broken and dirty like any common peasant woman. Christina enjoyed the open air, she felt less a captive in the gardens. "Really Chrissy, you're always digging and delving, I believe I recognize your bent rear more than I do your face." Christina always laughed for she was good-humoured and would wipe her dirty hands on her dirty dress and say, "Are you here again to steal my plants?"

Marjorie found it difficult in the convent during the early months of her arrival at Sixhills. She was a young woman, an age when she could have expected her father to be considering her betrothal. In her London prison she had been denied the company of other young maids and her manners had become somewhat coarse and morose, but as the months passed the easier captivity with her aunt and stepmother removed the tensions. She settled to being the good-humoured and forthright, young person, which in happier times, had been her character. She had always had a fondness for animals and without the restrictions that the daughter of a great earl or king had to endure, she followed her own desires. Every day, summer or winter she could be found around the byres and stables of the abbey, feeding and milking the cows and goats or busy grooming the few ponies kept by the abbey. When the spring came she was usually to be found with the shepherd in the lambing pens. At first her aunt and stepmother had tried to guide her into activities more suited to a maid of gentle birth, but Marjorie laughed, saying that there would be time enough to play the great lady if her father sent for her.

They settled into their quiet lives until the news of the great victory over the English. Then they left their work and went to the chapel to pray for the souls of the fallen and God's protection on themselves. For the rest of that summer they waited patiently for their fates to be decided. Captivity had taught Elizabeth and Christina patience, but Marjorie's restless spirit found those final months longer than the whole of her captivity put together. She could be heard talking to her favourite pony as she groomed him, questioning the animal how long he thought it would be before her father arranged her release. When her aunt heard her she laughed, for Marjorie had long ago lost her Scottish speech and sounded for all the world like a farmer's wench from eastern England. Then she would exclaim, "Marjorie, what are we to do with you? Your father will find it hard to believe you are his own young maid." Marjorie shrugged and continued to brush the animal's flank.

Fragile and gentle Mary Bruce had endured imprisonment in her cage at Roxburgh Castle for four years. Yet if her body was weak her spirit was indomitable and her dignified calm and thanks for any small kindness that her jailers showed her gained their respect. Towards the end of her imprisonment in the castle, she spent more time out than in her cage. Only when the governor expected visitors would they hurriedly put her back into the cruel device on the battlements well supplied with fur wraps, until the autumn of 1310 when Mary was sent to the Carmalite Convent in Berwick. A few weeks later Isabelle, Countess of Fife, joined her.

Isabelle's captivity had continued to be harsh so that Mary hardly recognized the poor creature. Captivating Isabelle was now so thin, her yellowing skin hung in wrinkled folds on her face and neck. Once she had been voluptuous, now her shrivelled breasts hung to her waist, whilst her once laughing eyes darted about in agitated, suspicious movements, sunken in her thin face. Her tangled and lice–infested hair had to be shorn from her head and she sat in her small chamber mumbling incomprehensibly to herself, rocking her body backwards and forwards. She refused to leave her chamber, not even to go into the garden and screamed loudly if they tried to take her outside.

The Carmalites were so stern, that Mary often found herself looking back at her captivity at Roxburgh with longing. Something had always been happening at the castle, people coming and going. She heard the minstrels playing and whenever she was confined to her cage the guards on the battlements, sheltering from the wind, stood and talked to her and she would hear all the gossip and news from the outside world. In the convent, when the weather was fine, Mary sat in the gardens embroidering and when the Holy women gave largesse to the sick and poor who came to their gate, Mary helped as best she could.

As the months passed there was no sign of improvement in Isabelle's condition. They kept her clean and her hair began to grow, but it was thin and grey and had lost all its beauty. Isabelle continued to mumble incomprehensibly to herself, rocking backwards and forwards and showing no interest in her surroundings.

One day when Mary had been brushing Isabelle's hair she began to cough again. That it gave her pain was apparent for she clutched her chest, screwing up her face, a bloody froth covering her lips. Mary wiped the blood and sweat from Isabelle's face, with a piece of linen, and knew for certain then that Isabelle would not recover. The convent was such a cold and cheerless place and Mary asked the Reverend Mother if Isabelle might have a small brassier in her cell, but Reverend Mother said, "The lady does not recognize her surroundings, a fire would be dangerous." "Then can she be moved, mother, to a chamber which is warmer? She is so cold and often lies at night without covering herself, for I have found her so." The Reverend Mother said she would consider it, but nothing happened and Isabelle remained in her cold and draughty chamber. Many nights she would spend coughing and Mary would creep into the sick woman, raising her pillows a little and giving her sips of warmed water.

When the snow was thick on the ground and a cold, north-easterly wind whistled through the convent and all who could were huddled around the fire in the refectory, Mary left Isabelle lying in her narrow bed, surrounded by hot stones and went to see the Reverend Mother. "Mother, the countess has a fever and grows weaker each day and she is nothing but skin and bone. For mercy sake find another chamber for her." "I am not free to make decisions for the countess's comfort, but I will seek the advice of others," said the woman. Mary had to be satisfied with the answer. Later that morning she sat with Isabelle. Her own feet were so cold that she could barely feel them and she decided not to wait for others to do their Christian duty. With lay sisters to help her, they carried the flimsy mattress with its skeletal patient, to the warmth of the refectory. Isabelle cried out, for she was fearful of leaving her cell, but was so weak that Mary and the others easily quietened her and they placed her close to the fire. When the Reverend Mother heard that Mary had moved Isabelle she swept into the chamber in a high rage, but Mary was ready for her, "Mother, the Countess is a sad, sick creature, who cannot wait for you to contact her jailer. She must have warmth now or her death will be on your shoulders." The outcome was that Isabelle was moved to a less draughty chamber, with a fire burning day and night and a servant to care for her.

The spring and summer came and Isabelle lingered on, but with the autumn the Reverend Mother worried, for it was certain the countess could not survive another winter. She paid a visit to Sir Henry de Beaumont, Isabelle's nephew. "I have done all I can for your aunt and I am commanded by the Bishop to ask that you take responsibility for her welfare." Sir Henry was as loathed as the church was to accept the burden of his dying aunt, but he thought, surely Isabelle, Countess of Fife, had long been forgotten by the outside world.

Mary Bruce had been very angry when the knight's men had come to take Isabelle away. "She's frightened when she's moved to a new room, let alone leaving the convent. How can you be so cruel? Hasn't she suffered enough already?" But they ignored her pleas. After that Mary rarely spoke to the Reverend Mother, whom she blamed for the lack of Christian charity to a sick woman.

Isabelle had hung on grimly to life, so that Sir Henry and his servants feared the old rumours were true. She was a witch, in league with the devil who would not let his handmaiden die. It was impossible that so frail a creature, wracked with bouts of coughing, could cling to life, but each morning her sunken eyes stared at them accusingly from her yellow face. On Twelfth Night, when the household was very merry, laughing, dancing and carefree, the old serving woman, ordered to care for Isabelle, slipped out of the chamber and down to the kitchen where she sat eating hot chestnuts and drinking mulled ale. It was so pleasant that, what with one thing and another, her chin slowly sunk on to her chest and she fell asleep. She awoke when the fire had burnt low. It would soon be morning and others would awake. She threw kindling onto the fire and selected some dry logs for it, then carrying a lighted taper, she went back to the sick woman's chamber.

The fire was barely alight, but in the glow from her taper she saw immediately that the countess was dead. At some time during the night Isabelle had got out of bed and lay beside the fire. She was cold and stiff; her sightless eyes fixed on the crucifix hanging on the chimneybreast. Blood stained her mouth and a pool of it had formed by her head. The old woman could not imagine how the countess had managed to leave her bed, for she had not moved since her arrival. She dragged the corpse back to the bed. There was no weight in it. She cleaned the floor and built up the fire, for she did not want them to know that she had left her charge unattended. Then she went in search of the steward.

In mid October 1314 horsemen arrived at the Convent of Sixhills. One of the knights who presented himself to the abbess was Donald, Earl of Mar, nephew to the King of Scots. His mother, Christina, had not seen him since she was dragged away weeping, on a cold winter's day in 1307. Donald had spent his childhood at King Edward's court and now, on the brink of manhood, was in his mannerisms and affections English.

Christina was in the still room rearranging bundles of herbs hanging from the rafters. She moved the bunches of lavender, harvested in summer and their perfume filled the air. A lay sister entered, "There are fine young lords here to see you, my lady." Christina found it hard to conceal her excitement as she removed the wadmal smock protecting her dark, woollen dress and adjusted her linen coif before walking without haste, but with a wildly beating heart, to the guests' chamber. Refreshments had been placed on the long table and Elizabeth was already present. Two knights stood up when Christina arrived. They were of a similar age, both finely dressed in kirtle's of richly dyed wool. Apart from the chaplain, who was nearing his three score years and the sick and old, men were rarely seen in the convent. Then Christina saw the look on Elizabeth's face. "Chrissy, your son is here my dear." Christina, breathing heavily, looked at the two young knights, tears welling up in her eyes. Then she recognized Donald for he looked so like his father. Donald took a step forward, uncertain how he should react, but his mother threw her arms about him, tears flowing down her cheeks, her coif slipping from her hair as she embraced her son.

In the middle of the reunion Marjorie arrived. She was nearly as tall as her cousin, her chestnut hair pulled back into a single plait. She had been outside with the ponies and her cheeks were red from the chill, autumn air. She gazed boldly at the two young men.

In her happiness Christina barely glanced at her son's companion, but he was Thomas, Earl of Norfolk, half-brother to King Edward. It was Marjorie who boldly asked the question, "Well cousin, what's going to happen to us?" The abbess, aware of her position and having had intimate knowledge of Marjorie's uncouth manners said, "Hush child, let our guests refresh themselves first, there's time enough." "Perhaps for you mother, but for me the news can't come too soon. Well cousin?"

The young Earl of Norfolk ignored Marjorie and turned to Elizabeth. "Lady, you and your companions are to be exchanged for the Earl of Hereford who is your husband's captive." His final words were nearly drowned by Marjorie who ran across the room and flung her arms around her stepmother, shouting loudly, "Freedom! Thank God, freedom." The two men looked embarrassed. The abbess, irritated by so much emotion clapped her hands and said, "Now, now, let our guests refresh themselves, but Marjorie was not to be silenced. "When are we leaving, we have little enough baggage?" Thomas answered in a peevish tone, "Lady, your escort will arrive tomorrow from Lincoln and then we shall escort you to the border." Even Marjorie was silenced by the news.

It was a large escort of men who accompanied the Bishop of Lincoln along the old, north road with the Scottish prisoners. Marjorie rode a chestnut mare and was so elated that she barely said farewell to the Holy women. Her saddest moment had been to say goodbye to the lay servants, for it was they whom she would miss and as she passed through the abbey gates she turned and waved to them. Elizabeth faced the journey with more trepidation. She was pleased to leave the cloistered life behind her but was returning to a home and husband who were strangers. The only contented traveller was Christina, returning to the kingdom of her birth and with her grown son at her side. It was true he was somewhat distant and shy towards his mother but that was to be expected, for he had been so young when he was taken from her.

They reached York and lodged in the archbishop's palace, before continuing the more difficult part of the journey through County Durham and Northumberland. Marjorie grew impatient and when three days had passed, she demanded of the Earl of Norfolk when they could expect to resume their journey. He looked irritated and answered her sharply, "Wait and see." Abruptly he walked away and Marjorie pulled a face at his retreating back. He really was a sullen boy and she did not think she liked him very much.

The following day a party of the king's men arrived and from a wagon stumbled a very old, frail, bent and blind Bishop Wishert, walking with the aid of a staff and a servant to guide his steps. The captured bishops, Lamberton and Wishert had been kept in chains for the first two years of their captivity, but after the death of his companion, Bishop Wishert had been moved to a monastery and like the Bruce womenfolk his imprisonment had become easier.

Two days later, accompanied by Archbishop Bek of York, their party continued slowly northwards, their speed dictated by the slow moving wagon, bumping and rattling along the rutted road, for the old man could not ride a horse.

During the first week of Advent the party arrived at Berwick and word was sent to Edward Bruce waiting their arrival on the Scottish side of the River Tweed. With him were the hostages, the Earl of Hereford and other prisoners for exchange.

Mary Bruce heard of the Scottish victory at Bannock, when the English king himself arrived after his sea voyage from Dunbar. For many weeks following the battle, survivors had been arriving in the town, tired and sick from illness or untended wounds. No one paid any attention to Mary and as summer turned to autumn she began to fear she had been forgotten and would be forced to spend the rest of her days in the cloister. She was plagued by thoughts of her husband, Neil Campbell. In the past she had not allowed herself the luxury of thinking about him. They had been wed in the late summer before the fateful murder of the Comyn at Greyfriars. Whilst in her cage she had lost count of time passing, but now in her secluded life she could reckon that she had seen four and twenty summers and she could barely remember her husband's features. What would he think of her, the passing years would have changed them both.

On a day in mid October, when she was sitting spinning, the Mother Superior came into the chamber. "Mary, prepare yourself they have come from the castle for you." Mary's heart began to pound. "What do they want of me?" she demanded. "That I have not been told, but make haste."

At Berwick Castle the governor came to her. "Lady, you are indeed fortunate, you are to be exchanged for a noble lord." Mary stood staring at the big man, hardly believing what she heard. Like so many of her male captors he felt sorry for the tiny, fragile–looking woman and softened his voice somewhat. "You must be patient for a little longer but soon you will be joined by your sisters."

The weeks following, Mary regularly ran up to the battlements to gaze along the road upon which her sisters and their escort would ride. Late one afternoon, when she had grown cold from her vigil on the battlements and had come down to sit close to the fire in the great hall, a man at arms, who had watched her waiting in all weathers, approached her. Mary recognized the man, he usually nodded to her whenever she climbed onto the wall. "My lady, I've seen what you search for, they'll arrive shortly." Joyfully she followed the soldier.

"Oh, Mary, Mary! God be praised you're alive," cried Christina Bruce. "They never would tell me what had become of you," she lamented. "Aye, no doubt they were ashamed to say," said Mary. Later when they sat together, Mary told them about her life during the previous seven years. Then Elizabeth asked, "Isabelle, what has become of her?" Mary looked sadly at her companions. "She suffered the most poor creature," And she told them about sad, sick Isabelle and her final years. "They made her pay the harshest of penalties for her disloyalty to her husband and his kinsmen. When God took her to himself it was a blessed relief from her torment." When she had finished her tale they all sat silent, even Marjorie, who could barely remember the countess who had served her father, making his claim to the kingdom legitimate at his inauguration. It was Marjorie who finally broke the silence. "She need not have sacrificed so much for father. His claim to the kingdom is through victory in battle." "Aye, but who could have known that then?" replied her stepmother.

During all the years of her captivity, Elizabeth had not been allowed a mirror and as the reunion with her husband drew closer she began to fret about her appearance. She had seen seven and twenty summers and the early years of her captivity had not been easy. What would Robert think when he saw her once again? She asked Christina her opinion. "Oh, Chrissy, tell me truly, have I faded?" Christina had looked at her sister-in-law for a long time with a serious expression on her face, until Elizabeth had exclaimed. "I knew it, I look old and you dare not tell me." Then Christina had laughed, "Beth, surely you have seen the looks that men give you. Why, you are lovelier than ever." As she left Elizabeth's chamber she said, "I think the cloistered life, free from men, has suited you." And she laughed again for she knew how much Elizabeth yearned for the outside world. When they had arrived in York, Elizabeth had asked for a mirror and with trepidation had breathed on the bright copper disk, wiped it and looked at her reflection. The face that stared back at her was less pale than she remembered and it had lost some of its fullness, but yes, Christina was not telling an untruth, the years without a husband had improved her countenance.

The day when they were to ride to the border, to be handed over to their kinsmen dawned, chill and damp. Christina, dressed in a warm, woollen mantle and heavy, fur cloak, walked with Elizabeth to the courtyard of Berwick Castle. The bishop was already in his carriage with Mary, while Marjorie, mounted on her palfrey, was plainly excited and impatient to leave. Donald stood beside the young Earl of Norfolk, dressed in a long, red, woollen kirtle but without outer clothing suitable for the journey. "Donald you must make haste," called his mother, "for your cousin is anxious to go," but Marjorie answered angrily. "Oh, Donald isn't coming aunt, he wants to stay with the English." Christina's face drained of colour. She swayed and Elizabeth took her arm to steady her sister-in-law. It was true that Donald had said little to his mother throughout the journey and had remained close to the English earl and his escort, but the women had thought this the natural shyness of a youth separated from his kinswomen for so long. Never had they thought that his loyalty now lay with England.

Christina cried out in anguish and ran to her boy, throwing her arms around him. "Don't you love your mother anymore Donald? They have taken all these years, am I now to lose, you forever." The men of the escort all looked embarrassed, turning their gaze away or found something in their horse's mane requiring attention. Elizabeth said, "How could you do this to your mother, Donald? How could you wait so long before telling her? Have you no courage? I see your companions have made you truly one of themselves." Mary ran to her sister and Bishop Wishert poked his head out from behind his curtains and called in a feeble voice, "What distresses the ladies?" Even Marjorie looked embarrassed because she had upset her aunt and dismounted to console her. Archbishop Bek took Donald on one side and talked to him for some time, but Donald could not be moved from his decision. He was sorry that he distressed his mother but his future lay with England and he asked that she would give him her blessing. Christina, trying to control her sobbing, walked with him to the gatehouse and in private she kissed him, took his hand and wished him happiness and good fortune.

She turned in her saddle just once to look back. He stood at the castle gate with Norfolk beside him and waved. She returned his farewell, then the mists of winter took him from her and in silence, with head bent so that the fur hood covered her face, she rode to meet her kinsmen.

THE HOMECOMING

Sir Marmaduke de Tweng, knight of Yorkshire, lost his horse in the battle of Bannockburn. However, he was determined not to be taken prisoner by just any Scotsman, for in spite of their victory, he still considered Scots to be inferior to a knight of Yorkshire. With his usual determination, after the battle he hid his arms and insignia and laid low throughout the night. Early the following morning he overheard two Scots discussing the many virtues of King Robert who, at that moment, they said was at prayer in St Ninian's chapel keeping vigil over the body of an English lord. Both agreed that their king had saintly qualities. That was just what de Tweng wanted to hear. With a Scottish plaid thrown around his shoulders and adopting the swagger of the victors he made his way towards St Ninians. It was plain that Bruce was still within the chapel, for his bodyguards sat about outside discussing the victory of the previous day. The same grey gelding, ridden by Bruce when de Tweng watched him strike the fatal blow to young de Bohun, stood placidly outside, one hoof raised, eyes half closed, ears relaxed and occasionally swishing its tail to ward off the flies, it rested in the warm sunshine.

The chapel door opened and the king emerged into the fresh summer morning. Marmaduke stepped from cover and walked towards him, but one of the king's men saw the unfamiliar face and reached for his battleaxe. The king held up his hand and said. "Welcome de Tweng, to which man are you a prisoner?" "To none my lord, I yield to you, to be at your will," replied the knight. "Then I receive you, Sir." Turning to his men King Robert said, "Treat this man with courtesy, for he and I were once friends and he's a gallant warrior."

After keeping his vigil over the body of the Earl of Gloucester, King Robert kept his promise to share the spoils of war with all his men. The fiery Murdo, Moira's husband, rode homewards on a fine pony, formerly the property of an English squire. He had a cooking pot for his lass, a bag of oats and a pouch with five English silver marks. It was his intention to use the money to buy another milking cow. He also carried a gift for Moira from the king. "Give this to your lass Murdo," the king had said, "as a token, for I still remember the kindness she once showed to a stranger. It was a small silver ring with a finely polished garnet.

Murdo travelled with other men from the west, all handsomely rewarded and loudly proclaiming the virtues of Good King Robert. They were well received in the villages, farmsteads and manors through which they passed. Fêted as heroes, everybody was eager to hear their stories which they were happy to retell, adding to their yarns with each new telling.

King Robert had now gained his kingdom through force of arms but he did not intend to let the English rest quietly for the question of Berwick still remained unsolved. Its easy access to trade with Flanders and the Hanseatic ports made it vital to Scotland's prosperity. He must regain Berwick and get King Edward to the negotiating table.

On 1st August after their victory at Bannockburn, the Scottish army invaded England's northern counties. Led by Edward Bruce and Douglas they bypassed Berwick, and swept through eastern England as far as the River Tees. They stole all cattle that had not been hidden and extorted ransoms from the terrified population in return for the promise not to burn towns, manors and farmsteads. They crossed the Pennines and returned home by the western route.

While the English were smarting from this latest outrage, King Robert sent a letter to the English king expressing his desire for peace and asking for a meeting to discuss terms. Edward, angry and humiliated, was forced to agree. His advisers included Archbishop Bek. The talks began in September and it was agreed to release the kinswomen of the Scottish king in exchange for Hereford and John Seagrave. The next item raised by the Scots was that King Edward should recognize King Robert as rightful King of Scots and Scotland as an independent kingdom, free from all claims by England. Archbishop Bek allowed the Scottish spokesman to have his say without interruption, but he then rose to his feet saying, "My lords, England's right to over-lordship of Scotland is not for discussion and to this end our Lord, King Edward and his noble father before him have fought honourably." He bowed and closely followed by his men swept from the chamber.

During the late autumn, when it was known that the queen would be returning to her husband, King Robert rode to Scone, ordering the palace to be prepared to receive his family. It was his intention to meet them and spend Christmas at Scone.

Robert considered himself an honourable man in all his dealings with women. Never had he taken a woman by force and had always shown courtesy to them. When there was a child he readily recognized it as his own and provided for the mother. Christine of Carrick and their children, Robert and Christine, had been his companions for the past four years and the children called him father. A visit to her manor and the warmth and comfort he found in her company, was the only relaxation he had allowed himself during the years of campaigning. With the imminent return of his wife he struggled with his restless conscience and pondered deeply about Christine's place in his heart. He loved her, he freely admitted, but Elizabeth was his queen and he must have a legitimate heir. Nay, Scotland must have an heir. He had passed his fortieth summer and after all his years of wandering, he desired peace in his personal life with all his heart and soul. Sadly, he came to a decision.

In mid October he visited Christine at her manor and she welcomed him with her usual warmth. He arrived at midday and sat with her and their children talking of the happenings in Scotland. He ate sparingly of the refreshments before asking Christine to walk with him. Their daughter made to follow, but her mother said, "Nay, do not come, I see your father has much he would say to me alone." Arm in arm they walked by the gushing, bubbling burn flowing merrily through the pasture, the black, shaggy cattle, grazing nearby watched them inquisitively. The king's men waited at a distance. Robert sat himself on a grey rock with willows at his back sheltering them from the view of onlookers and he pulled her down beside him. They sat in silence for a while, Robert throwing small pebbles and twigs into the peat-brown pool. He knew what he must say to her, but was loathed to say it, not because his courage failed him but because of his love for her. Eventually, Christine herself said, "Oh Robert, I know what you've come to say. Speak for pity's sake." "Sweetheart, you and I have shared much, but Elizabeth returns to me and I must be a husband to her. I've done her much harm and her youth will soon be gone." Christine said nothing. When years before he had told her that he was to marry the daughter of a great earl she had flown into a rage, ranting and raving, boxing his ears and throwing her best pottery at his retreating back. Their love had changed since those early days of youthful passion. What remained was a warmth and contentment between them and even if it hurt her she understood his dilemma. She knew he loved her and cared about her and the children, but a king could not behave like other men.

He did not stay the night with her, that would have been too cruel for both of them to bear, but with promises that he would send her regular messages and support, he rode away taking their son with him. Young Robert, so like his father, was ready to leave his mother and sister and with his father's help would make his way in the world. Christine watched until they were out of sight. She felt numb, tears moistening her cheeks, but her daughter standing beside her said with confidence, "Don't fret mother, father will come again." Her son turned in the saddle to wave, he was happy to be leaving home; it was a great adventure for him whose life as a grown man was just beginning. At Scone the king made his confession and received absolution from Abbot Bernard for the sin of fornication.

The palace was bright with lights, the great hall and king's chamber freshly swept and the cold, flag floors strewn with dried, sweet-smelling herbs. Fine, richly coloured tapestries were freshly hung and soft cushions arranged on the chairs and settle. The steward had been busy for many days arranging for the provisioning of the kitchens for the welcoming feasts. Fish, game, fowls, fruits and sweetmeats were being prepared for the feasting.

The king had been restless, but now that he knew she was just a mile away from Scone he ordered his horse to be saddled and rode out to meet her with James Douglas and Walter Stewart beside him. They reached the crest of a hill, the highway stretching before them, and at a little distance along the road they could see the queen's party. The king quickened the pace but before he had reached the travellers he reined in his horse, dismounted, handed the reins to Douglas and walked alone towards his family.

He looked a fine sight, his surcoat was the colour of ripe rowanberries and on his breast the Lion of Scotland was embroidered in golden threads. A wide, dark red, embossed leather belt, with the patterns picked out in gold and semi-precious stones encircled his waist. It was a bright but cold day and he wore a black mantle lined with the white fur of the mountain hare and held at the shoulder with a gold broach set with a central ruby. On his head he wore the same simple gold circlet which he had received at his inauguration. His hair and beard were now flecked with grey and the lines on his face showed the harshness of the life he had led since he had last seen his family, but his bearing was straight and vigorous and he was still a very handsome man.

As the riders drew closer he could see Elizabeth. She waved and smiled at him. By her side rode a young woman with a face tanned by the sun, which he recognized as Marjorie while Christina and little

Mary rode behind them. Marjorie jumped from her pony and hoisting her skirts, as she had as a young maid, sprinted like a boy towards her father, the hood from her cape fell from her chestnut hair which streamed behind her. She ran around the large puddles but the smaller ones she jumped across and upon reaching her amused father, she flung her arms about him and he swung her around so that her feet left the ground. "Sweetheart, your father has awaited this moment for so long." His voice broke with emotion. She gazed up into his face and saw that there were tears in his eyes. He took her arm, "Let's walk to meet your stepmother, Marjorie." Father and daughter walked along the road over which she had so recently flown.

"Hallo, Robert," was Elizabeth's simple greeting to her husband as he looked up at her. He was too overcome with emotion to say anything, but held out his arms to lift her from her mare. He greeted his sisters and surrounded by the happy throng, King Robert of Scots rode back the short distance to Scone.

At the feasting held in her honour, it was generally agreed by all that never could they remember seeing Elizabeth looking so fair. People had always thought Elizabeth delicate, but now her fair skin had lost its translucent look and her blue eyes sparkled at her husband, as she listened attentively to him. Her copper hair shone under a coif of the finest linen gauze, which was held in place by a gold circlet studded with pearls, a gift from her husband. That night they lay together, her body soft and silken-skinned beside his muscular, iron hard frame. For all the years of her imprisonment, staved of love, she had dreamt of the moment when he would stroke her thighs and kiss her breasts as once he had. She gasped like a small bird with pleasure and curled her arms and legs around him. Now, her dearest hope was that she would conceive and give him his heir.

Marjorie lay in her bed unable to sleep for she was so excited. James Douglas had rode by her side on the way back to Scone and during the feast she had been aware of his dark eyes watching her. When their glance met she smiled and he had raised his goblet to her. She remembered him as a pale youth chatting to her and making her laugh as they fled from their pursuers. Now, he was one of her father's most trusted captains and oh, so handsome. It was thoughts of Douglas that kept her awake.

Only Christina lay sadly in her bed thinking about her son and her husband, whom they told her had been so cruelly executed and her own wasted years in England.

During the twelve days of the Christmas feast, for the first time since his great adventure had begun, Robert Bruce, now undoubted King of Scots, surrounded by his loved ones, relaxed and enjoyed the peace of Christmas. He danced and sang, watched mummers, listened to his minstrels and laughed at his jester, but when the festival came to an end he met his councillors and captains to discuss business once again.

The young people, ignoring the dismal, winter weather, rode through the park in the brief hours of the afternoon. Marjorie with James Douglas, riding beside her, Thomas Randolph, the young Walter Stewart, Mary Bruce and others laughed and chatted. Randolph and Douglas were bitter rivals although they respected each other's military skills but neither man was as yet married. To both men the idea of becoming the king's son-in-law appeared a just reward for their loyal and distinguished careers in his service.

Marjorie, who had been forced to spend her most formative years isolated from men, particularly young and active men, found their attentions irresistible, but it was James Douglas whom she thought of when she was alone. Her father would be considering her marriage and she began to hope that James would be his choice. His lineage was not as noble as that of Thomas Randolph she knew that, but the Douglas's were an old family. Members of the king's household became aware of the mutual affection between the man and maid and Elizabeth mentioned to her husband that even the servants knew of Marjorie's fondness for James Douglas.

If the king had had many daughters he would gladly have given one each to Randolph and Douglas in recognition of their service. As things stood, to give Marjorie to one would give offence to the other and both had many loyal followers. Nor was it appropriate that the heir to the throne should be a young woman, for there was still hard fighting to be done before the kingdom was secure. The succession must be assured with a son-in-law acceptable to all.

The king sent both rivals to the border country to continue harassing the enemy and while they were away he held the betrothal feast for his daughter Marjorie to young Walter Stewart. There were angry scenes between Marjorie and her father and she stamped and raged and threatened to run back to England, until her father's patience began to wear thin. "Elizabeth, talk to her, make her understand that she must marry a man who will not pose a threat to other nobles, for she will not listen to me," the king had said to his wife, after yet another stormy meeting with his daughter. "She understands that Robert, but she has an affection for James Douglas and he for her. She is ruled by her heart and set beside Douglas, Walter Stewart is to her a poor substitute." But her husband looked irritated and angry and she said no more. Secretly she felt pity for her stepdaughter. The poor girl had suffered already because she was daughter to The Bruce and now to please her father she must marry an inexperienced youth five years her junior.

King Robert's parliament had already banned all Scottish lords from owning land in both England and Scotland. In the past it had been the main cause of all disloyalty and conflicts but from now on Scotland's nobles would know from whom they would gain the most rewards. In the spring of 1315, when Parliament met at Ayr, Edward Bruce was confirmed as the natural successor to the king in recognition of his steadfast loyalty to his brother and Scotland. Parliament also agreed the marriage between Marjorie Bruce and Walter Stewart.

That year the spring was very wet. It rained and rained until the oldest people said they could not remember such weather. The Rivers were in spate and the fields flooded in the low farmland in the east of the kingdom. The ground was so waterlogged it was impossible to plough or sow. If the weather did not improve soon the harvest would be sparse that summer.

The threat from the English lessened, for the English king was once again in dispute with the Earl of Lancaster and other lords. England also suffered from the effects of the bad weather. Since his defeat in Scotland and with so many problems, it was doubtful if King Edward would gain support for a renewed attack on Scotland, but steadfastly he continued to refuse to recognize King Robert's right to the throne of Scotland. Doggedly he upheld his own claim to the over-lordship of that kingdom. When John of Lorn approached him, proposing that he occupy the Isle of Man and attack western Scotland, King Edward gave him aid.

Edward Bruce lived in his elder brother's shadow and although his loyalty was never in doubt, after Bannockburn, he had grown somewhat restless and ambitious to follow his own destiny. When Edward proposed that he invade Ireland, King Robert readily agreed and offered to help him with an invasion fleet. If the English were forced to spend valuable time and resources defending Ireland, they would have little enough left to prepare a further invasion of Scotland. Envoys were sent to the Irish kings pointing out the shared heritage of Ireland and Scotland and offering to help recover their liberty from the English. The O'Neill's replied enthusiastically and offered the crown of the High King of all Ireland to Edward Bruce should he be successful. In the excitement it was overlooked that other Irish kings were lukewarm with their support.

Rhuri Macgillivery provided the warships and in May the fleet set sail for Larne with a large force of fighting men. Among them was Philip Mowbray who, after the battle at Bannock, had sworn allegiance to King Robert.

Domnal O'Neill, King of Tyrone, met Edward with great affection for they had been friends as boys and together they marched through Ulster with many local chieftains joining them. They sacked Dundalk and in September defeated the Earl of Ulster himself, father of Queen Elizabeth and the English were forced to flee.

That summer King Robert celebrated the marriage of his daughter to Walter Stewart. All the guests agreed they had never seen such a lovely bride. Her thick, curling, chestnut hair, brushed and shining, spread around her shoulders and reached down to her waist. Around her head she wore the maiden's golden circlet, a royal-blue, close fitting dress, with a golden belt worn low around her hips. Below this her dress fell in rich folds and lay upon the ground around her feet. The sleeves were long and split to the elbow, showing beneath the ruffled sleeves of her pale cream, silk shift. Yet in spite of all the finery she was a somewhat joyless bride. As her young husband took her hand at the abbey door she did not smile and her look was more one of resignation than maidenly modesty. Afterwards, at the bridal feast, she sat beside her husband saying little. People noticed that many times young Stewart tried to gain her attention but she smiled, saying nothing. There were those present who felt sadness for the young woman for she had been held in captivity for so long and now was obliged to marry a man for whom she had no affection. The few who were in Marjorie's confidence knew that in private she had referred to Walter Stewart as "just a silly boy." On this occasion some said the king had been very harsh with his only legitimate child. For her part Marjorie played a game with herself and when she and Walter lay together she imagined that he was James Douglas. By September her father was told she was already with child and duty done, Walter Stewart left on campaign with his father-in-law. Marjorie dutifully waved goodbye and breathed a sigh of relief that she would be able to lay in her bed alone, free from his fumbling, passionless hands.

The summer of 1316 had been so wet that it had barely been possible to ride on the soaked ground, but when the frosts came and the sickness which had marred the first weeks of her pregnancy had passed, Marjorie ordered her mare to be saddled. Ignoring the warnings from her nurse she rode in the crisp, morning air, happy and carefree, putting her husband's return out of her mind.

Scotland's byres and storehouses were barely half-full so that there would be serious famine in the coming winter and spring. Douglas and Randolph wasted no time and crossed the eastern border raiding as far as Durham, extorting ransoms and stealing cattle, sheep, corn and barley. That autumn a constant stream of animals and goods crossed the border back to Scotland.

The freeholders and burgesses of Northumberland and County Durham pleaded with their king to send them reinforcements to halt the Scottish attacks, but help did not arrive and the king's men, garrisoned in nearby fortresses, did not ride out to defend their countrymen. That year the men of the North Country did not pay taxes to their king for they had paid all they had to the Scots on condition that they would leave them in peace.

King Robert rode to Carlisle and laid siege to the city, intending to gain control of the western seas. The king usually viewed besieging cities as a waste of time and resources, but control of Carlisle served a double purpose. It would be useful as a bargaining pawn for the return of Berwick.

Carlisle had eight stone–throwing machines positioned around the city walls and the king was forced to keep his men well out of range of the large rocks which hurtled towards his lines. He had but one siege engine throwing stones at the northern gate and the rocks that King Robert sent across the battlements were quickly returned by the defenders with loud laughter and abuse. Only under cover of darkness was it safe to attempt an assault. He ordered trees to be felled and an assault tower built, that could be pushed closer to the city walls, but it was so heavy the wheels sank under its weight in the soft, rain–soaked earth and he was forced to abandon it. In the early morning light when the English saw the tower stuck firmly in the mud, listing crazily to one side, they hooted with laughter, whistling and yelling insults at the angry Scots.

On a moonless night the king led a massed assault on the east gate, setting many houses alight. While the defenders were preoccupied with the fires Douglas, who had recently joined the king, launched an attack on a different section of the wall using scaling ladders. The governor of Carlisle, Andrew Harclay was not so easily fooled and led the English defence pushing Douglas and his men back until the only Scots left on the Carlisle walls were dead men. King Robert called off the attack and the following morning, swallowing their pride, he and his men marched back to their own land, leaving behind the debris of war, catapult and tower, still trapped in the mud.

Shortly after crossing the border, a messenger brought the king news that John of Lorn had attacked the Argyll coast from his base in the Isle of Man and was trying to raise support among the chieftains against King Robert. Accompanied by his young son-in-law he sailed along the Sound of Bute to the mouth of Loch Fyne and through into Loch Tarbert. The open sea lay across a narrow strip of land with the western isles beyond. The king remembered the old prophecy that whoever sailed from shore to shore was rightful lord of the Isles. To impress his men he ordered the felling of the tallest of the Caledonian pines growing on the hillside. These they laid side by side across the narrow isthmus separating land from sea. On a fine, sunny day with a stiff south-easterly breeze each galley, with its awning still set, was dragged from the water and onto the logs. The wind blew into the rigged sails and each vessel was hauled across the causeway. "Heave, heave," bellowed Bruce and once onto the rollers the boats slithered across with ease. "Sir, never would I have thought it possible," said Walter Stewart. The king replied, "When I was a boy I had a nurse who came from these parts. She told me stories of the Viking warriors who dragged their longships across the land in such a manner. If they could do it so can we."

That the northmen had carried their vessels from place to place mattered little to the men of the isles. It was King Robert of Scotland, who had fulfilled the old prophecy and to their way of thinking, as the old saying said, 'by force of arms shall none withstand,' and forgetting their recent promises to John of Lorn, they came before the king as his liegemen.

The king spent the rest of the year with his family, for Elizabeth was with child, but when the Christmas feast had come to an end he rode with James Douglas to the eastern marches. Their target was Berwick.

On a cold and cloudy night in January the king led the attack while Douglas came from the sea into Berwick harbour. Cloth had been wrapped around the oars to muffle the noise as they moved in the oarlocks. Once they were close to the harbour wall they stopped pulling altogether and allowed their boats to drift to land. Douglas's task was to overpower the guards by the eastern and southern gates and allow Bruce and his men in, but as they made land the clouds suddenly parted and a full moon shone forth. The guards on the battlements clearly saw Bruces's men assembling beneath them and raised the alarm. Douglas had but a few men under his command. Once spotted there was nothing for it but to flee back to the boats and hurriedly put out to sea, with an English galley pursuing them for some distance up the coast before it gave up the chase.

Later that day, the King and Douglas met and agreed that Douglas would remain in the border country harassing the English around Berwick, while the king would arrange a blockade of the town from the sea. "Keep up the pressure," said the king as he prepared to depart. As always, Douglas carried out the king's instructions with singular dedication and by the end of February the townsfolk and garrison of Berwick found it difficult to get provisions through. The brave Berwick fishermen who were prepared to face wild seas found Scottish galleys waiting just outside the harbour to chase them back before they could cast their nets.

On the last day of February, when food was low and starvation becoming a very real possibility, a knight garrisoned at Berwick, declared it to be his intention to comb the surrounding hills for cattle, boar or deer.

James Douglas had built himself a lodge in the forests where he could keep watch on Berwick. He heard about the foraging party and with a small group of followers set an ambush in Teviotdale.

The Scots lay hidden among the trees in the late afternoon. A brisk, northerly wind threatened snow and the waiting men were cold to the bone. One of Douglas's men rode up in a great hurry. "My lord, they're coming this way and they're at least twice the number we are." In an hour it would be dark and Douglas reasoned that a lightening attack when the night was closing in had a chance of success.

The English came into view. Outnumbering the Scots, they were herding half a dozen scrawny beasts, no doubt stolen from some poor peasant. Douglas waited until their commander, a swarthy, arrogant-looking man, was almost passed him. Douglas went for the leader. Sir Edmund de Caillan was from Gascony and prided himself on his fighting prowess, especially using a battleaxe, which was the weapon of his choice and he kept two strapped to his saddle. He did not know Douglas by sight, but was left in little doubt that the knight, who hurtled towards him was indeed he, for he bellowed, "Douglas! Douglas!" De Caillan took up the challenge, pulled his destiere's head round and spurred him forward, axe in hand. Douglas brought up his shield to fend off the blow from the long handled axe and turned his horse. It was a smaller, lighter animal than that ridden by the Gascon and Douglas wore only chain mail and a padded haubeck, whereas de Caillan was protected by heavy body armour and did not have Douglas's agility.

Douglas was already thundering towards him before he could complete his turn. Once more the two men clashed but neither harmed the other. Again they met, but Douglas deliberately held his smaller animal well apart from the huge, armoured stallion, so that the Gascon knight was forced to lean well over in an attempt to strike his opponent. As de Caillan passed him, Douglas brought his broadsword across the knight's lower back. So forceful was the blow, that his armour was dented and he was knocked forward over his horse's neck. His feet came out of his stirrups and he lost his balance. As his mount continued its wild prancing, the rider fell to the frosty ground. He staggered to his feet, but Douglas rode straight at him bringing his axe down on the crown of the helmet, splitting both helmet and head in two. The man fell like a poleaxed ox. Douglas did not wait but turned his attention to the remaining Englishmen. The cattle, alarmed by all the noise and confusion, fled into the cover of the trees and the sergeant yelled to his men "Withdraw! Withdraw!" And fled along the track with his men thundering after him. As they disappeared into the twilight a shower of small stones flew in all directions from the hooves of their horses.

When the mauled foraging party returned to Berwick, they told their tale to the castle governor. Edmund de Caillan had been a popular man in the garrison, particularly with the Neville brothers, who questioned the sergeant closely about the knight's death. That Douglas had not shown Edmund the courtesy of dismounting and fighting him on equal terms was quite outrageous. Did Douglas follow any rules of chivalry? Was he a complete barbarian? The Nevilles were determined to avenge Edmund without delay. Sir Robert Neville was a fine fellow, tall and handsome, he bathed regularly and was always exquisitely dressed in brightly coloured surcoat and hose. His comrades laughed at his flamboyant appearance, saying he looked like a Frenchman and nicknamed him the 'Peacock.' Sir Robert sent a challenge to Douglas offering to meet him in personal combat to the death.

Robert Boyd had recently joined Douglas in his forest lodge and had been out hunting with him. The cold, early March weather had tired him and when Neville's challenge arrived, Boyd was sitting by the fire, chin resting on chest, eyes closed, his long legs stretched out before him so that his feet could take full advantage of the warmth. He snored gently; the only other sound in the hall came from the crackling flames. Douglas, a younger man and notorious for his excessive energy, was out in the yard overseeing the building of another barn to accommodate his growing number of followers. James rushed into the hall, laughing loudly and Boyd woke with a start. "Hey, Boyd. Those fools at Berwick have challenged me to combat. Imagine that, after all that has happened. They still do not understand this war." Boyd smiled at Douglas's contemptuous opinion of the English. He stretched, yawned and was about to reply but Douglas continued angrily. "Even though we've beaten them fair and square in battle and all that is left to them is Berwick, still they arrogantly offer personal challenges." Boyd, smiling said, "and what will be your answer?" "Why, I'll accept, of course, and win." This was said with supreme confidence. "The king wouldn't give his blessing to you pursuing a personal vendetta, Douglas, particularly if he loses one of his most valued captains." Douglas stared coldly at Boyd. "I won't fail," he said and abruptly returned to his work outside. Boyd could hear him angrily rebuking a man who had not completed a task to his high standards. Boyd decided that the contest would be too good a spectacle to miss and that he would not return north until he had witnessed the event.

After the wettest and coldest winter that anyone could remember, the ground around Berwick was so waterlogged that fighting from horseback would be no easy task. The Scots arrived at the appointed time and venue, out of arrow range of the town walls. Only then did the Neville brothers and their retinue of ten knights set forth. Their squires, boldly holding their standards, stayed a little back from the designated battleground to await the return of their masters. The Scots carried only one standard with the lion of Scotland emblazoned upon it, which they drove firmly into the ground. They drew up in a single line facing their enemy, ready for battle. The young, English squires, excited by the event and confident of victory, began to call out insults and whistle. The Scots, lacking supporters, banged on their shields to drown the abuse from the other side. There was no great distance between the two opposing groups of fighting men and Douglas gave the command to advance without waiting to observe the usual formalities of chivalry. The English rode taller, heavier stallions and each animal wanted to be the lead horse and required little prompting from its rider to advance. The citizens of Berwick lined the town walls to watch the event.

Douglas marked Sir Robert Neville as his opponent. They whirled around each other, battleaxes crunching on shields. The ground was so muddy that very quickly horses began to flounder on the slippery morass. Neville was unhorsed, lost his battleaxe, but managed to regain his feet quickly, and gripped his sword. Douglas, in chivalrous mood and aware of the spectators, jumped from his lighter mount prepared to fight on equal terms. He drew his broadsword, which had been strapped to his back and the two men circled around each other watching for an opportunity to strike. Around them knights fought, as in an ancient gladiatorial contest, the English squires and Berwick's population their audience. Douglas and Neville were of similar age, both agile men, but as usual Douglas was lightly clad and he moved forward with such aggression that the English knight was forced backwards and stumbled in the mud, falling heavily, his helmet flying from his head. Douglas took the advantage, as Neville tried to regain his feet and swung his broadsword in an arch. As it cut through the air the ringing sound was the last noise that the English knight heard. It cut deeply into the side of his head and he fell back, blood and brains spreading in the mud. Douglas jumped nimbly over the sprawling body to attack another victim.

Robert Boyd had not taken part in the fighting, but sat at a little distance watching the English squires and the distant gates of Berwick. When Robert Neville's squire saw his lord fall, he spurred his horse to join in the affray, but Boyd, sitting impassively watching the fight sent an arrow towards the young man. It stuck fast in his upper arm and he abandoned his attempt to assist his comrades.

Nevilles's younger brother was knocked from his horse and threw down his sword in a sign of surrender. His companions followed suit. Before the eyes of the citizens of Berwick the English knights were led away as prisoners. Later a messenger arrived at Berwick demanding ransom for their return.

March began in traditional style with high winds and driving rain sweeping across the land. The lowland shepherds were preparing for the lambing and as many ewes as possible were brought under cover, but some remained in the open and dropped their lambs onto the sodden grass. The bedraggled bundles of woolly life quickly succumbed to the biting cold. Cattle stood listlessly in the byres, their ribs clearly seen, their gaunt haunches protruding, leaving deep hollows in their flanks. They hung their heads dejectedly, lowing plaintively and cows close to calving, dropped stillborn young. Throughout Lent the people prayed for an early change in the weather. Another bad year would bring serious famine and misery with it, for it was said that the whole of Christendom suffered as Scotland did.

Marjorie was nearing the end of her pregnancy and her father's physician, after visiting her many times, declared that the king's grandchild would arrive before Lent was ended. On their advice she did not observe the Lenten fast for she would need all her strength for the forthcoming birth.

Towards the end of the first week of March the rain ceased.

"Praise be," cried Marjorie, "I think God has answered my prayers and has told the sun to shine, for he knows I hate sitting indoors," and she put her embroidery to one side and ordered her mare to be saddled. Her ladies looked shocked and tried to stop her and with one voice said "Lady, you mustn't ride so close to your time," but Marjorie ignored them, brushing aside their protests. "Alice, all of you, stop. I will ride in the park and shall come to no harm. Although the sun shone the wind was strong, roaring through the trees, their bare branches swaying in the wild gusts. Marjorie's grey mare pranced about on the muddy path, ears flattened, champing on the bit and tossing her head. The grooms who accompanied her found their mounts just as spirited. The horses in the palace stables had been on short rations since Christmas and in their stables they had stood dispirited and depressed, but out in the open the gale made them agitated and eager to gallop with the wind. Marjorie glanced over her shoulder at her escort, calling out "Let them have their heads and I'll race you all up to the bend in the track." John, the most senior of the men called, "Nay lady, the ground is poor and the wind makes them wild." He came level with her and tried to take her rein to steady her restless animal, but Marjorie laughed, brushed the man's hand away and slapped her mount with her crop. Away went Marjorie, followed by the men, but the faster they went the faster galloped Marjorie's spirited animal, its rider laughing and calling out to her escort behind her, until John shouted to his companions, "Hold back, we're frightening the Lady's mare." The wind raged around and in her mad headlong dash Marjorie's mantle billowed about her. She called out "See, even now I can beat you." The trees lining the path flashed by.

It happened without warning as she came to the bend. A large branch, weakened by the gale came crashing down onto both horse and rider. The horrified men watched as the terrified mare reared and floundered among the debris, legs flaying the air before it crashed to the ground. Marjorie was thrown clear and at first the men thought she was stunned, but they could not waken her. The mare was in a poor state, raising its head from among the broken branch and whinnying, pitifully pinned down by the weight of the branch, it was unable to raise itself. To speed its end, for mercy's sake, one of the grooms slit its throat. John took Marjorie in his arms and carried her before him. Cradling her like a small child, he rode back to the palace as fast as his burden would permit, sending one of his men ahead. "Tell them to call Master Mabinus the physician, for I fear for her."

In her chamber her women stood around in confusion. They burnt feathers under her nose but Marjorie did not stir. The physician arrived and placed his hand on her swollen belly. Inside the child still moved, but when a bronze mirror was placed to Marjorie's lips it was seen that breath did not cloud the reflection nor did her bosom rise and fall.

The king was away from Scone and it was Abbot Bernard who gave absolution to the departed soul of the king's daughter before ordering Master Mabinus to take out the child. The physician cut a deep wound into Marjorie's taunt white skin and removed a small, red, male child. The umbilicus was cut, the mucus removed from his tiny nose and mouth and above the noise of the wailing women the baby took its first breath and cried long and shrill. The doctor squeezed the dead mother's breasts, but fluid had not begun to fill them. A wet nurse had already been brought to the chamber and the boy, wrapped tightly in linen and wool was laid to her ample breast.

When the king heard the news he sat silent, tears brimming in his eyes. Always she had been a restless, spirited and headstrong maid, yet she had been dutiful to his wishes, for he knew that she would have had James Douglas for a husband, had she had her way. Well, he had a male grandchild, but at what a cost? His son-in-law showed suitable grief at her funeral mass, but there had been little affection between the two and he quickly recovered from his loss. His little son, named Robert, survived the trauma of his birth, gained weight and cried lustily for his nurse's breast.

In June, just before the king left on campaign, after a long labour Queen Elizabeth delivered her child. A lady ran to the great hall where the king sat with his men and breathlessly she cried, "My lord, the queen has been safely delivered. It's a strong maid." He could not help but show his disappointment that it was not a son, but ill temper was not his way and then he said. "She is well?" "She is tired, but the child has already been put to the breast." When the mother had rested her husband went to her. The chamber was very hot with a large fire burning in the hearth. Elizabeth lay quietly, the coverlet folded back under her breasts and the babe lying in the crook of her arm. She was gently singing to her daughter when the father came in. She smiled up at him as he stood looking down at the radiant mother and peaceful babe. The mother said. "She is healthy Robert and we may look to have a son next time," Her husband sat on the edge of the bed and stroked the child's silken cheek. Then he took his wife's soft hand, "As you say, sweetheart, there's time yet for many more and you are well. We will call her Margaret after the sainted queen and she will grow into a fine woman." In spite of his kindly words it worried him that the child was female, for he had seen forty-two summers and Scotland badly needed a male heir.

The weather had continued wet and cold with high winds and at midsummer King Robert collected an army together once again to invade England. In England he would capture meat and grain for the following winter.

Towards the end of the month, before the queen had had her churching, he led his army across the border, through the eastern marches and into the once rich county of Northumberland as far south as County Durham. Whereever they went the Scots demanded ransom from the English. Farmers and merchants willingly gave money for they knew their own king would not send out his soldiers to protect them from the invaders.

Haymaking had finished but the yield was poor and few haystacks were seen in the fields. Those there were already showing signs of mildew would not last beyond the autumn. Barley and oat crops were sparse and the high winds and heavy rains of the spring and early summer had flattened much of it. There was no sign of it ripening. At Barnard Castle, James Douglas led a division across the Pennines and burnt Penrith, while Walter Stewart, accompanied by Robert Boyd, marched into Wensleydale, extracting ransoms and burning and pillaging as they went.

King Robert took his division to Richmond Castle where the local merchants and nobility had already taken refuge, but in return for a large ransom he promised to leave them in peace and not burn the manors and farmsteads in the area. Then he turned north, rejoined the rest of his men and the whole army crossed over the western border heavily laden with gold, jewels and iron goods for there was a shortage of iron in Scotland.

The queen was at Dunfermline where the two royal babies were being nursed. The king spent that autumn and Christmas with his family, but in January he left, accompanied by his son, Robert Bruce, who had now seen eighteen winters, and Thomas Randolph. There was a warm friendship between father and son and Robert was often in the king's company, but when the queen was present the young man remained in the background and was modest and gallant and because of this he was liked by all. Elizabeth was aware of his presence and as each month came and went and she was not once again with child, she suffered bouts of anger and jealousy towards Christine of Carrick. However, she was not a woman to dwell on supposed injuries and her husband had, after all, begotten the boy with Christine of Carrick before she and he had wed.

Edward Bruce was now High King of Ireland and according to custom declared that it was his intention to progress around the provinces of Ulster, Meath, Leinster, Munster and Connaught and invited his brother, the King of Scots, to accompany him.

The powerful Bisset kinsmen of Ulster welcomed the Bruces, as they had when the King of Scots had led a vagrant's life, but Robert had to admit that on the whole there was little or no support for Edward from the Celtic Irish. Their chiefs were suspicious of the Scots and did not bring out their men in great numbers.

The Bruces marched south towards Dublin attacking Anglo-Irish forces and many English families and their supporters fled to Dublin which they intended to defend, but a siege was as distasteful to the Bruces as it had always been, and they turned westward to meet up with the chief of the O'Briens, who had promised his support, but when they arrived at Shannon they found the O'Briens had fallen out among themselves and were now arrayed in battle gear ready to fight the Scots.

One evening King Robert said to his brother, "We must return north, our supplies are low and foraging parties return, empty-handed. Look at the land." He waved an arm at the countryside, "It's bare." The great famine, which had struck all of Europe, had hit Ireland badly and the people, particularly the children, were thin with hollow cheeks and eyes sunken into their pale faces. Never had King Robert seen such hunger and the following day Edward Bruce gave the command to retreat back to Ulster. Each man packed his gear with relief. The sooner they left the barren land, where no living creature, neither fowl nor hoofed beast could be found, the better.

King Robert had already mounted, when above the general noise of an army preparing to march, he heard the screams and pleading of a woman's voice. It was plain something was amiss with one of the women who served the army in various ways. The screams and plaintive wailing continued and the king turned to his son, Robert, "Find out what ails that woman. Is murder being committed?" The screaming continued and young Robert Bruce quickly returned grinning. "It's nothing father, just a washerwoman who has come to her time and will be left behind. She begs someone to stay with her, but none will." Young Bruce jumped onto his horse preparing to move off with the other young men. "Nay, Robert," called his father, "There's no such great haste that we must leave the poor creature behind," and to the wonder of his son he ordered the army to wait until the child had been delivered. Edward Bruce and the other men, who had campaigned with the king for many years, did not find his generosity so surprising.

It was the aspect of his character that men found so attractive. It began to rain again and King Robert ordered that a tent be erected for the labouring woman, then the two kings and their whole army sat down to await nature. For most of that day the woman lay gripped with birth pains, but as the light began to fade a strong, male child was delivered. The waiting men, who heard its plaintive cries, all breathed a sigh of relief, for in the morning they could march north. At the king's command, mother and babe rode on a pony. A man, walking beside her, led the animal.

That evening as they rested, the woman begged to speak with King Robert and was taken before him. It was the closest she had ever been to her king and she fell on her knees. "Noble lord, I thank you for your kindness to a poor woman. I would be dead now had you not spared me." "Nay, mother, rise up, it's no more a kindness than I hope others would show to any Christian soul." There were tears in her eyes as she gazed at the bright, blue eyes and weather-beaten face of her king. "Lord, may I call my boy after you?" At that the king laughed out loud, "If it pleases you, may he have a more peaceful life than I have had."

During the march to Ulster, they were in more danger from the effects of famine than attack from the enemy, and were forced to kill and eat their horses before finally reaching Carrickfergus. News awaited them that the English had again crossed Scotland's border and in May, King Robert returned to his own kingdom, leaving Edward to continue his campaign throughout the summer.

James Douglas had been in command of Scotland's defence whilst the king was away. Once again he had outmanoeuvred the invading English. Their commander was the Earl of Arundel who had been forced to retreat back to England having gained very little booty. King Robert was happy to relax after the hardships of his march through Ireland and content to leave the mopping up to Douglas whilst he joined the queen at Dunfermline. Before the year came to an end Elizabeth was once again with child.

One day during Advent the king went to the private chapel in Dunfermline to pray. He found that with Scotland securely in his hands, he now had even less time to think and be alone than in the dark days when he had been a hunted man. There were so many matters of state that needed his attention and men were always seeking an audience with him. He heard a movement behind him and turning saw John Blair whom he had last seen after the battle at Bannockburn. The friar was a similar age to the king and had spent most of his life in Scotland's service, first with the Lord Wallace, who had been his friend, and later with Robert Bruce when he had been a hunted man hiding in the heather. "John Blair, my dear friend. How are you?" "My lord, I did not intend to disturb your contemplation." In his hand he held fresh candles for the altar. "For such as yourself, I always have time. I'd finished anyway." They walked together into the cloister, talking as they went. "How do you spend your time now, John?" "I teach, my lord and work for Abbot Bernard." "And your own writing, John, what of that? You spent many hours scribbling, if I remember correctly. What has become of it?" John Blair smiled. "Aye, I have written many stories of the heroic exploits of Wallace and yourself, sir and of Scotland's struggles. Men who come after us may read of these things." "It's a worthy task for sure, John. I'll speak to the abbot that he should give you time to complete your work. Scots, who are yet to live, should know of these matters and we none of us get any younger."

That Berwick was still in English hands was a great irritation to King Robert and he could not rest until that Scottish town had been reclaimed. In April he sent an advanced division of young and eager knights to recapture the town and with the help of a Scot, living within Berwick, during the night climbed the walls. The mainly English citizens, young tradesmen and merchants, resisted the Scots with great courage and William Keith found it no easy task to break through to open the gates and allow the king and his army to enter. The Berwick garrison refused to submit and the king was forced to besiege the castle until mid summer when the starving defenders finally surrendered.

He did not destroy Berwick Castle as was his usual habit, but ordered it to be re-provisioned for one year and left his son-in-law Walter Stewart as governor, while his son Robert Bruce, whom he had made Lord of Carrick, was second in command. The English would not suffer the indignity of Berwick's loss and would surely attempt to retake such an important trading town. He employed a Fleming, Master John Crab, to construct six springalds, with a great supply of iron–tipped darts, similar to those used by the defenders of Carlisle against his forces. The weapons were placed around the castle walls in readiness for the English attack.

The king retired to Scone Palace complaining of fever and headaches and where his chain mail had rubbed and chaffed his skin he had developed sores that would not heal. Master Mabinus recommended the king to rest. Elizabeth was with him with the three royal babes, Robert Stewart, and his daughters, Margaret and little Matilda, born a few weeks earlier. Robert sat in the garden enjoying the last golden days of autumn. Shortly the first frosts would claim the green foliage of the shrubs and herbs, but for the moment he could sit in peace, sheltered from the chill of the wind by the surrounding stone walls and watch the two fair infants as they played. They were both walking on unsteady, chubby legs. The boy stamped along the stony path, clutching a handful of dead leaves and pulling roughly at dead flower heads, putting them into his mouth with stumpy fingers. Young Robert watched his nurse and when she tried to take his treasures from him, he giggled happily and trotted away hoping to evade her outstretched arms. The chase usually ended when Robbie lost his balance and sat down heavily on the path, while his watching grandfather smiled benevolently as, at the same time, he watched his own little maid, Margaret, collecting pebbles and small pieces of moss which she placed in her father's lap. The new child slept placidly in her nurse's arms. The sores on his calf and neck had not yet healed but he had no pain and the fever had gone and with Elizabeth sitting quietly at his side he felt at ease with himself and his world.

October came and just before All Souls Day, while he sat by a blazing fire listening to the crackling of the flames and his harpist playing his favourite tunes, his chancellor came into the hall. The expression on Bernard's face informed the king that he was about to receive some bad news, but he had had many such messages in his time and he tried to prepare himself for it. Breathlessly, the abbot, with saddened eyes at the pain which he was about to inflict on his king, said, "Lord, a messenger has arrived from Ulster. The Lord Edward, your brother, has been killed in battle near Dunkeld." With bent head the king walked hurriedly to the Abbey and prostrated himself before the altar, humbled ready to submit himself to God's will, if he gave him a sign. He lay on the cold slabs until his body was stiff and aching, but no one dared to come close to him or interrupt his grief. "There's a curse on my kinsmen," he murmured. "God has allowed me to lead Scotland to victory and freedom from the English, but will not let me forget I have committed sacrilege in a Holy place. He continues to punish me for my pride and arrogance." It had been dark for some time before slowly he raised himself. He ate and drank sparingly before returning to the altar to pass the night in prayer and contemplation.

When Abbot Bernard saw the king the following morning, he thought he had never seen King Robert looking so tired and distressed. Not even at his daughter's death had the King of Scots appeared so forlorn. His cheerful and open face was drawn, his weathered skin yellow, his eyes, normally twinkling with good humour, were dull and dark from lack of sleep. He had the look of a beaten man.

The abbot listened to the king's confession of his sins and when he had finished Bernard said, "My lord, you cannot take the burden for all mankind's sins onto your shoulders. Our Lord, Jesus Christ, does that for us. You are a great king, but you are also a man who, like us all, sins. If you humbly confess and make penance He will hear. Has he not already shown the special favour he holds for his servant, Robert Bruce and the Scottish people? What you must now do, my lord, is to ask the Holy Father, in Rome, to raise his ban of excommunication against yourself and your people. Only when this ban has been raised, will you find spiritual peace." For some days after this the king remained in seclusion, seeing only his confessor and eating and drinking sparingly.

Parliament met at Scone at the beginning of December and agreed that Robert Stewart should be declared his grandfather's heir should the queen fail to produce a male child. Thomas Randolph, Earl of Moray, should be guardian if the king died while his heir was still a minor and that should Thomas Randolph die, Lord James Douglas would take over the administration and defence of the kingdom.

In England, King Edward, angry and humiliated by the loss of Berwick, mustered his army near Newcastle and prepared for a new offensive. He left his queen, Isabella and the exchequer in safety at York and by August was besieging Berwick with ten thousand men, whilst a fleet from England's eastern ports blockaded the sea approaches to the town.

Since the death of his wife Marjorie, the 'silly little boy' had grown up under his father-in-law's watchful eye and he commanded Berwick garrison energetically, replying aggressively to King Edward's assaults, using Master Crab's war machines to create the maximum possible confusion among the attacking English.

King Edward continued with the siege but in November, when Berwick garrison still remained stubborn and showed no sign of giving up the town, he heard that Douglas had invaded the West Coast of England and was marching across Lancashire. Savagely the Scots were attacking, burning what little harvest had been carried in after the wet summer and seizing all livestock.

King Edward raised the siege and withdrew his army to the River Trent, sending envoys to King Robert with instructions to negotiate a truce. During December the Earl of Pembroke and the Bishop of Ely led the English delegation to Newcastle and at Christmas, Sir Thomas Randolph swore, on behalf of King Robert, to uphold peace for two years.

THE LION AND
THE LEOPARD

The papal envoys had arrived from France two days previously and were told that King Robert would receive them when they had rested after their long journey. Accordingly, they presented themselves in the great hall at Scone Palace on a pleasant morning in early spring.

The palace was busy with the king's council, nobles, knights, squires, grooms and men hoping to place a petition before the king. It seemed that all men of consequence and those anxious to become men of consequence, had arrived to hear the letters from his Holiness. Rumours had already spread that the Holy Father had not addressed the king as king, but simple Robert Bruce. If this were true it was an affront to King Robert and to Scotland. All men knew whom to blame for the denial of Scotland's independence – the English, for in spite of their defeat at Bannockburn and loss of Berwick, they still clung to their arrogant claims.

The great hall was packed with barely space to walk through to the raised dais at the far end, where the king sat awaiting the papal emissaries, with a patient expression on his face. He wore a simple, gold crown, symbol of his authority, and full-length royal-blue surcoat edged with ermine.

The crowd of onlookers parted to make way for two eminent Frenchmen, the Bishop of Corbeil and the Archdeacon of Perpignan. The assembly carefully closed ranks again so that a solid wall of humanity stood watching as their king respectfully listened to the Pope's message. "And have you written letters from the Holy Father for us?" enquired the king mildly. The Bishop of Corbeil held out the parchment to the chancellor who scrutinized the seals and the opening preamble before saying to his king, "This document is most certainly from the Holy Father, my lord, but I fear it is not addressed to yourself." The king raised an eyebrow, took the document and glanced at it with only passing interest before handing it back to Abbot Bernard. He said to the emissary, "I see that it is addressed to Robert Bruce, but you must know there are many men of that name in my kingdom. Who can say which man this is addressed to? It cannot be I, for I am King Robert of Scotland and can't receive letters which are not addressed to me." There was a general murmur of dissatisfaction in the hall and the messengers shuffled uneasily, looking nervously around. The king raised his hand for silence and patiently waited for the emissary to reply.

"My lord, the omission of your title of king was not meant as an insult. Holy Church cannot write or say anything which can be misunderstood until a claim has been substantiated." There were raised voices amongst the listeners. "Shame," and "Nonsense," were among the milder comments but the king remained calm and replied with patient irony. "I am in possession of this kingdom, sirs. All my people call me king and foreign princes give me that title, excepting the English. It would seem that Mother Church has more partiality towards the English whom they try to please. Had you presented such letters to any other sovereign prince you might have received a harsher reply. Take back your letters, for I shall only receive them when I am treated as King of Scots. As it is I respect you as messengers from the Holy Father." The noise from the body of the hall grew louder, but the king rose and still benevolent and dignified, departed.

Later in the day the envoys were summoned before the king's council. Chancellor Bernard was courteous, but Douglas and Randolph were furious and made no attempt to hide it. Douglas said, "By birth and trial in battle, our lord has the right to be addressed as king. You insult all of us because you side with the English." The poor envoys, red in the face, tried to defend their master, but to no avail and Chancellor Bernard, after calming the situation, at the king's insistence escorted the Frenchmen to Berwick on the first stage of their return journey.

At a council meeting, held near Edinburgh and presided over by the king, the questions of Scotland's independence from England and the recognition of King Robert of Scots and how best to represent these points to the Pope, were discussed. The chancellor said, "It's true that his Holiness believes King Robert and you, my lords are rebels, because the English tell him that this is so. We must clear muddy waters and change his mind. The Holy Father must understand that Scotland has not rebelled against her lawful lord, King Edward of England, but that Scots are loyal subjects to their own king, and that they are and always have been a separate people from the English, although they remain obedient sons of the Church. "Aye, but how can we get him to understand this?" replied Thomas Randolph. The chancellor said, "I have given this matter careful thought. We must send him a great declaration that sets out our historical origins. It must tell the Holy

Father how we have become the people we are and how we have always been separate from England and her king. We should tell him that St Andrew himself converted us to Christianity and therefore the church especially blesses us. We should point out to him that only when our land was left kingless, without a leader, did the English king, whom until then we had considered a friend, turn on us with war and bloodshed." There were noises of approval around the room, but before continuing, the abbot looked towards the king who nodded his approval. The chancellor held up his hand for silence. "Finally we will point out that we have been set free from the evils of warfare by our lord, King Robert, who has fought tirelessly for his people and we hold him in lordship over us." There were again sounds of approval from his listeners, but he had not finished and continued. "It is essential that His Holiness understands it is the people of Scotland who welcome and revere the Lord Robert as king. That it is in our name he continues to place his immortal soul in jeopardy by leading us to freedom. Therefore, we will state that should he ever agree to make us subjects of the King of England, we will drive him from us as an enemy and will make another man king who will defend our freedom."

From the council members who were not within the inner circle of the king's advisers, there were gasps of surprise at such audacious speech before the king, but he just smiled. He had been silent since his arrival at the meeting, but held up his hand and said, "This declaration has been formulated with my full agreement. I believe it should be the Community of Scotland who appeals to the Holy Father for his protection against the persecution of the English. For this reason it will not be signed with the royal seal, but I will ask that you, my lords, set your own seals to it and that it is sent in your names."

All were in agreement that the document should be prepared and that the seals of the Earls of Ross, Fife, Strathearn, Lennox, Moray, Sutherland, Caithness and Patrick, Earl of Dunbar, should be affixed, along with the seals of many barons and freeman of Scotland. The envoys were chosen with great care. To deliver such an important document only men representing wide support now enjoyed by King Robert should be sent. Sir Adam Gordon had served the English until Bannockburn, before transferring his loyalty to King Robert. Odard de Maubisson, an envoy from the French Court, emphasized the support which the French gave to King Robert and Scotland and Alexander Kinnimonth, a lawyer, possessed of a rich and vibrant voice, who would read the Declaration to His Holiness, set out in early spring. They arrived at the Papal Court in Avignon towards the end of June 1320.

Pope John listened to the impressive document and its sentiments and noble ideals. He could not help but admire it, but was not entirely won over to the Scottish cause because of his own political aims. He was planning another crusade against the infidels and had requested the help of the kings of Christendom. King Robert had hinted that were he sure his kingdom would be free from English invasion, he would gladly lead a crusade from Scotland. However, King Edward of England had made a similar promise and there was no doubt that more help would be forthcoming from England than might be expected from the kingdom of the Scots, for England was a wealthier land. To offend the English was not in Pope John's interests, therefore he sent his reply to 'that illustrious man Robert, who assumes the title and position of King of Scotland.' In it he promised to use all his powers to make the English seek peace and that he would send a papal representative to the peace talks. This reply, he felt, satisfied the honour of both Scots and English and to appease King Robert he lifted the decree of excommunication. That autumn King Robert's messengers arrived back in Scotland, hopeful that peace would soon be declared.

Malais, Earl of Strathearn had been grateful to his king when he allowed him to take his parents to his own lands where they could live in peace and comfort. His father had never quite recovered from the shame he endured after his surrender to King Robert at Perth Castle. When his son was at home, he occasionally hunted in the parklands, but mostly he remained in his chamber, morose and speaking to few. He rarely visited his wife's chamber nor were their rumours that he visited any other women. When they took their food together he spoke little to her so that his brooding silence and black despair made meals a sad time. The servants looked forward to the return of their young lord and his followers, they lifted the atmosphere in the great hall, filling it with their jokes and youthful enthusiasm.

After Scotland's victory at Bannock, the old earl's mood became even more despairing. Once he had been a large, powerful man but he began to waste, his face drawn and pale, and took little interest in his appearance. His son, on a lightening visit to his castle, was so worried by his father's health, he asked his mother, "What ails father? Surely we can get a doctor to him." "A doctor cannot help your father, I believe a spell has been caste on him. When he sleeps at night he is chased by demons and he spends much time pacing up and down his chamber. Besides, he will not listen to me and we rarely say more than half a dozen words to each other." Malais found the atmosphere so oppressive that he was pleased to finish his business and return to the king's service.

He spent Christmas in the king's company. It was a jolly affair for he was a good friend with both Douglas and Randolph. The three drank together and rode in the king's company. In the New Year when the festivities were ended, he received news that his father's health had deteriorated further and he travelled to his estate to see his parents. His father was in bed and had been there for some weeks. He did not stir nor show any sign of recognition when his son bent over him. "Father, can you hear me?" There was no hint that the older man had knowledge of his surroundings. That night, Malais sat by his father's bedside, for he feared that when he came home again his father would no longer be there.

The old earl died quietly, early on a cold, February morning. He was quite alone when it happened. In his later years he had sought solitude and his former followers, men who had once called him lord, barely noticed his passing. Only his son mourned his departure.

The atmosphere in the castle lifted after the late earl's death. The Lady Agnes, his widow, although still vocal in her condemnation of King Robert, became more cheerful and pleased when her son came to see her and she took over the management of the household as she had done in happier years. She oversaw the preserving and setting aside of provisions, the re-hanging of heavy winter tapestries and the sweeping of the floors, strewing them with fresh herbs which she dried in her still room and she began to work on an elaborately embroidered surcoat for her son. It was full length, to reach to his ankles and when Malais saw it, he grunted saying, "Aye, it's fine mother but I'll hardly need it for I spend all my time in the saddle." His mother smiled and said nothing for Malais was the only one of her children left for her to fuss over.

After his father's death, Malais felt under less threat, certain that with the passage of time folk would forget his father's lack of enthusiasm for King Robert, and the rumours of treason which had troubled his family name, would soon be forgotten.

In June 1320, Strathearn was at his estate and sat one evening with his hounds at his feet and a goblet of Burgundian wine on a side table. His mother had already retired to her chamber. It was rare for him to be alone, kinsmen and followers usually surrounded him, but on this night they were away on various errands. During the day he had flown his falcon in the park and it was pleasant to sit before his own fireside, listening to his harpist. He became aware of the household steward, a man who had served the family since Malais had been a small boy. "My lord, I have heard something which I feel you should know." It was plain from the man's furtive glances around the hall that he did not want to be overheard. Malais led him to the chapel, which was quiet at that time of the evening. Murdoch, the steward, looked embarrassed and fidgeted before he finally told the earl his problem. "Sir, recently we have had many visits from noble lords." Strathearn looked startled. "Who would visit here when I am away from home?" Murdoch looked at the floor, tracing the outline of the flagstone with the toe of his boot. "They visit the lady, your mother, sir." Malais looked even more astonished. "Come Murdoch, spit it out. Undoubtedly you know why they come." Murdoch looked at his lord and when he spoke there was pity in his eyes. He used his lord's personal name as he had when the earl was a boy. "Malaise, they talk of treason. They plot to kill the king." A look of disbelief appeared on the earl's face, then he began to laugh. "Nay, it's not possible. I would have heard rumours had there been unrest in the kingdom. Name these men who have visited her and conspired against the king," he challenged. "The Lords Patrick Graham, Roger de Mowbray, Sir David Brechin and the Sheriff of Aberdeen conspire to set William de Soules on the throne after they have killed good King Robert." The earl's face turned an ashen hue, for William de Soules was his cousin; their mothers were both daughters of Alexander Comyn, Earl of Buchan. He thanked his steward for his loyalty and promised he would deal with the accusation without delay. He remembered that his aunt had recently stayed with his mother and the two had sat in her chamber blathering as women do. Now, he could see that their talk was more sinister. What should he do? Foolish he knew her to be, but she was still his mother. He sat late into the night and when at last he retired to his bed, he tossed and turned, unable to sleep. At first light, he arose went out to the stables and ordered the horses to be saddled.

His mother was still in bed, but stirred and sat up when her son appeared. She patted the bed inviting him to sit down, but he continued to stand, staring down at her with troubled eyes. "You look very serious, Malais. What's amiss?" He did not speak gently, "Mother, I hear you've been very busy during the past weeks, plotting with traitors against our king." She looked shocked and at first he thought she was going to deny the accusations. He said, "Don't try to lie to me mother." There was a long silence before she said, "Your cousin William would bring power back to his Comyn kinsmen if he replaced Bruce and you would be among his closest advisers. I meant to speak to you after the deed had been done, for I was sure once William had the crown, you would see the wisdom of joining him." "So you thought to drag me into your scheme. Don't you see that the power of the Comyn's has ended? King Robert is accepted by all. How could you be so foolish? You've ruined everything and we can only hope that when you've confessed to the king, he'll allow us to keep what we have without forfeiture or punishment." "Malais, you would have me tell Bruce? Never!" "Never could be a long time mother, if I pay with my life and you with imprisonment." His mother looked stunned. "How can that be when none know?" "How do you think I've found out? The servants know. Do you think they'll remain silent if I don't act?" spat her son. Yet his mother continued to argue angrily, reminding him that his father had fought bravely with Wallace, to support Scotland's freedom from the English, but Malais remained firm, ordering her to prepare for the journey to see the king. By the time she was ready, she was sobbing loudly and refused all assistance from him as she mounted her horse, but when she had composed herself, they began their journey in silence, for in truth there was little more to be said.

The king was at Dunfermline and Strathearn begged to see him immediately. The Lady Agnes looked frightened and her son was forced to take her arm to steady her. She stood before the king with her eyes downcast because she could not bring herself to return his enquiring gaze. She told him all and when he questioned her, she said, "Aye, they intended to kill you. The deed was to have been carried out by Gilbert Malherbe, John Logie and his squire Richard Brown. It was he who was to have struck the fatal blow." She had spoken with downcast eyes but, when she spoke of the king's murder she had looked up at him and was surprised to see that far from looking angry, his face bore an expression of great sadness. All he said to her when she had finished was, "I had thought that since I had left you and yours in peace to enjoy your estates, possessions and title you would be content. I see that in this I have misjudged you." Malais said, "My lord, king, I have been well content with all you have given me and have been loyal to you these past ten years. Never have I had cause to regret my allegiance." The king raised his hand to halt the earl's justification. "Malais, I know well your loyalty to me. I will make you responsible for your mother while she is here and you and I will talk later."

Agnes of Strathearn was confined to her chamber and her son placed a guard on her door. The king discussed the conspiracy secretly with his closest commanders and before the news of the lady's confinement became widely known the conspirators were arrested.

Douglas was sent to apprehend Mowbray, but when he arrived at the knight's manor, de Mowbray, fearing betrayal when he saw

Douglas, left his armed men in the courtyard and taking his broadsword tried to escape. Douglas caught him, but in the fighting Mowbray received a wound to his thigh. At first it appeared to be of little consequence, but as the days went by, the wound began to ooze foul smelling pus and became hot, the flesh around it black and putrid. Within a week he was dead.

On the 4th August, parliament met at Scone to hear the trial of the conspirators for treason. It was a noisy session, everybody wanted to have his say and show loyalty to King Robert. De Soules confessed and begged the king's forgiveness. His life was spared, but he was sent in chains to Dumburton Castle. Malherbe, Logie and Brown were all found guilty and since it was they who would have struck the fatal blow to their king, they received the death sentence. Roger de Mowbray posed a problem. He was legally as guilty as the others but had escaped justice because of his death. Parliament ordered that his body be brought before them so that they could pass a posthumous sentence on him. When the king heard that de Mowbray's corpse was to be symbolically hung and beheaded he refused to sign the warrant declaring that his death from Douglas's sword was sufficient punishment. "It's enough," he said irritably, that the records show him to be treacherous to Scotland and its king. When Mowbray's wife asked if she might take his body for burial, the king gave his consent.

News of the conspiracy spread throughout the shocked kingdom. Nobody could understand why they should conspire to kill Good King Robert, just when the kingdom was beginning to prosper and after so many years of warfare and famine. At the condemned men's executions, held in Perth, large crowds came to watch. Everyone agreed that the king was benevolent for there had been few executions beyond those of common felons.

The crowd was good-natured, but as each man was brought forward, they hissed and booed to show their displeasure and when the head was held high by the axeman they shouted their approval. It was the final execution that caused the most excitement. Sir David Brechin, they said, had not participated in the plot but had knowledge of it and had not informed the king. At his trial he said he had given his pledge to the conspirators that he would not betray their confidence although he would not join them. Parliament found that even though a man had given his word to remain silent, it was nonetheless his duty to inform the lord, his king, to whom he had given an earlier pledge of loyalty. The Perth crowd did not care for the finer points of the Code of Chivalry, the king had signed Brechin's execution warrant and if the king thought him guilty that was enough for them. Brechin died well, kneeling before the priest, he said his prayers and in a loud voice declared himself innocent of treason, committed his soul to God and said, "Oh God, give me the strength to do this well." As the executioner held his severed head high, the crowd cheered loudly.

Ingram de Umfraville was a close friend of Brechin and he had given his support to the doomed man by attending the execution. He was very bitter and considered it an over harsh sentence. He asked the king if he could take Brechin's body for an honourable burial, which the king granted but Umfraville's bitterness continued and on a fine day in late August, he sought an audience with the king. "My lord, I seek your permission to leave Scotland and to dispose of my estates and possessions."

The king looked surprised. It was true that the knight had fought for King Edward at the Bannockburn, but he had sworn allegiance to the King of Scots and had been loyal in his service since then. "Tell me what ails you, Sir Ingram, for I value your loyalty." For a few moments the man stood looking at his king with a defiant expression on his face, then he said. "Since you ask me, I'll tell you straight. David de Brechin was a fine and brave man and a good friend. I'll not stay to serve a king who values these virtues so little." The king stirred in his chair and considered for a few moments before giving his reply. "If you must go then I give my consent for you to sell your estates and leave the kingdom, for I will have none in my following who doesn't give me his oath wholeheartedly." Then he added, "There are few kings in Christendom to whom you could have spoken thus, sir." Umfraville flushed angrily, but the king continued to regard him with calm unflustered eyes until the man was forced to lower his gaze and asked for leave to withdraw.

The king walked in the gardens accompanied by his wife. It was a pleasant evening. After the heat of the day, the air was heavy with the sweet scent of roses, lavender and honeysuckle climbing over the warm, red bricks of the wall. "You're very quiet this evening, Robert. Are you planning another campaign for this autumn? I thought the English had a truce with us." Her husband smiled for he knew she did not like him leaving her and the children. He took her hand and raised it to his lips, "Nay, Beth. I was just thinking that to be a good king a man must have many virtues. I do believe it's easier to lead men into battle than to sit in judgement over them. A king must regret nothing. What's done is done." Elizabeth thought for a while before saying, "You need have no fear when you meet Our Lord on Judgement Day, Robert. You have been and are a most humane and steadfast man." A fine, red rose bloomed close by and the king picked it, removed its sharp thorns and with a small bow presented it to her. Then they continued their stroll, walking hand in hand like two young lovers.

A few weeks after this, Umfraville presented himself once again before the king. "My lord, I've come to say farewell," declared the knight. The hall was full and a hush fell on the assembly. "Have you completed your business to your satisfaction, sir?" said the king. "Aye, there's nothing now to keep me here. My family's prepared and we leave for England tomorrow." "Then Umfraville, I give you my safe conduct to the border. Let's hope that England greets you fairly." There was angry murmuring from the listeners, but the king raised his hand to silence any troublemakers. Umfraville bowed very low and left, looking to neither right nor left as he passed through the throng. As was expected the English king, who was always keen to hear bad news of Robert Bruce, welcomed Umfraville.

The conspiracy was talked about for many months. No one doubted that the king had acted correctly in condemning the conspirators, but the matter of David Brechin divided the king's subjects. Some said, that if a man knows a crime is to be committed and says nothing, he is as guilty as the conspirators and others said that if a man has given his word then he cannot break that trust. Only a few declared that a man's first duty was the oath he had sworn to his lord the king, who represented the realm of Scotland, and that it took precedence over all other loyalties.

In the New Year 1321 envoys from the Pope arrived in Scotland to lead the peace discussions between Scotland and England. The opening talks were held in Newcastle. The Scottish envoys were full of hope for the papal envoys plainly intended to help Scotland in her claim that she was an independent kingdom. Therefore, it came as a bitter blow when once again the English claimed overlordship of Scotland and that Scottish kings must pay homage to England. By mid February the talks were in deadlock and both sides retired to take advice. In March they returned to the talks, but this time in the Scottish town of Berwick. Neither side brought any new proposals to the meetings and very quickly, tempers flared. As the English laboured the old point of overlordship, the Scots declared that since King Edward was descended from a bastard, Duke William of Normandy, he was not true king of the English anyway and they would not discuss peace with his representatives any longer. To a man the Scots arose and left the chamber without agreeing to any further meetings. The Earl of

Pembroke, who led the English delegation, wrote to his king that the Scots spoke of peace but their behaviour was to the contrary, for they still agreed to nothing. Exasperated, the English made ready to return south, but before leaving they demanded that the Pope should reinstate the ban of excommunication for Robert Bruce and the Scottish people. "You have witnessed," said Pembroke, "that we have tried to be reasonable with them, but they have no intention of seeking peace. They prefer the old ways. They'll find we don't lack the courage," he threatened. In April the papal envoys arrived back in Avignon and recommended that King Robert and his people be excommunicated once again. Since the Pope could not afford to antagonize the English, he did as he was bid.

King Robert did not call his men to arms. The truce, negotiated two years previously, still had some months to run and he doubted that King Edward would break the truce, for he faced many troubles in his own land. If Scotland bided her time it might be hoped that the English lords would settle Scotland's problems for her.

In the autumn of that year, James Douglas came to the king with some interesting information. Representatives of Thomas, Earl of Lancaster had brought a message from their lord. Lancaster, cousin to the King of England, had not appeared at the English muster before the invasion preceding the battle of Bannockburn and it was well known that the two had barely spoken since and then only in the company of many supporters.

"Well James, what does the noble earl want?" King Robert could guess and was not surprised when Douglas confirmed that Lancaster wanted the throne of England for himself. "What does he offer us for our support, recognition?" "Aye, my lord, he seeks our aid and will recognize your claim to Scotland in return." Bruce smiled, "Nay, nay, how can such a man be loyal to his promises to me, if he is prepared to betray his own lord, but continue your discussions with him, James. Encourage him a little, it can do our cause nothing but good."

When the truce came to an end Randolph, Douglas and Walter Stewart crossed the border and began to pillage and burn the northern counties. In desperation Sir Andrew Harclay, Governor of Carlisle and men of those counties turned to the Earl of Lancaster in his castle at Pontefract and asked for his help against the invading Scots, but angrily Lancaster sent them away telling them to ask their lord, King Edward. Harclay knew the king would not send them help to fight the Scots and once again they were forced to pay ransom for their safety.

Since his defeat in battle at Bannockburn, the English king had become increasingly dependent on Hugh Despenser for his advice and friendship. By 1322 they had become very close indeed. Queen Isabella had recently given birth to a little maid, Joan, but when she had had her churching and was again comely and in full health, the king did not visit her in her chamber and rarely spent time in her company. Isabella brooded, often preoccupied with ways in which she might avenge her wounded and humiliated pride. If he had taken a mistress from among her ladies she would have been angry, but nothing more. Many men had mistresses and kings more than most, but that a noble lord should usurp her, for a second time, – never. When she and the king met she lashed him with her tongue. His reply was to leave her altogether with Despenser riding at his side. She watched them go from the window of her chamber. Well, there had never been love between them although she had borne him four children. Anyway, Despenser would probably go the same way as Gavaston, for he was widely hated by the nobles, particularly Lancaster and Hereford, she mused.

Queen Isabella was correct in her belief that many powerful men loathed Gavaston and it surprised no one when Lancaster and Hereford marched on London demanding the banishment of Despenser. Anxiously parliament banishment the king's favourite from the land. Isabella was delighted, not because she wanted the king back in her bed, but because she was vindicated. She was alarmed therefore, when she heard that the king had gained support from his young half-brothers and the great Earls of Pembroke and Surrey. With an army of many thousand men, the king marched to Cirencester where he spent Christmas and immediately after Twelfth Night, he marched through the Welsh border country driving the rebel earls before him. Lancaster had returned to his castle of Pontefract during Christmas and Hereford intended to join up with him once more. Many men surrendered to the king as he progressed, but Hereford and his men retreated northwards.

February arrived, bitterly cold with a biting northeasterly wind buffeting trees, men and horses alike. Shepherds gathered their flocks from the hillsides, closer to abbey, manor and farmstead, for the lambing was not far off and the ewes needed the protection of the lambing pens in such weather.

As the king prepared to follow the rebels to Pontefract, Andrew Harclay, Governor of Carlisle, rode into the yard begging to see the king. "My lord, after Twelfth Night the Scots came again and have brought great misery to the northern counties. My men cannot help the people for we dare not leave Carlisle and when I heard that you had mustered your army I came to ask for your help to drive off the Scots." The king heard him out, but said, "Andrew, the Scots are not my most urgent enemy at present. If I turn my back on the traitors in my own kingdom, who can say what they will do? You must return north and hold the castles and towns of importance. When I've defeated my treacherous lords then I'll deal with the Scots." During Harclay's cold ride to search for the king, he had been certain the king would give him support. Now he felt angry and frustrated. He understood his king's predicament, but as he saw the situation, until the Scots were sent packing and peace terms agreed between the two kingdoms, the people of the north country could not prosper as once they had. The following day he rode back to Carlisle, vowing to hold that town and send extra help to the king so that the rebellion would come to a speedy end. Then the king could turn his attention on the invaders. Harclay was a determined and able soldier, who had watched the mayhem in the north for the past ten years and would go to any lengths to bring peace to the region. As soon as he arrived in Carlisle he sent out orders for the levies to muster.

By the end of the month King Edward had arrived in Coventry and prepared for the final march to Burton upon Trent where the army of Lancaster and Hereford was awaiting him. Lancaster had positioned his men by the bridge over the Trent, the only crossing point, but the Earl of Pembroke who rode with the king, sent spies to enquire of the local people where the Trent could be forded. They marched up River from Burton until they reached a ford and after crossing swung north–east, intent on catching the rebels in their rear.

Lancaster became restless when the vanguard of the king's army did not appear as he had expected it to. When he heard the news that the king had crossed upstream and was marching rapidly towards him, he ordered a retreat. By marching throughout the night they outmanoeuvre the king's men, but were forced to leave behind their stores, carrying only their weapons back to Pontefract Castle. They arrived safely but the earl would not stay to defend it. "If we remain here, Hereford, the king will besiege us and without outside help we must surrender eventually. We'll march north and join up with the Scots. Then united we can defeat Edward in his own land. We'll leave tomorrow and join Thomas Randolph at Darlington."

When Andrew Harclay heard that Stewart and Douglas were in Teesdale demanding ransom from the people of Carlisle he left the defence of the city to his second in command. He led the men of

Cumberland and Westmorland across the Pennines to Boroughbridge where he could make a stand against Lancaster's men and prevent them joining the Scots.

At the north side of the bridge over the River Ure, Harclay drew up his mounted men and blocked Lancaster's advance. Upstream by the ford, he deployed his pikemen, in Scottish fashion. It would be their job to stop Lancaster's cavalry. Along the hillside he positioned his archers ready to harass the enemy. Then they sat down to wait for Lancaster to appear.

Lancaster set a gruelling pace, the sooner he met with the Earl of Moray and the Scots, the happier he would be. He increased the speed of the cavalry until his infantry were forced to run to keep up with their comrades.

Boroughbridge came into view and the earl caught sight of Harclay and his men commanding the crossing. Lancaster pulled up his horse so that the beast came to a slithering halt, nostrils flared, its breath coming in a grey vapour in the chill, afternoon air. Hereford reined in beside him. "Are the Scots this far south?" he enquired, gazing at Harclay's battle formation. "Don't be ridiculous man, since when did the Scots dress thus? They're our own, come to support the king. I'll talk to their commander, perhaps we can come to an understanding." Just short of the bridge the earl stopped and called out, "Who's your commander?" A tall fair, man rode forward calling out, "I, Harclay, Governor of Carlisle. You can go no further, my lord, stop now and make your peace with the king." Lancaster laughed unpleasantly. "There's no peace that can be forged between that bugger and I. You must join with us sir, together we can turn on him, for you can't make bargains with such a man as this king." The earl was right in his assessment of Edward's character, but Harclay was a loyal Englishman and not prepared to betray that trust.

Lancaster rode back to his men, determined to fight his way through. Hereford took command of the infantry and dismounted to lead them onto the bridge, whilst Lancaster led the cavalry to the ford.

Harclay also ordered his knights to dismount and fight on foot because the bridge was so narrow that barely two men at anytime could cross. Hereford, with broadsword firmly gripped and his standard bearer close behind, led his men onto the bridge. Harclay came forward barring their way.

The fighting, Englishman against Englishman was bloody. Hereford fell from a blow to the head. His standard bearer fell at his side. The fighting ebbed and flowed across the narrow bridge but

Harclay and his men did not give ground and as the afternoon wore on, the bridge became blocked with bodies. The River and its banks were littered with the corpses of men who had jumped or were thrown over the parapet.

Lancaster found it impossible to cross by the ford. Time and time again his mounted men were driven back by the pikemen and the incessant rain of arrows which fell upon them. He withdrew and returned to the bridge. There he saw the piles of bodies and called over to Harclay, asking for an amnesty until the following morning. Harclay called back, "My lord, think before you return tomorrow for you'll receive the same reply from my men. Make peace before it's too late." That night Lancaster's men bivouacked on the south bank whilst the men of Cumberland and Westmorland rested on the northern bank of the River Ure. Campfires burned merrily and each army could see the other in the glow from the flames. They prepared their food and sharpened weapons ready for the morrow and when they had satisfied their hunger, they sang and joked and each side could hear the other. At the entrance to the bridge and along the banks, the guards called out to one another across the River, trying to persuade their opponents to save their lives and desert before morning.

The Earl of Lancaster was not a popular lord. His men found him harsh and mean–minded. As they discussed the day's events, the prospect of taking on Harclay and his men again became increasingly unwelcome. The general opinion was 'why should we fight another Englishman' and as the night wore on, they left their firesides and crept away into the darkness.

Lancaster had had every intention of continuing the fight when morning came, but as dawn broke it was clear that large numbers of his men had deserted. Harclay called to the earl. "My lord, surrender and make your peace with the king." Lancaster, bemused by the rapid decline in his fortunes looked across the River dividing them. He did not know Harclay personally, but he looked a sound fellow and had handled his command with cool courage. Lancaster asked, "The men, who remain loyal to me, do you promise your protection to them?" Harclay nodded his agreement, held up his arm and said, "I swear."

Harclay escorted the earl back to Pontefract Castle, which was now occupied by the king. He fully expected the noble lord, cousin to the king, to be reprimanded and possibly held in detention for sometime. He was, therefore, unprepared for the sentence which the king passed on the unfortunate Lancaster.

The great hall of the castle was packed with lords and Lancaster's men who had paid homage to the king and that he had promised could return to their estates and farms. The king sat in the earl's chair and stared at his cousin. Lancaster was accused of high treason to his lord the king and of attempting to ally himself to England's enemy, Robert Bruce and the Scottish rebels. He was not permitted to speak in his own defence and in desperation he called out that the proceedings were illegal. "I've the right to put my case before parliament." Of course it was his right, thought Harclay, as he stood behind his agitated prisoner, but nobody listened. To save themselves Lancaster's men were prepared to remain silent. The King passed sentence of death, to be carried out immediately. The ferocity of King Edward's voice and the expression of hatred on his face jolted Harclay back from his own thoughts. Lancaster looked resigned and as he was escorted from the hall the earl said, "No more than could have been expected once he had me in his power."

They followed the king's instructions and placed Lancaster on an old mule that usually carried bags of wheat up to the mill. The man was heavier than its usual burdens and the animal moved very slowly out of the castle, barely managing to struggle up the hill to the place of execution.

Executions were not a task Hartlay had performed before, but as a great lord, the earl was not to face the hangman's noose but to be beheaded. After he had been shriven, Lancaster said to Harclay, "Make your aim true and be quick, sir." Reluctantly, Harclay balanced his broadsword in both hands, raised it high and carried out his task. He found it unpleasant and rode away from the scene at some speed. For the remainder of the day he sat in his own chamber with a flagon of wine as his companion. Evening arrived and his squire came to him. "My lord, the king demands that you attend him." Harclay slowly raised a flushed face from the table where he had rested his head. "Sir, you must revive yourself," said his squire. A pitcher of water stood in the corner and Harclay ordered his man to pour it over his sore head after which he declared himself to be clear in his thoughts. His squire noted that Sir Andrew had little control over his long legs and staggered as he navigated the narrow stairs down to the great hall. The fresh air on the draughty stairway revived him somewhat and by the time he reached the hall, his drunkenness was less obvious, but to a close observer Harclay's red face was evidence that the knight had looked deeply into his goblet.

The king was sitting as Harclay had last seen him, "Ah, Andrew," he called, "we owe you a great deal and your reward will fit your service to us. Come forward." Cautiously, taking care not to stagger, Andrew Harclay made his way up the hall and stood before his king. "We make you Earl of Carlisle, Sir Andrew Harclay, with all the estates and dues which come with this status." Around the hall men cheered, for without doubt Harclay had saved them all. If Lancaster had joined the Scots who could tell what the outcome would have been? That night the king gave a great feast in honour of the new earl, but Harclay appeared to be unmoved by his good luck and although he sat close to the king he was silent and preoccupied with his own thoughts. Late in the evening, when most men had drunk heavily, a messenger arrived with the news that after Lancaster's defeat, Douglas and the other Scottish commanders, with all their men, were retreating to their own country. Then the king announced that he would lead a new campaign to Scotland. Along the tables men cheered and banged the table with their knife handles, tankards or any other object close by.

True to his word the English king advanced to Newcastle to prepare for the new invasion and to await the arrival of further reinforcements from the southern counties.

When King Robert heard that the English were mustering along his eastern border he led a raid into the north–west of England, destroying crops, burning and plundering. Apart from Harclay, who held Carlisle, the Scots were unopposed, but the English king could not be enticed to alter his plans and defend his own territory. In July, a huge English army crossed into Scotland by the eastern route and Bruce returned to his own land heavily laden with booty.

By August King Edward was south of Edinburgh, but the countryside throughout Lothian was empty of both humans and animals and all crops had been either burned or removed by the retreating Scots. The English were forced to rely on their own provisions. Resting at Musselburgh, they had to await the arrival of supply ships, but the heavily laden, slow–moving ships had been attacked by Flemings, who were allies of the Scots, and the few which did escape were scattered along the east coast by unseasonable storms. Starvation and sickness began to claim English lives and James Douglas kept up a relentless attack until King Edward was forced to give the order to turn for home. Empty–handed and having achieved nothing, the tempers of the English men-at-arms became very fragile and daily arguments and fights broke out among the disgruntled men. By the end of August they arrived back in Newcastle and were disbanded. A frustrated and angry king Edward moved south to Durham. No sooner had he arrived in that city, than the Scots crossed the border and began raising havoc in Northumberland.

Hurriedly the king sent out orders to muster the men of the northern counties to oppose the threat.

Andrew Harclay sat in the great hall of Carlisle Castle, angry and bemused by his king's ineffectual handling of the troublesome Scots. How could he muster the levies of Cumberland and Westmorland again? He had already demanded the statutory forty days service from the men of these counties when he had gone to the king's aid at Boroughbridge. He knew the men would not come out again without payment for their service and he did not have money to pay them. He was fairly sure the king would not pay them. If he took the men from the garrison it would leave Carlisle undefended and the Scots would not miss such an opportunity. There was nothing for it but to raise the levies of Lancashire. The following day an angry Harclay rode south, declaring he would join the king as soon as he had the men. He left the defence of the city in his cousin's care, which was just as well, for no sooner had he left the county than the Scots appeared led by their king and began burning and plundering.

When King Robert heard that the English army was mustering again near Northallerton and that King Edward was with them he gave orders to cross the Pennines, into Yorkshire, where he hoped to catch the English king unawares. King Edward heard that the Scots were fast approaching his camp and realizing the danger he sent a division of mounted knights and foot soldiers to stop the advancing enemy.

At Scawton Moor the English took up position along the top of the escarpment overlooking the moor, across which the Scots would have to come. It was a good defensive position and they collected rocks and other missiles ready to hurl down at the enemy. The king had put his cousin, the Earl of Richmond, in command and when all were ready they sat down to await the Scots. It was a fine day for the time of year, sunny with white, scudding clouds. The wind was high and the men sat sheltered from it in the lee of the boulders. Just before noon the lookouts caught their first sight of the enemy.

King Robert halted his men and gazed along the escarpment edge. It would be no easy task to dislodge the defending English. Douglas, as usual, was at his side. "Well James, this'll not be easy, perhaps I should forget the idea of fighting Edward in his own territory." "Nay sir, think if we could but capture the English king you could make any demand you wished. I'll lead my men up yon bank and while they're busy trying to dislodge us from the cliff face you could lead an attack further along and take them in the flank." As Douglas spoke Thomas Randolph joined them and overheard the conversation. Both men continued to be jealous of the king's affection for the other and competed for his attention. Therefore, it came as no surprise to the king when Thomas said that he and his men would join Douglas in the frontal attack. In daylight, with clear visibility and no cover to speak of, it could be suicidal. The two men dismounted and remained in front of their men. As they reached the foot of the cliffs, arrows began to rain down on them so that it was necessary for each man to hold his shield above his head, having only one hand free to hold onto the rock face, as they scrambled upwards. Rocks and boulders cascaded downwards and there were many casualties as men lost their grip and fell.

The king watched their progress for a while, but when he was certain that the English were busy with the task in hand, he led his highlanders and islanders round to Roulston Scar and using ropes they scaled the cliff face and circled round, catching the English flank. Forced to defend themselves against a second Scottish attack took the pressure off Douglas and Randolph and their men rapidly covered the remaining ground between themselves and their enemy. The English stood back to back and fought ferociously against the Scottish onslaught until they lost heart and were chased across the moor.

Walter Stewart and his horsemen had remained in reserve and the king despatched him to Rievaulx Abbey where the English king was said to be staying. "Ride fast, Walter before he gets wind of the defeat here." He waved a hand in the direction of the fleeing English. "Try to capture him, then we can put a rapid end to this bloodshed."

When Stewart arrived the monastery was deserted. Even the old and sick had been taken from their beds in the infirmary and carried to safe hiding places. In his haste the English king had left behind his silver plate and other items of great value. Stewart paused long enough to collect these together, before continuing with his hunt, until he reached Beverley where they told him that Edward had ridden on to Holderness by the River Humber. To go further south into enemy territory was unwise and he contented himself with threatening to burn Beverley unless the burgesses paid ransom for their town. Then he withdrew his force to rejoin his king.

At Scrawton Moor many important prisoners were taken and King Robert, now resting at Rievaulx Abbey had them brought before him. Some of the knights were French and after cordially welcoming them to his presence the king offered them honourable hospitality until they could be sent back to France, because he did not want to alienate the French King. These men had been prisoners of James Douglas, who was irritated that the king should relieve him of such lucrative captives from whom he could have expected to gain large ransoms. King Robert, however, was adamant that the French knights should be treated with respect. "Come James, surely you understand my decision. We need allies," but Douglas knew Randolph had captured many English knights and that he would receive large ransoms from their families. The king saw the expression on his lieutenant's face and placing his hand on the man's shoulder said, "James, in compensation for your loss, you may hold your lands free from tax and when we return home I will command a charter to be drawn up stating this. As a sign of my pledge take this ring." He drew a gold and emerald ring from his finger and gave it to Douglas.

Amongst the English prisoners was the Earl of Richmond. When he was first captured he had taunted his captors, jeering and shouting insults about Robert Bruce and all Scots in general. Randolph had had to grit his teeth together, for he had been tempted to order the earl's execution. Richmond stood before Bruce, with a contemptuous sneer upon his face and Randolph, standing beside his king said, "My lord, Richmond looks as if he has an unpleasant smell at the end of his nose." "Aye, Thomas, I've never known that lord to look any other way, but his arrogance shelters a hollow man." Randolph was surprised by his king's damning words for rarely did he pass harsh judgement on his fellow men. "Chain him and take him as a prisoner to Scotland. He'll not see freedom until his face bears a different expression and he's learnt to curb his tongue," snapped the king. Towards the end of October the Scottish army turned northwards.

After raising the levies of Lancashire, Harclay marched with all speed to York where King Edward had taken up residence. "My lord, I've brought you fresh men eager to pursue the Scots at your command." Harclay was vigorous and enthusiastic, but he had not been in Edward's company for long before he became uneasy and disillusioned. Andrew had not been born into a noble family. He was a blunt soldier, nay more than blunt, for he called a spade a spade, and looked men straight in the eyes when he spoke to them. He was not a politician, for he saw what needed to be done and got on and did it. It was his strength, but also his weakness, for in court, surrounded by Gavaston and the others within the king's intimate circle, honest Harclay was out of his depth.

The king was visibly shaken by the rout of his forces at Scawton Moor and searched for a reason for their failure. Gavaston quickly pointed out that if the new Earl of Carlisle had arrived earlier with his northern levies, the outcome would have been different. Harclay defended his actions vigorously, but the king remained unmoved. Harclay said, "My lord, I know we can put an end to the Scottish invasions. They're decimating your northern counties and your people are very weary," but the king made no reply and later complained peevishly to Gavaston. "He's none of the knightly virtues, Hugh. A crude man, of little account." Gavaston agreed with him. The following day Sir Andrew presented himself before his king. "Lord, have I your permission to seek out the Scots and renew the truce with them? "If it pleases you Harclay, but I doubt your ability to come to terms with those traitors." A disappointed Harclay disbanded his men and told them to go home and prepare their homesteads for further attacks from the north. He himself returned to Carlisle and settled down to planning how he could contact the Scottish leaders to talk about a truce.

One evening he sat with his brother John. "Andrew, be careful. They say the king is not his own master. Leave policy to men who have experience of such things. Do what you're good at, commanding men," but Harclay was nothing if not single–minded. In January 1323, he crossed the border to Bruce's castle at Lochmaben and met Bruce. They discussed the terms for peace and the ability of the Scottish king and his commanders impressed Andrew. Quickly he came to an understanding with them on behalf of his own king, after reassuring King Robert that he had gained the English king's permission to enter into negotiations. When he was back in Carlisle, he received an angry letter from his king and said to his anxious brother, "The agreement is not binding until the king has signed it but they are honourable terms. They'll pay our king to drop his claim of sovereignty over Scotland. Just think, it will bring peace and God knows here in the North Country we badly need it. Besides, if someone doesn't act soon to end this madness, they'll overrun these northern counties and extend their lands down to the Humber. I can't believe that's what King Edward wants." John Harclay replied, "Then brother, why has the king responded to your letter in such unfriendly terms?" Harclay frowned. It was true he had expected a warmer response from the king, but perhaps he had misunderstood the terms of the treaty. When he had explained it fully to him, Andrew was sure he would ratify it. A simple man of action, Andrew Harclay ceased to worry about the problem, poured himself more ale and changed the topic of conversation.

Towards the end of February, when a bitter northeasterly wind and rain buffeted the ramparts of Carlisle Castle, a visitor arrived. Sir Andrew, who stood on the ramparts, recognized Anthony de Lucy and ran down to the yard to welcome him, for they had known each other since childhood and he greeted de Lucy as a friend. The knight had a large company of men with him, but Harclay, ever open handed, saw nothing odd in this. It came as a bitter blow when de Lucy arrested him on the king's orders charged with high treason. "Are you mad, I asked the king's permission to talk to the Scots and he agreed. Never have I pursued peace secretly and I have not put my name to the treaty." De Lucy found it hard to look the man in the eyes and remained silent.

Until the trial the following week Harclay remained optimistic, convinced that it was a misunderstanding which could be sorted out, but at the trial he realized he had been a doomed man even before his arrest.

The day following his trial, Sir Andrew Harclay stood on the scaffold gazing at the spectators to his execution. The citizens of Carlisle had gathered, for he was a popular figure. They were silent and looked dangerous, so that de Lucy had posted many guards around the scaffold and the Town Square to prevent any attempt to rescue the prisoner. Everybody knew that Harclay had admitted talking to the Scots, but to his confessor he steadfastly claimed that it had been with the king's approval.

He stood calmly, in command of his emotions, as he always had been and spoke to them. "People, you see before you a fool, who put too much trust in his king and friend. I die a loyal Englishman who desired peace." He was not allowed to say any more and the noose was placed around his neck. There were angry shouts from the crowd as they hoisted him high. He was cut down still breathing, the executioner ready with his tools of further torture. Women began to sob and faint while a man's voice called out "He only did what our king should be doing. Shame on you." The final acts of butchery were nonetheless carried out.

The execution of Andrew Harclay left the northern population sullen and angry. No one was surprised when they heard that John Harclay had fled across the border, taking his brother's wife and family with him and that he had taken service with the Scottish king. At Carlisle, King Edward was forced to double the strength of the garrison for fear that the citizens would hand their city over to the Scots.

Hastily, King Edward initiated peace talks to quell the unrest in the north and Henry de Scully, one of the French knights still with King Robert, undertook the negotiations on his behalf. When he returned to the Scottish king, he had further letters from King Edward. "Henry, my good friend." King Robert took his hand. "I'm pleased to see you again, but sorry your efforts have borne no fruit." Scully said, "No one will change that man's mind, he wears blinkers and cannot grasp the reality of his situation." The king laughed. "Do you know that his latest letters are addressed to, 'The people of Scotland,' not their king? I do believe he's lost his wits." De Scully replied, "He's influenced by fools and is unable to make his own decisions." Then the king said. "Go back to them, Henry and make them understand that there will be no peace until he addresses me as ruler of this kingdom.

Three months after Andrew Harclay's execution, a truce was signed to last for thirteen years and King Robert, on behalf of the Scottish people, signed his name. Robert, King of Scotland.

DEATH IS A
DEBT WE ALL MUST PAY

The king climbed to the crest of the hillock and slowly turned a full circle. To the south, the waters of the Clyde shone with many thousand diamonds. A merchant vessel, under full sail, was making its way up the Clyde towards Glasgow Harbour. To the east the Kilpatrick Hills, northwards more hills and forests, whilst beyond, although he could not see it, lay Loch Lomond. With the wind fanning his weather-beaten face, he turned towards the west and the lochs and islands of Gaelic Scotland. After the recent light shower there arose the sweetest smell from the damp earth and bracken and in the distance a curlew called. The scene captivated him as it had years before when he had began his great adventure. It was more than fifteen years since those frantic days. They were the worst of times and the happiest of times. So many good men had helped him and he had been pleased to call them friend. God rest their souls.

He was pleased with this land and strolled back towards the Clyde, planning his new house as he went. Over there would be his hunting park and here his house would stand, within a walled garden, with plants which scented the air. Elizabeth would like that. He would have a slipway built over by the River were his galley could be moored and he would have a separate house for his falcons. There would be glass in the windows of the house and the walls would be painted with lime and hung with tapestries. The floor of the great hall would be flagged, not earthen and there would be a proper fireplace with mantle. He would not have a smoke-filled home. In his mind's eye he pictured himself sitting in the hall listening to his minstrels.

His chancellor was waiting for him by the bank of the Clyde. "My lord, it's a peaceful setting, ideal for yourself and the queen." "Aye, the children will enjoy it here." He referred to his two daughters, Margaret, the elder, had seen seven summers and Elizabeth was once again pregnant. They both dared to hope that this child would be a son.

"Bernard, arrange for the payments to Lennox and David Graham for their lands. They're perfect for my manor. Send the masons and carpenters to me, I would have them begin work as soon as possible."

Throughout the Clyde and the Lennox, the King's new house became the most interesting topic of gossip. Fishermen and ship's crews passing up and down the Clyde paused on their oars to watch the progress of the work. It was an impressive building with many rooms. Its thick walls were limed on the outside and the roof thatched with the best reeds. In March 1324, there was a break in the weather and passing ship's crews saw Gilbert, the gardener laying out the garden, while the early morning sun glinted on the window glass.

In the second week of March, the Queen was safely delivered of a healthy son. The boy was named David and the kingdom rejoiced that the king had a legitimate heir. Everyone hoped that the boy would live to inherit from his father.

Elizabeth lay at Dumfermline, the sleeping babe cradled in the crook of her arm. She gazed at the tiny nose and rosebud mouth. That such an innocent and vulnerable being would grow into a man, nay a king, startled her. She wanted to keep him safe, nestled to her breast where no harm could come to him. Elizabeth had seen thirty six winters and they had almost given up hope of having a son.

Her women took the sleeping babe from her and placed him in a cradle. It was carved with animals and birds and inlaid with walrus ivory. On the headboard had been carved the rampart lion of Scotland.

They helped her from her bed. It was the first time since she had given birth. She had bled profusely after the boy's delivery and now she felt dizzy and tired. Her heavy, full breasts hurt her so and she asked to be seated near to the fire to rest. They wrapped her in furs with cushions to support her aching back and rearranged her thick plait of hair.

The door opened and the king and his daughters entered. The two girls greeted their mother and then ran to the cradle and began talking and laughing to their tiny brother. Robert pulled a stool close to the mother, sat and took her thin hand in his, pressing it to his lips. To those watching, it was a pleasant family scene and there were few in the kingdom who did not wish husband and wife well. Yet many womenfolk felt sorry for Elizabeth. She had endured years of enforced barrenness in England and since her return to Scotland, the king had barely rested in the same place for more than three nights at a time. No one had an unkind word to say of the queen. She was unfailingly cheerful and gentle, with kind words for all, no matter what their position in the royal household. Of course, everyone knew the king had other sons whom he recognized, but they could not inherit the throne.

Now when he was entering his fiftieth year, David had been born.

Elizabeth slowly regained her health and beauty and a little extra weight which suited her. Her face was less thin and her skin lost its translucent look whilst her wonderful, bronze hair, now streaked at the temples with a little silver, nevertheless, remained thick and shining beneath her fine linen gauze coif.

Occasionally the king strayed back to his Christine, but theirs was such a long-standing union that men and not a few women, would have been surprised if he had given her up completely. Elizabeth knew of his visits, but said nothing, preferring to have him on his terms rather than lose him altogether. After her churching he resumed his visits to her in her chamber.

The family spent much of its time in the new house at Cardross, Robert hunting and flying his falcons, whilst Elizabeth was pleased to sit enjoying the warmth of her garden, taking deep breaths of the perfumed air and listening to the bees droning in the flower beds. The year following David's birth, it was announced that Elizabeth was once again with child.

The king was a contented man, happy in his private life, respected by his nobles and common folk and recognized as ruler of Scotland by foreign princes throughout Christendom, excepting the English. Scotland was free and Robert firmly believed that if God spared him he could bring the kingdom to a lasting peace.

Scotland's pride was mirrored by England's despair. The nobles were frustrated by the weakness of their obstinate king, who clung to his claim of overlordship of Scotland and refused to recognize King Robert, listening to the flattering of his favourites and ignoring all prudent council and common sense. Whilst Hugh Despenser continued to strut the corridors of power, convinced of his own invulnerability for as long as he held the king's affection.

Queen Isabella's brother, Charles, was now King of France and relations between the two kingdoms had deteriorated since the death of Isabella's father and the new French king had formed an alliance with Scotland. Many Scottish lords visited the French court and surreptitiously whispered into King Charles' ear, but in 1324 he invited his brother-in-law to his kingdom to pay homage for his French territories.

King Edward was suspicious of his nobles' loyalties and loathed to leave England. The only noble whom he trusted was the Earl of Pembroke, but he was getting old and was in poor health.

King Charles grew impatient with his brother-in-law's failure to respond to his command and threatened to attack English territories in France. In desperation Edward dispatched Pembroke to France with instructions to reassure Charles. The crossing was rough and when the old warrior arrived in Calais he was taken ill and died, his wife by his side.

When King Robert heard of Pembroke's death he was saddened, for excluding Pembroke's act of dishonour at Methven, Robert had always respected Pembroke, whom he had known when they were both young and he knew the earl to have been a man of sound common sense and valour.

Pembroke's death was a bitter blow to King Edward, he had no other whom he trusted and who was also trusted by his contemporaries. He even feared the loyalty of his archbishops who were unlikely to work for their king's advantage. Frantically Edward searched for a replacement. He sat alone pondering his options when Hugh Despenser entered the chamber. "Edward, I've the answer to your problem. Send the queen. She can speak to her brother on your behalf." It was so simple that Edward wondered why he had not thought of that himself, but it was what he loved so much in Hugh, they complemented one another. Isabella was sure to accept the task, particularly since she would see her homeland. Yet when he approached his wife, she was not enthusiastic and made many excuses why she should not undertake the mission. "Come Bella, Joan is happy with her nurse and the child thrives, she's a fine, little maid," but Isabella pouted and tossed her head, looking at him with dark, cold, angry eyes. "If you need to send someone so desperately, why not send your dear Hugh? I don't want to go at this time of the year. The channel will be so rough and you know I don't like the sea." She snapped. She stormed from the room and when he angrily called to her to remain, she refused to heed him. When Despenser heard he said, "The bitch, she continues to make problems for me and embarrasses you, her own husband."

That evening, the king went to her chamber and more sharp words passed between them. Once again he demanded that she should go on his behalf to France. She gazed at him for some little while before saying, "Alright, but I'll take Edward with me and he can pay homage on your behalf and see how things are done in a real king's court." Her husband slapped her face and she staggered back, falling against the bedpost. There were tears in her eyes and her cheek was very red where he had hit her. "I've cried myself to sleep too many times because of your behaviour towards me, but never will I cry again for you, Edward," she snapped.

In March 1324 Queen Isabella, her son Edward and all their households sailed for France. For the remainder of that year in spite of her anger towards her husband, Isabella worked hard to sooth her brother and dispel any doubts he might have had about the King of England's good intentions towards him. She enjoyed herself and was loathed to return home to her humiliating life.

In her husband's court, Hugh Despenser continued his arrogant progress as the king's favourite and without Pembroke's wise council the dissatisfaction and restlessness among the nobles grew daily worse. Many noblemen left England to live in exile in France and these malcontents formed a band of plotters around the queen, among them Edward's half-brother and many others who had been loyal to the king throughout all his tribulations with the Scots, but Hugh Despenser taxed their loyalty too far.

Among these men was the marcher lord, Roger Mortimer and it was not long before the queen's household knew exactly why she now refused to return to her husband. The passion burning between the two could not be hidden. They barely took their eyes from one another and were always in each other's company. Isabella had never enjoyed the hunt, but when Lord Mortimer rode out with his hunting dogs, Isabella rode with him. Often they were to be seen in the garden talking quietly together and whenever he made a small joke she would tilt her head towards his and smile up at him, gently laughing at his cleverness. They were like fresh, young lovers although neither was in their first youth. Young Prince Edward noticed his mother's affection for the man and when he saw them together his face flushed deep crimson.

King Charles was shocked by his sister's behaviour. One morning he ordered her to his presence and immediately came to the point. "I'm told that you entertain the Lord Mortimer alone in your bed chamber, sister." Isabella stared at her brother with much the same expression, close to loathing, which she had displayed towards her husband. "And if I do, am I betraying my husband more than he has betrayed me? Never before have I forgotten my duty to him, and I have borne him four children, yet he loves his favourites and humiliates me," she spat. "There's a difference Bella, you are a woman and to cuckold your husband, the king, is high treason." She turned her back on him, gazing from the window out onto the gardens bathed in warm sunshine. In France she was so happy and carefree and had not felt that way since she left her homeland as a young bride. Tears welled up in her eyes, she could not, no she would not, give it all up. Roger had to be part of her life. He would make the decisions for them both. She turned a defiant gaze on her brother. "I cannot return to the life I once led, Charles." Her brother said coldly, "Then you must leave my protection, Isabella. I will not shelter a wife who betrays her husband."

Isabella, Edward and all their households, accompanied by the English lords, left France for Hainault where Count William offered them military aid to take the throne of England by force, on the condition that Prince Edward would be betrothed to his daughter, Philippa. In September 1326, Isabella's invasion force landed on the Orwell estuary. East Anglian nobles and Henry, Earl of Leicester, brother of the executed Thomas Earl of Lancaster, declared for the queen and the prince as they marched towards London. London gave their support to the queen and King Edward, with a handful of supporters, fled west. As always, he was unrealistic in his understanding of the seriousness of his situation, as he had been in his negotiation with the Scots. By the middle of October Bristol had also declared for the queen.

The King fled to Chepstow and among his supporters was Donald, Earl of Mar, who had stayed behind when his mother Christina Bruce had returned to Scotland after Bannockburn. He had great affection for King Edward and tried to hold Bristol for him, but when the town fell, he followed the king to the Welsh border country.

He was shocked by his friend's despair. Edward had lost weight and was very restless, walking nervously up and down his chamber. He had always been so strong and energetic with a noble bearing, eager to hunt, swim, fish and row and never happier than with a group of close friends. The changes in him shocked Donald. Edward greeted Donald with friendship but the haunted look remained in his eyes.

Donald did not stay long, but promised he would return to Scotland and seek the aid of Robert Bruce. "Tell him, that if he'll give me assistance against Isabella and Mortimer, I'll recognize the realm of Scotland as independent from England and King Robert as its lord. I'll also cede Northumberland to Scotland. Ride with all haste, Donald, for I fear my hiding places are becoming fewer."

Donald Mar was now nearing thirty and was received with great rejoicing by his Scottish relatives, particularly his mother. The king greeted him warmly and listened attentively to the English king's message. Finally he said, "Donald, I've personal sympathy for Edward and naturally I'm interested in his proposals. They are after all what I have fought for, for these past twenty years. You have my permission to seek any help from among my nobles which they may wish to give, but officially I will not help the English king."

In November news came that Edward had been betrayed by a Welsh noble and taken as a prisoner to Kenilworth Castle. He was ordered to hand over the great seal of the kingdom to the Bishop of Hereford and his fourteen year old son, Edward III, held his coronation with great splendour on 1st February 1327. On that same day Douglas crossed the border attacking the castle of Norham.

During the next few weeks, border towns and fortresses were systematically attacked and the northern garrisons were put under great pressure. Guards were doubled and lookouts posted on the top of all high hills.

Donald of Mar was relieved that his uncle, Robert of Scotland, had put military pressure on the "she wolf" and her lover and he took command of one of the three brigades of the Scottish army.

Mortimer, on behalf of the young King Edward III, mustered the English levies at York. It was an impressive army that included cavalry from Hainault and by mid July the army was camped near Durham.

The Scots crossed the border at two points. Moray and Mar marched through the Kielder Gap and advanced rapidly down the north Tyne Valley, while Douglas' brigade came through the western route. By-passing Carlisle, he swung east across the Pennines.

From their camp, the young, English king and his commanders could see the smoke from burning manors and villages. Scouts were hurriedly sent out, but they reported that although they had seen the destruction caused by the enemy, they had not found the Scots themselves. People had said they were last seen heading towards the Tyne, probably bound for Scotland. Mortimer, in overall command, ordered a forced march to cut off the enemy from their route back towards the border. To improve the speed of the army, he left the baggage train behind, issuing each man with a loaf of bread, rations for their journey. When they arrived at Haydon Bridge the army made camp, to await the Scots.

It was mid summer, but the weather was uncommonly cold, with threatening, grey clouds and a high wind so that it took a number of attempts to erect the king's tent. The wind came in strong gusts pulling the heavily oiled canvas from their hands, it billowed out like a huge sail and threatened to blow away altogether. That night, it began to rain heavily and continued the following day, flattening the crops in the surrounding fields. The men, on alert awaiting the Scots, could find no shelter from the deluge. "Where are the bleeders?" was the general moan. More scouts were sent out, but this time none returned, which convinced the men that the Scots were hiding somewhere close and watching their every move.

There was no let up in the weather, leaden skies and driving rain continued day and night for a week. The clothes of the men were sodden, their bread wet and covered with mildew. It was impossible to find bran for the horses that stood in a sea of mud with lowered heads and drooping ears. Occasionally they shook their heads and a shower of water flew in all directions. Consequently, the men continued to be bad tempered and fought among themselves.

Towards the end of a miserable week, a young squire called Rokeby returned with news of Douglas and his men. Rokeby had been captured and dragged before their leader. Douglas sat under a shelter, built from branches and thatched with a light covering of bracken, protecting him from the worst of the weather. They had built a fire in front of his shelter and he sat with his bare feet stretched out in front of him. His boots had been turned upside down and steamed by the fire. On his lap was a wooden bowl filled with boiled meat and hungrily he stabbed at each piece of meat with his knife. In his other hand was an oaten cake. His men were busy baking on the fire.

Rokeby, wet and hungry, thought that if he were about to die he would rather have a good meal inside him first. "You look hungry," said Douglas. "I've had a hard ride," replied his prisoner. Douglas indicated another bowl lying nearby, "Help yourself." Rokeby sat himself on a fallen log opposite his captor and for a while the two men sat eating without speaking, as if they had been life–long friends. The heat from the fire was intense and the front of Rokeby's leather jerkin began to steam, whilst his back, on which the rain still fell, glistened black and droplets of rain found their way inside and ran down his back. Douglas finished his meal and although he scrutinized his prisoner, he waited courteously until he had also finished eating. Then Douglas said, "You look as if you want nothing better than a dry bed, what on earth made you volunteer for this mission?" Rokeby, a Yorkshireman, who believed in direct speaking, replied, "Well now, they offered a knighthood and land to any man who could bring back news of your whereabouts. I can do with a helping hand, so here I am." "Ah!" exclaimed Douglas. "Aye, inducements always help a difficult situation. Well, if you help me, I'll see if I can help you. Take a message back to Mortimer for me and then you can claim your reward." Rokeby could hardly believe his good fortune and readily gave Douglas his word. "Tell Mortimer that we'll greet him on the banks of the River Wear and do battle with him there."

When Rokeby returned to his bedraggled comrades, he was

welcomed as their saviour. Everybody wanted to get the job over and done with and go home. Joyfully the army broke camp and left the morass of mud and filth behind them to march back to the River Wear. Sir Thomas Rokeby rode with them and blessed the good fortune that had led him to be captured by Douglas.

Sure enough, they could see the Scots camped on a small hill overlooking the River but on the southern bank, opposite them. Robesby was ordered before Mortimer. "Since you've already spoken to Douglas, you can ride over and challenge him to cross over and fight us on equal ground," commanded the lord. "From what I've seen of that Scot he'll laugh in my face, sir," replied Rokeby. "I've not asked for your opinion, Rokeby. Just do it." With that he turned his attention to other matters, expecting Rokeby to carry out his order.

Douglas himself rode to meet Rokeby, but when he heard Mortimer's demand he laughed. "Tell your commander that it's for him to seek us out, then we'll fight." Rokeby shrugged and grinned. "I more or less told him you would say that."

It was early August and night did not fall till late into the evening. The English could see the Scottish campfires on the hillside opposite and they could hear them laughing and singing loudly. "Damn them, they're laughing at us," swore Mortimer.

There was heavy cloud that night and both camps gradually settled to sleep. Fires on the hillside burnt brightly, but it became plain when dawn broke that, although smoke still spiralled upwards, the birds had flown. During the morning an exasperated Mortimer sent out scouts to search for the enemy but few returned. In the late afternoon a sergeant came back into camp, with news that he had found the enemy camped on the English side of the River upstream, at Stanhope. "It's a good defensive position, my lord." Mortimer with the young king beside him, sat listening to the sergeant. The king said, "Mortimer, they're playing a game of catch with us." Mortimer said nothing but looked angry and frustrated. A decisive victory against such a famous commander as James Douglas would seal his position as chief advisor to the young king.

It was growing too late in the day to move the men once more, but Mortimer decided that on the following morning the army would march to Stanhope and meet the Scots. Night fell. Guards were posted and men turned in to catch a few hours sleep before an early start the following day.

James Douglas had no intention of meeting the English in formal battle, for their numbers were much greater than his own. When night fell, with one hundred mounted men, he rode to the English camp. Reining in his horse, at some distance from the slumbering army, he gave orders in a hushed voice. Guards were silenced and they entered the camp on horseback, riding in pairs and hacking at the tent ropes so that the canvas collapsed onto the occupants. While they struggled to free themselves, they were struck with spears. In the confusion the Scots found many victims.

The royal pavilion was tumbled, but Edward, young and nimble, managed to struggle free. Many of his nobles and servants of his household surrounded the youthful king, but Douglas himself confronted the royal bodyguard and cut down any that tried to stand in his way. None were spared from his furious onslaught. Even the king's chaplain, who did not carry weapons, received a fatal blow from Douglas' battleaxe. The whole camp was in uproar with dazed men, many without their outer garments, running about in confusion, fighting with any weapon that came to hand by the light from the fires started by the Scots. Heavily outnumbered and aware that the element of surprise had passed, Douglas blew his hunting horn as a signal to withdraw.

In the cold light of morning, the full extent of the Scottish raid could be seen. The king gazed at the corpse of his chaplain, whom he had known since early childhood and tears welled up in his eyes, but they were also tears of anger because of the mismanagement that had led to the death of his dear friend. The men sat on the damp ground tending to their wounds as best they could, while the bodies of their dead comrades lay in piles beside them. They spent the rest of that day burying their dead in consecrated ground.

That night the Scottish army silently deserted their camp and withdrew northwards, while Mortimer led his army to York. Short of rations, hungry, angry and humiliated, they were disbanded.

During August, King Edward II had escaped from his prison and Earl Donald of Mar, in command of a handful of men loyal to the deposed King, rode south to the Welsh border. King Robert had given permission to find Edward and escort him to safety in Scotland, but before Earl Donald could carry out the rescue, Edward was recaptured by Mortimer's men and imprisoned in Berkeley Castle.

Determined that the deposed king would not get a second chance, Mortimer planned his murder, but how could it be done, without murder being suspected? Edward was well known for his famous good health. Mortimer did not discuss his plan with Isabella, she would make a fuss if he told her what had to be done. She despised her husband, but Edward was the father of her children.

At the beginning of September, Mortimer received news that the Scots had once again crossed the border. This time the Scottish king was in command and it was reported that he was taking all of England's northern counties under his protection. There was no time to lose. A message was sent to Edward's jailers at Berkeley Castle. They were to dispose of their captive forthwith.

Henry Percy, Lord of Alnwick, meanwhile was ordered to seek out the Scottish king who was then besieging Norham and immediately sue for peace.

The news spread that Edward II was dead, but no one could quite believe it. He was such a healthy man. For sure he must have been murdered by the she-wolf, the queen mother. His naked corpse was displayed to show that it was free from all wounds, but rumours continued spreading that his death had been manipulated by foul means. It was whispered that red hot pokers had entered his body by unnatural methods so that none could see the scars. Others said that the queen mother had sent him poisoned sweetmeats. Everyone knew she was a witch. However, his death had come about, Edward was gone and his young son was king. Generally the people hoped the new king would be more like his grandfather and lead England to victory and lasting peace, instead of the succession of defeats which had marked his father's reign.

When the new peace talks began, Scotland's aim was to secure sovereign independence and freedom from English interference for King Robert's son, David when he came to the throne. King Robert pursued the same terms he had agreed with the ill-fated Andrew Harclay. Marriage between David and the English king's sister, Joan, was agreed between the two realms and at last peace documents were signed.

King Robert left all negotiations to his council while he remained at his manor of Cardross. He loved the place. No matter what time of year, Cardross held his affection. The smell of the sea, the breeze blowing in from the west, bringing with it the smell of seaweed, heather and wild thyme and the clouds skimming across a blue sky. In autumn, he could hear the challenging bellows from the red deer in the hills and glens behind the house and always the melancholy call of the sea birds. Each and every smell and sound revived memories of times past. At the estuary of the small river bordering his manor, the king moored his galley and during the long hours of summer he visited his old haunts in the western isles. Christiana on Bara, like her king now advancing in years, her brother Rhuri, whom time had mellowed and Angus Og, who was still keen to pit his galley against the king's in a mad race along Loch Long.

In July 1326, the queen gave birth to a boy whom they baptized John. The labour was long and painful and towards the end the doctor, fearing for her life, asked the chaplain to give her absolution and the king came to say goodbye. He sat on her bed holding her hot, thin hand in his. She was perspiring, her eyes dark, filled with pain. Her once beautiful hair had been tightly braided and hung in two plaits and wisps of loose hair, wet with perspiration, clung to her temples. Robert lent forward, pressing his lips lightly on her forehead. Another bout of pain gripped her and she gasped before crying out and pressing down in an attempt to expel the hapless babe. "Oh Rob, help me, please help me," she wailed. He felt helpless and afraid. He had seen many men die and had been the cause of many men's death, but the pain and anguish at the very beginning of life, he had always found a difficult experience. He turned to the physician, "Is there nothing you can do?" "My lord, the child comes feet first and she's very tired." "Don't leave me Robert," called Elizabeth plaintively. The king patted her hand but as another pain enveloped her, he withdrew and sat himself on the window seat where she could still see him. A woman ran into the chamber carrying a bowl of goose fat and a jar containing pepper. Fresh pains began and the midwife, her hands smothered in the thick fat, shook pepper under the mother's nose and gripped the infant. Elizabeth, poor, tormented soul, sneezed, cried and pushed and pushed and sneezed again, whilst the midwife pulled and the physician pressed hard on her abdomen. Finally, amid the mother's wails of fear and pain, the midwife's soothing voice of encouragement and the commanding tones of the doctor a small, thin cry arose from the newly born boy.

The babe was well formed, but blue. They showed him to his father who gazed at the small wrinkled face. "Give him to his mother, she has fought hard for him," he said. He stood by her bed as they placed the boy in the crook of the mother's arm, but she lay in a swoon, weakened by the effort of giving birth. John, son to Robert Bruce, lived for a few hours.

Elizabeth lay pale and tired in her bed. Whenever they tried to move her, she cried out in pain and fresh blood flowed from her. Throughout the summer she languished, growing thin with sores on her heels and buttocks, but she bore all her tribulations with courage.

One golden evening in early September, when her husband sat beside her bed, she said, "Robert, I cannot recover and shortly, God willing, I will join our child in paradise." "Hush sweetheart, your husband doesn't want to lose you." "I don't want to leave you and the children, but Our Lord decides these matters. We've always been honest with one another, Rob, let's be honest to the end and not waste precious time." After this they talked more openly, like friends who had shared a long and dangerous journey together. Sometimes, they laughed about past events and arguments they had had which seemed so important at the time. One afternoon when he was visiting, she asked him to read to her from their book about the Noble Roland. She lay, his hand in hers, listening to his rich baritone voice, as she had when they were young.

As the days passed, she suffered from bouts of fever and when her women changed her linen, she shivered uncontrollably and by the first week of October had lapsed into a delirious sleep. Her husband still visited each afternoon and last thing at night, but she did not know him. The children were brought to see their mother for the last time. Matilda and Margaret were old enough to understand they would not see her again in this world and they clung to each other crying and distressed, but little David Bruce hardly knew her for she had lain in her bed for the past three months, unable to move. The little fellow of barely three, could not sit quietly by the sick woman's bed and his nurse carried him away to play in the garden.

Two days later Elizabeth slipped quietly away to paradise. Her husband kissed her white brow and murmured a small prayer before turning away with tears in his eyes. She had been his for twenty five years. There had been many partings and he had been the cause of many of her sorrows. At times, he knew he had bruised her heart but she had always been a gentle and loving wife and was very dear to him.

The funeral mass of Elizabeth, Queen of Scotland, was held at Dumfermline Abbey and her husband ordered a fine tomb to be built, so that all generations yet to come could see the love which King Robert had had for her. When all the pomp and fuss was ended he stood by her grave alone. Since the peace with England, the Holy Father had raised the ban of excommunication and it was a relief that she had died within the protection of the Church. With bent head he whispered, "I think it'll not be long before I join you sweetheart."

In March of the following year, the king lay at the Abbey of Holyrood. His health had been deteriorating for some time. He had sores on his body, which would not heal, and bouts of paralysis when he was unable to move or do anything for himself.

Douglas was a regular visitor. On one occasion the king had smiled cheerfully saying, "When a man has spent as much time in the saddle as I have, it's a pleasure to rest quietly in a dry feather bed." Yet all could see that his patience was sorely tested, particularly when they came to attend to his bodily needs. The paralysis came and went and the king fitted as much as he could into those periods when his body would obey his instructions.

The Peace Treaty required his royal seal and they brought the English Commissioners to his bedchamber. His advisors stood around him, men who had supported him and Scotland for so long, Douglas, Randolph, Boyd, Sir Andrew Murray, son of Wallace's comrade at the battle of Stirling, and many other noble earls and churchmen.

As the northern spring flooded Scotland with light and colour, yellow daffodils and primroses giving way to bluebells, the king recovered somewhat. The paralysis and stiffness in his body slowly disappeared. At first he walked with slow, shuffling steps, supported by a servant, but each day the distance grew greater until he stood by his bed, with a staff in each hand ready to take his first unassisted steps. He said to his chancellor, "Bernard, I'll attend my son's wedding yet. How are my wedding clothes progressing?"

The wedding preparations were well under way. David Bruce was nearly four, his bride Joan, sister to Edward III of England, just seven. At the beginning of July, Queen Isabella journeyed with her young daughter to Berwick. Among the bridal procession were many great earls and nobles, including Mortimer and William, Earl of Ulster, uncle to the young bridegroom. As they rode through Yorkshire and on into Northumberland, the folk who saw them felt a sense of relief and hope for future peace. There had always been peace, when the kings of Scotland had taken wives from within the English royal family, they reasoned, but a few noticed that King Edward himself was not among the wedding guests. Isabella had had furious arguments with her eldest son. "You and your amoroso have signed away my inheritance," he shouted at his mother. Edward and Mortimer were constantly at loggerheads and whenever Mortimer was in the king's company, the young man was argumentative and sulky. Whatever they arranged he opposed and he could not be moved in his opposition to the marriage with Scotland. On the day when the bridal procession was to depart, Edward and his men left early for the hunt without saying farewell to his sister and mother.

King Robert was at Holyrood Abbey, preparing to leave for Berwick when they brought him the news that the English king was not among the English guests. It was a bitter blow to him and he called Douglas and Randolph to his presence. "It's likely he's just showing his opposition to Mortimer," said Randolph. "He's at an age when he'll not take kindly to interference from his mother's lover." The king replied, "Whatever the reason, I fear it's an ill omen for the future." He gave a deep sigh, "I had hoped that I would leave the kingdom a legacy of peace." There was an air of despondency about him that they had not seen before. "Well, I'll not attend the ceremony either. You may be my witnesses to the union of Scotland and England." Both men understood their king so well that they said nothing and the following day, they escorted David Bruce to Berwick. The little lad loved both men and they took it in turns to have him perched on their saddle in front of them. He chatted incessantly about everything and anything, until both lords were relieved to hand him over to his nurse at the end of each day. Meanwhile, the king rode slowly to Cardross, happy to relax in the peace of his estate.

On a beautiful summer's day in July, the marriage between Scotland and England was solemnized by the church door in Berwick, watched by a congregation of Scottish and English nobles, who had so recently been deadly enemies.

The bride looked very solemn and just a little frightened, but answered her vows as she was instructed to do. David jumped up and down, refusing to hold Joan's hand and more interested in gazing around at the splendidly dressed English nobles, who smiled down at him benevolently. After the exchanging of the vows, the whole congregation trooped into the church to receive the sacrament together. In the evening, when their nurses had put the children to bed, the wedding guests sat down together for the bridal feast. None wore their weapons and their escorts, both Scots and English, were stationed well apart that none might, in a drunken state, spoil the peace and gladness existing between them.

The English guests returned to their own country with both Douglas and Randolph escorting them to the border. Before they parted, Scots and English gave each other their hands in a peaceful farewell. After this, Douglas and Randolph escorted the two children back to the King at Cardross.

Joan was tearful in her strange new surroundings. English servants had remained with her, but she was old enough to understand that this was now her new home and for a long time she remained very homesick. At Cardross the Scottish king's daughters were her playmates and gradually she forgot her shyness and began to play in the gardens and fields around the manor. The serious grown-up events, which had occurred at Berwick, became a memory.

During the Christmas feast the king remained at Cardross, but he became increasingly frail. He accepted his illness and imminent death with quiet submission and good humour. When his personal servants administered to his most intimate needs he did not complain. To his confessor, he admitted that his illness was a penance for his sins and years of bloodshed that his actions had brought upon the people of Scotland. He called his chancellor to him. "Bernard, we both know this will probably be my last Christmas. I must accept that this is God's will and put Scotland's affairs in order." Bernard said nothing for the king was a man who needed neither flattery nor false promises. "As soon as the worst of the winter is passed, I shall make a pilgrimage to Whithorn, to prepare my soul for the next life. While I'm away, write letters to my nobles ordering them to visit me here at Cardross."

There was a break in the weather in February and the king was carried onto his galley. With great care they rowed him down the coast to Girvan. From beneath his awning, King Robert watched the Clyde slip away and saw the hills and islands passing gently by. He remembered the other journey, more than twenty years earlier, when they had rowed from Cardross, fleeing from Pembroke. Then the people, curious to see Bruce's warships, had come out and lined the shore. Now, as the king's galley glided gracefully past, the people stopped whatever they were doing in the byre or smithy and ran down to the shoreline to wave and call out a greeting to their king and he waved back.

However gently they lifted him from the galley, he quietly moaned with pain. At Lochinch the weather grew particularly bleak, cold with heavy rain and low cloud. On his physicians instructions he rested for three weeks before slowly continuing his journey to the Saints, chapel at Whithorn. At St Ninian's sacred shine, he prayed for forgiveness for his many sins. After five days, sadly he said farewell to the Holy brothers, for he knew he would not return.

He ordered his servants to carry him by Glen Trool, for he had a great desire to see the battlefield where he had his first victory against English forces. It had been at the same time of the year, early spring. He was no longer able to kneel, but they carried him to the loch-side and he said a prayer for the souls of the fallen on both sides.

His nobles had gathered at Cardross, ready to say farewell to their king. A bed had been prepared in the great hall and all men of importance knelt before the dying man. In a weak voice, he began to speak to them and the chancellor loudly repeated each sentence so that everyone could hear the king's words. "This sickness of mine will shortly take me on that journey we all must make. Do not feel sad, for I've enjoyed every moment of the time I've spent in this life. If I have unwittingly injured any and have not acknowledged this, they should speak now so that I may make recompense, for I would not wish to leave unfinished business." No one spoke. "I ask all present, to swear upon their honour and the loyalty which they have for Scotland, to preserve faithfully the kingdom as it is now administered and will in due time pass to my son David." They all held up their right hand and loudly swore their loyalty to David Bruce. Then the king turned his eyes towards James Douglas who stood close by his bed. "You know we two vowed to go on crusade together when our work here was done. Now, I fear this is an impossible wish on my part, James. When at last my body no longer needs my heart, it is my desire that it be placed in a casket and that you take it on crusade."

The Lord James, tough, relentless warrior could not keep back his tears. It had been twenty three years since he had first fallen on his knees in the mud before Robert Bruce and he found it hard to say goodbye, but he gave his promise.

They carried the king back to his bedchamber where he lay for the next week, hovering between life and death. Sometimes in his dreams he saw those whom he had loved standing around his bed, smiling and beckoning. Elizabeth, as fresh and young as she had been when he wedded her, his brothers and John of Atholl, his dear loyal friend. Then one evening Wallace stood by his bed. "Is it you?" murmured the king. The chancellor, who sat close by, lent near to his lord trying to catch what the sick man said. The king continued to murmur but those about could not catch his words. "Do you come to take me with you, Wallace?" "Soon, my lord." The king said, "I've been remembering our meeting at Lammington. I laughed at you when you said I should make a bid for Scotland's crown. I was feckless in my youth, too quick to choose the easy path. So many fine men and women suffered whilst I learnt how to command myself before I could command them. In that you were the finer man, Wallace." "Perhaps, lord, but you bore the name that all men could follow."

The vision faded and the king opened his eyes. The men waiting around him leant forward. He recognized them, Randolph, his faithful James, and solid dependable Boyd, his nephew Donald of Mar and Robert, his and Christine's son. He managed to smile before drifting off once again into his world of spirits.

It was June; the short northern night had barely passed when Good

King Robert breathed his last. James Douglas, in his misery, lifted King Robert's hunting horn from its hook above the bed. Blinded by his tears, he stumbled from the king's hall out into the dewy garden. Placing the silver mouthpiece to his lips, he blew long and loud, so that Scotland might know that Robert Bruce had embarked on a journey where they could not follow.

Randolph, Boyd and the others joined him and stood in a silent semi-circle, lost without the man who had inspired them for nearly twenty five years. James had promised he would take Robert's heart with him on crusade. He would keep that promise, it would be his last service to his friend.

EPILOGUE

The deeds of men like Bruce, Wallace, Douglas, Boyd and Pilche have all been recorded in Scotland's Chronicles and it was through their sacrifices that Scotland remained an independent state, with a unique identity, which it has maintained throughout the turbulent years since those heroic days.

It would be satisfying to write that Scotland and England became the best of friends and lived happily ever after but the stories of nations rarely end tidily. From the bloodshed, injustices, misery and despair, the Scottish people developed a national personae. These ideals were beautifully encapsulated in the Declaration of Arbroath, which explained to the Pope the aspirations of the Scottish people, which were Wallace's and Bruce's legacy.

The sentiments set forth in the Declaration of Arbroath are easily understood by people of the twenty first century, however, they were unique concepts to the average medieval mind. The idea that a ruler represents the will of his people and could be deposed by those people if he betrayed their trust, was revolutionary in fourteenth century Europe. The whole script of the Declaration is a valuable read by anyone who would like to understand more fully medieval Scotland's view about its past, present and future.

After Robert's death, Scotland was left in the capable hands of Thomas Randolph. On his death, Sir Andrew Murray, son of Wallace's comrade at the battle of Stirling, and third husband to Christina Bruce, King Robert's sister, became Regent of Scotland until David Bruce came of age.

David Bruce did not have his father's strength of character, whilst King Edward III of England was a more capable ruler than his unfortunate father. Cross–border raids and retaliatory skirmishes continued. England remained the stronger nation with a larger population, more fertile land and a prosperous trade with Flanders. Yet in spite of this Scotland retained her independence, free from English domination, whilst England became embroiled in wars with the French, thus relieving Scotland from serious attack.

King David died without an heir and the Scottish crown passed to Robert Stewart, grandson of Robert the Bruce by his daughter Marjorie

Bruce and began the reign of the Stewart kings.

The year following King Robert's death, James Douglas kept his promise and went on crusade carrying the king's heart in a silver casket. The route led him through Spain, where he and other Scottish knights were involved in fighting against the Muslim Moors. Douglas was killed. A sad end to a loyal knight whose career had been devoted to Scotland's cause. King Robert's heart, however, was found on the battlefield and brought home to Scotland to be buried in Melrose Abbey, its rightful resting-place.

James Douglas had never married and his estates passed to his younger brother, William, who also died without an heir. The Douglas inheritance then passed to Archibald Douglas, illegitimate son of James Douglas. His contemporaries called him Archibald the Grim, and he carried on the Douglas reputation as tough, fighting men.

Robert Bruce, Earl of Carrick did have an estate in Tottenham, today in North London. The station is still called Bruce Grove to record this. During the sixteenth century, the Crown sold the royal manor of Burstwick, where Elizabeth Bruce began her captivity, to the Constable family and the site where Sixhills Convent once stood, is now a quiet Lincolnshire hamlet surrounded by fertile, agricultural land and a wonderful view of distant Lincoln Cathedral.

Historians have speculated upon the nature of King Robert's illness. The chronicles have described fevers, temporary paralysis and skin sores and for many years it was suggested that he suffered from leprosy. Even medieval kings with leprosy were strictly segregated, but King Robert lived with his family and was free to move among his people. In recent years it has been considered that a more likely diagnosis was syphilis.

Recent research has shown that syphilis has been a scourge in Europe since Roman times and given Robert's known charm, fondness for the lassies and the symptoms, it would seem likely. It would also account for his inability to father heirs in his later years and his son David's apparent sterility.

The king's enemies declared that Isabella of Fife had left her husband and run to the king's crowning because she was his mistress. There is no actual evidence for this, although I have made her so in King Robert's story. Perhaps I do the lady an injustice and she was merely a loyal Scot.

The Author, 2004